NOTHING GOOD

R. J. Piper

For Ron DeSantis

Contents

Chapter 1

Florida Man Commits Murder, Public Indecency

R ainy's evening was turning out to be sort of a mixed bag. On the one hand, he'd gotten what was probably the best blowjob of his life. On the other, his date had followed it up by pulling a gun on him.

Really fifty-fifty, if he thought about it.

It had started out as a pretty typical workday. Rainy had pulled up to the valet station of the five-star hotel, pushing his sunglasses up on his head. It was October, tail end of the rainy season, and the Miami air was so thick with humidity that you could taste it, rub it between your tongue and the roof of your mouth. Rainy's shirt stuck to his back as he climbed out onto the pavement. He checked his kit in the trunk of the silver convertible, making sure everything was in place before zipping the suitcase shut and lifting it out.

The valet was a skinny Latino kid who grinned when Rainy tossed him the keys, and Rainy felt a flash of pleasant nostalgia, like digging through the closet for an umbrella and finding an old photo album instead. He winked and told the kid to take it for a little spin. He'd be a few hours at least.

The lobby was vaulted and airy with a clean white aesthetic that did little to hide old-money sensibilities. Rainy breezed through the off-season denizens of the hotel, the businesspeople and wealthy retirees, all white and gracelessly aging. They were the furniture of

Rainy's city—the static and interchangeable backdrop around and over which the locals moved.

As a rule, Rainy never dressed up for work. His half-buttoned Hawaiian shirt, sneakers, and tattoos earned him a dubious glance from the receptionist, but a subtle one. In this part of town, you never knew which trashy streetwear hid a surprise tech millionaire or trust-fund kid.

"Do you have a reservation?" she asked, smoothing a hand down her uniform blouse.

"Luis Pliego," he told her, rolling the syllables of the fake name like a handful of dice. She clacked primly at her desktop, then beamed at him, satisfied that he was, in fact, a paying customer. Her smile was whitewashed and genial as the lobby itself.

"I have you for one night. Room 1243."

"Lovely," he said, and accepted the key.

His room was taken up by a king-sized bed upholstered in the most ridiculous eggshell duvet set he had ever seen. It looked like a fucking wedding cake. He heaved the suitcase up onto it and started unpacking.

His pearl-inlaid Colt 1911 got set aside for now. Rainy gave it an affectionate pat before letting it sink into the froth of the bedspread. Next came two prescription pill bottles—benzos and the strongest muscle relaxant he'd been able to get his hands on. He picked each up with a handkerchief, then folded it around them and set them down.

The final two items were a small plastic baggie and an unopened bottle of top-shelf, thirty-five-year-old scotch.

Whistling to himself, he cracked open the scotch and took a swig. It burned smooth, splashing warmth along his jaw and down into the center of his chest. He set the bottle down on the dresser and opened the baggie.

Inside were two plastic capsules, each about the length of his pinkie and half as thick. They were filled with fine white powder. Rainy tore the seam of one pouch and tipped its contents into the bottle. He wiped the excess from the rim, then recapped the bottle and swirled it until the silt disappeared.

The powder was a mix of the pills from the two prescription bottles, which he'd crushed by hand earlier that day and premeasured into two extra-hefty doses. He tucked the empty capsule back into his bag and dropped the full one into his shirt pocket.

You never knew when something like that might come in handy.

The spreadsheet Malia had typed up for him was pulled up on his phone. According to her—and she was never wrong—Holister would be arriving back to the lobby from his client dinner right about now. Rainy tucked the bottle under his arm and went out into the hall.

He'd asked for room 1243 because it was exactly one turn from the elevator. He stood just behind the corner, drumming his nails on the neck of the bottle, until he heard the elevator chime. Then he counted to ten under his breath and stepped out.

Dean Holister was a salt-and-pepper man in his late fifties with a haughty expression and a bad habit of fucking over people he wasn't remotely prepared to get away with fucking over. His tie was loosened against the humidity, and he pawed at the lock to his room as Rainy approached.

There was an art to homicide. There was also a structure to it—best practices, maybe. Rainy liked to call them the three Rs: research, relax, and relocate.

Malia handled the first step, research. There were all sorts of interesting things to learn about Holister. For example, his schedule. His chronic back pain that required prescription meds. His fondness for a certain label of top-shelf scotch.

"Oh, thank God," Rainy said, hurrying up to him just as he got the door open. "I thought I was going to have to go down to the lobby."

Holister squinted at him. Rainy plowed on:

"Came out to get my delivery and locked myself out of my room. Could I use the phone in yours? I don't want to trek all the way back down."

He shook the bottle at Holister, double-checking that it was unclouded. The man's eyes caught on the label, and his skeptical frown eased.

"That an '85?"

"A '90," Rainy offered. He uncapped the bottle and brought it to his lips, pressing his thumb over its mouth to pretend to drink. "Trade you some for a minute on the phone?"

Holister shrugged and pushed open the door.

"Be my guest."

That was the trick to the second R—approaching the mark in a role that felt unassuming, unthreatening. Getting them to relax.

Holister left the door propped open, tossing his tie and room key onto the table in the entryway. The suite had a sitting area with plush carpet and a sideboard with glasses and champagne already sitting on ice. Rainy plunked the bottle down there and strode toward the bedroom.

"Help yourself."

He paused for a moment in the next room, listening to Holister shuffling around. There was a clink of glass. Satisfied that he was sufficiently occupied, Rainy planted his hands on his hips and said to the empty air:

"Hi, yeah, locked out. Room 1247." He waited, drumming his fingers on his pants. "Great; I'll be waiting."

He walked back into the sitting area to find Holister already halfway through a tumbler of scotch. "Thanks, man, you saved my ass. That good stuff?"

"The best," Holister sighed.

Rainy laughed and passed the bottle to him again. "Pour yourself a taller glass. Least I can do."

Holister agreeably poured himself *quite* a tall glass and sipped it with a blissful expression. Rainy screwed the cap back onto the bottle and saluted him. "Thanks again."

On his way out, he pulled a handkerchief from his pocket and picked Holister's room key up off the table. He kicked the door shut behind himself without touching the handle.

Rainy returned to his room and packed the scotch back into his bag. He sat on the bed and checked the time. When the minute hand on his watch made it to the spot he'd marked, he tucked his Colt into the back of his jeans and tugged his shirt down over it. Then he snapped on a pair of latex gloves from his handy 120-count medical-grade box and stuffed the two prescription bottles into his pocket.

He checked to make sure there was nobody in the hall before using the swiped keycard to open Holister's door. A pause to listen yielded nothing but silence. Rainy closed the door behind himself and moved to the bedroom.

Holister was sprawled across the top of the duvet—a matched set with Rainy's, huzzah—with his eyes half-lidded and drool gathering at the corner of his mouth. His face had the slack deadness of unnatural sleep. Rainy sighed, cracked his neck, and went to work.

Unlike many, he actually liked this kind of job. It didn't need to be flashy and bloody; Emilio Espinosa, Rainy's employer for this hit, wasn't trying to send a message. He just needed Holister out of the way. That meant Rainy had the opportunity to get creative with it.

Holister wasn't a small guy, but Rainy had a linebacker's build. He'd spent his teen years playing Mike on the varsity football team, making a full-time gig of throwing around guys twice Holister's mass, and his post-high school career had ended up being much of the same. He picked Holister up off the bed and carried him to the bathroom, only bowing a little under the weight. Holister stirred but couldn't do much more than mumble his discontent.

He made quick work of Holister's suit and underwear, dumping them onto the counter. Holister groaned when Rainy dropped him into the tub and turned the water on. While it filled, he withdrew the pill bottles and placed them on the counter, unscrewing one lid. By the time the water had risen to cover Holister's chest, the man was squirming ineffectually toward the lip of the tub, fingers clumsy.

"Ah-ah," Rainy chastised, coming to sit on the bathmat. He placed his palm on Holister's forehead and pushed him under.

To his credit, Holister did try to wriggle away, but those pills were good shit. The fight went out of him quickly, and Rainy watched as the bubbles slowed from a roiling stream to an occasional *blop*. Once they stopped, he kept one hand under the water and checked his watch. When he'd counted out the appropriate number of minutes, he stood. Holister looked pale and small under the water. His eyes were closed. Rainy gave him a final poke, just for good measure, and turned away.

He dropped the keycard on the entryway table and let the door lock behind him.

It wasn't perfect—it rarely was—but it was a satisfying enough story to keep the cops occupied. Wealthy man gets his hands on some prescriptions he shouldn't have, gets drunk at dinner, and goes overboard self-medicating his aching back. Takes ill-advised bath. Accidents happen.

Whether or not the cops bought it in the end, Rainy's hands would be clean of it by morning.

Back in his room, he texted Malia, *Back from swimming. Time for a drink.*

You're such a freak, she replied. *Be back by three.*

Rainy mussed his dark hair in the mirror and undid another button on his shirt so the tattoo over the hard line of his left pec peeked out. Satisfied, he packed his kit into the suitcase and left it on the bed along with his gun.

The hotel's restaurant had crisp white tablecloths, a few tasteful crystal light fixtures, and a long backlit bar. It was the end of the dinner rush, and the scrapes of cutlery on plates were few and far between as diners leaned back in their seats, occupied with wine.

Rainy sidled up to the bar and leaned his back against it, surveying the field. At first, it was just his instinctual recon—noting the exits and checking for suspicious body language or too-bulky clothing. Then he let his gaze linger on a few of the other single patrons. A woman in a green cocktail dress eyed him from the end of the bar, and he winked at her.

His job meant that he was often stuck working when the rest of the city was having its fun, scattered, neon-saturated, across the bars and clubs and beachside cabanas. As such, Rainy had developed a bit of a tradition: whenever he pulled off a job at a place with a bar, he was obligated to pick someone up there for a quickie before heading out for the cleanup. It had started as a competition with Marco, but then Marco's affections had been drawn... elsewhere. Now, Rainy saw it almost as an integral part of pulling off a successful hit—like a kiss for luck.

The woman at the end of the bar had curly black hair and a ballerina's silhouette. Every graceful angle of her seated position on the stool, back curved and ankles crossed, gave an impression of careful arrangement. Rainy rumpled his hair again as he watched her, feeling that familiar dance of mutual awareness, the weight of her gaze sliding like water over his skin.

He waved absently for the bartender, who approached from the corner of the bar. He was tall and dressed in a tailored gray three-piece suit rather than the hotel uniform, but there was a name tag pinned to his breast pocket. When Rainy turned to face him, he had to bite down on a wince. The man had a brutal scar on his face, a pink line that puckered the skin from the corner of his mouth to his right ear.

"Yes?" the bartender asked. In the unusually open slide of the syllable, Rainy sensed an accent.

Already distracted by the woman still watching him, running her cocktail pick around the rim of her empty glass, Rainy nodded and dug for his wallet.

"Two Manhattans. One for me and one for the lady."

The bartender made a small, skeptical noise in the back of his throat. Rainy turned to him, incredulous.

"What?"

The man pulled two glasses and a cocktail shaker from under the bar top, shrugging.

"I didn't say nothing."

The accent was thick and Deep South—Alabama, if Rainy had to guess.

"You *hmm*-ed something," he accused.

"Well. Don't you think she's a little out of your league?"

Rainy's jaw dropped. "Excuse me?"

The bartender's gaze, burnt-coffee brown, was unimpressed. He dragged it pointedly over Rainy's patterned shirt and too-bright sneakers.

"I might be crazy," Rainy said, "but aren't you supposed to be polite to me?"

"Oh, yes, sir. Of course, sir." The bartender's voice was deadpan as he selected a bottle of bourbon without looking at it. "I'm assuming you like a heavy pour?"

Rainy leaned over the bar, woman briefly forgotten. He dragged the shaker away so the bartender was forced to look at him. The man clunked the bottle down on the bar and held Rainy's gaze.

He had short brown hair with a hint of curl to it and a flat, stern expression, like he was gearing up to tell Rainy to sit down and button his shirt. His neck was elegant and just a little too long in a way that made him interesting to look at. The scar on his face distracted from the handsome angles of him—a painting of an angel someone had slashed with a box cutter. He was long and wiry and stood with his feet a little too far apart. His hands had come to rest behind his back. Perfect, perfect posture. Rainy wanted to push him over.

His name tag read: *Jesse*.

"For your information, *Jesse*, I belong here plenty." Rainy turned on a megawatt smile, one he had on good authority should be labeled an air traffic hazard up there with fireworks and high-powered lasers. "I just closed on a big contract, and I wanted to celebrate by blowing some money on someone pretty."

Jesse reclaimed the shaker and started making the drinks. "Oh? And what is it that you do for a living?"

"High-profile talent agent." The lie came smooth and familiar as ever as Rainy watched Jesse pour the liquor with careless efficiency, barely glancing down while he worked. His hands were deft and long-fingered. There were freckles and white flecks of old scars across the knuckles.

"Mm," Jesse said. "With that shirt, that was gonna be my second guess after 'ten-dollar escort.'"

Rainy couldn't help the laugh that startled out of him like a puff of kicked-up dust. "Does insulting customers get you off, or do you just have a terrible personality?"

Jesse's mouth finally tilted up at the corner, smug and mean. "Both."

His accent was starting to get under Rainy's skin. The lazy stretch of the vowels was like a hand running down his shoulders, up the back of his neck. Rainy wanted to bite that snide little expression off his face.

"Shit," he said. "Forget the girl. Can I buy *you* a drink?"

"Hitting on the help? Classy."

"Oh, now you're concerned with appropriate employee-customer interactions?"

Jesse leaned against the bar, languidly uninterested, and shook the drinks. Rainy listened to the rattle and crunch of ice, watched the amber-red liquor trickle into the glasses. When it settled, he pushed one back across the bar.

"Come on. I said I wanted to buy a drink for someone pretty, and you're starting to look like the prettiest person here."

Jesse rolled his eyes. "Flattery won't get you nowhere."

"What will?"

"Depends on what you're offering."

Rainy leaned in on an elbow. "Sweetheart, you can have anything you want from me."

"Don't call me that."

There was a flash of fight in Jesse's eyes now, feral and deadly. The cut of his teeth made something hotter and heavier than gravity tug at Rainy's stomach.

"All right," Rainy said with false ease. "I'll go test my luck else-where, then." He picked up the glasses and turned away toward the end of the bar, where the woman in the green dress was starting to look annoyed at her empty glass.

"Wait," Jesse said.

Rainy bit down on his smirk and turned. "Yes?"

Jesse plunked a jar of Luxardo cherries onto the bar. "You forgot the most important part."

Rainy set the drinks back down and watched Jesse spear cherries with gold-enameled cocktail picks, dropping one into each glass. He felt a pleasant rush in his ears, a warmth starting to radiate up his neck, like the scotch he'd drunk earlier had suddenly decided to make him tipsy after all.

"I'm Luis, by the way. And you're—don't tell me—Jesse."

"Amazing. How'd you guess?"

"I'm observant like that." Rainy took a sip from his glass and raised his eyebrows. "This is fantastic." The bourbon and bitters were perfectly balanced by the sweetness of the vermouth and the rich curl of cherry.

"I'm a man of many talents," Jesse said drily.

"Oh, I bet you are."

A pair of businessmen had walked up to the other end of the bar and were trying to get Jesse's attention. He ignored them.

"Look. I don't got patience for people who dance around words. So just look me in the eye and tell me you wanna fuck me." His voice dragged derisively over the word *fuck*. "So I can turn you down and we can both get on with our nights."

The bite in his tone was more challenge than irritability, smug-ness and sharp teeth. That was the best part, Rainy thought—the way Jesse talked like they were playing a secret game that he'd already won.

"I'm not sure you *would* turn me down. And if you did, I think you'd regret it."

"Mister Luis, you wouldn't last two minutes with me."

"No? I'm a strong boy." Rainy demonstratively flexed a tanned forearm, where the outline of a boxer was tattooed with only the red, red gloves filled in. He enjoyed the way Jesse followed the movement with his eyes and then tried to pretend he hadn't. "I can take it."

Jesse plucked the cocktail pick from Rainy's drink and closed his lips around it. He drew it out slowly, gold glinting against the wet pink of his bottom lip. A drop of juice gathered there. He chewed the cherries, then tipped his chin back to swallow. With that neck on him, it was a whole spectacle.

"Excuse me," one of the men down the bar called.

"Fuck off," Rainy told them mildly, eyes still locked on the spot where Jesse's throat disappeared under his collar. Fuck, he wanted to get under that collar.

"Come on. Anything you want, remember?" And then he added, deliberately, "Sweetheart."

Jesse's eyes smoldered, deep and dark enough to swallow all the light in the room.

"I told you not to call me that," he said, voice all fangs.

Rainy's pulse was a wild thing under his skin. He wondered if Jesse could see it jumping against his sternum.

"You going to stop me?" he challenged.

Jesse tipped his head. He had a strange way of holding it, Rainy had noticed—chin tilted slightly to the right, scarred side canted away, so he was always looking at Rainy a little bit sideways. He turned to face him fully now. The cool lighting of the bar silvered the scar tissue on his cheek.

"Finish your drink," he ordered.

Rainy lifted it for a sip and sputtered when Jesse's hand suddenly covered his, tipping the glass further, forcing him to drink it all. Bourbon ran out of the corner of his mouth, burned in his sinuses. He met Jesse's eyes over the glass as he swallowed. They were black and shuttered, unreadable. Rainy's jeans were much too tight.

When the glass was empty and the pick clinked against Rainy's teeth, Jesse pulled it away and set it on the bar.

"I'm gonna take my thirty-minute break, now," he said. "Are you coming?"

"I sure fucking hope so."

Jesse turned primly on his heel and stalked to the corner of the bar, where he flipped up the top and walked out. Rainy enjoyed the lithe line of his back and the way his pants were tailored across his ass.

"Hey, man, we're still waiting on drinks!" one of the men down the bar complained. Jesse pushed through the swinging door into the kitchen without a word.

Rainy offered the two men a shrug. *What can you do?* Then he hopped off his stool and all but scampered after.

On his way, he passed the woman in the green cocktail dress. Her gamine figure was stiff with irritation. Rainy gave her an apologetic wince before following Jesse into the kitchen.

Steam and sound, the smell of pan-fried fish and fresh-baked soufflé. Rainy hurried down a whitewashed hall past the kitchen proper, following Jesse's retreating back. It skipped a dish room and a pantry, rounding a corner. Rainy made the same tight turn—then the world jerked around him, and he found himself pinned against the wall.

Adrenaline flashed along his limbs like lightning, and he started to go for his Colt before remembering he hadn't brought it. Fine, then—his knife, or his hands. Rainy, as Marco fondly told him, was built like a pile of bricks. He could put Jesse on the ground easily enough, and Jesse—

And Jesse was kissing him. Sliding their mouths together and biting down on Rainy's lower lip. It was forceful, aggressive. Challenging. Rainy's adrenaline had never shifted faster from one priority to another. He kissed back hard, his blood rising higher at the delicious contrast between Jesse's soft lips and the sharp, insistent tug of his teeth. His mouth tasted like cherry syrup, sickening-sweet.

The wall at Rainy's back was gloss-painted and slippery against his sweat-dampened shirt. The drab, unopulent innards of the service side of the hotel were stifling. He didn't know how Jesse was surviving in all those designer layers. The narrow bones and lean muscle of his body where he pressed Rainy into the wall were burning hot.

A hand slid up into Rainy's hair, tightening at the scalp. Jesse dragged his head to the side, exposing the arch of his throat. He leaned back and examined him, eyes more black than brown. The collar of Rainy's shirt had slid down to bare most of one shoulder and the tattoo on his chest. He watched Jesse take it in—a tangled burst of wild violets inked over his left pec, like his skin had split open and they'd come spilling out. Rainy swallowed, and it felt too thick, vulnerable.

"Are you—" he started, and then forgot what he was going to ask, because Jesse leaned down to the juncture between his neck and shoulder and bit him.

"*Fuck.*" Rainy's hips bucked involuntarily.

Jesse's teeth dug in punishingly hard, enough that Rainy thought in a flashbulb of fear and arousal that he might actually break the skin. Then they released, and his tongue swept in to soothe over the damp, bruised skin. He found the line of spilled bourbon and followed it up Rainy's throat, then paused, open-mouthed, at the pulse point under his jaw. Rainy's heart was pounding, and he could feel the blood rushing just below the soft skin of his neck, against Jesse's hot mouth and the skate of his bared teeth.

Jesus Christ, he thought, *this man is going to kill me.*

Then Jesse kissed him there, gentle and unhurried, and Rainy needed to touch him now, now, *now.* He slid his hands over the surprisingly powerful curve of Jesse's shoulders. The wool twill of his suit jacket was soft.

When Rainy went to lean forward, Jesse let him, releasing his hair. He nuzzled Jesse's chin back until his head was tilted at a devastating angle. His Adam's apple jutted out sharp as a broken neck. Rainy latched onto it with his mouth. God, that neck was really something. Jesse shuddered as Rainy sucked his way down it, tasted the hollow of his collarbone and then the spot behind his ear. He ground their hips together.

Rainy was almost fully hard now, dick hot and aching. The sharp press of his zipper and the friction of rough denim was unbearable. He wanted to get under that bespoke suit of armor, starting with the jacket. His hands roamed down Jesse's back to the tailored dip of his waist—

Jesse spun out of his grip. Rainy's skin smarted at the loss, his hips pushing forward into empty air. He stared at Jesse in the white fluorescent light of the service hallway. His suit was still immaculately pressed, but below the surface, his face was flushed and his chest was heaving, and there was a red mark on his neck from Rainy's mouth. Rainy reached for him.

He stepped back. "Let's take this somewhere more private."

"I have a room," Rainy offered immediately.

Jesse scowled. "I'm not waiting that long. Come on."

He grabbed Rainy by the arm and dragged him up the hall, away from the kitchens. His grip was strong, enough to break Rainy's wrist if he so chose. Rainy followed eagerly.

"I like the way you think, Jesse."

Jesse led him down a set of concrete stairs, the air turning a little drier as they descended. The hotel was built on a rise, and on the backside there was a small lower level where the building sprawled down over the hill. They hurried down the narrow hallway that ran its length, Jesse's fingers digging into Rainy's skin hard enough to bruise.

In the center of the hall was a door that opened with a key Jesse fished out of his pocket. It swung inward to reveal a wine cellar. It was a deep room with brick-covered walls. Low light glinted off rows and rows of dark green and aubergine glass. There must have been some kind of atmosphere-control system, because the air was dry as chalk against Rainy's sweat-slicked skin when Jesse tugged him inside and closed the door behind them.

"Take your pants off," he ordered.

"Well, someone's e—"

Jesse pushed him back until his knees hit a stack of pallets and he sprawled across them. By the time Rainy managed to scramble up into a sitting position, Jesse was already on his knees in front of him, wrestling with the zipper of his jeans.

"Okay, Jesus, okay." Rainy wriggled out of his pants. His breath was coming frantic, everything high-contrast, gilded with alcohol-warmth. He was painfully aware of every centimeter of himself, every nerve and capillary, the hot damp of Jesse's breath on the inside of his thigh. There were tattoos there too, geometric mandala patterns that wrapped around and up the insides of his thighs, and Jesse traced one with a finger.

Looking down on the top of his head, Rainy could see that there was gel in Jesse's hair, taming the soft natural curl of it into a meticulous sweep. He wanted to run his hand through and ruin it. He forgot about that pretty quickly when Jesse dragged down his underwear and took him in hand.

His hands were strong, broad, and surprisingly rough, the calluses on his palm scraping over the flushed, sensitive skin. He squeezed with his thumb and tilted his wrist in long, torturous strokes that had Rainy arching his hips off the pallets, a drop of precome gathering at his tip. Jesse bent down to lap it up.

Rainy had to bite down on his own wrist to keep from moaning when Jesse's mouth latched onto him, hot and wet and soft. His tongue ran a teasing sweep and then he sank down, taking Rainy in all the way.

"Oh my God." Jesse's mouth was tight and warm. His lips slid all the way down to the base and he swallowed. Rainy's body drew tight at the feeling.

He set a brutal pace, drawing his mouth and tongue and teeth over Rainy until Rainy was shaking with the effort to keep himself from thrusting up into Jesse's throat. The heat that had built up in his hips was spreading through the rest of him, warm and liquid and throbbing with his pulse. Electricity was arcing over his bones, ready to bite and fry.

Jesse's hands gripped his hips. He used them as leverage to guide Rainy's cock up into his open mouth, gliding in and out. Rainy took the hint. He tried a tentative thrust, and Jesse sank in close around him, coaxing and pliant. He rolled his hips again and again until he was fucking his mouth roughly, Jesse's fingers still digging into his hip bones.

He made the mistake of looking down just as Jesse looked up, and the breath was punched out of him. Jesse's eyes were round and wet, with long, long lashes that were sinfully pretty. Innocent as an angel's, while his lips were stretched wet and pink over Rainy's cock. Rainy brought a hand up to cup his cheek. He traced his thumb gently over the scar.

Jesse bit him. Fucking *bit* him.

Rainy grabbed him by the back of the neck instead and snapped his hips forward hard, hard enough that he hit the inside of Jesse's throat. Jesse's eyes blew wide, and Rainy leaned back on his other elbow for leverage, thrusting deep enough to choke.

Jesse was moaning now. Rainy could feel it vibrating against him. His skin felt flash-boiled. His whole body was pulsing, the pleasure surging and stretching. Every bit of smug sternness was gone from Jesse's face. He looked desperate and fucked-out as Rainy thrust into his mouth. Rainy wanted to pull out and come on his face, watch the mess drip down the front of his still-immaculate suit. The image was so overwhelming that he felt that low ache crest like a breaking wave.

"Fuck, I'm going to—"

He tried to pull back, but Jesse chased him with his mouth. Rainy bit down on his palm hard enough to bruise as he came buried in Jesse's throat. The orgasm lit his whole body up in an incandescent wave and he was left raw as a burnt-out filament. He whimpered as Jesse kept sucking, drinking him down.

When Jesse finally pulled away, there was a smear of come at the corner of his mouth. He wiped it demurely away with a thumb and checked his watch.

"I guess you did break two minutes. Not by much, though."

Rainy had to tip back against the wall, boneless, while his breath caught back up to his body. As he gasped there like a dying fish, chest slick with sweat, Jesse stood and brushed off the knees of his suit. His movements were calm, but Rainy could see the outline of his own dick straining against his pants. Rainy tilted forward to feel him, going to slide his hands under the tailored vest and shirt.

Jesse skirted out of his grip again. "Sorry, I don't give it up to guys who ain't even bought me a drink yet."

Rainy laughed. "God, you're a bastard. Are you going to let me buy you one now?"

His body was loose and shaky with the lingering sensation of Jesse on him, and he needed more. Normally, he preferred giving to receiving, but right now all he wanted was this awful, beautiful man to hold him down and call him nasty things while he fucked Rainy raw.

Jesse made a show of considering, teeth sliding over his lip. "Maybe."

Rainy took him in, how his eyes crinkled, smug and satisfied and a little cruel. The scar on his face, the tall, lithe arch of him, the tiny spatter of freckles across the bridge of his straight nose.

God, this man was really something.

It was too bad, Rainy thought, that Jesse was here to kill him.

Chapter 2

Florida Man, Bartender Cause Public Disturbance

The first clue had been the way Jesse stood relaxed behind the bar—feet spread too far apart, hands drifting toward his back. Old habits died hard. His sharp, economical movements confirmed Rainy's suspicion—ex-military, definitely. That had invited further scrutiny of the way he was dressed, out of uniform and too expensive for this job, wearing a jacket when he had to be nearly sweating through it. Packing, certainly, which was supported by his refusal to let Rainy feel him up too closely.

But, really, what had done it was watching Jesse make his drink. The precise motion of his hands, the sinew and stretch and certainty of them, easy in their old scars. People always thought they'd be able to spot a murderer by the eyes, the demeanor, the empty smile. But that wasn't true. You never knew, just talking to a person, just looking at their face. Faces could hide anything—it was in the hands.

Rainy knew a killer's hands when he saw them.

So, Jesse was an assassin. And, like all good ones, he followed a predictable pattern—Rainy's three Rs. He'd done his research, known Rainy was going to be at this hotel on this night, and that he would follow through on tradition by going down to the bar to pick someone up. He'd put himself in a place where Rainy would have to talk to him, in a role most people would overlook.

And then he'd lured Rainy to the back.

20

Generally, Rainy preferred to deal with things head-on, so he'd been inclined to follow wherever Jesse led and get the confrontation over with. He hadn't been expecting to actually get a blowjob out of it. It turned out that Jesse was full of all sorts of surprises.

Now, Rainy reclined on the stack of pallets, carefully relaxed, watching Jesse recompose himself. The wine cellar was cool, and the lingering sweat on his skin slid cold down his back, making him shiver. The post-orgasmic relaxation was fighting with the edge on his nerves. His eyes stayed glued to the movement of Jesse's hands.

He was sure from the way Jesse had moved with him that his jacket concealed a gun. Best to keep from tipping his hand for as long as possible. Rainy's Colt was still resting on his bed upstairs. All he had was his knife, and...

And.

"Are you sure you don't want me to do anything for you?" he asked, watching Jesse straighten his tie.

"You know, most men wouldn't be complaining too hard about getting a BJ with nothing expected in return," Jesse drawled. He cracked his neck, where there was still a faint pink mark under his jaw from Rainy's mouth.

Being forbidden to touch him, Rainy thought, was definitely cause for complaint.

"I don't like owing people things," he said.

It was true, and nagging at the back of his mind. He didn't think he was wrong about Jesse's purpose here, but why the blowjob? Why actually follow through on the flirtation, if it had just been a ploy to lure him here?

"That's sad for you," Jesse told him.

"But I still have a chance. You're going to let me buy you a drink now, right? That's plenty for me to work with."

Jesse's expression stayed flat. "I don't think I wanna go back to the bar just yet. My break's not over."

No, Rainy wouldn't be able to coax him back into public now. Most likely, one of them was never going to see that bar again. But—

He pushed himself off the pallets, buttoning up his jeans. "No need. I like it just fine here. As long as nobody's going to disturb us?"

"No," Jesse said. "No one's coming."

Rainy didn't let his smile flicker. "Good." He crossed to one of the racks of wine.

"You can't steal that," Jesse told him, disgusted.

"I'm not. I'm buying you a drink, remember? Put it on my tab."

Rainy stepped along the length of the rack, keeping his shoulders loose, his back unguarded. He watched Jesse's reflection on the dark, glossy curves of the bottles. He was a distorted pale smudge in their glass worlds, a ghost in the dark. Unease made the hair on the back of Rainy's neck prickle, but he forced himself to hum nonchalantly.

He selected a bottle with a pink and white label that he liked the look of and pulled it out with a flourish.

"That's a three-thousand-dollar bottle of wine," Jesse informed him.

Rainy replaced it wordlessly on the rack and skimmed his fingers a few bottles down, then looked over his shoulder. Jesse nodded.

He tugged the bottle free with a dull glassy ring and held it up to the light.

"Toss me a bottle opener?" he asked.

Jesse's eyes cut a quick, assessing glance around the room. Rainy pretended not to notice, just squinted down and fiddled with the cork as Jesse locked onto a cabinet near the door and went to rifle through it. He came up with a bottle opener, which he tossed to Rainy.

"That's a Burgundy, low tannins. Don't have to decant it."

"Perfect," Rainy said, digging the bottle opener into the cork. "Do you keep tasting glasses in here?"

Jesse extracted two glasses from the cabinet and approached. Rainy managed to free the cork and set it aside. He accepted a glass from Jesse and filled it. Wine splashed up its sides like storm-tossed waves and then receded, dark red as old blood. He passed the glass to Jesse and watched as he swirled it idly. While Jesse's eyes tracked the motion of the liquid in his glass, Rainy's fingers slipped into his own shirt pocket.

He took the second glass from Jesse's hand and set it on the shelf next to him, going to fill it. "Well? How's that drink taste?"

Jesse snorted, but took a sip. His eyes drifted shut as he did, focused on the taste. When the glass lowered, Rainy watched his tongue sweep along his lower lip, erasing the red sheen of wine there.

"Not bad," he said. "But I've had better."

Rainy laughed and took the glass from him. He turned the rim so the smudge from Jesse's mouth faced him and closed his own lips over it, drinking deep. The wine was heady and a little bitter, something once sweet changed by years in the dark. It made the room gather in closer, stuffy.

"Funny," he said. "I don't think I have had better."

Jesse rolled his eyes, but a pink flush crept along the tips of his ears. Instead of replying, he reached between them to pick up the other glass, the one Rainy had poured while he'd been distracted. Rainy watched him drink from it, then slid down until he was seated on the cool concrete floor, back braced against the shelf.

"You weren't bluffing. You are really good with your mouth."

"Mmhm." Jesse settled on the stack of pallets, lounging like a cat between Rainy and the door. Outwardly relaxed, but with an undercurrent of feralness to the angle of his limbs that suggested he would be ready to pounce at a moment's notice. Pleasant warmth bloomed in Rainy's stomach despite his wariness. The image of Jesse's mouth wrapped around him, eyes hazy with lust, was superimposed over the image of him demurely sipping his wine.

"I don't think it's fair not to let me have a chance to show you how good I am," Rainy said.

"Mm. Best not to let you embarrass yourself, I think."

Rainy grinned. "You've got to at least let me buy you dinner."

"Let's not get ahead of ourselves."

Rainy pulled out his phone and opened the menu of the upstairs restaurant, scrolling through.

"What do you think about scallops? Or lobster? That classy enough for you?"

"Cute."

"Ooh, I bet they make a mean eggs benedict. You know, you add a little ketchup, a little hot sauce, you might have something there."

Jesse stared at him like he'd just suggested fileting a puppy. "Good God, is there a way to take back a blowjob?"

"You mock me now, but we'll see who's laughing when you try it."

The wine seemed to be seeping its warmth into Jesse, staining his mouth red and sending a pleasant flush spreading over his cheeks, down his neck. Rainy watched it creep below his collar and out of sight, and imagined peeling Jesse out of those fancy clothes, spreading him out on the concrete floor and working him with his fingers just to enjoy the sight of that flush spreading down his chest, down—

Rainy took a gulp of wine to recenter himself. Jesse watched the motion with predatory disinterest. He was still holding his head that same way, slightly crooked so the scar was tilted away.

"So, Jesse. How long have you worked here?"

"Oh, not long. Just moved to town a couple weeks ago."

"Really?" Rainy finished his glass, set it down. "You need a real Miami local to show you around. Take you to the good spots, catch you up on the local racket..."

"You know, there is something I've been dying to know since I got to town. Is there a story behind the nickname 'Rainy'? Because if there is, I ain't been around long enough to hear it."

The cool dryness of the cellar froze around them. Time hung suspended like snow in the air. Rainy breathed, counted, felt his lungs expand and release. His body hummed.

Jesse's gaze on his, dark and swift and deadly, felt like darts pinning him to the wall.

"How'd you hear that name?" Rainy asked.

Jesse tipped his head and emptied the last of his wineglass. He set it aside, angled its base just so. Then he reached into his jacket and pulled out a gun.

"I think you already know the answer to that question, Mister Rainy. No need for either of us to keep playing dumb."

Rainy kept his gaze even on the pistol angled casually at his heart, the single black eye of it, swallowing up the light of the room. He arranged his muscles, let the adrenaline tension seep into them.

"Who do you work for?"

His mind clicked through the possibilities: disgruntled family member, Andy Parish, the Vees, that one deputy mayor he'd pissed off? If he could just get Jesse to—

"Seong," Jesse said.

Oh. Well, that was easier than expected. Also, not surprising. Seong was new in town and stepping on a lot of toes—most notably, Emilio Espinosa's. Rainy had been sent two weeks ago to deliver a few gentle warning shots through the heads of some of Seong's enforcers. There were a lot of questions he should have been asking, information he could sell to the Espinosas. At the bottom of the list was:

"Why'd you blow me in a cellar if you were just planning on killing me?"

Jesse shrugged. "I had a little extra time. Besides, it seems only polite, don't you think?"

Rainy felt a stupid grin spread across his face. It really was a shame that one of them was going to be dead at the end of this.

He started to inch the hand on his hidden side toward the knife strapped to his ankle. "So, what happened to the real bartender?"

Jesse remained seated, his gun hand steady. Left-handed.

"He found himself unexpectedly indisposed before his shift this evening. Luckily, I came highly recommended."

Rainy thumbed up the hem of his jeans. "Who's Jesse?"

Jesse—not Jesse, really—looked down at the name tag pinned to his breast pocket. "Fuck if I know." He unpinned it with one hand and tossed it over his shoulder.

In his moment of distraction, Rainy leaned down to seize the knife's handle and tug it free.

His fingers closed around an empty strap.

When he looked back at Jesse, the other man was smiling at him. Without breaking eye contact, he reached into his pocket and produced Rainy's knife. Rainy swallowed.

Well. Okay. Maybe he'd let himself get a little too distracted while Jesse was giving him mind-blowing oral sex.

He retracted his hand and closed it into a quiet fist at his side. He forced a smile. "You've got good hands."

"Too bad you won't get to find out how good. Now, let's go." Jesse gestured with his gun toward the door.

"Not here?"

"It would be a shame to risk ruining those vintages. I'd prefer to spill your blood on a cheaper surface. Suits you better, don't you think?"

Rainy licked his lips. He had no weapon, but that was okay, if he played it right. What he needed was time.

Slowly, telegraphing his movements, he pushed to his feet. Jesse rose too, and Rainy passed him on his way out the door.

"Left," Jesse ordered. Rainy moved down the hall, away from the stairs. Ahead, the concrete was marked with signage for a loading dock. He checked his watch with a barely-there flick of his eyes as they went. The walls grew sparser and more utilitarian, culminating in a set of metal steps.

"Down the stairs," Jesse told him. His accent had turned a little doughy at the corners, like the wine was getting to him. Rainy bit down on his lip to hide a smile.

Each of Rainy's steps clanged heavily on the stairs, echoing the rising pound of his heart. The loading bay was dim, and his eyes had to adjust. He breathed in low and steady through his nose. He reached the grimy concrete floor. Behind him, there was a whisper of fabric.

Here goes nothing, he thought.

He spun and slammed Jesse's wrist against the railing. Bones ground under skin. Jesse grunted and his hand spasmed, sending the gun clattering to the floor. Rainy lunged for it.

Jesse's foot flashed in before he could reach it. With a neat flick of his toe, the gun jumped right back into his waiting hand.

"Holy shit—I think that was the coolest thing I've ever seen," Rainy said, then tackled him.

They went rolling across the floor and the gun was lost again. Rainy ended up on his back, Jesse straddling him. A hard blow snapped his head to the side, then another. Jesse's knuckles were an unforgiving edge against his cheekbone, orbit, temple. The pain brought a lightning flash of certainty, popped behind an eye like a blown bulb, that this man had killed people with his bare hands. Rainy's vision swam.

Then, a heartbeat of reprieve. Jesse was rearing back for a stronger blow, but it was an opening. Rainy wrenched his body, leveraging his superior weight, and threw him off.

Jesse bounced off the concrete and was scrambling up again in half a second, but Rainy was already on his feet, putting him back down with a hard kick to the side of his head.

It was a nasty shot, but, well, fight to the death and all. Rainy prayed that it would speed this up.

His head was throbbing and the vision in his right eye was already going spotty from the battering he'd taken. Not-Jesse Last-name-unknown sure knew how to suck a man's dick and beat the ever-loving shit out of him. Well-rounded guy.

Speaking of, he was already jumping up, mouth bloody. There was a matching smear of red on the white rubber toe of Rainy's sneaker.

"Don't make this harder on yourself," he told Rainy. There was a definite slur to his words now, like he'd had a lot more than one glass of wine. He was tilting a little, off-balance.

It didn't deter him as much as Rainy had hoped it would. Jesse lunged—a feint that Rainy bought, going to catch him head-on. Jesse ducked under his guard and behind his back. Panic stabbed up into Rainy's gut like tripping onto a rusty spike, but before he could turn, Jesse's leg swept through his knees and he fell straight into the garotte threaded around his neck.

White-hot pain and pressure in a line across his throat. The wire cut deep. Rainy's *stupid fucking* gripless shoes slid on the concrete, and he couldn't get his feet under him to push away from the *squeeze squeeze squeeze—*

A breath of air, a split second of slack. Jesse's hands were fumbling, a little clumsy on the ends of the wire. It was all Rainy needed to throw him off, and Jesse tripped and landed on his ass.

Rainy panted and rubbed his throat, watching Jesse struggle to a standing position. His feet were braced too wide, his hands stretched out warily to either side of Rainy like he was seeing double. *Finally*, Rainy thought, looking back down at his watch.

"Feeling all right, sweetheart?" he called.

Jesse snarled, a feral animal sound like he was going to go for Rainy's throat with his teeth if he had to. The effect was surprisingly undiminished by the fact that his eyes were a little unfocused. He went in for a tackle, and completely missed Rainy's center of gravity. All it took was a small shove to send him sprawling again. He was cursing now, tipping over on his way up and landing back on his stomach. Rainy watched the realization move over his face in a ripple of hatred.

"You fuggin'... roofied me," he slurred.

Rainy pulled the leftover packet he'd prepared for Holister, now empty, from his shirt pocket.

"In my defense," he said, "it was a self-defense roofie."

"I'll fucking kill you," Jesse hissed. Well, actually, it was more of a mushy string of syllables, but Rainy got the gist when his stolen knife was suddenly in Jesse's hand.

He narrowly dodged a messy swipe that could have disemboweled him and caught Jesse's wrist, twisting the knife away. He pinned Jesse's arms to his sides. Jesse kicked and struggled, but his movements were sluggish. His head kept lolling against Rainy's chest.

With the last scraps of his lucidity, he threw a shocking amount of strength into what appeared to be an attempt to rip out Rainy's kidneys with his bare hands. God, he was a vicious little fucker. It was kind of adorable, actually. Rainy put a knee on his back and held him down on the concrete until he finally went limp.

Once he was well and truly out, eyes rolled back behind half-closed lids, Rainy fished around in his pockets until he found his cell phone and wallet. Password protected, credit cards and ID all with *James Montgomery* printed on them. No room key. Rainy retrieved his knife, then picked up the gun—Beretta M9; army-pedigree goon for sure—and checked the magazine before sticking it into his waistband and tugging his shirt down over it.

Held up, he texted Malia. *Be there in two hours.*

Rainy stood over Jesse's immaculately dressed, unconscious form and considered the logistics of killing him. It would be easy to bring the car around and stuff him into the trunk, drive out to the spot on the edge of the Everglades he favored for dumping, and put a bullet in his skull. Leave him for the gators, who understood the arrangement as well as he did. If Jesse was Seong's muscle, the legal heat wouldn't be too bad. It would escalate things with Seong, but if he'd put out a hit on Rainy, those bridges were already flamed half to the waterline.

Jesse looked softer in his sleep. His brow was open, his lips parted. He twitched a little, like a sleeping puppy, then his face pinched minutely and his lip curled like he was biting someone in a dream.

Rainy sighed.

"Now we're even," he told him. Let it never be said that he was a selfish lover.

He tugged Jesse's tie out from his vest and used it to mop the blood off of Jesse's mouth and chin where Rainy's shoe had sliced the inside of his lip open. He wasn't that heavy, and Rainy easily got him up off the concrete and over his shoulder. He crossed the bay to the service elevator and dumped him inside, hitting the button for the second floor.

The plain, whitewashed staff corridor was empty when the doors opened, so Rainy scooped his charge up in a bridal carry. Jesse's head lolled against his shoulder, mouth open, which might have been endearing if it weren't for the stream of blood running down into Rainy's shirt.

He ducked around a laundry cart and into the main hallway, making for his room. It was two corners to 1243. Luckily, the key was in his front pocket, so he just had to bump his hip against the sensor to unlock the door. He pushed it open and dumped Jesse onto the bed.

A few doors down, Dean Holister was starting to go cold and stiff in the tub. Rainy threw the deadbolt and flipped the light on to survey his situation, hands on his hips.

Jesse was half-buried in the hideous white confection that was the comforter, totally dead to the world. He looked ridiculous. Rainy snapped a picture before tugging off his expensive-looking leather shoes and sitting him up to strip off his jacket. Jesse mumbled in his sleep as Rainy arranged him on his side so he wouldn't drown in blood or vomit.

His phone buzzed in his pocket. Malia: *I swear to God, if you're making me wait here so you can make it with some stupid hotel bar slut...*

Not exactly, Rainy replied. He looked down at Jesse, whose lashes were soft against his cheeks, blond and feathery at the tips.

He's a special hotel bar slut.

The cocktail of depressants he'd whipped up for Holister had the potential to kill a man all on its own, so he settled into a chair and flicked idly through Malia's notes, glancing up occasionally to make sure Jesse's breathing hadn't stopped. After ten minutes, he became restless. He paced a bit, then had an idea. He laid his Colt on the rug and tried to kick it up into his hand. It went skittering off into a corner.

"Motherfucker made it look so easy," he complained, and went to retrieve it.

After an hour, he had managed several dings in the wood furniture legs and not one single sick gun-soccer trick, so he gave up. Jesse had started to twitch more restlessly, muttering into the pillow's taffeta roses. Rainy checked his watch again, then walked to the phone on the nightstand and placed an order with the front desk.

"Charge it to the same card," he told them. It was about time to scrap the Luis Pliego identity, anyway.

Fifteen minutes later, there was a knock at the door and Rainy opened it to accept the room service cart with its silver-lidded dish. He lifted the cover to reveal a picture-perfect eggs benedict. Then he picked up the requested bottles from the corner of the cart and, with extreme prejudice, smothered the plate in ketchup and hot sauce.

Jesse had rolled closer to the side of the bed at the smell of food, and his hand was doing a sort of weird little spasm on the mattress next to him. Rainy tore a page from the pad on the nightstand and stuck a note to the room service cart.

Room is paid for 'til 10, he wrote. *Eggs not poisoned. Promise.*

After a beat, he added, *See you around.*

Then he stacked Jesse's things on the counter, gathered up his suitcase, and closed the door quietly on his way out. When he hit the street, the same young valet brought his car around, and Rainy pressed a hefty tip into his hand before tearing off into the night.

Chapter 3

Florida Man: Crime Means Bad Coworkers

Rainy was awoken when Marco Espinosa dropped onto the couch next to him with enough force to cause a tidal wave, bouncing Rainy's head against the armrest. He sat up, groaning.

"Jesus, have some respect for your betters." Swinging his feet to the linoleum floor, he fumbled for his sneakers.

He'd gotten back to the Rattrap, the office kept by himself, Malia, and a few other mercenaries, well after midnight. He and Malia had spent two hours polishing off the Holister contract until she went home and he passed out on the couch. Now, he had a terrible crick in his neck and his clothes smelled like mildew.

He and the others who hung around the Rattrap were technically freelance, but the lines in Miami were drawn pretty clearly—they were Espinosa-loyal, which meant no Vees or any other Espinosa enemies. Fortunately, they still got plenty of business; unfortunately, this meant that Rainy had to deal with Emilio Espinosa's darling third child.

Marco rolled onto his back, feet propped up against the wall and head dangling off the couch, and pointed at Rainy's face. "What the hell happened to you?"

Rainy probed his swollen right eye, wincing. When he flipped on his phone camera, it was mottled an ugly shade of purple. "Had some trouble."

"From Dean Holister?" Marco asked. "Fucking *how?*"

"No, not from Holister," Rainy snapped, offended.

Before Marco could reply, a new voice cut in.

"Fuck, it looks way worse this morning. Why didn't you ice it like I told you?" Malia strode through the ajar door, petite and delicate, looking unfairly fresh and rested in a clean pair of flared jeans with her butterfly locs pulled back into a ponytail. She dumped her bag in front of her desk with its bank of desktop monitors and flopped into her five-hundred-dollar gaming chair, which Marco was forbidden from touching under any circumstances.

"We don't have an ice maker here," Rainy protested.

"Then go home, you hooligan. This isn't a halfway house." She swiveled to address Marco. "Also, why is your sister lurking the entryway like a wraith?"

Marco sighed theatrically and flopped face down on the couch, which was gross considering Rainy was pretty sure it had been there when they'd bought the place. "I owe her twenty bucks."

"Then pay the woman. She scares me."

Marco turned a pair of watery brown puppy eyes on them.

"Oh, hell no." Rainy shoved off the couch and crossed to the plastic jar of lollipops on Malia's desk. It had a peeling masking-tape label that read *Rainy's*. He unwrapped one and stuck it in his mouth. "Your dad is a millionaire. You can cough up twenty bucks."

"You guys never let me in on anything with a decent payout."

"That's because your dad is a millionaire. Also, a crime lord. Only softballs for you, Junior." Malia flicked on one of her monitors, then pointed at Rainy. "All you. I need to pay for a ride to class later."

Rainy sighed and fished a twenty out of his wallet while Marco made a disgusted face at Malia.

"I can't believe you have one of the coolest jobs ever, and to you it's just a side gig to put you through undergrad."

"That's because, unlike you, I actually *wanted* to go to school."

Emilio Espinosa, Puerto Rican expat and patriarch of the most powerful crime family in Florida, was a firm believer that his children were above ordinary grunt work. His elder son Felix was the heir to the empire, his daughter Catalina was the family's personal defense attorney, and his youngest child Marco had sabotaged his own pre-med career until Emilio finally caved and accepted that his son's dream was to be a lowly contract killer.

"I'm a man of the people," Marco frequently told them, sweeping his arms expansively. A pain in the ass was what he was.

Lina Espinosa herself had pushed through the unlocked door and was now clacking across the floor in her shiny black stilettos. She and Marco had the same strong nose and thick, dark hair, though Marco had, in a delightful twist of fate, been passed over by the height that Lina and Felix had both inherited.

Rainy wordlessly handed her the twenty-dollar bill and she tucked it into the pocket of her smart black skirt suit.

"Thanks for the ride," Marco called.

"Why did you need a ride, anyway?" Rainy asked. "Where's your car?"

Lina rolled her eyes. "I had to bail him out of jail. Again. For jaywalking."

"How do you even get arrested for jaywalking?"

"I just kept doing it in front of them until I disrupted traffic and they had to bring me in," Marco told him cheerfully.

"Let me guess: the arresting officer was Sergeant Tessa?"

Marco sighed dreamily. "I actually got her to laugh at one of my jokes while I was cuffed in the back of the squad car this time. Next time, I bet I can get a real smile."

Lina brandished her car keys at Rainy. "Please tell me that after last night, I don't have to get you out of another homicide charge."

She squinted at his black eye. "Double homicide? I know that's not from Holister."

"No, I ran into this other guy. Apparently, Seong's put out a hit on me."

Malia let her feet drop to the floor. "Oh my God, you didn't tell me it was *Adler*."

"Adler." Rainy rolled the name around his mouth with the sweet-tart artificial taste of green apple.

"Spooky guy with the facial scar?"

Rainy pointed his lollipop at her. "That's him."

"Who's Adler?" Marco asked.

"Seong's assassin-on-retainer," Malia said. "He has the Vees pissing their pants. If this turf war between Seong and you guys keeps escalating, he'll probably be chewing his way through your ranks soon too."

Rainy leaned a hip against Malia's desk. *Adler.* He tested the name against his memory of the man from the previous night. His sarcastic drawl, his haughty eyes, the way he'd pushed Rainy back on the pallets and taken him apart with his mouth.

Adler.

"He's ex-military, for sure," Rainy offered. "What else do you know? First name?"

Malia shook her head. "No first name. If you put any stock in word on the street, he either used to be super-duper special ops, or Seong fished him out of some third-world prison. Either way, Adler's been loyal as a dog to the guy for years."

Lina snorted. "If you put any stock in word on the street, he once bit a guy's pinkie off and just swallowed it instead of bothering to spit it out."

"That one might actually be true," Rainy said. "He's a fucking terror." He settled fully onto Malia's desk. "Find me what you can on him."

"If he really was military, it shouldn't be hard to pull records. I just need some data other than the surname."

Rainy pictured Adler in his mind's eye. There were a few choice images that weren't at all hard to conjure up. "White with brown hair. Thirty-ish, six-foot, but skinny. Dresses like a fucking Edwardian gentleman. Scar, obviously. Deep South accent. Montgomery was his alias, so I'm ninety percent on Alabama." He paused. "Wait, hold on; I have a picture."

The image he'd snapped in the hotel room was even funnier in the light of day. Adler was snuggled into the ugly, frothy bedspread, lips parted to show his bloody teeth. Rainy felt a weird flash of fondness.

The others leaned in to look at it. "Jesus," Malia said, "did you kill him?"

"No, just knocked him out."

Lina scowled. "You knocked him out and didn't kill him while he was unconscious?"

"It just didn't seem sporting."

"You literally drowned an unconscious man earlier last night."

Marco squinted at Rainy's phone. "Is he in bed? Oh, shit, did you hit that?" He straightened and gave Rainy a high five.

"Confusingly, yes. Although not during the bed part." Rainy frowned. "And especially not during the unconscious part. He was very conscious."

"Ugh, I do *not* want to hear this." Malia swiped Rainy's phone and texted the photo to herself. "I'll find you everything there is to know about this guy if you promise to never tell me about it."

"Deal." Rainy crunched the rest of his lollipop and tossed the stick. "Lina, you on your way out?"

He left Malia and Marco to bicker and walked with Lina into the Rattrap's garage. His car was waiting there for him, sandwiched behind Lina's SUV. It was his baby and by far the most expensive thing he owned, sleek and silver and lovely. He pulled out of the garage and drove with the top down, enjoying the sunshine and sticky air. There were thunderheads on the horizon, and it looked like afternoon showers.

His place was in Riverside, as close to downtown as he could get without edging out of Espinosa turf. Ever since he'd been a kid, the city had been divided up that way—Espinosas in the south, Vees in the north. Brickell, with its waterfront high-rises and business centers, belonged solidly to Andy Parish. And now Hyun-woo Seong had begun carving out his own slice of the waterfront, in the Upper East Side and northern edge of downtown.

Contrary to Malia's insistence, it would have been hard to call Rainy's apartment a home. It was a space for him to store his stuff and occasionally shower; other than that, he wasn't around much. The apartment was on the fourth floor and was essentially unchanged from when he'd bought it years ago—airy, bright, and mostly empty. As soon as he stepped through the door, he began mentally calculating the quickest excuse he could come up with to leave again.

Minimizing the time he spent here made him less antsy. Rainy had been like that all his adult life—always feeling like he needed to shift, move, run, do whatever was necessary to stay in motion.

He dumped his kit onto the couch and went to rummage through the kitchen. There was some cereal, but the milk carton was empty where he'd put it back in the fridge as a reminder to himself to buy more milk. There was also a box of Chinese takeout that was no longer fit for human consumption. Rainy carried it to the balcony while crunching on a handful of dry cereal.

The week-old beef dish was pungent when he opened the box and set it on the balcony, a flat concrete platform with a wrought-iron railing that overlooked the shimmering glass skyscrapers of downtown. Rainy settled in the doorway and began to make sharp clicking noises with his tongue.

"Ay, Patoso!"

There was a set of scaffolding, left over from months-ago construction, that led up to Rainy's balcony from a nearby alley. Presently, a plump, scarred tomcat came hobbling up it, awkward on the twisted foot of an old injury. He wound through the bars just out of arm's reach, pretending not to be interested in the food. Rainy turned his head away and continued on his cereal. Patoso darted forward and dug into the beef, making gross feline chewing noises. When he finished, he deigned to allow Rainy one scratch of his ears before scooting off down the scaffolding, tail high in alarm.

Finished with his breakfast, Rainy moved into his bedroom, which was just as sparsely furnished as the rest of his space. It wasn't that Rainy didn't like things, per se; he certainly had the money to decorate the place however he wanted. It was just that he preferred to be out and about, and the thought of this place being cozy and comforting somewhere behind him filled him with an inexplicable unease. He preferred it as it was.

There were two big black suitcases under the bed. Rainy pulled one out and unzipped it to reveal a loosely organized stash of guns, ammo, knives, brass knuckles, assorted nasty chemicals, and an aluminum softball bat with a smiley face painted on the barrel. He selected another .45 semi-auto and laid it on the bed next to his Colt. If someone like Adler had it out for him, better safe than sorry.

Next, blessedly, shower. Rainy grabbed a fresh shirt from his closet (this one patterned with flamingos wearing leis) and stepped into the bathroom. He was running up a truly unholy olfactory mixture of murder sweat, fight-to-the-death sweat, general post-blowjob stickiness, alcohol, blood, and old couch smell. When he took off his shirt, there was a red wine splatter across the stomach and a patch of dried blood on the shoulder.

While he waited for the water to heat, he examined his face in the mirror. His right eye wasn't swollen so badly that he couldn't see, but it was a nasty red-purple. The bruise extended along the dip between his cheekbone and brow back into his hairline. No biggie; Rainy was used to shiners. If anything, they added a certain *je ne sais quoi* to his whole charming-boyish-rogue ensemble. His black hair, which was floppy at best and shaggy at worst, was long enough to flick over some of the damage anyway.

With his shirt out of the way, he evaluated the rest. There was a shallow bruise on his side, over the ridges of his obliques, from where Adler had tackled him. It was already going green. There was one high across his neck, too, where his throat was hoarse from the choking attempt. And then there was the dark mark on his shoulder, over the arch of his trapezius. Rainy's fingers hovered, hesitant to touch it. He remembered the feel of Adler's teeth there, the heat of his breath as he'd smoothed the pain away with an open-mouthed kiss.

When Rainy finally worked up the nerve to run a finger over it, he shivered at the muscle-deep ache.

The steam of the shower slowly loosened his stiff muscles, leaving him wrung out as an old washcloth. The heat made his face and shoulder throb again, and he rested his forehead against the wall, letting the water run through his hair.

The image of Adler's eyes, cold and deadly as any predator's, should have washed away the sweetness of the muscle memory of his weight pressing Rainy against the wall. And yet, Rainy couldn't stop his hand from drifting up to skim over the bruise, again and again.

He was freshly dressed and about to go retrieve a new carton of milk when his phone buzzed with a message from "Big E." He knocked milk down to the bottom of his to-do list and got into the car.

The Espinosa estate was a sprawling three-story in North Beach. It was barricaded with tall wrought-iron fences and a pair of grunts was always on patrol around the perimeter, rain or shine. Eduardo, one of the men on duty, fist-bumped Rainy as he opened the gate.

The driveway was modern, a spread of big white pavers gridded with neatly manicured grass. He parked next to Emilio's beloved Tor Red 1970s Plymouth Barracuda and turned off his engine, pushing his sunglasses up onto his head.

The big, brass-bound front door with its thorny-rose knocker was opened by Jazz McCormick, Emilio's longtime girlfriend.

"Rainy!" she exclaimed happily in her heavy Jersey accent, drawing him in to kiss him on both cheeks.

Jazz was a busty forty-ish bottle blonde who wore far too much leopard print. She was boisterous and friendly and entirely too open about her previous career as a sex worker, and Emilio doted on her like a princess, though anyone who came around was warned on pain of broken fingers never to bring up marriage.

"Emilio's waiting for you," she gushed. "He's in the study. Can I bring you some lemonade? Splash a little rum and triple sec in there?" She tittered and threw up her hands. "It's two o'clock some-where!"

"Not today, Jazz," Rainy said, extricating himself gently. "I'll just show myself in."

The Espinosas' home was tastefully but lavishly decorated. Rainy passed through the marble-tiled foyer and the sitting room with its heavy oak furniture to the room adjoining Emilio's study. There was a black duffel bag sitting on the table, with two men bent over it. The older one straightened when Rainy entered.

"Ay, Rainy! R-man!" He shot some finger guns. "Killing hard, or hardly killing?"

Rainy forced a laugh. "You got me, Felix."

The eldest Espinosa sibling was tall and hawk-faced like his sister, but with his father's prematurely receding hairline. He patted the kid next to him on the shoulder.

"Javi and I were just talking about a slipup he made, but now that he knows what's up, no harm done, right?"

"Uh, yeah. Sure, Felix," the kid replied.

"We're going to have to dock your pay until we're reimbursed for the quarter-kilo you lost, though."

Javi made big eyes at him. "But, Felix, I can't afford to lose that much. I need that money for my mom."

Felix waffled. "Well, Javi, I'm trying to be stern with you here—"

The study door swung open, and all three spines in the room stiffened. Emilio Espinosa strode out. Barrel-chested and balding with a thick, dark mustache, he went right to the table and placed a hand on Javi's shoulder.

"So, Javi. Losing merchandise, now, are we?" His tone was jovial, but the lightness of it was drowned in the bass of his voice.

Javi seemed to have shrunk several inches, as though Emilio's hand were heavy enough to push his ankles down through the tile floor. "I had to run, and I lost track of it."

Emilio grunted. Letting go of the boy's shoulder, he reached into the duffel bag and pulled out a white, plastic-wrapped bundle. "I'm just a little fucking curious how you lose twenty-five grand of heroin." He tossed the brick to Javi, who fumbled and almost dropped it.

"It was an accident. I swear on my life." Javi looked to Felix, who had suddenly become very interested in the woodwork of the table.

Emilio boomed out a laugh, one that rumbled in the high-ceilinged room like thunder. "You hear that, Rainy? What a funny choice of words."

Javi licked his lips and let out a reedy answering laugh, several seconds too late. It dropped out of his mouth stone-dead when Emilio pulled out his gun and set it on the table between them.

"You don't do things on accident, ever. You do what I fucking tell you, or you do nothing at all. And, now, I'm telling you to get out there and find that fucking merchandise. Understand?"

"Yes," Javi said thinly.

"Good. And next time you decide to do something on accident, I'll have Julian cut off your thumbs. Now get out of my house."

Javi scampered out of the room so fast that he practically left skid marks on the floor. Emilio sighed and stowed his gun, then kicked a fallen brick of heroin so it slid across the floor and hit the wall. Felix cleared his throat.

"I was, ah, handling it."

"Just get down to the fucking Hub and make sure nobody else is *losing* anything."

Felix nodded awkwardly to Rainy and marched toward the front door. Emilio waved Rainy into his study. He had gone all heavy, arrogant amusement again, the darkness from before shut glibly away behind a door.

The door, like most that people constructed with their expressions and words, was transparent to Rainy.

"They don't make kids like they used to, I tell you," Emilio said. "I got runners and enforcers making fucking videos on their phones. Why don't they come like you were when you were that age? Smart and scrappy and grateful."

"I remember being called impudent pretty often, though," Rainy offered.

"Fucking funny too. Why did I ever let you go freelance?" Emilio settled into his desk chair with a resounding creak and folded his hands over his belly. "Sit down."

Rainy sank into one of the plush chairs in front of Emilio's massive lacquered wood desk. "Is this about Adler?"

"It's about Seong in general. But, yeah. Marco tattled on you. You kicked the guy's ass last night?"

Rainy wondered how heavily edited the version of events Marco had given his father was. "Uh, in a sense."

"Good. I'm going to be frank with you. Seong has only been in town a couple months, but he's already making the Vees his bitch. Now he's edging in on the docks, and the only good fronting is between me and Andy Parish. Seong's the type who got rich and then went dirty, not the other way around, and he's full of all kinds of nasty corporate tricks. I don't have the kind of above-the-board connections Parish has, so Seong is gunning for our share. He's new in town; he doesn't respect the understanding between us and the crooked bigwigs like Parish. I want to put him in his place before he gets any more ideas."

"What happens to businessmen who don't understand the way things work around here is what I did to Dean Holister last night," Rainy said. "You want me to ice Seong? That's a big ask."

"No, no, nothing like that. I just want to warn him not to stick his hand in our cookie jar. Nice job with Holister, by the way. Painkillers in the bathtub. Classic. My hands aren't going to turn up dirty on that, are they?"

"When have I ever let you down?"

Emilio grinned a toothy, predatory grin. "That's why you're here. Two days ago, Seong had one of my DA's office guys put down. You know how long it took me to put him there? Now they're after you. So, I want you to take care of Seong's lap dog."

Understanding crept, cautious, up Rainy's neck. "You want me to kill Adler."

"I'll give you double the Holister job."

"Triple," Rainy said immediately. "What, you want a friends and family discount?"

"He's already got a target on you. You need to deal with this anyway."

"Lying low until they lose interest isn't the same as gunning for the guy. Triple."

"Double and some change."

"I heard he ate a man's pinkie."

Emilio sighed. "Fine, fine. Just get it done before Seong pushes it too far. If I have to mop Marco or Lina up off a warehouse floor, this city is going to burn."

Rainy thought of Adler in the docking bay, quick and efficient and brutal despite the drugs in his system. He was no joke. But Rainy had offed plenty of professional killers. He just had to find a weak spot. Everyone had one.

The thought of killing Adler wasn't particularly troubling either. Sure, he gave great head, but he was a world-class asshole and clearly didn't have any qualms about killing Rainy. And for triple the Holister payout, there weren't many people Rainy *wouldn't* kill.

"All right," he said.

"Good," Emilio said. "Before you go, though, I think you should remember that I'm not particularly sympathetic to *accidents* right about now."

"Please, E, it's me you're talking to. Nice and smooth. No accidents, no distractions."

Emilio smiled. "That's what I like to hear. Now, bring me his head."

Rainy spread his arms magnanimously.
"Medium or rare?"

Chapter 4

Florida Man Revealed as Incompetent Stalker

R ainy didn't mind committing murder as much as he probably should have.

It wasn't that he saw people as objects, or anything like that. He knew that the people he killed had souls and lives and dreams. It was just that, in the end, it was a lot easier to do calculus with the value of those lives than most people would be willing to admit.

The first man he'd killed had been with his bare hands. It had been easy, so ridiculously easy that he hadn't been able to believe it. Human bodies were so fragile, if you had the willpower. He had knelt there in the gravel, soaked to the skin, over a limp body. It hadn't been exhilarating, and it hadn't been soul-crushing. It was just doing as nature intended.

Didn't hurt that it paid well, either.

So he didn't lose any sleep over making plans to kill Adler, who was just as much a stone-cold killer as he was. He was going to have to make this one good. Rainy was proud of the Holister job; it had been neat, quick, and creative. He was going to have to do a lot better than that for someone like Adler, so this was going to be one for the books.

Killing was mostly in the preparation. That first R—research—was the weightiest. Malia carried out her end of it in her invisible world of bank statements and insurance records. Rainy was a little more

47

traditional. He learned by watching. That was the trick to being a really effective killer—being able to look at someone and know them, inside and out. Rainy had always had that. It was what his mentor, Rezakova, had seen in him years ago.

Rainy knew that Adler was physically dangerous, and that he knew his stuff. He'd done his own research, enough to know Rainy's schedule and predict his movements. The "ex-military" was written all over him, from the way he stood to the gun he favored. He hadn't figured out his craft through trial and error—he'd had it taught to him.

This all gave Rainy an idea of the essence of who Adler was. Exacting, thorough, regimented. Clever, but not creative. Inflexible. He was all raw ferocity, confident in his deadliness. That was how Rainy had gotten the drop on him; Adler was used to solving problems by ramming his head against them until they broke, and had never had a use for thinking outside the box.

Still, there was an elusiveness to the picture that made Rainy uneasy. That gleam of feral viciousness that had nearly killed Rainy despite his upper hand. The fact that Adler had followed through on their flirtation before going in for the kill.

It seems only polite, don't you think?

But why? Certainly not just to steal Rainy's knife. Was it a weird power thing that he got off on? Was he just that bored and horny?

There was something missing from his picture. Something that made Adler unpredictable. And there was nothing Rainy hated in other people more than unpredictability. Unpredictability got you killed.

So, it was time for some good old-fashioned recon.

The morning after he got the assignment from Emilio, Rainy put on a toned-down shirt and a pair of sunglasses and found, with Malia's directions, Seong's downtown offices. They were located in a glass-and-steel neo-futurist monstrosity that had a vaguely phallic suggestion to it. He parked across the street and snapped a picture to send to the Rattrap group chat.

Grow up, Malia replied, at the same time that Marco said, *Nice*.

Malia was still trawling for any kind of address on Adler, but Rainy figured that if Adler and Seong were as joined at the hip as everyone seemed to think, he would eventually be found here.

He only had to wait two hours. Around ten, Rainy glanced up from the sudoku he was idly completing on his phone to watch a tall, narrow figure in a tweed three-piece suit stride out onto the sidewalk. Fucking tweed. *This* was the man who'd given Rainy head so good that it kept randomly popping into his brain days later to drive him to distraction.

Fucking *tweed*.

It didn't help that he looked fantastic in it. The suit was classy and professional and tailored to within an inch of its life, but it was the way Adler wore it that made it unbearable. With his physique, he should've been lanky, but he prowled around like a big cat, all lithe, deadly grace. He stood on the curb and checked his watch, and suddenly Rainy was having war flashbacks to watching him do the same thing while kneeling on the floor between Rainy's open thighs, looking snide at Rainy's boneless post-orgasmic bliss.

Rainy was so distracted by the memory that he almost missed the black car pulling up alongside the curb. He turned on his engine as Adler climbed inside, then counted out the appropriate number of cars between them before pulling out to follow.

The car took Adler south, out of downtown and into the city's tiny Korean enclave. It took a turn down a narrow street and dropped him off in front of the kind of weather-grimy, battered shopping center only locals ever frequented. Rainy frowned, watching him walk in through the entrance archway before circling the block for parking.

It was a partially overcast day, but Rainy kept his dark glasses on as he entered the shopping center. Luckily, it was busy for a Friday morning. He kept to the edge of the two-tiered courtyard layout, passing through the shadow of shops whose signs were written almost exclusively in Hangul. He paused behind the natural blind formed by a line of customers for a eomuk stand.

Adler was easy to spot, with his formal suit and relatively tall stature. He was on the top level of the center, where a balcony with a sun-bleached wooden railing overlooked the courtyard below. He walked purposefully into a storefront that had no discernible English signage, and Rainy cut across the courtyard toward the large concrete staircase to follow.

He made himself inconspicuous on a bench across from and to the right of the storefront, keeping his head lowered to his phone. Inside the store, Adler was leaning against the counter, talking to the elderly, stooped Korean man who stood behind the register.

Rainy wondered what Adler was doing here. The man didn't look particularly frightened, so Adler probably wasn't here to kill him. More than likely, he was carrying out some business for Seong. It didn't seem like a shakedown, and Seong wasn't the type to play with small fish like that anyway. Was this an underground business contact? Maybe an informant?

Adler handed the man a slip of paper from his pocket. The man glanced at it before disappearing behind a curtain into the back of the store. Some kind of supplier, then. Weapons? Drugs? Information?

The man returned with something large draped over his arm—a pair of long fabric bags on hangers.

Dry cleaning.

He had followed Adler here to watch him pick up his fucking dry cleaning.

Adler accepted the bags and exited the store, headed the opposite direction from Rainy's bench. Rainy rose after a few beats and trailed him at a distance, making sure to keep at least fifty feet between them. Adler descended the steps again and turned right into another store with solely Hangul signage. This one, though, was obviously a grocery store. Tall shelves formed a maze inside, packed with brightly packaged products Rainy couldn't read the labels of. Adler vanished into the labyrinth, and Rainy waited outside for a full minute before following.

He hung back in a snack aisle, watching Adler fill a bag with produce and some canned goods. Before walking up to the register, he grabbed a bouquet of tulips.

The woman at the register greeted Adler by name. When she named a price for the produce he'd set down, he started saying something to her that had the distinctive sound of haggling, but Rainy couldn't understand the words. The woman laughed at something he said and waved him off, her words just as nonsensical to Rainy.

He speaks Korean! he texted Malia.

Bitch, I am in econ lecture. Do not bother me unless you've been shot.

When Rainy looked up, Adler was gone. He cursed under his breath and exited the store, but the bastard must have hightailed it somewhere. He couldn't spot him anywhere in the crowd that milled around the courtyard.

He made a full circuit around the center, keeping to the edges to seek unobserved, but he couldn't find Adler. Finally, he stepped back onto the street, but a brief venture in both directions turned up no clues. He'd lost him. Get distracted for twenty seconds, and boom! Adler was a slippery fucker, Rainy had to give him that.

Resigning himself to hunting down another lead, he made one last inquisitive circle around the block before returning to his car. As soon as he approached, an odd feeling of wrongness tangled its fingers in his hair and tugged at the back of his skull. He'd parallel parked between two sedans, and the same cars were there, only now they looked... taller.

"Shit! Oh, no, no, no." Rainy raced over to his car, which was riding unusually low against the curb. He crouched down, a hand braced on his baby's glossy silver paint job, and ran the other hand over the first tire he reached. "God damn it!"

There was a straight puncture several inches long gouged into the sidewall of his tire. Upon further inspection, all four of his tires had been irreparably slashed. Rainy grabbed two fistfuls of his hair.

"Fuck!" He threw his sunglasses down on the pavement, where one of the lenses cracked. "Fucking hell!"

There was a note pinned under the windshield wiper closest to the driver's door.

In neat, looping cursive, it read: *Stop following me.*

Eight hours later, Rainy was fuming on a rooftop.

Twelve hundred dollars. Twelve hundred dollars, plus whatever the tow bill was going to be. Threaten Rainy's life, fine. Even fucking kill him, whatever. But mess with his car? Oh, hell no. That was not going to fly. Twelve *hundred* dollars.

Screw not getting a rush from killing. Rainy was going to fucking enjoy this.

He needed something really, really nasty. Electrocution, maybe. Burying Adler alive. Tossing him off a bridge in lead shoes. In an area with sharks. With some holes poked in him to let the blood out. And a hair dryer thrown in for good measure.

Rainy had had a lot of time to think about it during the five hours he'd sat at the dealership.

As he sweated on the cement lip of the roof in the muggy autumn evening, he distracted himself by daydreaming about ripping up one of Adler's fancy tailored suits in front of him. Tearing it limb from lapel. Maybe taking a butane torch to that crisp tweed jacket while Adler begged for its life. Also, in this dream Adler may or may not have been tied up. And naked.

It was a multifaceted fantasy.

The good thing about the time he'd been forced to sit around getting new tires was that it had given him the opportunity to puzzle out where to look for Adler next.

He'd really bought quite a lot of produce for one person. He might have been stocking up for the week, but Rainy thought it was more likely that he was cooking for someone else. Then, the flowers. Adler didn't really seem like the type of person to buy flowers for himself, and, with his impeccable taste in suits, Rainy assumed he wouldn't be getting tulips for a date. That meant either he was visiting his mother—not likely, given the accent—or they were a hostess gift for an older woman he knew.

Well, that gave Rainy an idea, at least.

So now he was camped out on the roof of the insurance company headquarters across from Seong's downtown penthouse. He'd bribed a security guard to let him up after business hours and now he was huddled up with a pair of binoculars.

Seong's apartment was almost entirely glass-faced on the edge closest to Rainy. It took up the whole top floor of the luxury apartment building and was done up in sleek modern appliances and tasteful furniture, and it had to cost a bajillion dollars. Currently taking up residence on a gravel roof, Rainy kind of hated it.

Through his binoculars, he watched the Seongs bustle about their giant, shiny chrome kitchen. Hyun-woo Seong himself was a slight man in his fifties, with mostly gray hair and a crinkly smile too gentle to be trustworthy. He'd shed his jacket and loosened his tie at the door, and he was currently frying something at the stove. His wife, Su-jin, was busy setting the table while their kids, ages eleven and eight, were on the huge L-shaped couch, engrossed in some indecipherable teen drama that Malia watched religiously.

Su-jin perked up and wiped her hands on a towel, then walked to the front door. Rainy checked his watch. Seven on the dot. Su-jin opened the door to reveal Adler in his same pristine suit, holding a large foil-covered bowl and the bouquet of tulips. He bent down to accept a kiss on the unscarred cheek, then presented the flowers to her with the tooth-rotting charm of a Southern gentleman.

Damn, Rainy was good. He high-fived himself mentally, and then, since he was alone, also physically.

Adler deposited his bowl in the kitchen, where Seong clapped him on the shoulder. The kids leaped up and ran to wrap themselves around his middle, and it might have been a fault in the binoculars, but it looked like Adler actually smiled. It made his eyes crinkle and his scar bunch up, and it looked better on him than his bespoke suit.

Hmph.

The Seong family plus Adler settled in at the table to eat. It occurred to Rainy that this was actually a pretty boring stakeout scenario. It was starting to get dark, Rainy's surroundings illuminated by the light through the penthouse windows, and they were just sitting there with their mouths moving soundlessly, eating from a spread that looked unfairly delicious. Rainy grumpily dug his hand into the bag of trail mix between his feet, which was just nuts and raisins now because he'd already eaten out all the candy.

In just twenty minutes or so, it was fully dark, and Rainy kept shifting uncomfortably on the gravel. Adler and the Seongs had cracked open a bottle of wine. Rainy was not looking forward to waiting through the whole bottle to follow Adler home. To occupy himself, he focused on watching Adler's mannerisms—food cut neatly with fork and knife, meat and sides eaten one by one instead of all together. He still held his head in that slightly crooked way Rainy had noticed at the bar, his chin tilted like he was always trying to angle his unscarred side toward whoever was speaking.

Rainy devoted entirely too much focus to watching him drink his wine, unhurried, tongue sliding over the rim of the glass to catch the last drop of Merlot, and remembering the way he'd looked in the wine cellar. More particularly, the way his tongue had looked on Rainy's skin.

Around eight thirty, Rainy was so bored that he started trying to read the Seongs' lips, then gave up after about five minutes in favor of making up his own dialogue.

So, Seong asked, *have you made any progress in taking down that devastatingly handsome and charming hitman I sent you to kill?*

While waving off the offer of a refill on wine, Adler replied, No; *now he's on my tail. I fear for my life because he is so spectacularly talented, yet I also feel a burning passion for him. Ever since our brief sexual encounter, I haven't been able to get him out of my head. I hope he's gentle when he inevitably kills me, and maybe lets me make sweet love to him beforehand.*

"Ha, in your dreams," Rainy muttered.

The boredom was maybe getting to him a little bit.

It was nearly nine when Adler finally excused himself and stood from the table, disappearing deeper into the penthouse. A minute or two later, he briefly passed in front of the windows again, carrying a long black parcel under his arm. Seong called something to him, and Adler waved vaguely before vanishing once more into the recesses of the apartment. Rainy frowned, waiting for him to reappear.

Several minutes later, he still hadn't. Rainy was getting antsy, and he'd taken to scanning the sidewalk below to see if Adler had used some unseen back exit to leave the building. So far, no luck. Where the hell had he gone?

His phone buzzed in his pocket, making him jump. Glancing around to make sure a nonexistent audience hadn't seen the slipup, he fumbled for his phone. If he was lucky, it was an old hookup looking for a booty call. If he was unlucky, it was Marco asking which color of diamonds Rainy thought would be most likely to make Sergeant Tessa realize her undying love for him. He pulled it out—unknown number—and answered.

"Now's not a great time."

"Hi, *Mister Rainy*," Adler drawled. Rainy was so startled that he nearly dropped the phone.

"How did you get this number?"

"*Come on. Don't embarrass yourself.*" There was a mechanical clicking and sliding sound from Adler's end. "*I just wanted to give you fair warning. You don't wanna keep fucking around with me.*"

"I'm not too worried. If I remember correctly, things worked out pretty well for me last time."

"*That's what the warning's for. Nobody gets the drop on me twice. Now, be polite and wave hello.*"

A flash of alarm ripped up Rainy's spine. Adler knew he was here. But could he really see him? He scanned the penthouse windows. No sign of Adler. The sidewalk below was clear, too, which left only...

Body going very still, Rainy moved only his neck muscles to tilt his head up. The roof of Seong's apartment building was approximately twenty feet above him, ringed with a concrete lip. Adler had his elbows propped up on it. He was holding a scoped rifle.

He snapped off a lazy salute.

"*Fuck.*" Rainy dropped, skinning himself on the gravel. A bullet slashed the air where his head had been. The shot echoed in the canyon between the buildings, and someone on the street shouted in alarm. Rainy was already moving.

Sending gravel flying off the roof, he scrabbled to his feet and took off for the concrete structure that housed the roof access door. Everything inside him was perfectly still, the calm at the heart of the storm that he felt when his body flew straight through panic and into life-or-death. Another shot cracked through the air, and he didn't see, didn't feel. Just ran.

A bullet hit the door shelter in front of him, showering him with chips of concrete. He dodged and kept going. The door swallowed him, wrapping him tight in the safety of concrete and steel. He felt his body, the air white and blistering in his lungs, checking for holes. His clothes were dry and clean. No hits.

He was safe.

He'd managed to hold on to his phone, but the binoculars and trail mix were a lost cause. Rainy cursed violently under his breath. He considered popping out with his Colt and squeezing off a few retaliatory shots, but Adler was well out of his range.

Bastard. Fucking bastard, stupid car-slashing, rifle-wielding, cock-sucking—

The phone was still connected. Rainy raised it to his ear, snarling.

"*See you around.*" Rainy could hear the smirk in Adler's voice before the line went dead. He pressed himself back into the concrete wall and squeezed his hands into fists until they stopped shaking.

It was possible that this was going to be more difficult than he had first anticipated.

Chapter 5

Florida Man Plots Revenge, Kidnapping

Rainy spent the next three days in a truly foul mood.

Over the weekend, he had to divert some of his attention to helping Novikov, one of the Rattrap's other in-house contractors, bleach down a warehouse where a hit had gone particularly poorly. There were no more half-baked attempts at tailing Adler. Rainy had accepted that the best course of action for now was to wait for Malia to finish working her magic.

And, of course, to stew.

Every time he saw his car, a hot red monster of rage gnawed its way deeper into his belly. And every time he read the note Adler had left on his windshield, which he'd crumpled up in his pocket, he wanted to drive his fist through the nearest wall.

It didn't help that the one number he didn't want to deal with at the moment kept blowing up his phone. He considered blocking it after it kept vibrating his jeans pocket for minutes at a time when he was wearing heavy rubber gloves coated in industrial chemicals and couldn't reach around to turn it off.

"You should answer," his friend Julian told him when they were out for drinks on Saturday night, watching Novikov trying to blunder his way into a bachelorette partygoer's pants.

"Do I look like I have time for that?" Rainy asked, cold. He wanted to shut the line of conversation down as efficiently as possible.

Marco, who Rainy had seen gut a man with a hunting knife with the disturbing glee of a little girl on Christmas morning, tipped his beer. "You are one stone-cold son of a bitch, Rainy." Then he cupped a hand around his mouth and shouted at Novikov's back, "You got this, Ilya!" Novikov turned red and scampered away from the bridesmaid like his cover had just been blown.

"Aw, come on, Marco," Malia scolded, nursing her own drink. "It's going to take the guy another thirty years to work up the nerve to talk to a girl again."

Novikov, despite being just about the right size to crush a man's skull in his fist like a pigeon egg, hid a shy and soft heart behind his mountain of prison-tattooed muscle.

Their booth at the club, forcibly cleared by a bouncer whenever Marco swaggered in, had started out the night crammed with Espinosa acquaintances—Rainy's old friends from coming up through the ranks and the young pups Marco hung around. Now, most had scattered to amorous pursuits or wandered off in some misguided drunken quest or other. Julian, a distant Espinosa cousin who'd been the one to show Rainy the ropes when he'd first joined up nine years ago, had already had to be restrained twice from chasing upstart frat bros out into the alley to "teach them a lesson." Tall but sort of rangy and unable to pack on muscle the way Rainy always had, Julian was always looking for a way to punch and stab out his insecurities. He was currently eyeing another loud group of twenty-somethings at the bar. Rainy stole his beer to distract him.

Malia never brought any friends around. In fact, Rainy knew next to nothing about the fine details of her life beyond the Rattrap. Once, Marco had spotted her on the street with a college friend and gone to say hello, and Malia had beaten him around the ears with a stapler at work the next day.

Don't so much as look at one of my real people again, do you hear me? she'd snapped, and that had made it clear enough.

That buried line of tension, though, was easy enough to ignore when they were all drunk and laughing at Marco as he diverted yet another giggling girl in a floral-print bustier off his lap.

"I'm sorry," he kept saying in what was apparently his approximation of a gentlemanly affectation. "I only have eyes for one woman."

Malia scrunched her nose at Rainy from across the table. "Ah, to be young and in love with the enemy."

"We're like, fucking... Romeo and Juliet," Marco supplied with drunken eloquence.

"What's your excuse, Rainy?" Malia smirked. "Can't keep up with the young bucks anymore?"

"Fuck you; I'm twenty-seven."

This was what he got for spending most of his time with two coworkers who were still college-aged. He turned to Julian for backup, only to find that he'd stolen away to find a fight while Rainy was distracted. Ah, well. He was in Lina's capable homicide-attorney hands now.

Just to prove Malia wrong, Rainy poached one of Marco's admirers and managed to spirit her as far as the nearest bathroom. He got a sloppy handjob and a damp, vodka-flavored makeout session for his trouble. His muscles stayed clenched the entire time with the effort of not letting his mind drift to the much more purposeful motion of Adler's wrist, the condescension in his eyes, and the way his mouth looked when he spoke Korean.

Professional frustrations, he told himself. Letting work collide with pleasure. Maybe Malia had the right of it.

The next morning, he woke alone in his own bed, the worst kind of waking. Rainy stared at the blank walls of his bedroom until he couldn't take it anymore and went to entertain himself by attempting the gun-kick move Adler had pulled in the hotel. He definitely hadn't been practicing. And certainly not every day.

On about the seven hundredth try, he managed to punt his Colt high enough to catch and crowed, "Take *that*," before he remembered that there was nobody around to hear.

He tried unsuccessfully to summon Patoso to the window before fleeing to the couch, the only piece of furniture in his main room, to watch the news on his phone. Reporting on the mysterious death of Dean Holister. Authorities were starting to suspect foul play and were looking for tips. At this point in the game, Rainy was as good as free and clear.

The news feed was interrupted by a call—the same old number. Rainy swiped it away before it had a chance to ring.

Please pick up, mijo, his mother texted. *You know how your father gets about Thanksgiving plans.*

Rainy ignored it and walked into the kitchen. He opened the fridge and stared at the brand-new, unopened carton of milk that sat alone on the shelf.

His parents lived in a moderately priced two-story in east Coconut Grove that he'd bought for them with the money from his first big contracts. His father still worked the occasional construction job, even though Rainy told him there was no need. His mother was as stay-at-home as she'd always been, though with her younger son moved out for a decade and her elder son dead just as long, she was bouncing off the walls with boredom.

Rafa works in entertainment management, she told her friends with the single-minded fervor of someone desperate to believe it. *You know the crazy hours they keep in that industry!*

He picked up his phone and fired off a message, barely glancing at the screen.

Busy with work right now. I'll call when I get the chance.

He threw the milk in the garbage can and left.

Halfway to the Rattrap, the touch display in his dash lit up with a text from Malia.

Merry Christmas, it said. Rainy grinned.

When he swanned into the office, she was perched smugly in her chair like a spider at the center of her web.

"Tell me you love me," she ordered.

"I love you, you goddess amongst lowly mortals."

Graciously, she swept a stack of paper off the printer and handed it over. Rainy fished a lollipop out of the jar. He always thought better when he had something to occupy his mouth.

"I thought it would be a little harder, at least," she began. "Seems like he didn't even try to cover his tracks. Adler's his real last name, as far as I can tell. Birth certificate and everything. I found an Adler off the Purple Heart roster who matched our guy straightaway. Army Special Forces, enlisted straight out of high school in rural Alabama. At first, I thought it was a dead end, though, because that Purple Heart? Posthumous. The Green Berets reported him KIA seven years ago after an IED detonation in Syria."

Rainy frowned. "But?"

"*But*, check this out: three months later, Hyun-woo Seong paid a visit to one of his IS-tied investors near Aleppo. Now, I won't speculate on what this all means, but let me lay out some facts for you. One week into the trip, Seong wires a neat little sum to a Syrian associate without explanation. He extends his trip by two weeks. Then, his favorite contact at the Ministry of Foreign Affairs buys himself a new Rolex, and a week later, Seong returns to Busan with a new friend sporting a mysteriously-appearing South Korean passport. American-born, twenty-two years old, occupation listed as *business attaché*." Malia tapped the packet with a violet-painted fingernail.

Rainy traced the name and birthday stamped in bold, black ink. It felt as stark and weirdly intimate as it always did, seeing a life laid out so easily in a few sentences.

"So, what, he faked his own death? Doesn't seem likely."

"No," Malia agreed. "I'm no expert, but the report the army filed on the incident seemed pretty sketchy. There were a lot of holes in the story, starting with the fact that the locations didn't really line up. My best guess is that they were up to a pretty big no-no, and when things went to shit, it was easier to write him off as dead than own up to it."

Rainy felt slightly queasy, until he remembered his slashed tires.

"So they left him to ISIS and then Seong, what, bought him? Doesn't really seem like the kind of thing to inspire undying loyalty."

"It might if you've been stuck in a Syrian prison for three months." Malia leaned over the desk and flipped open the packet to the second page, where there was a thumb-sized photograph. "That's our guy, right?"

It was an old army photo, dated from early in the year he'd been reported dead. Adler was twenty-two and despite his pristine uniform, he looked hopelessly young. Baby fat softened his jaw, and both his cheeks were smooth and downy as a puppy's ear. Rainy swallowed around the weird feeling in his throat.

"Yeah, that's him. Do you have an address?"

"Oh, Rainy. Rainy, Rainy, Rainy."

"Yeah, yeah, just fork it over."

And fork it over she did.

On Monday, Rainy got the bill from the tow company. It cemented his resolve that despite the fact that Adler had once been a very cute and wide-eyed cadet, he deserved to die a very nasty death.

Luckily, Rainy had a plan.

There were three important things that he'd taken away from the failed recon mission: one, Adler knew Rainy was after him. Two, he was very confident in his ability to outmatch Rainy. And three, everything about him, from the creases of his suit to his rifle etiquette, was regulation. That was the kind of thing that stuck in a man's mind. That was the kind of thing Rainy could exploit.

But his run-in with Adler's rifle on the roof had been a wake-up call, and despite the first impression he usually gave, Rainy wasn't dumb. Once he had Adler's schedule staked down, he cut Marco and Novikov in. It meant splitting the money, but this was a three-man job.

"I wouldn't normally let you anywhere near this, but I need the backup," he told Marco.

"Relax," Marco replied, puffing a cloud of raspberry-flavored vape in his face. "I'm a professional."

"You do everything I say. And don't lose your cool. He's... trying."

Marco smirked. "Sounded like you had a pretty good time with him. If I didn't have Tessa, maybe I'd let him get on his knees for me too."

Rainy felt an unexpected urge to slam Marco's face against the wall. It was irrational, obviously, but the image of Adler looking up through his lashes at Marco the way he'd looked up at Rainy made him want to throttle Marco almost as badly as he wanted to throttle Adler.

And, boy, had he fantasized about throttling Adler. Wrapping his hands around that long, elegant neck—so delicate, compared to the rest of him—and squeezing and squeezing until the skin turned black-and-blue and something snapped under his hands. Watching the spite go out of Adler's narrow, dark eyes.

"I don't know why I even told you about the blowjob thing," he said instead.

That was how he found himself crouching in the bushes at eleven at night, waiting.

Adler's apartment was set back from the street, with a walkway that cut to it through twin lines of shrubbery. Nice place. Tactically, weak. The only light on this portion of sidewalk was from the front exterior lights of the building, so there were plenty of shadows pooling among the foliage. Rainy arranged himself in one, still and poised for violence. His hand was clenched around a fistful of pebbles, so tight they dug indents into the flesh of his palm.

The clip of Italian leather shoes on the pavement had him stiffening. Adler opted for a sturdier dress boot rather than traditional Oxfords, and his step was distinctive. Rainy checked his watch. Punctual as ever.

Adler appeared at the end of the sidewalk, recognizable by the neatly tailored lines of his silhouette. Three paces closer. Rainy breathed deep to steady himself. He loosened his grip and let some of the pebbles clatter onto the pavement.

Adler had a gun in his hand before he'd even stiffened at the noise, but Rainy was already moving. Through sheer momentum, he knocked Adler's Beretta off into the brush, and then they were grappling, arms locked.

With strength alone, Adler shouldn't have stood a chance against Rainy, who must have had thirty pounds on him. But he was so damned fast. He diverted Rainy with an elbow while his left hand flashed back for his concealed shoulder holster. He might have blown Rainy's head off if Rainy hadn't caught him and wrestled his arm behind his back, twisting the elbow. Adler grunted in pain. Rainy felt flush with the victory for a split second, until Adler's knee came around and slammed into his groin.

He doubled over, pain and nausea a hot spike up into his abdomen. He narrowly dodged a second knee to the nose before Adler kicked him and sent him sprawling on the cement.

Rainy went easily, let himself be laid out flat. He scrambled backward on his elbows, keeping himself in a vulnerable position. Adler took the bait. He strode forward and planted his knee in Rainy's stomach to hold him in place.

"I told you not to fuck with me," he said. Smug, assured. "You know I'll get back around to killing you. Just wait your turn."

His hand came down to wrap around Rainy's throat. Just holding.

"Couldn't keep away," Rainy told him, trying not to wheeze against the lingering ache in his balls. "I just needed you to know that I'm the one."

Adler snorted. He slid his knee down so it was pressed against Rainy's dick and leaned his weight on it until Rainy winced. His hand moved up Rainy's throat until he gripped his jaw, fingertips digging into the skin. He held Rainy's face still while he examined it, eyes impassive and black in the low light.

Rainy didn't have to fake whatever it was that he saw there, because Adler's cool expression combined with the places he was putting pressure were taking him there. Fear, resentment, arousal. Adler read it there and smiled.

"You're the one who's *what*, Mister Rainy?"

Rainy smiled back. "I'm the one who's going to get the drop on you twice."

Adler's expression pinched then, uncertainty flashing in his eyes. That was exactly the moment that Marco pulled the bag down over his head.

Adler flew into frenzied motion instantly, releasing Rainy to scrabble at the opaque fabric over his face. Unfortunately for him, Marco had cinched it closed at his neck. The seconds Adler wasted trying to get it off allowed Marco to wrap himself around Adler's back like a baby sloth.

It would have been best to try to get away first, and Adler would have known that. But he still went for the bag.

Interesting.

His distraction didn't last long. Even as Rainy went to help grapple him, Adler shoved off his chest with both hands and dropped straight back toward the pavement, going to crush Marco beneath him. Marco let go, alarmed, and Adler hit the sidewalk. He took the rib-crushing impact like a champ and rolled to his feet to take off.

He was foiled when Novikov grabbed him from behind, pinning his arms to his sides in a bear hug. Adler struggled, still blinded by the bag. His fingers dipped into his left sleeve, where Rainy saw the flash of a strap but didn't have time to call out a warning before Adler had a knife in his hand and was sinking it into Novikov's thigh.

Novikov bellowed in pain but kept hold of him. Rainy seized Adler's legs, and was wholly unprepared for the violence of the resistance he was met with. He had to wrap himself entirely around them just to keep from getting kicked off. Novikov seemed to be having a similar issue with his torso; Adler was bucking and kicking like a prize-winning rodeo horse.

Marco had zip ties in his hand now and twisted Adler's wrists behind his back so he had no leverage to fight as he bound them together. Adler spat at them from under his hood.

"Come on," Rainy said, still holding his legs. "Let's go."

They bundled him through the bushes to the side street where they'd parked the van. Marco jumped behind the wheel while Rainy and Novikov shoved Adler into the back.

"Fuck, Rainy, you said he was crazy, but you didn't tell us he was a fucking monster," Marco chattered.

"He stabbed me," Novikov agreed, giving Rainy a reproachful look.

"Only a little," Rainy placated, grabbing the handle of the knife and giving it a little tug. Fresh blood sloughed down Novikov's leg. "Uh, actually, you might want to leave that in."

Now that his heaving breaths were echoing in the enclosed space, Rainy was feeling the adrenaline surge, the throbbing pain in his groin and his back where he'd fallen on the cement. There was the familiar bite under his skin, the urge to grab and shake and shake and shake until whoever hurt him got their comeuppance. It was like a high.

Rainy looked at Adler on the floor of the van. Smug, sure Adler. *Nobody gets the drop on me twice.* Well, well, look where we are now. He was struggling against his restraints, trying to work his wrists out. Rainy leaned down and tugged the bag off of his head. Adler blinked for a moment in the light before Rainy's Colt was pressed to his forehead.

"Hold still," he ordered.

Adler fell still and looked up at them, eyes cold. As always, he was wearing a trim mid-weight suit. This one was scuffed and stained in places with Novikov's blood. This was the first time Rainy had seen him up close since the night of the Holister job, and he was just as infuriating as the first time. With his tie untucked and his hair mussed out of its gel, he looked feral. Rainy's attention snagged on his bottom lip, the way it was a little chapped and chewed in a way he hadn't noticed before.

"Miss me?" he asked, tracing the muzzle of his gun along it.

Adler's jaw clenched so tight, Rainy swore he heard a tooth crack. "You need your friends to help you? Can't face me like a man?"

"Like a soldier, you mean," Rainy corrected. "You're in Miami now, sweetheart. You've got to learn to play dirty. Not that you'll get the chance, now."

"So you got two plays to get your dates home," Adler drawled, undaunted. "Kidnapping as well as drugging."

Rainy couldn't restrain a grin, the high gamboling and doubling back on itself. "I already told you—it was a self-defense roofie. Besides, I was a perfect gentleman. I put you up in a fancy room, watched you the whole time you were sleeping, paid for room service. That's better aftercare than most could dream of."

In the front seat, Marco snorted. "That's adorable."

Rainy felt himself flush. He hadn't meant to let that part slip, actually—the intimacy of it felt like a secret meant to be held close to his chest. *I watched over you while you were sleeping.*

It might have been the new, dim light of the van, or just the new information, but Adler's scar looked different tonight. More severe. Rainy was now noticing the way the skin was stretched too tight over the right side of his jaw, how the muscles twitched the corner of his mouth up into a facsimile of a smile whenever he squinted. The scar tissue was so thick and stiff; the wound must have been deep. Too deep. It was jagged and curving, nothing of the clean, straight cut of a blade in it, and the edges were marbled with the evidence of old infection.

I watched over you while you were sleeping.

"Did you like the eggs?" Rainy asked.

"Fuck off."

"Oh, you so did."

Adler ignored him, sizing up the others. "Novikov and the little Espinosa, I presume."

Marco saluted from the driver's seat. "Nice try, *asere*. Short king and proud."

"And let me guess, Mister Rainy: by the end of tonight, you think I'll be dead."

"Oh, sweetheart, you'll be more than dead." Basking in the glow of the hatred that sparked in Adler's eyes, Rainy pulled out his phone and opened the file that Malia had emailed him, the name and birthday, printed in stark black. "But you fucked with my car. So first, *Nathaniel*, we're going to have a little fun."

Chapter 6

Florida Man's Ventures in Water Torture

Adler was nothing if not a consummate professional; Rainy had to give him that. He kept quiet, face carefully neutral, the whole way to the Rattrap. Didn't fuss over the dig of the zip ties into his wrists, didn't even raise an eyebrow when they steered him inside and secured him to a chair.

The building the Rattrap occupied had once been a dance school. It was the butt of many jokes, but the space suited them just fine. Malia's desk was situated in the old reception area, and they pulled Adler through it into what the Rattrap's band of rogues affectionately referred to as the "multipurpose room." It was the old studio, a large and windowless room whose wooden floor had been pried up to expose the slab of rubbery linoleum beneath. It was secluded, easy to clean, and had soundproof walls.

The purposes it could be used for were, indeed, multi.

When Rainy's mentor Rezakova had bought the place, she'd pulled out the floors and barre but left up the floor-to-ceiling mirror that covered one wall. Rainy watched Adler's expression in its reflection. His chair was the only piece of furniture and faced the mirror directly. In the mirror's silver expanse, the room looked wide and stark under the harsh fluorescents; the only thing for miles was Adler, tied to the chair, and Rainy at his shoulder. Adler's face was perfectly calm, but under the fabric of his pants, his thighs were straining against the tension of his bonds.

It was a checkmate position. The kind of position that those in their line of work dreaded finding themselves in, because it meant the end of the line. And yet, Adler still had that expression on his face—not haughty or arrogant like Rainy had first supposed. Just flat. Cool, measured. Rainy got the sense that Adler was a careful construction, something painstakingly put together and kept locked down tight. Perfectly in control of himself, in a way Rainy had never been from the moment he first drew air.

Rainy had always been a sort of quilt, or a bazaar. Most load-bearing pieces of him were borrowed from someone else, and he traded and swapped and shared with everyone around him all the time, shuffling into the bliss of not recognizing himself. Adler, though, was a closed system. Every piece of him belonged to him alone. Rainy had known plenty of people like him—those who built themselves walls to protect something inside. It drove him crazy with the urge to poke and prod and pry. He wondered what the soft, fragile center of Adler was.

Then again, maybe Adler was a special sort of wall-builder. Maybe he'd doubled in and over himself until there was no center, and walls were all he was.

They were alone in the room. Marco and Novikov were conferring outside for the moment. Rainy sucked hard on the lollipop he'd snagged from Malia's desk, felt it clatter against his teeth in a satisfyingly annoying way. Adler's eye twitched.

"Cherry," Rainy offered, trying to school his voice to hide the adrenaline still capering up and down his sinews and veins, the throb of his heart at the base of his throat.

"Charming." Adler's mouth stayed flat, pinned in at the corners. Rainy wanted to peel that expression away, to wrench apart the walls until Adler was finished, totally undone.

He was going to do it, before he killed him. Before he put Adler in the ground, he was going to pry that flat look off his face, make him look at Rainy with desperation in his eyes. Yes, that was what he wanted. He could get it, too—he could break Adler's kneecaps, each delicate bone in his fingers, crush his nose against the linoleum floor. If Adler gave him the word, Rainy could pin him against the wall and fuck him until he forgot every word except for Rainy's name.

With Rainy's blood coursing as high as it was, either option felt perfectly acceptable at the moment.

He walked a slow circle around the chair, taking the scene in from each angle. The flex of Adler's wrists against his bonds. The slight involuntary part of his thighs where each ankle was lashed to a chair leg.

He opened the file on his phone again. "Sergeant Nathaniel Adler, Jr.," he read aloud. "Parents call you Junior? That's pretty cute."

Adler's teeth ground, just a little. Rainy dragged the lollipop along his cheek again, making a flat clack against each tooth. Starting right from his big brother, everyone he'd ever met could confirm that Rainy had a special talent for getting under people's skin. And that was even before he'd started *literally* getting under people's skin.

"Age twenty-nine, born and raised in Hedrick, Alabama. Kind of a shithole, if I'm being honest. I'm not surprised you didn't want to limp back there after getting half your face blown off."

"Am I supposed to be impressed by this?" Adler drawled. "I'm an open book. Any moron with a computer could've cobbled this together."

"I just like to know who I'm dealing with. And, after reading your whole file…" Rainy clicked his tongue. "Honestly, not as impressive as I was expecting."

He stopped just behind the chair. Their eyes met in the mirror, and there was something behind Adler's gaze now, that stoked-up hot-coal bite to his coiled reservation.

"Sorry to disappoint," he said. "Now, can we get this over with? I really don't wanna hear the sound of your voice any longer than necessary."

The temper lurking under Rainy's skin jumped, flushing him hot and cold just subdermal. Adler's hair was a little longer than it looked, shaken out of its careful styling. Long enough for Rainy to get a good grip on it, blood-white tight right at the scalp. He pulled Adler's head back firmly, exposing the vulnerable arch of his neck.

His hair was stiff and sticky with styling gel against Rainy's fingers. There was sweat and blood beaded on his brow. His eyes were like a knife between Rainy's ribs. Lips parted involuntarily.

"You've got such a mouth on you," Rainy murmured, something dark and fluid uncoiling in his chest. "I remember that."

With his free hand, he pulled the lollipop from his own mouth and pressed it against Adler's lips where he was held in place. It poised there for a moment, glistening red and clear under the fluorescents like a precious jewel or a drop of blood. Pushing in, insistent. Then Adler parted his teeth and it slid down into his mouth, slick and easy as if it belonged there.

Rainy could feel Adler's eyes on him, but he was watching his mouth as his lips closed around the white stick just a breath from Rainy's fingers. His cheeks dipped in, scar tugging the corner of his mouth. Rainy felt the tremor in the stick when his tongue traced over it and he sucked, once. Then Rainy tugged and he relinquished it, letting it slide back between his lips. Rainy pressed the head of the lollipop, dragging his bottom lip down. The moment hung heavy, stretched out with the slide of the candy against Adler's lip, the tiny wet part of his mouth.

Rainy finally dared a glance at Adler's expression. His eyes were hazy and violent. An electric-red dab of artificial dye gathered at the corner of his mouth. Rainy was struck by the sudden urge to lean in and kiss the taste of cherry out of his mouth. He might have, too, if he hadn't known Adler would bite him bloody.

"Rainy," a voice alerted. Rainy released Adler's hair roughly and stepped back to look at Marco framed in the door. "Conference."

Out in the office, Novikov was sitting on the musty green-brown couch, poking at his knife wound with a mild frown. Malia was hunkered behind her desktop monitors, looking alarmed.

"Jesus, he's going to bleed out on the couch," she hissed. "This is why you guys are supposed to take care of things in the *field*."

"Not going to bleed out," Novikov assured her. "Not good, though."

Malia looked doubtful and was carefully averting her eyes from the blood. Marco folded his arms.

"Ilya needs to tap out. That stab wound could be a problem if he doesn't get it looked at soon."

"I can finish," Novikov insisted.

Rainy sighed. "No, you need to get out of here. Go get Nasrin to stitch you up."

"She's not admitting anyone right now. Says she's not to be disturbed on maternity leave."

Marco ducked under Novikov's arm and steadied him upright. "Tell her it's a favor for her favorite brother-in-law."

They got Novikov mobile and out, and then Rainy was cracking his knuckles.

"All right," he said, thinking of the red on Adler's lips. "I've been looking forward to this all week."

Rezakova had told him years ago that there was a special line that a professional killer had to straddle. You had to be cold enough to do it without hesitation, but you could never start to get off on it, or take pleasure from the act for the act's sake. If you tipped off that tightrope in either direction, it would drag you under.

As pissed-off as he was about his tires, he wasn't going to find it entirely pleasurable to wring the life out of Adler.

Not entirely—but a little bit.

He had been considering how to do it. A bullet was too quick and easy. A knife too slow, too difficult to clean up after. Rainy had been leaning toward strangulation. He'd put on a pair of gloves and wrap his hands around Adler's throat, squeeze until it took. Watch the desperation come into his eyes and then go out, along with everything else.

The thought made his pulse pick up again. Not exactly with excitement, or with dread. Just... something.

"Hold on," Marco said. "We don't want to start with the killing yet."

"No, actually, I do want to start with the killing. Were you not paying attention?"

"Hold on, Rainy. Don't you think we should start with—" He made a gruesome twisting gesture. "Let's not waste an opportunity here. You said this guy has dinner at Seong's house. Hugs his kids. He'll definitely know something worthwhile."

Displeasure crept up Rainy's back. "This is my job, Marco. We're not torturing him."

"Come on."

"If your dad wanted the full bundle, he should've offered me more money. That wasn't part of the deal."

Marco stepped in closer, angling Malia out of the conversation. "Please, man? Look—Andy Parish is now trying to strong-arm us into selling him a portion of our dockfront, and we know Seong is almost definitely involved. My dad is hard-pressed right now, which means he's riding Felix's ass, which means Felix is riding mine. I need this. You'd be doing the family a favor."

"I don't do favors," Rainy hissed. He dragged a hand through his hair, thinking. "You owe me back half the cut I offered you. And when I say you're done, you're done, understand?"

Marco clasped his hands together. "You're my hero. Come on, Malia," he called over his shoulder. "Novikov's gone; you're spotting us."

Malia's brown skin went several shades paler. "What? No, I'm not going in there."

"You work here, too, don't you?"

"Not like that," she snapped.

"Well, congrats. You've been promoted," Rainy said. He pushed back into the multipurpose room, blood fizzing with irritation. Adler met his eyes in the mirror and arched a brow, like he knew Rainy's delightfully organized plans were starting to slip.

On second thought, roughing him up was maybe an excellent idea on Marco's part.

He crunched down on his lollipop and swallowed, the jagged pieces scraping his throat, then tossed the crumpled stick into the corner. Malia dodged it and made a face as she slunk into the room.

Marco crossed to stand in front of Adler, looming over him in the small metal chair. Adler just looked up at him with narrow, hooded eyes.

"We're going to have a chat about Seong's dealings with Andy Parish," Marco said.

Adler stared up at him evenly. His gaze slid to Rainy, checking something, and back.

Then he laughed.

It was a short, sharp bark, more taunt than mirth. He kept laughing right up until Marco struck him in the face.

The blow hit so hard that Adler's chair toppled sideways, and he landed on the floor. He grunted, and then Rainy was pulling the chair back upright, bracing the back with his hands and the legs with his feet.

"If you think this is a joke, you're about to have a rude awakening," Rainy murmured in his right ear, the side with the scar.

In the mirror, Adler's face changed a little. A wrinkle between his brows, a slight tilt of his head. Not fear, but something like misunderstanding. Before Rainy could puzzle it out, though, Marco was hitting Adler again, snapping his head back against Rainy's chest. Adler let out a rough noise. Malia jumped.

"Fucking Jesus," she yelped, turning her back. "Oh God."

"Really, Malia?" Marco asked, massaging his knuckles. "Fuck, grow a pair already."

To drive the point home, apparently, he grabbed Adler by the shoulders and drove his knee up hard under his ribs, sinking into the unprotected softness of his abdomen. Once, twice. Bruisingly. Adler doubled over, coughing, until Rainy grabbed him by the back of his neck and pulled him back up.

"Get it moving, Marco," he said. "I'm not going to wait all night."

The involuntary noise of pain Adler had made was doing something to him. Rainy's breath was coming hard now, static buzzing between his ears. He didn't know if it was anger or satisfaction or arousal, but he wanted Marco to hit him again. He felt like breaking something if Marco hit him again.

"Start thinking," Marco advised Adler. "Seong. Parish. That bomb didn't knock your brain loose, did it?"

Adler snorted, tilting back into Rainy's rough grip on his neck. "Fuck off."

"If that's how it's going to be," Marco said, slipping a set of rings from his left hand to his right.

His next hit knocked Adler's head back again. And again. The sounds of violence were so familiar. The dull thud of colliding bones cushioned by flesh. The clack of teeth being forced together. With each impact, Adler let out another tamped-down grunt, caged behind clenched teeth.

Marco was smiling, a familiar, feral thing. Emilio had never understood him; this was Marco's natural element. This was what he was made for. Rings flashed on his fingers, wet with blood.

Each punch knocked Adler's head back against Rainy's sternum. Hard enough that he felt the hit in his own bones. He felt each one.

When Marco's frenzy subsided, Adler's face was red and raw. Blood trickled from his nose and sliced lip, from the patch where Marco's ring had skinned his brow. He tilted his head and spat a clot of blood and saliva onto the floor, bright and candy-red.

If Rainy kissed him now, would he taste like cherries?

During the onslaught, Malia had hidden her face in the crook of her elbow. Now she looked up and immediately started gagging.

"Are you fucking serious?" Marco asked, letting his bloody knuckles fall to his sides.

"Miss Malia," Adler said gently, despite the nasal gargle in his voice, "would it be better if you waited outside for this part?"

Malia nodded and stumbled toward the door.

"Hey!" Marco snapped, darting after her. "That's not—"

Rainy sighed and released Adler to slump in the chair. "Wait here," he ordered, patting him on his bruised cheek.

Outside, Malia was cramming things into her backpack.

"Grow the fuck up," Marco told her. "This is kind of what we do here, remember?"

"Not me," she snapped. "I'm not involved in that shit."

Irritation was a hot wire around Rainy's skull, pulling tighter. The confusing mix of anger and excitement and displeasure that had been crashing through him all night was igniting everything white-hot.

"Really? What did you think we do with the information you give us? On the hits you help us set up?"

Malia turned to Rainy, startled at the outburst. "I'm not like you."

And that was too fucking much.

"What, you think your hands are clean? You think that one day you'll just up and leave, and this place won't stick to you?"

"Fuck you." Her voice was ice and flint as she stuffed the last piece of paper into her bag. "This isn't in my job description. I'll see you tomorrow." She pointed at Marco. "And you're a fucking idiot if you think you can just break some of that guy's fingers like you would with any random ghetto kid and he'll talk to you. He was a fucking Green Beret, moron. He's probably been trained to resist torture."

She grabbed her car keys off the desk and stormed past Rainy out into the night. Marco looked at him helplessly.

"I didn't think of that, actually."

"God, you're an idiot." Rainy pinched his brow. "I'm giving you five more minutes. That's it."

"I—"

"He's my contract. I call the shots, and I'm getting tired of this. Five minutes."

Marco had that look in his eyes still, that ugly glint that Rainy sometimes thought was less than human. In a family full of fairly awful people, Marco Espinosa might just have been the scariest.

"She's right," he said. "We need to go all 'enhanced interrogation techniques' on his ass." He crossed to the bathroom adjoining the office and emerged with a pink floral hand towel.

Rainy paused. The wild crash of anticipation and vicious delight was still surging inside him, lapping a question at his ears: *How much further does this go?* Questions of death and pain and flesh, Rainy usually didn't have any trouble parsing. He wasn't supposed to feel guilt or joy at killing. Killing just was. But with this, he *felt.*

"Marco," he warned.

Ignoring him, Marco jostled the water cooler in the corner, lifting out the five-gallon plastic jug. Water splashed across his sneakers. Tucking it under his arm, he looked at Rainy.

Rainy clenched his fist at his side, popping each of his knuckles in turn. He could shut it down right now; Marco would give him shit for the next month, but he could do it. With any other target, it wouldn't have mattered, but part of him wanted to say no. For the life of him, though, Rainy couldn't figure out why, so he said:

"Fine. Five minutes."

This wasn't supposed to be conflicting. He wasn't supposed to be confused. He followed Marco back into the room where Adler was bound. As they approached from the right, Adler tilted his head as if to angle his good side toward them again.

"I've always wanted to try this," Marco gushed.

"God, you're such a psycho. Fuck." Rainy swallowed at the sight of Adler's eyes following them in the mirror, dark with understanding and challenge. He tipped his chin up.

"Hold his head," Marco instructed.

Rainy's palms hovered on either side of Adler's temples. His face was starting to bruise, and there was blood in his hairline. Despite his composed expression, he was breathing hard. Gently, Rainy grasped his head and tilted it back. Adler's neck stiffened with resistance, then released. Like he knew this was inevitable. Like he wanted to get it over with.

Rainy knelt on the floor and tipped the chair back until Adler was braced against him. It was almost like holding him.

"Seong. Parish," Marco repeated. "Last chance." He was soaking the hand towel in water.

Adler's eyes latched onto Rainy's, unreadable.

I watched over you while you were sleeping.

"Deep breath, sweetheart," Rainy whispered.

Marco laid the wet cloth over Adler's mouth and nose. Rainy saw the moment the cold composure in his eyes slipped, the way memory flashed across them, bright as terror.

Wait, hold on, stop— he thought.

Marco stood and poured the water in a low arc onto Adler's face. For a single second, his eyes went wide enough to swallow all the light in the room. Then they closed, and he was thrashing, struggling against the ropes, the chair, Rainy's hands. The water splashed over Rainy, cold and shocking, and Adler was gasping and choking, fighting like Rainy was killing him. The cloth bowed as he futilely tried to suck in through his mouth, and—

And Marco stopped pouring. Rainy tore the cloth away, and Adler bucked in his arms, sputtering and coughing. Bloody water splattered Rainy's face.

Marco was beaming. "Holy shit, it works! Feel like talking now?"

Something like panic was squeezing Rainy's lungs. That wild feeling inside him was shaken up like too much carbonation, ready to pop. "Marco—" he warned.

Adler spat on Marco's already-soaked shoes.

Then Marco's weight was pressing the chair back into Rainy, and he had the cloth back over Adler's face, and he was splashing water, a torrent rather than a stream. Adler was writhing again, his head punching Rainy in the ribs, his breathing a wet scream. His eyes were open, and they were a dying man's eyes. Desperation. Desperation was what Rainy had wanted.

"*Fuck!*" Rainy shoved Marco, sending him stumbling back against the mirror. The jug of water went rolling across the floor, mostly empty. "That's it! That's enough!"

Adler kept struggling until Rainy peeled the towel away, then spat up a stream of pink water. Rainy turned him onto his side to help him cough.

"Jesus, what does it matter?" Marco pushed himself up with a squelch. He was wet, but not as soaked as Rainy, whose clothes felt like plastic wrap and whose hair was a drenched black sheet.

Adler was still heaving on the floor, but he looked up at Marco anyway. His voice was bloody-hoarse.

"If you wanna get something out of my head," he said evenly, "you're gonna have to use an ice pick." He spat more water onto the linoleum. "Fucking amateur."

Marco's hand was at his belt, then he was holding a switchblade. In two steps, he had Adler by the neck.

"How about I carve up the rest of your face, asshole? See how you like being symmetrical."

One second, Rainy was watching the knife scrape along Adler's left cheek, Marco's fingers digging into Adler's neck hard enough to bruise. The next, something was popping in him like a sudden change in atmosphere, and he was hauling Marco away with one hand in his belt and the other on the back of his neck.

He threw him toward the other end of the room hard enough that he stumbled and fell. Sometimes, Marco needed to be reminded that he wasn't the biggest fucker around.

"You're done," Rainy shouted. "You're done. Go home."

Marco gestured with his knife, furious. "I'm not—"

"*Go the fuck home.*"

Marco glared at him for a moment, but throwing his weight around had worked. He backed down with one last kick at Adler, splashing water, and stalked out of the room. Rainy paused, breathing hard, and squeezed his head between his hands hard enough to hold himself together. There was a clatter of office supplies being swept to the floor, then the front door slammed and the deadbolt clunked.

Rainy looked at Adler, who looked at him. The blood had mostly washed away from his face, leaving it flushed and bruised. His hair was completely wrecked, hanging limp around his ears, and his skin glistened with water. His beautiful suit was completely soaked, collar turned pink with blood. He looked—well, drowned.

"You got excellent taste in coworkers," he told Rainy.

"Yeah. He's a real gem, huh?"

And just like that, Rainy realized, for the first time since the night they'd met, they were completely and utterly alone.

Chapter 7

Florida Man Apologizes for Waterboarding Incident

R ainy found a towel and dried Adler off a bit after setting his chair back upright, then gave his own hair a quick once-over before kicking the towel around the floor to soak up some of the spilled water. Despite his best efforts, Adler was still shivering and choking a little. Rainy didn't say anything, letting him cough up the last of the water with some dignity left intact.

Adler looked smaller when wet, like he looked smaller asleep. All the rage had leaked out of Rainy, all the righteous conviction. When he called up the image of his slashed tires, the adrenaline of dodging rifle shots on the roof, it felt flimsy and hollow compared to the immediate sense memory of holding Adler almost in his lap, close as a lover. Watching him thrash. Rainy felt oddly sick. He didn't usually care much about fair play; you couldn't really have a code of honor in his line of work. Still, the look in Adler's eyes...

"You've been waterboarded before," he said. Adler glared at him in the mirror.

"The Syrians thought it was funny to give Americans a taste of their own medicine. Like I said—your friend's an amateur."

"Didn't seem so casual when it was happening."

"Yeah. Well."

The slightly sick twinge to his stomach was identifiable now. It was shame. He felt a sudden need to explain himself, to make it clear to Adler.

"It wasn't my idea," he said.

"I gathered that much."

"I'm... sorry."

Adler's eyes flicked over him, unreadable. "Don't ever apologize, Mister Rainy. It don't look good on you."

Rainy felt a smile tug at his mouth. "Are you okay?"

"Does it matter? I thought you were gonna kill me."

"I like to know what I'm up against."

Adler didn't humor him with a response, but Rainy could have sworn that the corner of his mouth twitched, just a little. The hot sea of emotion he'd thought had entirely drained away lapped at his ribs. He wanted to drag that smile out kicking and screaming.

"I'll consider your emotional suffering payment for my tires," he offered.

"We're square, then?"

"Nah. Pain and suffering caps out at five hundred. You still owe me four hundred."

Adler blinked. "Seems cheap for that nice of tires."

"Well, I did take three hundred bucks from your wallet while you were being tied up."

"Ah."

Adler seemed just fine now, the lines of his terror and pain smoothed away as easily as he might iron the wrinkles out of a dress shirt. It was almost as if the whole thing hadn't happened. It wasn't exactly the same, though. There was something a little softer in the way Adler was holding himself, as though Marco's First Water Torture had shaken something loose in him. He seemed less tightly wrapped, like Rainy could peel up a corner and unravel him, just a little.

Then he remembered why Adler was here.

He glanced at his watch. It was nearing one, and he needed to wrap this up by dawn. Now, though, he couldn't summon the fury that had made him want to make this particularly creative. It still felt personal, but in the wrong way.

"I'm going to kill you, you know," he said.

"So you keep saying."

Rainy sighed, rubbed his neck. "Can I get you anything first?"

It seemed only polite.

Adler eyed him, that little crease between his brows. "Seriously?"

"Yeah."

Adler seemed to genuinely consider it, cocking his head and wrinkling his nose a little. It was a startlingly adorable thinking face and not at all what Rainy needed at the moment.

"A cigarette," he decided.

Rainy was embarrassed by the force of his own surprise. "You smoke?"

"Not since I got out of prison. But if it's my last chance..." Adler shrugged.

"I think I can make that happen." Rainy had avoided smoking like the plague in high school to keep his body in tip-top football shape and never picked it up after. But it was a common enough vice around here. "I might only be able to find Marco's vape, though."

"I would rather you just shot me now."

Luckily, Novikov had a battered pack of cigarettes and a lighter in his locker. Rainy pocketed them and returned to the multipurpose room.

Bending over the chair with his back to the mirror, he shook out a cigarette and held it out. Adler took it between his teeth, and the faded bruise on Rainy's shoulder throbbed. Adler's mouth was still bleeding; a dribble of red ran down his chin. The lighter took a few tries.

When the tip of the cigarette lit up orange, Adler sucked in deep, a foreign, blissed-out expression kind of like the one he'd made right before Rainy came in his mouth crossing his face. Rainy watched, enthralled, as he held the smoke in and then let it out in a slow stream. He nudged with his lips, and Rainy obediently took the cigarette back.

"Fuck, that's good," Adler said, and the hoarse pleasure in his voice made Rainy's dick stir. "And after all that time I wasted quitting. I guess we do always end up our parents."

"I'm nothing like my parents," Rainy said, going to sit on the still-drying floor on Adler's right.

"Everyone's like their parents. Don't sit there."

"Why?"

"'Cause I said so." Adler jerked his head to the left.

Rainy shrugged and moved around the chair to sit on the other side. He lifted the hand with the cigarette in offering, and Adler leaned forward for another drag. His lips brushed Rainy's fingers.

"I don't really see any way I'm like my parents."

"Let me guess: you got either stupidly hardheaded assholes, or ones who insist on being blind to what they don't wanna believe."

"One of each, actually."

"Well, there you go, Mr. 'I don't see any resemblance.'"

Rainy grinned. "You're actually kind of funny, you know that?"

Adler snorted. "Cigarette," he ordered, and Rainy held it up to his lips again. Whatever the water incident had shaken loose in him, the cigarette seemed to relax even further. Adler blew smoke out through his nose like a dragon and rolled his long, pretty neck to work a kink out of it.

This version of him... well, Rainy actually sort of liked him.

Too bad he had to die.

"It's getting to be that time," he said.

"Mm."

Rainy hesitated, feeling like he was teetering on a whisker-thin edge. "How do you want it?"

"Are you for real?"

Rainy stared into the mirror, the image of the two of them close together in the wide, empty room. "I always kind of wanted to get decapitated. Or blown up. Something really flashy. I want people to be talking about it for years, like, 'Oh, that Rainy guy. You know, the one who got his head chopped off and then a building dropped on him.'"

He was hoping that would draw out another half smile, but Adler just looked pensive.

"You ever been real close to dying?" he asked.

"Nah. Been shot a few times, but not big-time. Shoulder, leg. What about you?"

Adler didn't answer. He'd tilted his head back to look at the ceiling, neck extended gracefully. With his hair plastered to his head and his scarred side facing away, he could have stepped out of that photo from Malia's file. Young, soft, and new.

"I've almost died alone on concrete floors too many times to count," he said. "Honestly? I just want someone to hold me while I go."

And Rainy... Rainy didn't know what to do with that. He didn't know how all these variables—Adler kissing him hard in a service hallway, firing down on him from a roof, looking up at him while he drowned, smoking a cigarette like it was his last—added up to the feeling in his chest. It wasn't affection, or even grudging respect. It was just a heaviness in his hand as he tugged his Colt free from his waistband. He glanced down at it, uncertain.

"I guess the real question is whether there's a way you don't want it."

Adler snorted. "Right. You think I'm that dumb?"

"No, seriously. I'm still going to kill you. But if there's a way you don't want it, then I'll pick something else."

"And I'm supposed to trust you?"

"Honor among thieves, right?"

"Mm."

"I mean, I already admitted I'm going to kill you," Rainy pointed out. "Is there any lesser need for dishonesty than between a man who's about to die and the man who's about to kill him?"

Adler was silent.

"I'd lie about a lot of things, but not about this. Trust me?"

Adler didn't answer for long enough that Rainy started to stand, checking his gun. He almost startled when Adler said, softly:

"Just nothing over the face. I don't like feeling trapped."

Rainy remembered the way Adler had scrabbled, panicked, at the bag over his head. He nodded.

"Noted."

He met Adler's eyes in the mirror. In his experience, looking into a man's eyes just before he died yielded all kinds of things—fear, desperation, hatred, resignation. He didn't find any of those things in Adler's gaze. Instead, even now, Adler looked calm and collected. His eyes gleamed with defiance. It was a shame, Rainy thought, that he'd only gotten the one chance to kiss him. That feeling was drawing in closer now, a heaviness in his gun hand, a pendular ticking at the inside of his ribs.

"Regret," he named it. "I think you might be the first person I'll ever regret having to kill."

"I got good news, then," Adler told him. "You're not actually gonna kill me."

"No?" Rainy was charmed despite himself by Adler's flat affect.

"No. You're gonna untie me." Adler's pensiveness had sunk back beneath the surface, subsumed by cool matter-of-factness.

"Why would I do that?" Rainy asked.

Adler smiled then. That big, full, mean smile from the wine cellar. Dimples. He had fucking dimples. And Rainy thought, *Uh-oh.*

"Because I'm better at this job than you are." Adler watched him in the mirror. "You seemed to have fun listing off your little fact sheet, earlier. Do you wanna hear mine?"

Rainy stood, uneasy, letting the half-smoked cigarette fall to the floor. His gun itched and bit at his palm.

"Rafael Perez," Adler drawled, and ice washed down Rainy's spine. "Age twenty-seven, born and raised in Miami, Florida."

"How did you find that out?" Rainy snapped. "Nobody knows that."

"Like I said: I'm better at my job than you. Shall I go on? Son of José and Esperanza Perez, of 238 Punnet Street. Lovely folks. I think that right about now, your mother will be asleep, but your father will be just getting to bed after catching up on his DVR. He'll walk upstairs and open the curtains to look out onto the street. Little basil in the window planter. They're big windows. Lots of room to see in."

Rainy's mind was blank. Here was that feeling again, that chasm of adrenaline just before death bit down. Adler's charm had fallen away like a cheap silk sheath, and Rainy couldn't believe that he'd thought for a second there was anything under there but this. Icy, deadly, calculating.

Killer's hands, he thought. He should have trusted the hands.

"I got two guys posted at 237. They're on standing orders. Seong's men are good at that. If I don't call them every three hours, well... you get the idea. I called them just as I was leaving work." Adler smirked. "If you hadn't offered me the cigarette, you might have had time to shoot me and get there in time. But you don't, now."

Rainy's tongue felt like lead, too heavy and sliding down his throat to choke him. He could see it so clearly—his father scratching his belly, peering at the empty street below, his mother fast asleep, hooked up to her CPAP machine.

Bullet. Bullet.

"So," Adler finished, "you're gonna untie me."

Rainy hated him. Fuck, did he hate him in that moment. He'd let himself fall for the guilt and the cigarette and the soft confessions. He'd let himself forget the rules of the game they were playing. And he'd been played like a fucking chump.

"I told you," Adler said, almost apologetic. "Nobody gets the drop on me twice."

The world was still.

"Okay," Rainy said. "You win."

He stuck his gun back into his waistband and crouched behind the chair, working his numb fingers into the zip tie that held Adler's wrists in place. He had to pull his knife to get it to fall away. Underneath, Adler's wrists were rubbed raw, and Rainy felt a flash of satisfaction. He undid the ankle restraints, and Adler stepped cleanly out of the chair, rubbing at the skin under his cuffs. Rainy dropped the knife. Adler kicked it away.

Rainy raised his hands, showing that they were empty. "Your phone's in the other room."

Adler nodded and crossed to the door to rifle through the pile of his things that they'd left on the table, pulling out his cell. He gestured to Rainy in the doorway.

"Gun, now. Both of them."

"Keep fucking dreaming."

"I need to know you ain't gonna shoot me as soon as I make the call."

"You're going to shoot me as soon as I hand you my guns."

Adler regarded him evenly. "Well, then. I guess it's you or your parents."

Rainy made a valiant effort to burn a hole through Adler's head with the sheer force of his hatred. Then he bent down and placed his Colt on the floor, pulling his other .45 from his shoulder holster to lay beside it. He kicked them both over.

Adler tossed the second gun off into the locker room and kept the Colt for himself. He ran a pleased finger along its pearled stock.

"Now make the call," Rainy gritted out.

"The call." Adler dropped his cell into his pocket derisively. "Here's a word of advice: never play poker, Mister Rainy. You're no good at it."

Oh. Oh, fucking *fuck.*

Rainy saw red. He lunged forward, hands outstretched for Adler's throat. He was going to throttle him, act out every fantasy he'd entertained in the last week and choke him until his neck snapped.

The Colt swung up between them, easy as a third hand. "Back up," Adler said calmly.

Fuming, Rainy stepped backward into the multipurpose room. Adler followed him, impassive.

"You're a better liar than you look," Rainy said, his fists clenched at his sides.

"You said I needed to learn to play dirty, right?" Adler smiled. "I'm a quick study."

Rainy's body was tensed in preparation for a bullet, and yet he almost laughed. He was weirdly impressed, and half-hysterical. His parents were safe, for now. It was a burst of relief against the conflagration. It was a mercy. His parents were safe, and he was about to die.

Why hadn't he just let Marco drown the bastard?

Adler flicked his wrist. Rainy dropped to one knee in the center of the linoleum floor.

The space between them closed, Adler stalking toward him. Everything echoed in the contained, shiny space of the old studio. Footsteps, heartbeats. The shot would echo. It would bounce around between the walls until it shattered the whole world apart with its roar.

If Adler got close enough, if Rainy lunged just right, he might get his hand around the gun before he was hit. Rainy gathered his weight, and breathed, and plotted his next move.

It was either that or nothing.

Rainy wasn't a quitter.

Adler stopped a little too far away in that at-ease stance of his, feet spread apart and free hand drifting back toward his hip. Rainy would have regretted killing Adler, if he'd done it five minutes ago. But not now.

There was no elation on Adler's face, no satisfaction. Only blankness. A killer through and through.

Rainy's heart was pounding hard enough to break his ribs and spear itself on the jagged edges. With fear and adrenaline, but also, Rainy realized, with thrill. Knowing that his parents were safe, it was a game again. The same game Rainy had loved half his life. And now, finally, he'd met his match.

Above him, Adler's finger was steady on the trigger. His hair was freed from its product completely, a dusty brown just long enough to brush the tops of his ears, fall forward into his eyes. There were bruises blooming along his cheekbone, his jaw, his brow. Charming, clever, smug, vicious, nasty Adler. There was a rosy flush in his cheeks, up his neck. A sheen of sweat glittered on his brow; water gathered in the hollow of his throat. His clothes were still soaked. His eyes were infinitely dark.

God, he was beautiful. Portrait of an avenging angel.

If Adler was pulling the trigger, Rainy supposed that it was a sufficiently legendary way to go.

He reached for something and found, as always, a joke.

"Not going to offer me any sexual favors this time?" he asked. "I mean, it's only polite, right?"

The muzzle of his own gun pondered his forehead. Adler tilted his head, considering. His gaze scraped like a straight razor down Rainy's body where he knelt on the floor. Rainy's clothes were still soaked, his shirt probably clinging to him and the outlines of his tattoos showing through the wet fabric.

The gun... faltered.

"All right," Adler said.

Rainy blinked. "What?"

"You're right." Adler's smile was sharp-edged and opaque. "It is only polite. Just so you know, though, the second we're finished, I *will* put a bullet in you. So make it count."

Then he tucked the Colt into the front of his waistband.

Rainy considered the pre-coiled tension in his muscles. He could launch himself now, grapple with Adler. He probably wouldn't be able to get the gun, but he could put up a good fight. Probably not a smart plan, considering how he'd fared in the hotel loading bay when Adler was already drugged. But it was what he had. Well, unless...

"You're actually going to blow me?" he asked.

Adler shrugged. "Don't have to be a blowjob, I guess."

"What, then?"

Adler was sliding out of his jacket. He stood in shirtsleeves and vest. The water turned his shirt translucent, clinging to the toned shape of his arms. He tossed the jacket aside.

"Dier's choice."

His pupils were dilated and his pulse jumped at his throat. And then it made sense—this and the wine cellar and the teasing interference. Because Adler loved this game like Rainy did, and maybe playing it well turned him on just as much.

Rainy looked up at him—his long, tailored lines, the narrow but strong set of his shoulders, the dark promise in his eyes. He remembered what he'd thought in the dim afterglow of the cellar, that he wanted to feel Adler inside him, wanted to know what it was like to have that haughtiness and single-minded ferocity focused entirely on taking him apart. And, God, just the image of it had Rainy half-hard. But if this might be his last time on Earth...

"I want to fuck you," he said. Blunt, the way Adler liked it.

Adler smirked and loosened his tie. "Good."

Rainy lost his breath a little. "There's, uh, supplies in my wallet. On the desk," he offered. Waiting for Adler to back down, write it off as a joke. Maybe just shoot him.

"Of course there are." Adler turned and walked back into the office. Rainy heard him pushing through the scattered supplies on Malia's desk.

He could run. There was a small chance he could make it to the door. He could just—

Ah, fuck, who was he kidding?

Adler reappeared in the doorway and tossed Rainy a condom and some packets of lube. Rainy caught them out of the air, grinning.

"Is this for real?"

In reply, Adler pulled Rainy's Colt from his belt and released the magazine, catching it deftly in his right hand. With his thumb, he flicked out the first round. Then the next. They landed on the linoleum with dull clicks. All the way down until there was a little glinting constellation around his polished black shoes, and one round left in the magazine. Adler showed it to him.

"This one's for you," he said, sliding the magazine home with a careless efficiency that did more for Rainy than it probably should have. He bent down and set the gun on the floor, right next to the door. "I'm gonna shoot you with it before I walk out of here. Now take your clothes off."

Chapter 8

Florida Man Seduces Prospective Killer

Rainy didn't need to be told twice. He unbuckled his shoulder holster and yanked his shirt over his head. Adler's eyes assessed him with interest, scraping hot over his body, the bullet scar on his shoulder and his tattoos—the violets on his chest, the Latin scripture on his ribs. The ring of thorns inked around one bicep, marking him as an Espinosa grunt, once upon a time. Adler picked his way neatly over the damp floor and dropped into his lap. Rainy groaned at the weight of him against his thighs. His fingers trailed down Rainy's chest, over his abs, to rest on the tiny twin revolvers tattooed there, angled down into the V of his hips.

"Original," he said, dry as dust.

"No one's complained yet."

"Well, it is Miami."

Rainy looped Adler's tie around his fist and dragged him in for a kiss, open and sloppy and angry. Then he pulled away, sputtering.

"You taste like an ashtray."

"Shut the hell up."

Adler shoved him flat on his back and rode him down for another kiss. He pushed his tongue into Rainy's mouth, demanding. The ashy flower taste of tobacco smoke was almost enough to gag on, but Rainy found that he could get over a lot when Adler was kissing him like that. Like he was about to kill him. Then Adler's tongue was teasing him forward and Rainy was on the offensive, pushing forward into Adler's mouth, biting his lip. It was bleeding still, and Rainy licked it away, the hot copper of blood and burnt-sweet acridity of smoke mixing into the heady taste of sex and violence.

They were laying on the cold linoleum floor where Rainy had probably shot a dozen men. Ah, well. They had bleached it just last week.

Rainy's hands found Adler's waist through his damp clothes, feeling in the way he hadn't been allowed to at the hotel. The dip of his waist, the sharp arch of his hip bones, the curve of his ribs. He was perfect. A well-oiled killing machine, lithe and precise and gorgeous.

Something frantic and hungry was surging under Rainy's skin, driving him forward with something close to desperation. It was the culmination of this week of cat-and-mouse, the memory of Adler's body and the adrenaline and planning, the pain and beatings and hatred, jealousy, humor, regret. Watching Adler sleep. Suddenly, it was all crashing together into this one hot, clear spike of feeling, and Rainy couldn't touch enough of Adler at once. He needed to get down to skin, deeper even, and run his hands and mouth over everything and feel and feel and feel.

He tugged Adler's shirt out from his belt and slid his hands up underneath. The skin of his back was warm, smooth, damp. Rainy could feel each notch of spine, the flex of his lats. He'd never hated Adler's fancy, expensive clothes more than he did at that moment. He scrabbled at the fabric, trying to get at more skin. So many goddamned *buttons*. The twill vest just wouldn't give, and his fingers were clumsy and shaking.

"Why do you have to wear so much clothing?" he grunted into the skin at the base of Adler's neck.

Adler planted both palms on Rainy's bare chest and pushed him back onto the floor, looking supremely unimpressed. Sitting back, he took about three seconds to get out of the vest.

"Sorry I don't find my clothes in the thrift store dumpster like you clearly do."

Rainy was so distracted by the deft movement of Adler's fingers that he almost forgot to reply.

"Aren't you supposed to be nice to me, or something?"

"This is a Make-A-Wish fuck, not our goddamn wedding night."

Adler was actually, honest-to-God pausing to fold his shirt and tie instead of just throwing them onto the floor. Yeah, that wasn't going to fly. Rainy pounced.

Skin on skin. Rainy rolled them over and over until they were out of the wet spot and he was pinning Adler to the floor. Adler was an inch or so taller, but Rainy was broad enough to cover him entirely—shoulders, chest, hips.

Under all those layers, Adler was pale, with a flush that spread down his chest just how Rainy had imagined it in the wine cellar. Rainy held him down with an arm across his collarbone and ran a hand up his side, admiring. Adler was trim and strong, muscular but not bulky like Rainy was. Just what was necessary and not a pound more. Practical and efficient—Adler to a tee. There were freckles, a mole at the bottom of his rib cage. And scars.

Rainy traced a finger along a thin, pale one that ran over the muscular plane of his abdomen, a silver-pink slash below his navel. The thickest was a stripe of puckered skin that climbed his right clavicle to the shoulder. It branched off, supported a satellite system of smaller parallel dips and pink marks. Like he'd been ripped open by a dozen tiny blades. *IED,* Rainy thought, and bent down to kiss it.

Adler shoved him away. Rainy was so startled that he sat back obediently, only to find Adler glaring at him.

"Don't fucking do that."

"I... sorry?" Rainy tried.

Adler's eyes were sharp. There were spots of red on his cheekbones. Rainy wasn't quite sure what he'd done wrong. He loved scars, loved to trace the stories of old battles and mistakes on skin. He flaunted his own with ludicrously embellished tales.

Though maybe they stopped being so fun once you got one you didn't have the option to hide.

He hadn't realized how pliant and relaxed Adler had been under him until he stiffened with unhappiness. Rainy pressed a kiss under his jaw and palmed at his hip, trying to get the tension to ease out of his muscles again. He lapped a drop of sweat out of the hollow at the bottom of Adler's throat, and his eyes landed on the red marks on either side of his trachea. Finger marks, clearly delineated. Marco's fingers. Rainy felt something hot and shifty flare inside him. He brought his hand up to cover the bruise, fitting his own fingers over the marks. Adler shivered.

Oh. So that's how it was. Rainy tightened his fingers a little. Used the grip to hold Adler down while he kissed down his chest, ignoring the scars this time.

A trail of dark hair ran from Adler's navel down into his waistband, right where Rainy wanted to go. He kissed it, stroked his hip bones where they angled in toward that same spot.

Abruptly, he sat back on his heels and curved a hand under Adler's right knee. He pulled it up to rest the ankle on his shoulder, then made a big show of removing Adler's shoe and sock and tossing them into the corner. He pressed a wet kiss to his ankle, and Adler rolled his eyes.

Once he'd finished with that, he started in on the belt. With them all wet and ridiculously tailored, taking Adler's pants off was like unpeeling cellophane. Knowing he'd be distracted, Rainy made himself get the pants all the way off Adler's ankles before looking down.

Distracted, he was. Like the rest of him, Adler's dick was long and slender. It had that same rosy flush to it where it rested, fully hard, against his toned stomach. Unable to resist, Rainy reached down and wrapped a hand around it, grinning when Adler's abdominal muscles jumped at the touch. He moved his hand in two long strokes, enjoying the way the roughness of his palm scraped over the velvety skin. Adler let out a stuttering exhale, and Rainy's own cock pressed against the zipper of his jeans.

"You're gorgeous; you know that?" Rainy told him. Adler huffed and turned his face away, but the tips of his ears went pink.

He tensed and writhed as Rainy kept working him, clearly trying to resist showing that he was in any way affected. Like a bad-tempered cat that had to be tricked into receiving and showing affection. Rainy had experience with those. He slicked two fingers in spit and brought them down to run lightly over Adler's balls. Adler made a sharp noise and tried to jerk away, but Rainy pinned him down by a hip.

"Relax," he murmured, leaning down to suck Adler's earlobe into his mouth. "How am I supposed to fuck you if you won't relax?"

Adler elbowed him in the ribs, earning a grunt. Well, it stood to reason that he would be just as much of a control freak in bed as he was everywhere else. When he started to roll away, Rainy grabbed him by the forearms and pinned him down on the linoleum.

Adler was quick and ferocious, but when it came to brute strength, Rainy's flashy muscles had him far outmatched. Rainy could feel him flex and shift, testing the pin. It would hold. Anywhere else, Adler could probably beat him. But here, if Rainy shifted to brace his knees, there was no way Adler would be able to fight out from under him short of going for the jugular with his teeth. In the furious cut of his eyes, Rainy could see him actually considering it.

Slowly, telegraphing his movements, Rainy leaned down to kiss him. Adler resisted for a moment, then opened his mouth. As they kissed lazily, Rainy released his arms and reached down, fumbling blindly across the floor. He found the lube and tore it open one-handed.

Adler gasped into his mouth when Rainy pressed a finger inside him, and Rainy drank it down. Adler's body was hot and tight, muscle clenching as Rainy slid in to the last knuckle. He drew out and back in, kissing the tiny noises out of Adler's mouth.

"Good," he murmured. "Just like that."

When he drew back, Adler's eyes were black with lust. His lips were parted, like he'd forgotten that Rainy had stopped kissing him.

He took the second finger eagerly, rolling his hips down onto Rainy's hand. Rainy could feel his heart between his ears as he stroked into the slick heat, massaging with his thumb. He watched his fingers disappear into Adler with something like wonder. When he started to pump faster, Adler made a pleased sound and moved his hips in time, abdominal muscles flexing.

Rainy's pants were starting to become painfully uncomfortable, but the way Adler was moving demanded his full attention. He couldn't tear his eyes away from how his back arched, the way his hand came down to grip the wrist Rainy had braced on the floor, strong enough to break bones.

"Hurry up," Adler commanded. Managing to sound imperious with another man's fingers up your ass was a special sort of talent.

"What if I'm not in a hurry to die?" Rainy retorted. Though, to be honest, dodging that final bullet was rapidly sliding down his list of priorities.

With a twist of movement too fast for Rainy's lust-addled brain to process, Adler was on top of him, wrestling him out of his jeans. Nails dragged deliciously down the tattooed insides of his thighs before shoving them apart. Rainy was still trying to gather enough working brain cells to protest the indignity of being manhandled when Adler got his underwear off and started demonstrating his impatience with a spit-slicked hand.

"Oh, God, you're amazing," Rainy gasped.

"I know," Adler drawled, then shoved him back flat on the floor with a knee to the chest. One hand still working, he ripped a condom open with his teeth and leaned down to roll it onto Rainy.

"Do your worst, sweetheart," Rainy told him.

Adler's eyes flashed. His hands were suddenly on Rainy's wrists, pinning them on either side of his head. "What did I tell you about calling me that?" he hissed. And then he shifted his weight back, still glaring, and sank onto Rainy's cock.

Rainy let out an embarrassing whimper, and his body arched up off the floor. The sudden transition from the snug, uncomfortable grip of the condom in open air to being buried in the hot, bruising tightness of Adler's body was almost too much to bear. Before he had a moment to recover, Adler was moving, shifting the angle to go deeper, grinding down with his hips. His head was tilted back and he was breathing hard, and Rainy wanted so badly to touch him.

Adler forced him back down with an authoritative hand on his chest. Then he really started moving.

He was so mind-bendingly slick and warm, moving with every thrust like a fucking professional. Every time Rainy started to get into a rhythm, Adler would shift his hips to throw him off, setting a new pace that suited him better. It was maddening. Rainy wasn't sure that he was in control of any part of his body anymore. His mouth kept saying a lot of very dirty words in combinations that probably didn't even make sense.

Everything inside him, that awful, confusing swirl of emotion and need, was suddenly clear as day, boiling and bubbling through him like a warm spring. This was what he'd been craving the whole time. The surge of heat under his skin was overwhelming.

Adler, of course, looked extremely pleased with himself. Rainy doubted anyone in history had ever looked so smug about riding someone's dick before. He was just giving Rainy that little lazy expression like he thought Rainy was the biggest bumbling idiot in the world, while he kept sliding up and down with that filthy rhythm, drawing fully off before sinking back to the base slow enough to make Rainy moan.

Rainy was an idiot, he realized, for fighting Adler at all. If Adler got it in his mind to kill Rainy, he could do as he damn well pleased. Rainy would let Adler do *anything* he pleased to him. Ride him raw and use him up and leave him bloodied. It was just the proper way of the world, Adler looking like the cat who got the canary, and Rainy wanted to give every last scrap of it to him. He remembered what he'd said to Adler, leaning against the bar, on the night they'd met:

Sweetheart, you can have anything you want from me.

"Can I make a request?" he gasped.

Adler pulled off a torturous twist of his hips. "It is your last meal."

"Mirror," Rainy managed to get out. "I want to watch."

Slowing, Adler made a big show of considering it. Then he nodded and rolled off. Rainy took several tries to get to his feet and grabbed Adler's hand to drag him over to the chair, nearly tripping over the jeans that were still tangled around his shins. The metal was freezing on his bare skin when he sat, facing the floor-to-ceiling mirror. Adler's skin was warm. He allowed himself to be reeled in and pulled back down onto Rainy's cock.

The angle was devastating. Rainy had to bite the inside of his cheek to stop himself from coming right then as Adler took him in almost eagerly, so deep it felt profane. He braced his feet and thrust up roughly, and Adler hissed.

It was a little awkward, since Adler was a couple of inches taller, but Rainy hooked his chin into the crook between Adler's neck and shoulder and stared into the mirror.

It was obscene. Adler's back was flush against Rainy's chest, Rainy's hand spread possessively over his sternum. His cock stood at full attention, looking flushed and almost painfully hard. Rainy met his eyes in the mirror and pushed up into him again and again, losing himself in the delicious, snug fit, the hot slide.

The warm sea of pleasure was rising with every thrust, filling him up, and Rainy thought, *Oh, I'm going to drown.* And then, *Oh, yes, I'm going to drown.*

Adler was shivering again, moving with him, finally submitting to Rainy's rhythm. Their breaths echoed in the wood-paneled room, the sound of panting and the filthy, slick noises when Rainy slipped out until just the head was inside, then slid back home. Adler was flushed red, bruised and shining with sweat. There was nothing he could hide in the mirror. His whole body was on display for Rainy, who drank it down with his eyes. He slid his palms up Adler's stomach, over his chest. Used both hands to part his thighs, wide enough that it had to hurt, to watch himself fuck up into him.

Adler's perfect composure was falling away piece by piece, and it was so unbelievably good that Rainy thought it would honestly be fitting if he were to die after this. Nothing left for him in life could possibly top Adler writhing against him, letting out those little panting whines.

"You feel amazing, sweetheart," he murmured directly into Adler's ear. Adler twisted his neck abruptly so Rainy's face was pressed into his opposite cheek, the unscarred one, and nuzzled like a cat.

Rainy's hand slid up Adler's belly, his chest, and settled on his neck. It was sweaty, all pounding pulse and tense muscles. But when Rainy tipped his chin back, it was so long, pretty and bruised and delicate. He wrapped his hand around it.

He could end this whole game now, if he really wanted. There would be no more need for desperate grappling, the uncertainty and fear for his life. There would be no need for the bullet on the other side of the room. Adler was in a bad position. If Rainy wanted, he could hold him here long enough to strangle him as he'd originally planned, watch his face go blue and the light fade from his eyes with Rainy still inside him.

"I could kill you, you know," he panted.

Adler stared him down in the mirror. Arched an eyebrow. "Then go ahead."

God, wasn't he something?

Rainy tightened his grip, digging his fingers in on either side of Adler's windpipe. Pressing in over Marco's bruises, stealing the air away. Adler's eyes widened. After a few seconds, his lips started to work, trying to draw in a breath. Rainy squeezed tighter, wrapping an arm tight as a steel band around his waist to hold him in place as he kept driving up into him, reveling in the twist and clench as Adler started to squirm. His hand was coming up, moving to claw at Rainy's wrist.

Rainy released the arm around his middle and wrapped his hand firmly around Adler's dick, stroking roughly. Adler gasped and writhed, thrusting desperately into his curled fingers. Rainy's hand on his neck went tighter, tighter, impeding the blood flow, crushing his own bruises to erase Marco's touch. If he kept it up, Adler was probably going to pass out. That was the edge he wanted to ride. He slid his hand down to where he was still buried inside Adler, slick and messy, and came back up to pump him again, hand wet with lube.

He released his grip on Adler's throat, and Adler gasped hoarsely as he came. Rainy could feel the orgasm shudder through his entire body, wet warmth spilling over his hand. He clenched down on Rainy's cock, and then Rainy was coming too. It was just on the edge of excruciating, the way the pleasure surged and burst inside of him, every muscle locking against the white-hot *yes*.

He rode it down with the overstimulating tease of Adler's muscles twitching helplessly around him, drawing out more shudders.

"Oh, God," he gasped, burying his face in the sweaty hollow of Adler's collarbone.

After a moment when the only inhabitant of the room was the mingled sound of their labored breathing, Adler pushed himself up. Rainy groaned at the feeling of their bodies slipping apart from the place they were connected. He couldn't quite summon the muscle coordination or clarity of mind to move.

He was supposed to be moving, wasn't he? There was a reason.

He tilted his head to watch as Adler walked back to where their clothes were heaped on the floor. Made a sound of protest as Adler wriggled back into his heinously tight pants without even bothering to wipe himself off. Then the shirt, and the belt, and Rainy thought, *Oh, that's right. Shit.*

Adler saw the realization in his eyes and snorted, tossing Rainy his jeans.

"Put your pants on," he said. "Unlike you, I don't make a habit of killing men while their dicks are out."

Mortal-peril fight-or-flight and post-orgasmic bliss. An incredibly bizarre cocktail. Rainy was up and scrambling for the gun before he could pull together a thought, but Adler was already there, leveling it at his head.

"Pants on," he repeated, toneless as ever.

Rainy peeled off the condom and put on his pants.

They stood facing each other, the gun trained between Rainy's eyes. Unspent rounds littered the floor around Adler's bare feet. Calmly, Adler bent to pick up his vest and jacket, draped them over his arm. Gathered both shoes and socks in his free hand.

"You're going to shoot me now?" Rainy's body was hot and cold, sore with the memory of skin on skin and the bite of adrenaline.

"I did promise you a bullet." Adler cocked his head lazily, let the Colt's muzzle drift down to Rainy's heart. Rainy's entire body was tensed, but he felt strangely detached from it. Like he was a balloon tied to his own wrist by a flimsy string, everything numb and floaty. Adler stroked the trigger like a lover.

Then he let the gun fall to his side, shrugging.

"I'll kill you tomorrow," he said, as bored as though he were announcing he'd take a trip to the supermarket.

A laugh startled out of Rainy's chest. "Fuck," he wheezed. "You're the worst person I've ever met."

Adler's mouth had that pinned-in quality to it. "I'm still gonna kill you. Just wouldn't be much fun if it's this easy. You're too interesting."

Oh. Oh, good fucking Lord. Rainy felt his biggest, most certified-shit-eating grin unfurl across his face. It was because—

"You like me," he said.

Adler scowled. "I don't fucking like you."

"You do! You like me and my delicious eggs and my comedic brilliance."

"First off, your eggs were disgusting—"

"You *did* try them!"

"—and, second, you're an irritating, uninspired, smarmy son of a bitch."

"You li—" Rainy shut up when Adler brandished the gun at him again.

"Don't make me change my mind." Adler turned and walked out into the office, then dropped his shoes onto the floor to slip them on. Rainy didn't follow.

"Bend over further," he called. "Give me something to remember you by."

"I *will* kill you."

Rainy folded his arms, almost giddy at Adler's tense, angry posture. "When I was fucking you, you didn't seem to have a problem with me calling you sweetheart."

Adler stood up straight, sharp as razor wire. His expression was murderous, and Rainy flinched back a little, wary of the sudden, definitive reappearance of Adler's finger on the trigger. Then his posture eased, the tiniest bit. Somehow, it was scarier. His eyes flicked over Rainy, deadly and lazy. Predatory.

"Don't get ahead of yourself," he said. "I said I would kill you later. I'm a man of my word. I also promised you this bullet before I walked out the door." He smiled, the most self-satisfied, vicious smile Rainy had seen on him yet. Dimpled and pretty and sharp as broken glass. "You want something to remember me by? Here you go."

And then he shot him.

The crack was infinitely loud in the enclosed room, just like he'd imagined. He felt the bullet, the burning path it carved through the air, and then force like a cracking bullwhip. Pain exploded across the side of his head, whiting out his vision, and Rainy fell to his knees with a scream.

He killed me. He killed me he shot me in the head he killed me oh god oh fuck

His hands were bloody, hot, trying to hold his head together. He was terrified when he shoved his fingers up into the bloody pain that he might find a chunk of skull. The floor was damp, was slippery and cold. His head was on fire. God, how was he alive?

Through the pain and shock, the roar and echo in his ears, he almost missed Adler calmly gathering up the rest of his things, tucking Rainy's gun away in his own belt.

Rainy was bleeding. Oh, he was bleeding, and he was… not dying. The pain was throbbing, red-hot, wild. Not dying. Fuck, there was so much blood, what—

He was still scrabbling around on the floor, fingers slipping in his bloody hair, when Adler closed the front door behind himself, the office echoing with his short, humorless laugh.

Chapter 9

Florida Man Mutilated in Lovers' Spat

"He shot me in the ear," Rainy said for the thousandth time. "He shot me in the fucking ear."

"Stop being such a sissy," Nasrin ordered, the words rolling smoothly in her thick Farsi accent. She dropped the gauze swab she was using on his right ear onto the soiled tray, then picked up another pad soaked in something that stung like a motherfucker.

"It hurts," he said defensively. "I've been shot."

"The baby is old enough to hear outside the womb now. If you keep whining, you're going to make her pathetic."

"All babies are pathetic. They're babies; that's their whole thing."

"Not as pathetic as you. You didn't even cry this much when I stitched up that bullet hole in your shoulder."

Rainy sniffed, trying not to wince at the fresh burn of antiseptic. "That time, some psycho hadn't shot half my ear off."

Nasrin scoffed. "Not half. Barely a quarter. Now hold still."

Nasrin Espinosa was one of the best trauma surgeons in Miami, Felix Espinosa's wife, and holder of his balls. She was also seven months pregnant, and had commandeered the operating table in the makeshift surgery in her and Felix's garage while she made Rainy stand. He had been tempted to argue the contrasting disability levels of pregnant versus freshly shot, but he did have an interest in keeping his ear as intact as possible.

Once the shock of a bullet passing an inch from his skull had worn off, Rainy had felt a bubbling panic as he fished a coin-sized piece of his own cartilage and skin out of the bloody puddle on the multipurpose room's floor. In the car on the way to Nasrin, the feeling had shifted into disbelief and, by the time he arrived, it had coalesced into rage.

"He laughed. He fucking *laughed*. Like it was funny. The *ear*."

"Yes, I heard you the first twenty times." Nasrin was finishing up, wrapping his entire ear in stiff white bandaging. The world went muffled. Rainy reached up to tentatively squeeze. An inch-long chunk of the outer helix had been ripped away, along with a ragged piece of the flat cartilage that made up the upper part of the ear.

"It's like someone took a bite out of me."

Nasrin snorted. "Maybe a baby."

She dropped to the bleach-scented concrete, rolling her swollen ankles. When he'd shown up in the deathly hours of the morning, ear in hand, she'd pulled on over her pajamas the white smock and sheer pink hijab that she always reserved for "backdoor calls." Somehow, her current state of unwieldy rotundness did nothing to lessen the effect of her glare.

"Are you sure you don't need the other piece?" Rainy asked, looking forlornly at the severed bit of ear lying next to a jar of cotton swabs.

"No point. Keep changing the bandages, don't get it wet. The skin will grow back fast."

"How soon will the rest of the ear grow back?"

"The cartilage won't grow back. It's cartilage."

Rainy gaped. "You mean my ear is going to look like this forever?"

"If you want to go throw money at a reconstructive surgeon for a graft, be my guest. I'm going back to sleep before my daughter decides to use my spleen as a punching bag again and Felix wakes up crying about how Andy Parish is all over him."

"How serious is this Parish situation, really?"

Nasrin sighed. "Serious enough that my husband won't shut up about it. Lina says that he has us way outmatched in the legal department, and if she can't organize to fight it just right, he could peel away some of our dockfront. He's never been this hostile before. It must be related to Seong moving to town. That's all I'm saying; I'm tired of hearing about it. I'll be writing up a bill, by the way. Go freelance, no free backdoor calls."

"If I'd known you were just going to stick a Band-Aid on it, I wouldn't have bothered."

Nasrin leveled a warning finger at him, thick eyebrows raised. Rainy lifted his hands in surrender.

"Okay, Jesus. Coming right up."

"Good. Now get out of my garage."

Rainy forked over one of the hundreds he'd taken from Adler's wallet and walked back out to his car. The dawn was just over the horizon, and the stars behind the boxy skyline of the city were being washed out in the pale gray spreading up from the direction of the Atlantic. Rainy sat in the driver's seat, resting his forehead against the wheel, until the street lamp overhead clicked off. His ear throbbed like someone was driving a hot spike into it. Like the bullet was ripping through again and again. It was a push pin stuck through his head to hold a reminder in place.

Adler had ruined his ear. Actually, honest-to-God mutilated him. He'd threatened the only thing in Rainy's world that really mattered, then given him the most mind-blowing sex of his life, and then mutilated him just for the hell of it. No, not for the hell of it—to remind him that he was serious when he told Rainy he'd kill him later. Because Rainy had forgotten. The pain was a blessing in disguise, because each time it washed over him in a fresh, copper-flavored wave, it made everything crystal clear.

This wasn't a game anymore. Not for Rainy. Adler might have been jerking him around just for the fun of toying with his food, but Rainy was done playing. This was kill or be killed.

He drove south, moving through the sparse early-morning streets of Coconut Grove, which had the air of a ghost town. Punnet Street was quiet, a painting of an idyllic palm-shaded neighborhood before the occupants were penciled in. He parked on the curb, hands white on the steering wheel. Despite the fact that he'd washed them at Nasrin's, his knuckles were still stained pink with his own blood.

It occurred to him then to look down at himself. He looked fucking terrible. His shirt was rumpled, buttoned wrong, and covered in bloody handprints. He was wearing one sock and his hair was a warzone. There was a smear of crusty white fingerprints on the waistband of his jeans that he was ninety percent sure was dried semen.

Sighing, he released his seatbelt and crawled into his tiny back seat, where he kept a duffel bag with an emergency change of clothes for just this reason. He exchanged his shirt and pants for a clean set, then crammed a baseball cap on, backwards, to hide the blood in his hair.

Feeling both clean and filthier than ever, he got out of the car to climb the steps.

The chime of the doorbell echoed distantly, and a minute later his father was at the door.

"Rafa?" he grumbled, squinting. "What are you doing here?"

Underneath the years of home cooking he'd put on, José Perez was still built like a steam engine. There were patches of black remaining in his hair, though the silver was quickly rising to swallow them. He'd grown his beard out since the last time Rainy had seen him.

"Hi, *Pa.* Can I come in?"

His father shrugged and stepped aside. Rainy cast one final glance around the empty street before ducking through the door.

The house that he'd bought his parents was always warm and a little stuffy with his mother's cheap incense. Their living room was cluttered, the couch smothered in blankets and one wall almost entirely covered by the collection of glazed ceramic crosses his mother had made over her years of pottery classes. They started from the top left corner and showed a marked progression in terms of symmetry and non-headache-inducing paint jobs. The shelf over the couch was lined with years and years of Rainy's old football trophies. In the center of the wall, like some kind of weird shrine, was the chalkboard chore chart his mother had made about twenty years ago, never gotten anyone to follow, and refused to get rid of. In the middle of the chart, just above *Rafa*, *Miguel* was written in faded blue chalk. Rainy swallowed roughly.

He hated this place.

"Is something going on?" his father asked. "You look fucking terrible."

"I'm fine," Rainy said. "Look—"

"*Mijo*, is that you?" His mother was coming down the stairs in her plaid pajamas, a thin red line from her breathing mask around her nose and mouth. She was a tiny, round woman with wide-set gray eyes that only Miguel had inherited. "What happened to your ear?"

"Hi, *Mami*. Accident at work. Actually, do you have some Tylenol I can borrow?"

"Yes, of course." She bundled into the downstairs bathroom. Rainy turned back to his father.

"Did anything happen here tonight?"

His father narrowed his eyes. "Your mother made cookies for the Kaufmans and I watched my shows. We went to bed. Was there something you were expecting to happen?"

"No, that's good. Listen: has anyone come around here asking questions in the past week?"

"I don't think so," his mother said, returning with a bottle of pills. Rainy tapped two into his palm and swallowed them dry. "I think I would have remembered something like that."

His father's voice was cold. "Why would someone have come around?"

"I—" Rainy swallowed. "I got into some trouble at work. I need you to be very careful for the next week or two. Don't talk to strangers, don't go out after dark. I'm going to have some friends hang around the neighborhood, just to keep an eye on things."

"You can't really have such a bad client?" his mother asked docilely, but his father looked livid.

"What have you done this time? What did I fucking tell you?"

Rainy sucked in a deep breath through his nose. He really didn't have the patience right now. "It won't be a problem. I'm handling it. Just, if you see any Espinosas near the house—"

"*Espinosas,*" his father ground out. "I don't want your *friends* here at all, Rafael. I don't want you dragging your bad decisions back here, just like I didn't want your fucking charity—"

The last clinging thread of Rainy's temper snapped. "But you needed it! And you need me now. You don't get to sit here, where I put you, and spit down on me."

"What I need is for my son to get an honest, decent job and stop running around like a thug, before I have no sons left!"

"No fighting!" his mother shouted. "No fighting in my house, and no using that language. Rafa is a good boy. I'm sure he'll get whatever this is sorted out." She smoothed her hair compulsively. "Now, how about I make us all some hot chocolate?"

"No thanks, *Mami*," Rainy sighed, adjusting his baseball cap. He couldn't manage to look his father in the eye.

"Are you sure you don't want me to look at that ear?" she asked. "It looks bad."

"I already went to the doctor. It's okay."

"What happened? I can't see some skinny little singer doing that to you."

"He got shot," his father said flatly.

"José, don't—"

"Oh, *discúlpeme*, I didn't realize it was a pretending night."

"I lied, actually," Rainy cut in. "It was a bad date."

His mother smoothed her hair again. "Now, that's where you're not a good boy. You'll be thirty soon; don't you think it's time to stop messing around and find a nice girl?"

"Or boy, Esperanza," his father corrected impatiently. "He likes both."

"Well, of course I remember *that*. But don't you want to give us grandbabies with the Gonzales eyes, *mijo*? And if you want to get married in the Church. You know, there's this sweet girl in my classes, pretty white Catholic girl named Amy..."

"No thanks, *Mami*." Begrudgingly, Rainy whispered to his father, "Thanks."

"Shut up. We're still fighting."

"Why don't you stay for breakfast?" his mother insisted, eager to keep changing the subject.

"Sorry—I need to get back to work." That was partly true, considering he had a big mess in the multipurpose room that he needed to clean up before Malia got in. But, mostly, it was the fact that he couldn't spend more than an hour in this house without wanting to crawl out of his skin.

"Well, before you go, we need to talk about Thanksgiving."

"Thanksgiving can wait," his father said. "He might not even be alive by then."

"José!"

The Tylenol had lessened the throbbing pain in his ear a little, but there was a tension headache building behind his eyes now. "I'll just go."

"Wait!" she exclaimed. "I have something to give you. Wait here." Then she scampered away up the stairs. Rainy sighed and pinched the bridge of his nose.

"I'm not fighting you on this," he said. "The Espinosas are going to look after you until I get this sorted out, and then my coworker is going to bury the leads between us deep enough that this doesn't happen again."

"Oh, that's lovely! My son, who has to hide his real name and his parents his whole life. That's what I always wanted!"

"*Pa.*"

His father's face was flushed with the righteous fury that Rainy had never quite seen even the fieriest preachers be able to match.

"I worked my whole life at a real job. I may not have been able to give you much, but what I did give you didn't come at the expense of anyone else. We came here to give you a better life, and look at what you've done with it. You think I couldn't have gone down that road? I never wanted this for my family. I never wanted this for your soul."

"*Pa.*"

His father was gripping him by the shoulders now. His hands were strong with years of hard labor, broad and dense the way Rainy had inherited. His eyes were dark with grief.

"You promised me, *mijo*. You promised me, when you started going down this path, that I wouldn't have to bury another son."

"And you won't." Rainy removed his father's hands gently. "You won't."

His mother stopped at the top of the stairs, taking in the scene—Rainy gripping his father's hands, their bodies tight with tension. They stepped apart.

"Here we go. We're working with photography right now in Delia's class," she said cheerfully. "I made us a whole set, but I want you to have this one for your place."

She handed Rainy a small ceramic dish, sleek with crimped edges. It was dark blue and green, painted in a marbled pattern. In the center of the dish, cut into a circle and preserved flush under the glaze somehow, was a picture. Two grinning, summer-browned boys standing in front of a lookout point sign against a canyon of fall-patterned foliage, arms slung around each other. Rainy and Miguel in the Appalachians, ages nine and twelve. He felt the quiet in him slide, roll off a shelf, and fall into the depths. As always, he waited for the crash that never came.

"It's nice. Thank you."

"I have more, if you want."

"Uh, no thanks," he said quickly. "This one would be special." He cleared his throat and tucked the bowl, roughly the size of his palm, into his back pocket. "I really do need to get back to work. I'll call you about Thanksgiving, okay?"

His mother wrapped him in a hug that didn't do anything good for his bruised ribs. Over the top of her head, Rainy's father leaned in the doorway to the kitchen, tense. Rainy attempted to meet his eyes, then let his gaze slide to the floor when he found in them what he'd been dreading.

Nine years was a long time, but not long enough to wash away the memory of the way his father had once looked at him as he jogged off the field, young and flushed with victory. He'd clapped Rainy—Rafa—on the back and laughed, and his eyes had shone with pride.

If you'd asked Rainy when he was that age, eighteen and immortal, he would have laughed at the idea that emotions had physical dimensions. But today, if you'd blindfolded him and placed in the palm of his hand the expression his father wore now, he would have guessed it right away, so familiar was he with the weight of disappointment.

After dodging a last-ditch attempt to dump some leftovers on him, he finally made it out the door and down the steps. Back at the car, he took a deep breath and let it out slowly. Remembered how Adler had blown smoke out of his nose the same way, and stopped.

The little house looked so obvious and defenseless. It was all too easy to imagine it crumbling to dust before his eyes. The basil in the upstairs planter box was starting to wilt.

It was one thing for Adler to slash Rainy's tires, even damage his ear. But if he laid a single finger on Rainy's parents, Rainy would eviscerate him. This wasn't funny, or flirty, or playful anymore. Adler had a bullet in Rainy's ear and a knife pressed against his blind spot. Rainy found the memories of the previous night—how amazing it had felt to be inside him, how frightened he'd looked when the water came down, how he'd pressed his cheek to Rainy's face at the word *sweetheart*—and shoved them down, hard.

Sex was just that. It had been good sex—brain-meltingly good, actually—but, in the end, that was all it was. Clearly, Adler had no problem making the distinction. Rainy wouldn't either.

Sex and blood. What the world turned on. Well, this game had run its course.

It was time for blood.

When Rainy dropped into the driver's seat, something jabbed him in the tailbone. He pulled out the little ceramic bowl, gleaming in the early dawn light, and placed it on the passenger seat. The two boys in the photo smiled up at him, remnants of a time long past. Rainy was struck by the feeling, heavy and sure as a hammer to the head, that both of the boys in that picture were dead.

Before he pulled onto the street, he tossed his jacket down onto the seat to cover their faces.

Chapter 10

Florida Man Losing Grip, Warns Coworker

"**C**ome on," Marco begged. "*Please* show it to us. You can just show it to me, if you want. You don't even have to let the crybaby see."

Malia dropped her pen with a sharp clack. "Rainy, tell Marco that if he can't be a mature and respectful workplace contributor, he can get out of my office."

"Tell *Malia* that she can suck my evil, murdering dick."

"Oh my God." Rainy set his disassembled gun on the mat. "I'm supposed to be the irreverent, flirty young assassin, and you two are turning me into a middle-aged mom. Shut up."

He had spread out a yoga mat in the corner of the Rattrap's office to clean his weapons while Malia assembled a complete movement map on Adler. Unfortunately, Marco had also set up shop upside-down on the couch to pester Rainy into taking off his ear bandage.

"I can't believe he took your gun."

"I kind of wish you would stop reminding me."

"I mean, that's your signature gun. Kind of emasculating."

Rainy slid his Glock back together with a satisfying click and pointed it at Marco. "Again: leave me alone unless you want Tessa to become a widow before you ever even score a date. I'm in full war mode here. And, honestly, I don't want you around if you can't control yourself."

"God, are you still upset about the waterboarding thing? I had it under control." Marco kicked the wall for a few seconds, growing visibly bored when nobody replied. "Felix said you didn't show up with your ear all fucked until past two. What were you doing that whole time if not torturing the dude?"

Rainy unhappily set in on sharpening his knives. "None of your business." He glared at Malia out of the corner of his eye. "But, no, I wasn't torturing him, if that's what you think."

Malia didn't look up from the monitor. "I didn't say that. You guys are blowing everything out of proportion. I just don't do well with blood, okay?"

"You work for a bunch of hitmen."

"Oh, but, Rainy, don't you know? She's a perfect angel who's never hurt a fly," Marco simpered.

Malia slammed her hand down on the desk. "I can stop helping you with this, if that's what you want."

Rainy dropped his sharpener onto the mat and raised his hands over his head to command the full attention of the room. "Please, let's all just pull it together for the ten more minutes we need to be in the same room, so I can make this guy dead as soon as possible."

The couch creaked as Marco rolled down to a sitting position. "Wow, you're really out for blood with this guy now. What's up with that?"

"Oh, I don't know—maybe it's because he shot me in the ear and threatened my family? Besides, I always had it out for him. It's my fucking job." Rainy started packing his weapons back up, sliding the everyday ones into their homes on his person.

"Nah, the sick fuck is right," Malia deadpanned, going back to her keyboard. "Before, you were totally acting like you had a crush on the guy or something."

"I do not have a crush on him. In case you missed the memo, my primary objective is to erase him from the face of the Earth."

There was a silence. "Don't you mean *ear*-rase?" Marco asked sweetly.

"Marco."

Malia was hiding behind her monitor. "Aw, come on, Rainy; he means well. Why don't you lend him an ear?"

"It's *not funny.*"

Marco and Malia exchanged a glance over the desk.

"Sorry, wouldn't want to get on the bad side of feared assassin Rainy Half-ear."

"Terrifying. Always up to his ears in murder."

Rainy snatched his duffel and mat off the ground and stormed into the locker room. Little shits. He was fucking mutilated for life, and here they were, laughing it up.

"Sorry, Rainy, were your ears burning?" Malia called after him.

"No, don't run out of *earshot.*"

There was wild cackling, and then the sound of a high five. At least Rainy wouldn't have to deal with their bickering anymore. His dignity was a small price to pay for peace in our time.

He took longer than necessary putting his things away, sulking in the locker room. When he returned to the office, Marco had wandered off to find attention elsewhere. Malia turned a monitor to face him.

"I've emailed the full report to you. This is the map of all the confirmed movements we have on him. It should be a good start. Now, we can start talking logistics, if you want..."

Rainy leaned in to examine the dots scattered across the uptown and midtown areas. "Sure. You can help me plan it all out, and then, when I'm committing violent homicide, I'll be sure to let Adler know how not-complicit you were in it."

Malia crossed her arms. "Really? Now?"

Rainy had been in a truly hellish mood since the ear incident and, with all the mocking, he was itching to stick a knife in something. If Adler wasn't here, Malia would do.

"I'm sorry," she gritted out, "that I'm not as used to casual violence as the rest of you."

"That's not the point."

"It's not?"

Rainy picked up a stress doll off Malia's desk and squeezed it until its eyes bulged. "No. The point is that you think you're better than me—" than *us*, he'd meant to say *us* "—because you just sit here in this chair and handle people as numbers. Because you're such a bright girl that you're going to be out of here in a couple years, and fuck off to the rest of us."

"I don't think I'm better than you. And you don't get to shame me for having a future beyond this place."

Rainy squeezed the doll until it let out a little screaming leak of air. It smothered his flinch.

"Just own up to it. You kill people, Malia. You murder people for money."

"It's not the same."

"What, just because you don't have to wash blood out from under your nails at the end of the night?" Rainy didn't know when he'd raised his voice. Malia was staring him down, cool and collected. It made him even angrier. "It's not so different."

"Fine," she snapped. "I think you're a horrible person. Is that what you want to hear? And maybe I'm just as bad. Maybe I've done things that are totally irredeemable. But that's not what this is about." She looked forlorn, suddenly. "I want to walk out of this place when I graduate. I don't want this to become my life. I mean, look at you."

"Me?"

Malia was so headstrong most of the time that Rainy forgot about the size difference between them, the way she was so tiny compared to him that he could have snapped her spine as easily as he would a baby animal's. Now, the imbalance was all he could see as she tugged at her crochet top, staring through him.

"You're the one who brought me in, Rainy. You're the first person I met who let this become their whole world. And you're fucking miserable. You're totally miserable, and you don't even know it."

Rainy was so stunned that he lost grip of his anger completely. "I'm not miserable. I'm—my life is fine."

Her lips twisted sadly. "Right. My mistake." With a press of her thumb, she powered down her monitors and picked up her bag. "Happy hunting, Rainy."

He wondered how, even while he was acutely aware of how big he was standing next to her, she could manage to make him feel so small.

Thankfully, he didn't have any time to spare worrying himself over whatever Malia thought she saw in him. She had one thing right—he was on the hunt. He had to get it right this time. The Rattrap became his base of operations; he only left to scrounge up food down the block before returning to the office to eat it. He spent hours staring at the files and maps Malia had built, studying. Memorizing. He mapped out the patterns in Adler's routine, studied every account by friends in the business who'd run across him.

It was sort of like studying wildlife, Rainy thought. Observing in the animal's natural habitat. Adler was a feral sort of creature, a jackal or some other elusive desert beast. Rainy could only read the tracks and the empty spaces, the places he'd been and hadn't been.

He was going a little crazy, maybe. Just a little.

Under his bandage, the skin was starting to web over the bloody-broken cartilage edges of his eartip. It itched like hell. Each time he unwrapped it to clean the wound, he was struck by how much it really did look like Adler had leaned in close and taken a bite out of him.

He learned Adler's schedule inside and out, including the horrifying fact that he got up at five every morning to run several miles and that he owned two dogs, which was a horrifying fact in that it was disturbingly human.

When he needed a break from reading because his eyes ached, he retreated to the back where they kept the boxing equipment and sparred with the punching bag until his knuckles split.

The déjà vu of it wasn't lost on him; it felt like an echo of last week, when he'd been preparing to intercept Adler the first time. But now, everything was heightened and more desperate. Like being stuck in a time loop, where each go-around became more frantic and panicked than the last. He was in a closed system filling with the fizzing static of entropy, and soon it was all going to pop like the cork out of a shaken bottle of champagne.

He was going to find a way to get ahead of the explosion, even if it killed him.

By the end of the week, he was ready. No backup this time—they'd only made things worse. He checked with the Espinosas guarding his parents, loaded himself down with his most reliable pieces, and staked out and waited and laid a trap on the way to a Vee hideout Adler was known to pop into regularly to police.

Nothing. He never showed.

Rainy went home and tried again the next night, at a different place. No dice. He tried all of Adler's usual haunts, every place he'd been spotted, growing sloppier and more desperate each time, but Adler never appeared. He even staked out Adler's apartment and didn't catch a glimpse of the man. It was like he'd vanished off the face of the Earth.

There were two possibilities, in Rainy's eyes: either Adler was avoiding him (which made him livid), or he was busy with something he deemed more important than Rainy (unbearable).

Maybe, in the intervening days, someone else had gotten off a lucky shot and Adler's body just hadn't washed up yet. Somehow, that was the worst possibility of all. Adler was his. Rainy was the one who got to finish this, to put a bullet between his eyes. It wasn't just about dueling contracts anymore, Adler being paid to kill Rainy, Rainy being paid to kill him. He felt like they were connected now. Magnetized. Epic final battle written in the stars, or whatever passed for them in the hazy, light-polluted skies over Miami.

When he got too keyed up, wired and so angry in the echoey post-midnight silence that it felt like something deep inside him was bleeding, he found himself retreating to the bathroom and jerking off in a frantic, strangled rush. Despite his best efforts, his mind always turned to the weight and warmth and obscene, desperate sounds Adler had made riding in his lap. Interspersed seamlessly were fantasies of choking Adler 'til he turned blue, slitting his throat from ear to ear. The sex and violence blurred together, turning him hot and cold, stuttering, until he couldn't tell them apart and didn't know which he was getting off on. He came unhappily with a bitten-off cry in the back of his throat, and collapsed into too-few hours of dreamless sleep on the couch.

In the muggy daylight hours, Malia brought him a pack of dollar-store lollipops and Marco snuck a box of lo mein onto his lap. Peace offerings. After a few days of Malia's loud side-eye, Rainy slunk back to his apartment to shower and change his clothes. He dished out the remaining lo mein to Patoso, then held still for the appropriate number of minutes for the cat to settle nearby and allow a few strokes down his spine before he capered away in overblown offense.

He sat in the middle of his empty living room, feeling the gray walls press in. The space felt too small and too large, made him seasick. He wanted to escape through the front door, run and run through the streets until the city washed the feeling away and he was anybody but himself. He squeezed the damaged tip of his ear until it bled again, just to feel the pain.

The floor was hard and unforgiving when he lay down on it and closed his eyes.

When he'd been taking his first, toddling baby steps away from the Espinosas, he had been enamored with Olga Rezakova. At that point, she'd been the only real independent assassin in the area. Nobody owned her—she was an artist of death who worked fully on commission. Rainy had wanted to be her. When he'd begged her to take him on as an apprentice, she'd made him play the same game she made all of her protégés play. She called it "magic bullet." It went like this:

You took the magazine out of your gun, removed every last round. Made sure the chamber was empty, and it was harmless as a child's toy. Then, you put the rounds in your pocket, held the gun to your temple, and pulled the trigger.

It was simple enough—a playground version of Russian roulette. But the trick wasn't in pulling the trigger; it was in the moment before. Because in the moment the gun kissed the side of your head and your finger hesitated on the trigger, doubt crept in. You'd made sure it was empty, but what if you'd made a mistake? In your mind, you knew that you hadn't, but *what if what if what if.* As long as the chamber was out of your sight, the chance that that space was occupied was never quite zero. Schrödinger's bullet, or whatever. And, like Rezakova said, even when it was empty, every time you thought about it for the rest of your life, you'd feel the phantom pain of what might have been right inside your skull. A shot that both was and wasn't, suspended in time.

Click.

Magic bullet.

These hours and days of frantic waiting to face Adler felt like that moment right before the trigger was pulled.

Adler probably wouldn't have gotten that game, Rainy thought bitterly. He was too controlled, too competent and self-contained. The doubt would have never occurred to him. If he had emptied the chamber, then there was no bullet. Rainy wondered what it was like, knowing exactly who and what you were. He wondered what it was like to want to know.

He sat up abruptly, his unbuttoned shirt sliding off of one shoulder. A thought had sparked, unbidden, from the crude smashing-together of rocks in the tumbler of his mind.

His problem was that he had been looking for Adler, when Adler controlled what the world saw of him. The trick was looking at the gun Adler *wasn't* holding. Looking at what he didn't control.

For example, Adler didn't control Hyun-woo Seong.

Gathering up his toothbrush and a change of underwear, Rainy hurried back to the office.

Seong's movements were much easier to follow once Rainy set Malia on them, since he was something of a public figure. One of the wealthiest men in the city, and all that. Most of it was boring and expected: meetings, dinners, a charity event at his children's new-age hippie private school. But, a few nights ago, Seong had made a brief, unexpected stop at an exclusive Brickell club, the kind of den of investment bankers and trust fund burners where the escorts wore Louboutins and fur. A popular place in those circles, but definitely not Seong's style.

"It pains me to say this," Rainy sighed when Malia turned her monitor to show him, "but I might have to dress up for work."

He bought a suit whose price was in very uncomfortable proportion to that of his car. It was French blue and paired with a pocket square, for God's sake. He had them tailor the pants close across his ass, just because. Might as well go all out, if he was going out at all.

It looked great on him—accentuated the breadth of his shoulders, the warm hue of his skin—but Rainy felt stuffy and trapped. He normally went for "charmingly rough around the edges" with his clothes; this made him look like he managed hedge funds for a living.

When he looked in the mirror, hair combed neatly back, the clothes felt like a lie, a game. With Rainy's usual clothing, everything was out in the open, and you got what you saw. Little left to the imagination, as it were. This was...

It was enough to pretend for a night.

On Sunday night, nearly a full week after the disaster with Adler, Rainy drove into Brickell to stake out the club. When he arrived, the place was already busy. Bodies milled and circled each other in a kind of orbital dance over the frosted-glass dance floor and the tables that lined the wide bank of windows. Over the bar was a panel of blue and green light fixtures that gave the whole place the air of an aquarium, complete with shark-nosed men in gray suits and glittering, scaly-sequined slips of girls.

Rainy settled at the bar and ordered himself a cosmo. The most badass of drinks it was not, but it was his favorite, and he might die tonight. Magic bullet, and all that. He sipped it as he surveyed the room, the bitter-citrus-vodka taste warming his nerves where they thrummed under his skin.

Seong wasn't here, but that was expected. It wasn't him, exactly, that Rainy was looking for—it was whatever business he had here. If it was important enough for Seong himself to pop in on, it was important enough for his favorite guard dog.

Songs changed. Rainy got to the bottom of his drink. He ordered another, scanned the room again and again, less hopefully each time. A woman named Charlotte sat next to him and he bought her a drink. They chatted a while, and she left, and Rainy scanned the room again, and Adler didn't show. After a few hours, he started to doubt that this had been a good idea after all. He felt embarrassingly like a date who'd been stood up.

When he was at the bottom of his third drink, a hand trailed over his shoulder and he tensed, thinking, *AdlerAdlerAdler*. But the man who settled next to him was no Adler. He was near fifty, with salt-and-pepper hair and laughing blue eyes and a casually unbuttoned collar, and Rainy almost choked on the disappointment.

"Buy you a drink?" the man asked, and Rainy's figurative choke nearly turned into a literal one, because he *recognized* the man. And this—this was, without a doubt, the reason Seong had appeared at this club. Fucking hell.

Rainy let a little heat curl in his gaze as he looked the man up and down, pushed some seductive roughness into the scuff of his syllables. "Sure," he said. "Name's Alex Guerrero."

The man grinned. "Andy Parish. What're you drinking, Alex?"

Rainy could tell just from the cant of his voice and his posture that Parish didn't recognize him. Of course he didn't; Andy Parish had no need to get his hands dirty in street play the way the Espinosas did. He didn't need to know who was doing the killing around the city when he hinted that things needed to get done—it was all arranged for him.

He didn't have a damn clue who Rainy was.

And that could be useful.

Adler wasn't here, but Rainy had no doubt that whatever Seong was up to around here was about Parish. Anything Rainy could get out of him would help him pin down Adler. And, more than that, Emilio would be willing to pay out in favors for any information on Parish's new business plans that Rainy could bring him. This night might not be a bust after all.

"Whatever you want me to be drinking," he replied.

Parish's smile grew. He waved over the bartender, ordered them both Sazeracs, and told him to leave the top-shelf bottle of absinthe on the bar.

While he did so, Rainy looked him over carefully. Parish wasn't a big man, and he'd approached Rainy, who was twenty years younger and about forty pounds heavier than him, all wrapped up in obvious muscle. The initial conclusion was that he wanted someone big, young, and strong to manhandle him, and that recommended confidence.

But that wasn't it. Everyone in this bar knew Parish, and Parish knew it. He knew that Rainy knew who he was, the strings he held. He dressed tastefully but indiscreetly: gold-accented watch, silk pocket square. Preening. He wanted to be looked at and admired. Same with the drink order. He knew that Rainy admired him, but he took it further—he wanted Rainy starstruck, cowed. It was about having big, physically powerful men bend the knee. His smile at being handed the reins on Rainy's drink was all the confirmation Rainy needed. By the time Parish turned back to him and handed him his Sazerac, he had already put together his plan of attack.

"I've never had one," he lied, fingering the condensation on the lip of his glass.

"Try it," Parish insisted. Rainy faked a shy glance down into the dark golden liquor and lifted it up for a sip. The orange peel tickled his nose, and when he smiled, he looked up into Parish's eyes.

"Good?" Parish asked.

"Good."

Parish sighed, downing a long sip of his own glass. "I love New Orleans. Greatest city on Earth, I think. You ever been?"

Rainy shook his head, rounding his eyes a little. He knew how to play coquettish, when it was wanted.

"That's a shame," Parish said. "I own a few high-end clubs there; that's where I got my start. So much cheap real estate after Katrina. You just have to be savvy enough to act when conditions are just right."

Rainy resisted the urge to grind his teeth. He could definitely dedicate a night to helping Emilio take this fucker down a peg.

"I always wanted to go," he said, easy and flirty. "Nobody to take me, and I never take vacations on my own. Always working."

"Take it from me," Parish said, leaning in conspiratorially. "A pretty young thing like you has to learn to indulge every once in a while, while you're still pretty and young." His hand ghosted over Rainy's knee in his fine, pressed blue slacks. Rainy butted up into the touch and smiled, indulgent and inviting.

Parish poured him a shot of absinthe, slid it over. Rainy examined the pale-greenish spirit. "None for you?"

"In a moment," Parish soothed. "I just want to watch."

Rainy threw back his head as he took the shot, exposing the line of his throat. He met Parish's eyes as he licked a drop off his bottom lip, and tried not to wince at the bitter licorice taste. Parish looked pleased with everything about Rainy: the sleek hair and neat suit with the too-tight pants. Rainy knew he looked excellent, square-jawed and handsome and moneyed and just exotic enough to fascinate a man like Andy Parish.

He wondered fleetingly whether Parish would still want him in his cheap street clothes, covered in another man's blood.

Rainy poured a second shot and held it straight up to Parish's lips. He tried not to think about the fact that he was pulling a page from Adler's playbook, or that instead of the authoritative way Adler had poured bourbon down Rainy's throat, he was coaxing against Parish, a shy thumb pressed to the corner of his mouth. It felt like a falsehood.

"Is it rude to ask about the ear?" Parish asked.

Rainy laughed. "My cat. Please tell anyone who asks that I was shot, though. My reputation is on the line."

"Your secret is safe with me." Parish watched Rainy take a sip of absinthe straight from the bottle, eyes dark. "You know, last time I was in New Orleans, I bought the most beautiful antique piano. Used to stand in a nineteenth-century brothel, and then a jazz club. If you close your eyes while listening, it's like being in the city itself. You can taste it."

Rainy let his lashes dip. They were his mother's lashes, long and dark. "Can I see?"

The next thing Rainy knew, Parish had paid the tab and was ushering him down to the street with jarring speed. A bodyguard peeled off from the wall to accompany them down in the elevator, but he didn't recognize Rainy either. He was private muscle from an above-the-board company. Not the kind that usually played with Rainy's type. Rainy made an excuse to duck into his own car, quickly stripping off his weapons and locking them inside. When he emerged, Parish was leaning against the wall, waiting.

He crawled half into Parish's lap in the back seat of the chauffeured car, pressing lazy, absinthe-sticky kisses against his neck. He didn't usually go for men Parish's age, but Parish was attractive enough and Rainy was plenty incentivized. Besides, the frustrated anticipation of another night waiting in vain to confront Adler was fizzling in his veins, making him hot and itchy with the need to do *something*. If that something had to be Parish—well, Rainy had done a lot worse.

He kept track of the car's turns while he made a show of panting into Parish's neck. He could feel Parish getting hard against him as he felt up Rainy's ass through his too-tight pants. The things were monstrous, honestly. He didn't know how Adler did it.

Parish owned an estate in North Beach not far from the Espinosas, with a long driveway and a manicured garden that ran down to the beachfront. Over the black water of Biscayne Bay, the lights of downtown rose like modern Towers of Babel, built in man's hubris to hang replacement stars. Parish's home was tall and elegant, all archways. There were more bodyguards lurking. Rainy counted the one who came with them, plus another who patted him down before entry and four more they encountered on their way through the house to the study, Parish's hand in Rainy's back pocket the whole way. That was all right; Rainy didn't plan on making any sort of trouble tonight that warranted the guarding of bodies. Just a little light snooping.

Parish's study, unlike the modern interior of the rest of the house, was very old-money, boys-with-cigars-club. It was all dark wood paneling and vintage banker's lamps, with a mantled fireplace and, as promised, an antique piano with a name stenciled in peeling gilded paint. Parish poured them some drinks (no more absinthe, thank God) and settled at the piano to play while Rainy lounged on a crushed velvet fainting couch that could have been pulled straight from a Victorian period drama.

The music was good, Rainy had to admit. Whether it transported one straight to New Orleans, he didn't know. He'd never been. Had never been much of anywhere other than Miami, really.

Parish watched him more and more as he played, traced his eyes over the careful arrangement of Rainy's body on the backless couch. In the warm, dark alcohol-slickness of his body, Rainy could feel the charge in the air, the tip in the scales when a moment between strangers turned from interest to Yes, *this is about to happen.* The room was too hot, so Rainy removed his tie and jacket, loosened the collar of his shirt. Parish's eyes devoured each new inch of skin revealed, growing hungrier at the glimpse of tattoo that peeked out from Rainy's open collar. And even if he wasn't someone Rainy would have approached, well—it was good to be admired.

Finally, Parish left the piano and settled on the arm of the couch to trace a finger up Rainy's thigh. He called out to a bodyguard hovering out of sight of the doorway, who Rainy had been keeping an eye on. "Can you send in Mark?" he asked, then returned his attention to Rainy.

"I've been told I'm a man of unusual tastes," he said without preamble.

Uh-oh.

Parish laughed at the involuntary look of alarm that must have crossed Rainy's features. "No, nothing gruesome, I promise." He smoothed Rainy's shirt with a hand. "It's just that I like to play with friends, if you know what I mean. Are you okay with that?"

Rainy nodded, relieved. Three-or-more-somes, while not generally his style, weren't entirely foreign territory.

"You could have just led with that," he admonished, taking Parish's drink.

"Where's the fun in that?" Parish glanced up as his friend appeared in the doorway. "Mark, there you are. Come and see what delightful thing I picked up at the bar. This is Alex."

Rainy glanced lazily over at the newcomer, tall and lean in his posh gray suit, and froze. The man's steps faltered in unison, a quickly concealed flinch ebbing across his face. They stared at each other.

"Hello, Alex," said Adler.

Chapter 11

Florida Man Tells All: Eccentric Billionaire Seduction

For all his meticulous planning, Rainy hadn't quite known what he would do when he saw Adler again. He was a creature of the moment, after all. And now Adler was right in front of him, in Andy Parish's study, of all places. He was a little undone, relaxed in his surroundings—jacket missing, tie loose, hair curling at his ears.

In that single, frozen moment, Rainy thought he might throw himself at him. That cacophony of fury and hatred, all the dread and misery of the past week, crescendoed inside him, and his muscles bunched to launch him at Adler's throat. He wanted to tear into his skin, lack of weapons and lurking guards be damned. The only thing that held him on the couch, rigid with rage, was Parish's hand on his thigh.

The moment passed, and Adler's face smoothed back to perfect composure. Rainy was sure that his own expression was giving too much away, but he couldn't help it. Adler was finally within arm's reach, and he wanted to taste blood.

"Do you know each other?" Parish asked, confused.

"No," Adler replied, "I don't think so." He stretched out a hand. "Mark Calhoun."

Rainy blinked. Why not rat him out? Because—because Parish had called him *Mark*.

Parish didn't know who Adler was, either.

Rainy couldn't fight the tiny smile that curled the edge of his lip. He could expose Adler to Parish right now, and there would be nothing Adler could do about it. Of course, that would require exposing himself in the process, and that was a little too suicidal a move for even him, with no guns on him.

He took Adler's hand. Instead of shaking it, Adler pulled it up to his lips and pressed a kiss against his knuckles. Rainy burned.

"Mark and I met in much the same way you and I did," Parish prattled happily. "But he's been such fun, I've kept him around. He makes the most brilliant cocktails."

He patted Adler's neatly gelled head like a dog's. The gesture made Rainy want to bite someone. Whom or why, he wasn't sure. He just wanted to sink his teeth in.

So Adler was here for the same reason Rainy was—recon. Digging around in Parish's personal affairs while he was distracted. Great minds think alike and all. If Seong was moving in on Brickell, then it made sense that he'd want to get inside the home of its baron. This meant that Seong and Parish weren't working together; that in itself was information that Emilio would pay well for. But there was more to be had.

Adler was staring at Rainy's ear where the tip was still wrapped in a thin white bandage. His eyes met Rainy's and he smirked. Rainy's hand tightened on the arm of the couch until it creaked.

"Come, sit," Parish said, beckoning. Adler stopped admiring his handiwork to pour himself a drink and perch on a chair. Parish had to curl a hand around Rainy's jaw and physically turn his head to get his eyes off Adler.

He drew him in for a kiss, deep and slow. Rainy could feel Adler's eyes burning into the side of his head, and he felt stiff, clumsy. He missed the cue when Parish ran his tongue over his bottom lip to ease his mouth open, and Parish pulled away.

"Relax," he coaxed.

"Feeling shy?" Adler drawled. "I can turn around, if you want."

Rainy glared at him, then yanked Parish in by the collar of his shirt. He kissed him rough and thorough, stroking his tongue into his mouth and biting his lip. Parish groaned approvingly and pressed forward, pinning Rainy to the couch. Rainy let him take charge, let himself be kissed. Parish's hand left his thigh to beckon somewhere off to his side, and then a warm weight was settling onto the couch at Rainy's back. Adler's hands smoothed up his spine, curved around his chest to work at the buttons of his shirt. His mouth landed on Rainy's neck, hot and wet, kissing his way up to suck Rainy's earlobe into his mouth. While Parish tugged on Rainy's lip with his teeth, Adler's lips skimmed up Rainy's ear and closed lightly around the bandaged tip.

Rainy stomped on his instep. Adler wheezed in pain, the puff of air hot against Rainy's wounded ear. Then he bent and bit down on Rainy's neck, hard enough that Rainy gasped into Parish's mouth. Parish made a pleased noise and spread his hands over Rainy's exposed chest.

The firelight kissed Rainy's skin as Adler eased the shirt off his shoulders. Parish's hands followed after, exploring the rippling muscle, the swells and ridges of him, but Rainy's attention was drawn by the soft snort that Adler let out behind him. His fingers skimmed over Rainy's upper back, tracing the tattoo there—a cowboy in corny Hollywood western regalia, napping in profile half-propped up against Rainy's shoulder blade with one knee up, his arms folded across his chest, and his hat tipped down over his face. Adler's thumb dug into a spot that throbbed with an old pain. Rainy had peered at it in the mirror enough times to picture it: the remnant of his last run-in with a bullet, a small cigarette-burn exit wound scar that went right through the cowboy's face. Rainy closed his eyes and felt the two sets of fingers pressing into his skin, overwhelming in the heat of the room.

And then Parish was sitting back, and Adler's were the only hands on him. Rainy hated these tight fucking pants for refusing to hide how turned-on he was. His blood was pounding in his ears, and the room felt like it was squeezing in.

Parish examined him, eyes not missing the bulge in the front of his pants. "Let me explain," he purred. "I'm a man of particular taste. I like my meals prepared well for me before I enjoy them."

Rainy blinked, not entirely following. Adler leaned into his ear.

"I'm the chef in this analogy, honey," he murmured, a light mocking tone in his voice. It made that same rage kick up white-hot in Rainy's chest. And yet, at the same time, he hated himself for the way the endearment, rolled in Adler's molasses-thick accent, made him shiver with arousal.

Adler's hand slid down to rest possessively on his hip, and Rainy stiffened.

He could leave now—stand up and politely say this wasn't his thing, retreat without blowing his cover. The door was right there, and with this weird rich-white-people sex bullshit, Parish and Adler had served him up an easy out. But Rainy had gotten himself here, inside Parish's house, with leverage to get himself out with information. Like hell was he going to let Adler ruin that for him.

"Whatever you like," he said, making his eyes wide and guileless. He could sense Adler's displeasure, but Parish grinned.

"Good boy." He topped off his glass and settled in the chair Adler had vacated, unbuckling his belt and spreading his legs for easy access. Rainy leaned back against Adler's chest, keeping his eyes on Parish.

Adler pressed his mouth to Rainy's ear. "Get out of here," he hissed, so soft that Rainy almost didn't catch it.

Rainy's only answer was his polished, plastic smile.

"Fine." Adler planted a palm in the center of Rainy's back and pushed him face down onto the couch. Rainy's entire body was buzzing with the urge to shove back, to wrestle Adler down and take a bite out of him. He forced himself to relax, pressed his cheek into the velvet, and bit down on his own tongue.

Across the plush carpet, backlit by the fireplace, he could see that Parish had opened his pants and taken himself in hand, stroking lazily. Rainy felt Adler's hands at his own belt where his hips were angled up in the air.

Adler was clearly practiced with too-tight slacks, because he had Rainy's off in half a heartbeat. Then his dry, calloused palm was on Rainy, coaxing him to full hardness. Rainy had to lock his muscles to stop himself from pushing forward into the tight, delicious grip. He bit down harder on his tongue, refusing to give Adler the satisfaction of groaning into the antique velvet.

It seemed to carry anyway, because he felt Adler huff a laugh against him. He twisted his grip, moving mercilessly. Rainy's hips stuttered forward.

"Easy, Mark," Parish chastised. "You know how I like it."

Adler pressed his thumb teasingly against Rainy's tip, then released him. He gripped Rainy's thighs, easing his knees out from under him so his hips fell flat. His cock throbbed, trapped between his stomach and the velvet cushion of the couch.

With a firm grasp on either hip bone, Adler dragged him backward until his hips were balanced on the edge of the couch, his legs falling to the floor. A broad palm pressed down on the small of his back, presumptive and claiming.

Rainy felt flushed and pulled-taut. If he was plucked, he would hum like a guitar string. *I'm going to kill you*, he thought, calm despite the wildfire raging over every nerve ending. *We're doing this now, but the second I get a chance, I'm going to kill you.*

Adler knelt on the rug between his legs. His hands slid up and down Rainy's thighs, strong fingertips digging into the muscle. Rainy tried to force himself to relax for the sake of the show, but he only felt his muscles winding tighter as Adler's warm breath ghosted over the delicate skin of his perineum.

His tongue followed with a firm, confident stroke. Rainy tried not to tremble at the little shivers that emanated from the point of contact, the gentle first ripple of pleasure as Adler mouthed over the most fragile, exposed part of him. *Fight*, his body insisted, confused and hot-blooded and wanting to push back into the contact.

He bit down harder on his tongue to keep from gasping when Adler dipped lower, sucking one and then both of Rainy's balls into his mouth with demure lightness. Rainy's whole body went numb and tingly with fight-or-flight and fizzy pleasure. Adler had his mouth closed around the most delicate part of him. Rainy could feel the light press of the ridges of his teeth where he was doing his level best to hold them out of the way, but they were just there, ready to snap closed at a moment's notice and inflict untold agony. But it was so, so good, the feeling of being surrounded and submerged in the plush wet heat of his mouth, feeling the press and stroke over every bit of too-sensitive skin as Adler *sucked*.

Rainy pressed his forehead into the velvet, nearly overstimulated, and writhed to try and get some friction. Adler's hands tightened on his thighs in warning, and he stilled. Parish was still touching himself unhurriedly, looking pleased at Rainy's tense writhing. Rainy focused on the wet, red head of the man's cock, trying to ignore the way his body was pulling tighter and tighter like a stretched rubber band, ready to snap.

Adler moved away, finally. Rainy hid a gasp of relief in the crook of his arm. His balls felt heavy and tingly, wet and bare in the hearth-warmed air.

In his chair, Parish was examining them appraisingly, one hand cradling his drink and the other still wrapped around himself.

"Your mouth," he seemed to decide, with the entitled delight of a spoiled child selecting chocolates from the glass case at the candy store.

"Yes," Adler acquiesced, and Rainy could hear the just barely bitten-off *sir* that dangled at the end. It gave him a little spark of satisfaction, the knowledge that despite his genteel wrapping, Adler was ultimately just a dog that followed orders. The meanness of the thought steadied him as he felt Adler's focus return.

Broad, rough hands slid up the curve of Rainy's ass. *Killer's hands.* Suddenly, the thought that Adler was just following orders wasn't comforting at all, not when he was sliding his calloused thumbs between Rainy's cheeks and parting them, clinical and efficient. Rainy felt the air and light touch the hidden clenched-muscle of him, and it set his insides squirming like a nest of worms in his abdomen. He felt terrifyingly exposed, opened to the world, and there Adler was, cold and professional and totally unaffected.

Parish drank down Rainy's expression eagerly. "Good," he said, voice husky. "Make him good and ready for me."

Adler's thumb dipped to brush over the tightly clenched muscle of his opening. Rainy had to marshal every second of his years of training in control and stamina not to jump at the touch. His brain whirred.

Rationally, he knew what he was getting himself into. As a rule, Rainy considered himself Up For Anything. This had led him into some bizarre situations; most enjoyable, others not so much. Because joint preferences usually ran to him topping whenever he hooked up with men, he'd only been eaten out once. He hadn't really been that into it; most of the enjoyment factor had come from how into it his partner *had* been. So, in theory, Rainy knew what was about to happen. He could prepare himself.

He clenched his fists until the knuckles blanched and set his teeth, determined not to react. He would not wriggle around or make any undignified noises.

The sound he made when Adler's tongue pressed against him crashed straight through *undignified* and came out as a whimper. He felt Adler's amused huff right up against him, almost *inside* him. Then his tongue was back, slicking over him in a hot, gliding press, teasing at his entrance with tiny kitten licks.

It was like being kissed, but *there*. The same sensation as if Adler had kissed him on the mouth, but a thousand times more intimate. It felt obscene, too private even for sex. Rainy pressed his face into the couch, flushed and shivery.

"Look at me," Parish said. "I want to see you." But Rainy couldn't bring himself to lift his head.

Rainy didn't know if the other partner who'd done this to him hadn't been good or if it was just *Adler*, but this was entirely new. Adler was idly circling his rim, licking and sucking, and then his tongue pressed in firm and insistent.

Rainy gasped when the tip of it pushed inside him, sliding through the ring of muscle. He tried to relax, but he felt like his spine was about to snap from the tension. Adler seemed to sense how little give he had and retreated, returning to gently kissing where he'd been before. He carried on with that for what felt like minutes, easing the tension from Rainy's muscles with his lips and tongue until Rainy was writhing and panting. He was leaking precome into a slick spot on his stomach, and he thought distantly that the velvet couch was going to be ruined. He felt like that spot inside him was aching for Adler now, and instead of clenching, his body felt eager to take him in, take him and take him until Rainy was full and wrecked.

When Adler's tongue pressed in again, he slid deeper in a smooth glide, Rainy's body welcoming him. Rainy moaned as he worked in and out, moving his tongue with short thrusts until Rainy was looser and his tongue went deep enough that Rainy could feel him on the inside.

He could feel Adler's cufflinks digging into his skin and the front of his expensive, starched shirt pressed against his bare thighs. The juxtaposition was dizzying; Adler immaculate and fully-dressed while he fucked Rainy with his tongue.

Every stroke sent purple-red sparks pinwheeling through his body, gathering in drifts deep in his belly, heavy and warm and unbearably good. Adler kept pressing in to the root of his tongue, coaxing. Opening Rainy up for him. The thought made him want to press back desperately, take more in.

He caught himself just before giving in to the urge. This was exactly what he'd been afraid of—getting distracted by the undeniable attraction he felt toward Adler, and letting his guard down again. He tried to wriggle forward, away from the sensation, but Adler's fingers tightened on his hips and dragged him back onto his tongue, deeper than before.

"Fuck," Rainy gasped brokenly. "Fuck me."

He'd meant it as an expletive, but once it hung in the air in front of him, it looked more like a plea. Adler hummed in satisfaction, and Rainy almost yelped at the vibration of it against the warm, loose muscle of him.

He almost forgot Parish was in the room until the man opened a drawer in the big oak desk and tossed something over Rainy's sprawled form. Adler caught it and the delicious pressure of his tongue disappeared. Rainy didn't have time to notice the relief before two long fingers were pushing past his entrance, slippery with lube. Even after Adler's ministrations, there was a slight burn at the intrusion, the stretch of muscles not used to stretching. But Rainy still wanted more. The fingers were more tangible than Adler's tongue, filling him deeper and more substantially.

Adler stroked and spread with his fingers, smoothing away the ache. He added more lube, smearing it liberally until Rainy felt slick and wet. A finger from his other hand flirted with Rainy's entrance, and Rainy's muscles rebelled at the stretch. But he was too slippery to fight the inexorable slide, and his body had no choice but to take the finger until it was in past the last knuckle. Rainy instantly relaxed, feeling pleased in some base, animal part of himself, clenching happily around the fullness.

Adler lapped at the taut skin around his fingers. What had been lazy sparks of pleasure was now a fire, leaping and scorching. A finger slid out, and then Adler's tongue was back in its place, stroking gently as he stretched Rainy open with his knuckles.

Rainy's thighs were trembling and he was lying completely flat, limbs too weak to push him up. He rolled his hips shamelessly, grinding down into the soft, scratchy velvet cushion.

I could come like this, he thought, and was abruptly right on the edge.

And then Adler was drawing away, slipping his fingers out. Rainy clenched futilely around their absence, but Adler was sitting back, admiring his work. Rainy felt exposed, sloppy and open to the world. His face burned as he pressed it into the couch.

"Good," Parish was saying, a little breathless. "Come on, Mark, I want you to sit here."

"Of course," Adler replied; no danger of dropping an accidental *sir*. But before stepping away, he leaned in again, almost disobediently, and pressed a kiss against Rainy's slippery, stretched entrance. It was gentle, affectionate, almost chaste, like a kiss goodnight on the doorstep of a first date.

Then there was a shuffling of feet, the crinkle of a condom being opened. Rainy opened his eyes in time to see Adler draping himself over the chair that Parish had vacated, looking flushed, his collar open and mouth glistening wet before he wiped it with the heel of his hand.

Rainy was still making eye contact with him, trying to push all the challenge and resentment he had into his gaze, when Parish pushed inside of him.

He'd forgotten how fingers didn't prepare you. Not for the thickness and length, the unyielding pressure as it slid home deep. The fullness was unbearable for a moment, almost agonizing. His body squeezed down, trying to accustom itself to the intrusion, but there was no reprieve. He was pressed open, filled, and it drove him straight out of his brain. It slid all the way home, pinning Rainy in place, and for a hot, frantic moment, he thought, *Adler, yes, fuck.*

But Adler was across the rug, sitting in the chair, drinking Parish's brandy. It was Parish inside him, and he was reminded when the man groaned appreciatively and slid out and back in, pushing the air from Rainy's lungs.

He set a quick but dragging pace at a low angle, clearly intent on wringing every bit of pleasure for himself out of how Adler had prepared Rainy's body. There was something arrogant and presumptive in the way he fucked, like Rainy's body belonged to him and he might deign to give it back only once he'd used it however he saw fit.

It was maddening. Rainy squirmed around the rough, too-deep thrusts. Each push inside, filling him and stretching him out, packed down those long-gathered sparks until the pressure was too much, and he was going to pop with it. The motion dragged his cock along the velvet of the couch enough to stimulate, but this... it wasn't as good. He'd been all the way on the edge with just Adler's hands and mouth, and the fucking was good, but it wasn't—

It wasn't the way Adler was looking at him now, eyes all pupil, black with lust. He was still fully dressed, dick pressing against his pants, but he made no move to touch himself. He just watched Rainy's face as Parish fucked him, mouth quirked in a slight smile.

He looked smug. Smug with the knowledge that despite the fact that Parish was the one fucking Rainy, it was Adler who'd brought him here. Adler who his body wanted inside, fucking every last tremor out of him with a hand flattened possessively over his spine. He felt like he was drowning in Adler's dark eyes, flailing and gasping for air. He was suddenly aware of the non-silence of the room, the slap of flesh and the slick, filthy sounds.

This is for you, he thought nonsensically. *You see what you do to me?* Adler seemed to understand, because his non-smile morphed into a real smirk. The sight made Rainy clench down around the hard length inside him, the inexorable movement, thinking, *Yes, God, Adler, yes.* Parish's angle was driving him down into the couch with sweet friction, and the pleasure was pressed so tight inside him that he wanted to die.

Adler slid off the chair, dropping to his knees on the carpet, and leaned in to kiss him. Hungry and deep and possessive. *Yes,* Rainy thought, and came.

The orgasm hit so hard his fingers went numb. It washed over him in waves as he rutted into the scratchy velvet, clenched down and found no relief as Parish kept thrusting mercilessly inside him. When he finally came down, shivering and weak, his face was buried in the crook of Adler's neck.

He just lay there limply as Parish kept fucking his orgasm-loose body until he tensed and came. He didn't move while Parish pressed his forehead into the sweaty dip of his back, then left to dispose of the condom. He wasn't sure he was connected to his body anymore. It came back to him in fits and starts, ending with the sensation of Adler lightly stroking the hair at the nape of his neck.

Rainy jerked away and went toppling off the couch, landing on the plush rug with a grunt. He had to lie there to collect himself for a moment before he registered the nasty sensation of his own come smeared up his abdomen.

Adler tossed him some cloth to wipe himself off, and he snatched it away, face burning.

The hatred was rushing back in in the post-coital emptiness, brighter and more jagged than before. The attraction didn't cancel it out, Rainy realized. The desperation with which he wanted Adler's body made him hate him all the more. The feeling was a fever pitch, and even in this sex-drunk relaxation, Rainy felt that he might throw himself at Adler's feet, take him out at the knees. Bash his head in on the hardwood or kiss him.

All the same, as long as one of them was dead at the end.

Then Parish's shoes were clicking back—he hadn't taken off his fucking *shoes*—and Rainy controlled himself. Not now. There would be time to fight later. Right now, he had other things to accomplish.

Parish helped him up and offered him a fresh glass of brandy.

Rainy started to speak, then had to clear his throat and try again. "Can you point me to the bathroom?" he asked. "I'd like to clean up a little."

Parish grinned, looking him up and down. "Just down the hall. Help yourself."

Rainy felt Adler's eyes on the back of his neck as he stuffed himself back into his clothes, but Parish was already dragging *Mark* into a dull conversation, demanding his attention. Rainy risked a sneer over his shoulder before he all but bolted from the study.

The bodyguards had drifted away out of sight to give them some privacy. Rainy could hear them echoing about on the staircase, so he hurried away down the hall, past the bathroom and around a corner.

The room they'd been in had been for entertaining; Parish would have another office, a real one. Rainy trailed his hand over the bamboo statement doors, peering inside at guest bedrooms, reading rooms, a goddamn *library*—then a more sober office, with heavy green drapes and a stuffed desk. Rainy glanced around to make sure nobody was watching and ducked inside, shutting the door with a soft click.

In the dim of the study, he allowed himself a moment to lean against the desk, evening his breathing. Trying to forget the hard clash of lips against his.

There wasn't much time. He got to work.

Chapter 12

Florida Man Joins Violent Spree; 3 Casualties

R ainy estimated that he had about five minutes before Parish would start to question his whereabouts, so he dug into the desk straightaway. There were stacks of papers secured by clips, printed memos, and a yellow legal pad with such enlightening shorthand missives as "call m" and "b street no." Rainy rifled through them all, pausing only to adjust himself uncomfortably every few moments.

He'd done a fair job of wiping himself off with the towel, but he still felt sticky and awful in those horribly tight pants. If this was how Adler had felt after they'd done it in the multipurpose room, Rainy was starting to understand why he'd felt the urge to shoot him.

There was a locked file drawer in the bottom of the desk, which Rainy picked open efficiently with a pilfered paper clip. Inside was the good stuff—files on Parish's holdings at the docks. Everything was legit, stamped with the letterheads of real, heavyweight property law firms, not legacy mob attorneys like Lina. Parish's was the kind of empire that was ironclad to everyone below his class. You couldn't touch him without pulling strings higher than the ones he already had looped up in his hands.

But Rainy had once been a rising star in the Espinosa ranks, and he may not have understood arcane contract law, but he did know illegal shit when he saw it. And he saw it all over—off-the-books ledgers with the names of suppliers he recognized, shady contractors, bribes. Very much the Espinosas' bread and butter.

Folded inside one envelope was a map of Parish's holdings on the docks, marked up in ballpoint shorthand. Off-the-books storage, the kind you couldn't register with the port authority. Rainy puffed out an impressed breath and snapped a photo with his phone.

Seong's presence in Miami had clearly emboldened Parish to press Emilio. That meant that he was afraid of Seong's connections in a way that he hadn't been afraid of Emilio's. And yet, Adler was here to spy on him, which meant that the two weren't working together. So Seong wasn't really a big enough threat for Parish to bargain with him. He was the inverse of Emilio—all connections, no brute force.

A delicate spiderweb of an idea began to spin itself into existence in the corner of his mind.

The door swung open on oiled-silent hinges and light leaped across the room, framing Rainy in a damning square of yellow. He jumped and, childishly, shoved the folded paper back into the drawer.

Adler closed the door behind himself, expression flat and humorless in a way that was all the worse because Rainy had now witnessed him displaying actual human emotion. He was still conspicuously unbuttoned, his tie loose. He folded his arms.

"Real subtle," he said. "Don't worry; I kicked a rug over the skid marks you left on the floor."

Rainy now found out what his body did without Parish there to keep him in check. He darted across the room and slammed Adler against the wall. A shelf of heavy glass awards rattled, and Adler sneered at him.

"Be quiet," he hissed.

"Fuck you."

"We're about even on that front now. Sore?" Adler grunted satisfyingly when Rainy crushed his slighter frame against the wall. "Now, hands off."

There was suddenly a knife pricking through the fine fabric of Rainy's shirt, pressing neatly into the divot between two ribs. He backed off, warily eyeing the five-inch fixed-blade Adler had magicked from somewhere on his person.

"How did you even get that thing in here? They practically cavity searched me."

"We've been over this, Mister Rainy. I'm better than you." Adler relaxed his wrist, holding the knife casually enough that it stung Rainy's pride a little. "Even so, I don't wanna make a mess of you all over this Turkish rug. So get the hell out of here before you blow my cover."

"I don't care about the rug," Rainy snarled. "I'm going to wring your giraffe neck like a dish towel."

"I'm busy." Adler waved his knife hand dismissively. "I'll deal with you later; just fuck off."

No. No, no, no. This bastard didn't get to put Rainy through what he had and then *dismiss* him like an afternoon appointment. He'd show him just how much of an afterthought he was. He stepped forward, hands raised, and was fended off again with the knife.

There was a crease between Adler's brows now. "You were in the desk. You saw the reports. The Espinosas are punching above their weight class trying anything with Parish. He'd tie them up in knots and take their house right out from under them, so run on home and tell them that."

"First off, I'm not some trained Espinosa dog. Sorry—I know that must be hard for you to wrap your brain around." Rainy let a smile slip across his face, felt it curdle and turn nasty. "You know, I figured you were just obedient enough to follow Seong when he called, but maybe this is your MO. Did you get your day job by letting him fuck you, too?"

He was prepared for Adler's lunge, all the viciousness behind it. He dodged the knife and tried to wrap his arms around from behind, binding Adler's hands to his sides, but he was too slow. Adler executed a startlingly graceful high side kick that sent Rainy stumbling back into the desk, and then he was on him, knife raised.

Rainy didn't let himself flinch. "You're just as screwed here as I am," he said. "That's what I saw in the desk. That's why you're still here. Parish told your boss to go fuck himself, and Seong has the connections to bite him back. But you don't have the ground game to liquidate his product, or handle his men. You don't know how to operate in this city yet."

Adler's eyes burned with resentment, but his silence was answer enough. Rainy was just starting to chortle with delight when the knife curved at the corner of his vision, and he remembered with a throb of his injured ear why it wasn't such a good idea to mock Adler while he was smarting.

That was how they were poised—Rainy half-thrown back across the desk and Adler over him with a knife—when one of Parish's bodyguards pushed the door open and flicked on the lights.

There was a brief, frozen moment that hung in the air, crystalline, as the man's eyes traveled over their grappled position to the knife in Adler's hand and the open desk drawer with papers spilling out of it. Then his hand slid toward his gun, and time unstuck.

Adler threw the knife. It tumbled gracefully blade over handle and lodged directly in the man's windpipe. He let out a horrible gargle and the gun in his hand went off into his own thigh before he crumpled loudly to the hallway floor. There was a shout of alarm from further up the hall.

"Fuck!" Rainy admonished. "You fucking—"

But Adler was already running, stooping to snatch his knife from the dying man's neck and sprinting off down the hall. Rainy cursed and grabbed one of the heavy glass trophies off the shelf.

The hallway, with its carved wooden molding and hand-woven runner, stretched off in either direction, lit by blown-glass wall sconces. To Rainy's right, there was the pounding of footsteps on hardwood as the other bodyguards came to investigate. To his left, Adler was running in the opposite direction and looking like he had at least some sense of where he was going. Rainy decided to follow him.

As men shouted at their heels, Adler looped around a corner. Rainy pushed himself to catch up right as Adler pulled open a door seemingly at random and slipped inside. Rainy stuck his foot out to stop it from closing.

"Get out of here," Adler hissed, wild-eyed, trying to close the door on Rainy's brand-new leather shoe. Fuck, did those things pinch.

"No," Rainy said petulantly. "I *will* rat."

Looking murderous, Adler yanked him inside by the tie and closed the door with a soft click. They both dropped into crouches in the dark, Adler bracing his right shoulder against the door.

The room was a half bath that was entirely too large. The toilet in its French tile alcove receded into distant gloom.

In the hall, there were voices and heavy footsteps. Adler shuffled his crouch around and pressed his left ear against the door.

"What are they saying?" Rainy whispered. Adler kicked him.

It didn't take a lot of imagination to figure out. Nearby, there was the thundering snap-thud of a door being kicked open. Then another. Rainy swallowed around the dry prickliness in his throat and adjusted his grip on the glass trophy where it was slippery with sweat.

Adler was shifting with those tight, economical military movements now, wiping the blade of his knife on a hand towel and evening his breath. Rainy could practically hear the clicks of tumblers and gears falling into place as his eyes took on that sharp, tactical look.

"You have a plan," Rainy murmured. "Tell me."

"Fuck you."

"Don't be stupid."

Adler may have been a lot of things, but he wasn't that. He made aggressive eye contact as he spoke, tilting his head toward Rainy. Maybe that was some weird military thing too.

"There's one stairway. We need to get through these men to double back. I estimate three." He held up three fingers, which was pretty unnecessary, in Rainy's opinion. "On my count. Just know I won't stop for you."

"I won't stop for you either," Rainy hissed, but then he couldn't speak as he tensed in anticipation, adrenaline thrumming. Adler was dropping down his three fingers slowly, one by one. That kick hit Rainy's bloodstream, the thrill of the fight. The only thing he'd ever been good at. Adler's long index finger curled down into his palm.

He threw open the door and rolled straightaway in the direction of the shouting and shuffling. Rainy followed, keeping low and hefting Parish's rich-fuck-of-the-year award.

There were indeed three guys, two of them already with guns in hand. Adler regained his feet fluidly in front of them and launched himself straight onto one of the armed ones, angling his knife into the man's stomach. They went down grappling, the man's gun useless when Adler was wrapped inside his reach.

The second gun went right to Adler's back. Then Rainy was there, body-checking the unarmed man out of his way to bring his trophy down on the gunman's head. He didn't have time to check the result before he was spinning back to face his other attacker, dodging a right hook. They traded blows, the man trying to wrestle him into a grapple and Rainy dancing out of reach.

But he wasn't particularly mobile in this constricting suit, and the guy was a lot quicker than him. Rainy took a hit to his chin and then to his solar plexus, and found himself up against the wall.

Over the man's shoulder, Adler was on his feet. Rainy's eyes caught his across the wide, wild gulf of the hall and, on instinct, he kicked the man advancing on him back like a passed soccer ball. Adler caught him easily with a knife in his back and looped an elbow around his throat to hold him. Behind him, there was movement—Rainy's blow with the trophy had only been glancing, and the man had found his gun, and Adler didn't—

"Duck!" Rainy shouted, and Adler just did, without question. Thank God for those military instincts. Rainy smashed his fist into the man's temple hard enough that he felt the skin on his knuckles split and slide, and then the man was down and Adler was dropping his opponent and they were running for the stairs.

Behind them, he could hear one of the guards up and coming after them, but they had a head start. They crashed down the stairway with its wrought-iron banisters, taking the stairs five at a time. In the foyer below, Rainy spotted a flash of rumpled suit as one of the bodyguards frog-marched Parish toward the safety of the den.

Six guards that he'd seen on the way in—that left one more un-accounted for. Rainy found him when the glossy-lacquered front door swung open and the guard burst in with his pistol raised.

Adler hit the foyer and swerved to the right, dodging the new-comer. Rainy followed, dress shoes sliding on the tile floor. They cut through a dining room and a kitchen, and then there was a mudroom and a door in front of them.

After the house's world-class air conditioning, the humidity hit like a sloppy, wet sucker punch. In the moonlight and the soft yellow glow of the house, the garden was a collection of loose, leafy shapes and pale gravel trails. Adler navigated it with the grace of a dancer. Rainy crashed through a rosebush, swearing a blue streak.

Two men were still on their tail, just reaching the edge of the garden. Outside, they seemed to have less scruples about discharging their weapons, because Rainy heard the crack of a shot and felt a hot zip of air pass by him. He drew in his shoulders and pushed himself harder. His hip flexors were smarting, and his feet would be blistered bloody from these goddamn shoes, but he reached the edge of the estate a second behind Adler.

Parish's property was bounded by a tall brick wall that butted the wrought-iron gate at the foot of the driveway. Seemingly without thinking, Adler dropped to a knee and laced his hands to boost Rainy over. More leftover military conditioning, probably—it was just instinct to not leave a man behind. Rainy wasn't about to waste time thinking about it. He planted his foot in the proffered brace and let Adler's lent strength carry him easily up onto the narrow, flat top of the wall.

Before he could even consider his options, he was twisting on his awkward perch, ignoring another close call with a bullet to drop both arms down. Adler leaped up and his strong, sure hands wrapped around Rainy's biceps. Rainy braced his feet and tipped back, using his own considerable weight as a lever to yank Adler up and over the wall with him.

They landed in a clumsy tangle on the cement on the other side. Whatever deep-trained fellow-feeling had possessed Adler seemed to leave him now, because he elbowed Rainy rudely out of his way and took off again, loping down the street. Rainy grit his teeth and followed.

He'd lost the trophy on his way out of the house. As the gate swung open and flashlights swept behind them, he followed Adler past the gated beginnings of several more driveways. At the end of the block—if it could be called that—there was a mansion still under construction, a palace of plywood, plastic siding, and exposed insulation. They both scrambled over the chain-link fence that guarded it and ducked through the missing front door.

Rainy pressed himself against an unfinished wall and slid down, panting. His suit was wrecked—torn and shredded by thorns and conspicuously bloody. Adler, leaning against the opposite wall, looked similarly awful. He was glaring daggers at Rainy even as he braced his hands on his knees to catch his breath. They sat in the beginnings of a foyer as voices bounced between the buildings outside, already moving further down the street.

"Were you dropped on your head as a baby?" Adler growled the moment he'd regained himself.

"Please," Rainy said. "I did you a favor. You weren't going to get anything else from that place."

He pushed to his feet, stripping out of his ruined jacket and tie. His feet were in agony inside those terrible shoes, and he briefly considered ditching them as well. Across the way, Adler was putting himself to rights, straightening his shirt and vest into as crisp of angles as he could. Rainy was reminded of the photo of a younger Adler in his clean, meticulously-kept military uniform. Maybe it wasn't just the combat instincts that had stuck around.

Parish's men had faded into the distance, and they were alone in this half-finished house. Rainy hazarded a glance at Adler and found him staring right back, silent. The air fizzled uneasily with the first hint of electricity.

It was almost identical to the tension that had flavored the air while Parish played the piano earlier—the tip of circumstance to mutual certainty of what was about to happen. Rainy's feet would have to wait; his wounded ear and pride demanded satisfaction.

"You know," he said, because something in the moment demanded it, "we don't make such a bad team, when it comes down to it."

"Shame," Adler replied.

They both stood perfectly still, waiting to see who would break the building tension. Rainy watched the expert shift of weight in Adler's body, the nearly imperceptible transition from relaxed to deadly, heralded by tiny adjustments in the angle of his hips and shoulders.

Rainy wanted something. He didn't know what it was, but he wanted it so badly it hurt.

In the end, he made the first move, if only to escape the swelling bubble of *something* in his chest. Rainy had never been called a patient man. He darted forward and swung.

Adler dodged him, but Rainy kept coming, a blitzkrieg of fists and elbows and knees. Adler had stowed the knife somewhere, but Rainy knew he still had it. He needed to make this too fast and hard for Adler to get it back in his hands. He pressed his advantage, which was in strength and brute force; when he landed a hit on Adler, it knocked him back into the wall. But Adler was so quick and tenacious. Any damage he took, he took and kept rolling with.

The first time they'd fought, in the hotel, Rainy hadn't gone as hard as he could have. He hadn't yet realized what a nightmare Adler was, and there was no point in really pounding a guy you'd already slipped a knockout dose. This was different. This time, one of them was going to be dead at the end of it, and Rainy knew that he had to fight as dirty as he could if he didn't want it to be him.

Unfortunately, Adler seemed to recognize the same thing. Even through Rainy's best onslaught, he managed to sneak in a few targeted shots to Rainy's liver and then a direct hit to his wounded ear.

Rainy stumbled, vision whiting. He could feel the new skin tearing and fresh blood soaking his bandage.

His rage was back, but, beyond it, he felt a deeper sense of immense gravity. His weeks of restlessness had solidified his anger into something heavy and dark that sat at the core of him, dragging down into his belly. The idea of this encounter as some kind of epic, fated battle didn't feel like a melodramatic late-night musing anymore. This felt inevitable as the force that brought every object inexorably back toward the center of the Earth. From the moment Rainy had locked eyes with Adler over that bar, there had been no avoiding this. Kill or be killed. The enormity of it funneled and sharpened, drawn in like all the background static of the universe narrowing to the radio antenna that was the red-hot pain in Rainy's ear.

He punched Adler between the eyes. It was so sharp and hard that Adler didn't even have a chance to block it. And Adler may have been a champ at taking hits, but not even a lifelong boxer could just shrug off a blow like that. He fell back against the wall, looking violently dizzy. After a second, his vision cleared and he was scrabbling for skin again, but Rainy wasn't a good enough sport to not press the advantage when he had it.

He grabbed Adler by the upper arms and slammed him against the wall over and over, hard enough that the plywood splintered and they almost fell through it. Adler wobbled, bloodied, and Rainy put him on the floor at the foot of the wall. Adler curled in to protect himself, a physical mirror of those internal walls, but he was too punch-drunk slow. Rainy brought his foot down, the heel of his leather dress shoe unforgiving.

The muffled, organic snap of breaking bones was so familiar that, most nights, Rainy heard it in his dreams. Adler's ribs made that sound now. He let out an involuntary keen of pain, the kind that was wrenched out of someone determined not to show they were hurting. Rainy kicked him again, and again.

Please stop, he thought as Adler made another rough noise. *Please, just let me kill you easy. Just let me get this over with.*

He'd thought he would enjoy this, even fantasized about it. But now he just wanted it to end. He wanted Adler to stop fighting, so he could stop hurting him. He wanted to be done.

Then, unexpectedly, Adler was wrapped around his legs and dragging him down. They ended up rolling across the concrete floor, struggling. Adler was long and wiry and hard to pin down. Rainy dug an elbow into his broken ribs and got him flat, but Adler kept fighting, writhing and kicking with everything he had, and Rainy could barely keep hold of him. He let his arm drift too high, trying to lever it against Adler's collarbone, and teeth sunk in deep enough to draw blood. Rainy yelped and pulled away, and then they were grappling across the floor again.

As they fought, Rainy's body burning with small abrasions and everything matted with sweat and sawdust, there was a split second where he tried to wrap an arm around Adler's neck and instead caught his eyes. They were feral and deadly and hard-sharp enough to cut glass. Rainy faltered for a moment, the breath knocked out of him.

It was exactly how he imagined encountering a grizzly bear or a mountain lion out in the wild would be—a sense of terrified awe, and peace with it. The sudden thought that fighting against something like that was like trying to fight a bolt of divine lightning. The proper thing to do was just roll over and die, and feel an appropriate sense of awe at the majesty of what had struck you down.

Just a moment, but that was enough. Adler lunged, rolled them over and over with an intent Rainy couldn't counter. And then Adler was up on his knees, and Rainy was looking up at him, and there was the cold stinging kiss of a knife between Rainy's ribs.

The world held its breath. The silence of the unfinished house echoed.

Rainy had a sudden sense memory of trailing after his mother across a stone floor as a child, hands fisted in her skirt. He'd been dressed neatly, hair combed, for his first confession. His mother had dragged him from their usual smaller church to the echoey old Cathedral of Saint Mary, a bastion of stained glass and drafts and the towering shadow of Christ suffering upon the cross, bloody wound in his side. He remembered that old building having a silence that smothered, that consumed. That reflected all one's sins and shortcomings back until you drowned in them.

That was the silence that gripped the world now.

Adler knelt in the center of the concrete floor. Rainy was draped over his lap, chest propped over one knee so his ribcage jutted up at the sky. One of Adler's scarred, long-fingered hands rested on his sternum through the open collar of his shirt. The other was pressing the knife into the space between his third and fourth ribs, angled inward with chilling familiarity. It was biting sharply into the skin, a tiny carnation of blood blooming on his white shirt like the one in a groom's buttonhole.

They would make an excellent marble church statue, Rainy thought. *Agony of a Saint.* Or maybe *Slaying of a Devil.*

He gave an experimental wriggle, but Adler just pressed the knife another quarter inch into his pectoral muscle. Sharp enough to cut bone like butter, was that knife. Adler *would* be fastidious about his blades. Rainy craned his neck to watch the red spot grow, just over his heart, where the violets bloomed across his skin.

He didn't try to move again. Adler met his gaze with characteristically grave eyes. Now, they didn't seem out of place. Their steady unhappiness was almost comforting. Rainy wanted to reach up and touch him.

So this was how it ended. There was no out this time. Rainy had always thought his death would come in a flash of fire and brimstone, a maelstrom of glory and violence. This felt as echoing and infinite as that cathedral of memory.

"Wait," he said. He didn't know what for. Last time, he'd pulled a joke out of the air, but this atmosphere was flat and humorless. This time, there were no games left, no delays or second chances. Just as Rainy had wanted, it ended here.

Adler shook his head. "Close your eyes," he said, not unkindly.

But Rainy didn't want to miss this. He didn't want to miss Adler, curved over him in the dim, the fine planes of his face picked out by the light of the distant city. The straight slope of his nose, the secret blond tips of his lashes, the silver-pink pucker of scar tissue. Rainy had never been a very good Catholic, but he knew something godsent when he saw it. Adler was penance, and oh, wasn't he lovely?

The knife dug in further, severing skin and tissue. Another inch, and Adler would pierce his heart, send his life spilling out across the floor. But Rainy felt the other hand leave his sternum to curl around his shoulders instead. He remembered what Adler had said while tied to that chair in the multipurpose room, cigarette smoke lingering around his lips.

I just want someone to hold me while I go.

And the knife was sliding home, but, with sudden clarity, all Rainy could think was: *Will you hold me while I go?*

Will you keep me in your arms until the last of me bleeds away, and even a little bit after?

Will you handle my body gently once I'm gone?

Will you kiss me goodnight?

The knife stung, but only a little. It was such a small pain, for the end of the world.

Nonsensically, with finality, he thought, *What a shame. We really did make a good team.*

With that thought, something that had been coalescing at the corner of his mind in Parish's study solidified into an idea.

"Wait," he gasped. His voice was wet with unshed tears he hadn't noticed gathering.

The knife paused, an inch into his chest. Adler shook his head, not meeting Rainy's eyes.

"Wait," Rainy repeated. "I have... I have a business proposition."

Adler stilled, expression grave as death. He stared at the point where he was piercing Rainy's chest, the red spot that had spread across the whole left side of his shirt's breast.

The knife slid out. Rainy felt it leave his flesh, its absence like an ache.

"You got two minutes," Adler said.

Chapter 13

Florida Man Charms End to Gang Violence

A dler retreated to the other end of the room, sticking his knife into an exposed two-by-four within arm's reach. Rainy watched a drop of his own blood roll down the wood as he pushed himself into a seated position on the concrete floor. He felt too weak and shaky to stand, like Adler really had nicked his heart and he was bleeding out.

Adler pulled a pack of cigarettes from his pocket and lit one. His fingers were trembling.

"I thought you quit," Rainy said, voice hoarse.

Adler took a long drag, closed his eyes, and exhaled through his nose. "You kicked me off the wagon. Talk fast, now."

Rainy pressed a hand to his throbbing chest, where the thin puncture wound dug down between his ribs. It was bleeding, but not terribly. It didn't even hurt that bad; not as bad as a broken bone, he thought, observing the way Adler was standing with an arm curved gingerly around one side of his chest, grimacing with each inhale.

"We're here because the Espinosas and Seong are fighting," Rainy started. "There's not enough to go around in this city, so Seong is trying to chip away at Emilio's slice and Emilio is fighting back."

Adler looked at him like he was an idiot. "Yeah?"

Rainy pulled his hand away from his shirt to examine the blood pooled in the creases of his palm. "What if they didn't have to be fighting?"

Adler's only response was a thoughtful flare of orange at the tip of his cigarette. Rainy pressed on.

"They can keep tearing chunks out of each other and get just that—chunks. But you saw Parish's papers. We're both here because Seong can't go after Parish effectively, and neither can the Espinosas, so their only choice is to fight each other. But, if they worked together..." Rainy smiled. "We could take it *all*."

Adler took another contemplative drag. Rainy had to mentally berate himself because, one, he needed to focus, and, two, there was absolutely no excuse for finding a man smoking a cigarette sexy. Cigarettes were fucking disgusting. And yet.

"This is a little above my pay grade," Adler said finally.

"No, really? I thought you were the brains of the operation."

Adler flipped him off idly with the hand that was babying his ribs. "But," he conceded, "there might be something there."

Rainy nodded. "I know you don't make calls for Seong, and I'm not even an Espinosa. So who knows if this could be a thing. But if they were to consider it, it would probably be easier for them to work something out if their favorite hired guns haven't murdered each other."

"You wanna call a ceasefire."

"Temporary truce," Rainy amended. "We walk now, and take what we found at Parish's back to our sides. If they don't go for it, we're back to square one, and you can go back to merrily impaling me to your heart's content."

It was a transparent ploy to get out of this building alive, and Rainy knew it. But he had something here, something that had the potential to be big. Something to shake up this game, and maybe end it.

There was something else, too, something that had lodged in him like a sliver of glass while he'd been driving his foot into Adler's stomach. *Please, please take it. Please take a ridiculous, wild chance on this stupid idea, because—*

Because Rainy needed him to.

Adler flicked some cinders onto the concrete floor. He watched them smolder for a moment before extinguishing them with the toe of his boot.

"All right," he said. "Temporary truce. Until I get clarifying orders."

Rainy swallowed down the bright, painful balloon of emotion that swelled in his throat. It tasted like relief. He watched as Adler crossed back to the center of the floor, leaving his knife stuck in the wall, and held out a hand. Rainy let himself be pulled to his feet and groaned. The pinchy shoes had chafed him raw, and he was pretty sure he'd split his pants open in a few places.

"I paid so much money for this outfit," he complained. "This is why I don't dress up for work."

"Didn't suit you, anyhow," Adler said. "I like your dumpster clothes better."

Rainy beamed when he realized that, under its insulting wrapping, that actually might have been a compliment.

"You like the way I dress."

Adler drifted out of the foyer and into what would probably become a dining room, a square empty space with an enormous cutout in one wall that heralded a future picture window. He propped his elbows on it, left hand poised by his jaw with its half-smoked cigarette. Rainy leaned against the window as well, leaving a cautious gap between them. Beyond the empty frame, the house's private beachfront dipped its toes into the water. The sparkling technicolor lights of downtown rose over the flat black expanse of the bay.

"I think you dress like a moron," Adler replied finally. "I'm starting to think you might be a little smarter than you look, though."

Normally, it didn't bother Rainy when people saw him as just a dumb lump of muscle. Usually, it played to his advantage. But, for some reason, the idea of Adler thinking he was stupid chafed. He was a lot smarter than people gave him credit for. He wouldn't have lived this long or been so successful if he wasn't. He was more observant than most, too; after all, he'd pegged Adler almost instantly. And there were plenty of things he'd noticed that he could point out to prove it, the chief among them being:

"You're deaf in your right ear."

Adler went rigid beside him.

"Who told you that?"

"Nobody. You're good at covering for it. I noticed that you always put people on your left side, though. At first, I thought it was just about the scar. But it's more than that—you have this weird way of holding your head when you're talking to people, like you have to tilt it to hear them. When I whispered in your right ear last week, you couldn't understand what I said. And earlier, in the bathroom, you were pressed right up against the door. You could have just put your right ear against it to listen, but you turned your body all the way around first." Rainy idly examined his nails, which were packed with sawdust and blood. "Am I right?"

Adler rolled his cigarette between thumb and forefinger, thinking.

"Not totally deaf. Everything's muffled, like it's underwater. I get real loud voices, and some music. Used to be just terrible tinnitus all the time, but it ain't so bad anymore."

I'm sorry, Rainy wanted to say, but he was pretty sure that if he did, Adler would burn him with his cigarette. So, instead, he said, "I won't tell anyone."

Adler exhaled a cloud of smoke that turned the glittering distant galaxy of the city lights briefly hazy. Rainy coughed, scowling.

"Those things will kill you, you know."

"Not faster than anything else in my life." Adler shifted and winced when the motion tugged on his busted ribs.

"How'd it happen?" Rainy blurted. It wasn't a very clear question, and was probably off-limits, but Adler just eyed him briefly and turned back to the view.

"We were on a mission north of Raqqa. Covert ops, real serious shit. There was no advance team to sweep for explosives. *Boom*." Adler flicked his cigarette so ash spiraled off into the night. "The blast gave away our position, so they had to get the hell out of Dodge. I don't really blame them for leaving me; I might as well have been dead."

Rainy stayed motionless, silently fishing for more. After a moment, Adler delivered.

"The first thing I remember is waking up on a damp concrete floor, in the dark. I was all freezing and sweaty and delirious with fever. My nose and throat were clogged with congealed blood, like someone tried to drown me in it. That was the first thought I had. And my face hurt so bad, I thought, 'Uh-oh, it might not be just a burn; there might be a cut too.' So I reached up to touch my cheek, and my fingers landed on my back molars."

Rainy flinched. Beside him, Adler was absently tracing the vicious slash of the scar across his face.

"I still dream about it. Took three reconstructive surgeries once I got to Busan to get it looking like this. Used to be much worse, after it healed the first time. I still had a hole in my face when Seong met me."

"You mean when he bought you."

"He didn't *buy* me," Adler said hotly. "I was held with a few other Western POWs. They—" He cleared his throat. "They beat us sometimes, but I wasn't much fun to mess with when I could barely stay conscious. They were mostly content to let me starve in peace. My cell was a six-by-six-by-six box. I went weeks without being able to straighten my legs all the way, in the pitch dark."

Rainy thought of Adler panicking when Marco pulled the bag over his head. *Just nothing over the face. I don't like feeling trapped.*

Adler's hand was curled around the plywood windowsill, knuckles white. Rainy slowly slid his own hand over until his pinky brushed Adler's. Adler didn't look away from the bay, but his hand unclenched a little.

"Anyhow, while they decided what to do with us, they would lend us out sometimes to do labor for this wealthy IS-tied businessman. I don't even remember what I was supposed to be doing, I was so weak at that point. But Seong was there and said, 'I haven't seen an American around here in ages.' And I told him his bodyguards looked too comfortable in a stranger's house. They'd been bought off. He gave me this look, and just walked straight out of the house. A week later, he'd paid for my release. He's always refused to tell me how much."

"I still don't see how this isn't buying," Rainy pointed out.

"Because he gave me a choice. He would buy me a plane ticket and send me back to America, or I could come to Busan and work for him. No questions asked."

"You could have come home, and you decided to run off and become an international criminal instead?"

Adler offered a bitter twist of a smile that Rainy didn't like at all.

"Home? I know for a fact that getting that folded flag was the happiest I've ever made my parents. Without the army, I had nothing and no one in the States."

And looking at him with his too-posh suit and drooping cigarette, Rainy felt suddenly, overwhelmingly *disappointed*. Because Adler was supposed to be this grand, enticing mystery, unknowable and tantalizing. But in this moment, everything about him was painfully transparent. Rainy could see the line of it so clearly: kid with a shitty home life runs off to join the army and feels, for the first time, a sense of purpose and belonging. Then they abandon him too, and he pins all that misplaced loyalty on the first person who gives him a hand up. Trades his combat fatigues for a bespoke three-piece, but it's all a uniform just the same.

"You're kind of a letdown," Rainy told him.

Adler's mouth twitched. Almost a smile, but not quite.

"Sorry to disappoint."

Rainy drummed his fingers on the plywood windowsill and stared out at the city. He imagined it as an abstract grid of streets and corners laid out at his feet, the way he'd seen it as a kid. He knew every block of it like the sinews of his own body. And yet, from this angle, it felt both claustrophobically familiar and entirely new.

Something about this felt off. It was the sudden power imbalance between them. He'd forced Adler into showing a little of his vulnerable underbelly, and Rainy thought it was only fair that he do the same.

For the spirit of the game, of course.

"When I was a kid, I played football," he said. Adler glanced at him, surprised. He picked at a splinter with his nail. "I was good. Varsity middle linebacker all through high school. State champions. There were scholarship offers. I was going places."

He gnawed his lip. It had been so long since he'd told this story. So long since anyone had told it, even his parents.

"My older brother, though. He was in with the Espinosas. He and my father fought about it constantly, but Miguel just knew he wasn't in over his head." Rainy snorted. "He was a big, dumb lug. A naïve sweetheart, like my mom. He was never cut out for this life. One day, he picked the wrong guy to trust. Brought him in on running some weapons for Emilio. The guy shot my brother in the back of the head and took the score."

"Shit," Adler said. He offered Rainy a pull from his cigarette. Rainy waved it away, grimacing.

"One of his friends called my parents, told them what happened." Rainy swallowed. "My mother cried and cried, but I remember my father just made this... sound. And he slid down onto the floor of our tiny apartment and wouldn't get up. The thing was, Miguel had told me where he was headed, and I may not have been involved in that shit, but I was a Miami kid and I knew how things were divided between the Espinosas and the Vees. So I took off for this gravel lot that skirts the river near the Espinosa-Vee boundary."

"I know the one," Adler murmured.

"I caught up to him there, where he was hunkered down under this shed, sorting out what to keep for himself. I remember it was dumping buckets raining even though it was only May, because that was the year Ana hit the coast. I found this guy, and I didn't even have to say anything. He just took one look at me and pointed a gun at my head. But I didn't give a fuck about anything that day. I tackled him into the gravel and pinned him, and I snapped his neck." Rainy mimed the motion now. He could still feel the grind and pop under his hands, the storm running in rivulets down his skin.

"Then I gathered up all the stuff he stole and walked all the way to the Hub. I'd never even been to the place before. My buddy Julian was on guard duty that day, and the way he tells it, I just appeared out of the sheets of rain with this duffel bag of guns, soaking wet, and walked right up to Felix and said, 'I think this is yours.'" Rainy smirked. "I wouldn't tell them who I was—I think I was in too much shock—so they just clapped me on the back and called me 'rainy boy.' And the next thing I knew, I was standing in front of Emilio Espinosa, and he was offering me a job. The rest is history."

Adler had finished his cigarette, and he dropped it onto the concrete to grind under his heel. He stared out the window for a long moment, silent, before glancing at Rainy out of the corner of his eye.

"Sorry about your brother."

"Yeah. Sorry about your face."

Adler snorted with involuntary force. Rainy looked over to find that he'd put a hand over his mouth. Rainy giggled at the childishness of it, and then Adler was laughing helplessly along with him. It was a nice laugh. Maybe a little rusty, but full and charming.

He broke off with a long-suffering curse in a language Rainy didn't recognize, which set Rainy off again.

"I can't believe you speak Korean."

Adler gave him that look like he was a moron again. Rainy was maybe starting to grow a little fond of it. "I lived in Busan for four years."

"What other languages do you speak?"

He thought about it for a moment. "Mandarin, Cantonese, Japanese, Russian... Levantine. Okay Spanish, since I spent a few months in Buenos Aires earlier this year."

"You've been to all those places?" Rainy asked him, in Spanish.

"Seong has business all over the world," Adler replied, passably. Rainy guffawed again.

"Your accent is terrible," he told him in English. Adler scowled.

Rainy drummed his fingers against the sill. "What's your favorite place you've ever visited?"

"I went to Prague once, with my ex," Adler mused. "That crashed and burned, but the trip was good. But, honestly, probably Fuji-Hakone-Izu. It ain't easy for someone like me to feel at peace, but there I just about managed it."

The concept of being at peace sounded as foreign to Rainy as the Japanese name. It made him uneasy, so he focused on the much more intriguing concept of Adler having an ex. What kind of person would Adler deign to say he'd dated? Rainy pictured him and another slinky international assassin in a tailored suit frolicking through Czechia.

He was distracted from the image when Adler asked, "How about you?"

Rainy laughed. "Oh, I've never really left Miami."

"Why? If you make half as much as Seong pays me, you can afford it."

"I..." Rainy paused, frowning at the distant cityscape. It had never occurred to him, really. "I'm just too busy, I guess."

Rainy's entire life had unfolded within the boundaries of this city. Every birthday, hookup, family gathering, hit—all of it had been contained within these few square miles. He'd only ever taken one overnight trip outside the city.

When he was nine and Miguel was twelve, their parents had taken them on a road trip to see the fall colors in the Appalachians. They'd camped for two nights in a tent whose capacity their parents had severely overestimated. His mother had absolutely hated it, and vowed that they would never try anything new ever again. But running through the red and gold woods, sniffing out babbling waterfalls and leaning over the guardrails of scenic overlooks to trace the rolling slopes with his outstretched finger, Rainy had fallen in love.

"There was this one time," he admitted, "when I was in Virginia with my family, out in the woods. I went off on my own and stumbled across this clearing that was just full of wild violets. Like a purple carpet. I just ran around and lay down and I—it was like that. Someplace where you feel things you never realized you could."

He unbuttoned his shirt to bare the tattoo on the left side of his chest, the violets that spilled over the skin like they'd been caged in by his ribs before the tattoo artist took a knife to him and let them out. Adler's blade had punctured right through the center of them, so it looked like the flowers themselves were bleeding.

The memory of the sunlight and clean mountain air and the smell of crushed stems underneath him was still vivid in his memory. Among the violets, he'd felt like something out of a fairy tale, some feral creature no longer beholden to the laws of mankind. And when his parents had physically dragged him out of the flowers and back to their campsite, he'd vowed to himself that he would see the whole world.

That hungry joy and wonder felt distant now, as if it had belonged to someone else. Like it was something he'd seen in a movie once, not felt himself.

It felt like the dream of a child.

He shrugged off his sudden melancholy, uncomfortable with the scratch of emotion behind the bridge of his nose, and covered the tattoo.

"Guess I'm just married to my job. Can't even tear myself away for a weekend. Real workaholic, am I."

"What about the cowboy one?" Adler asked.

Rainy laughed and rolled his shoulders where the tattoo stretched across his upper back. "What, you mean Cherry? I did a couple-month stint in the county correctional when I was nineteen—practically a rite of passage for Espinosa boys. Twice a week, they had movie night, but the only movie they ever showed was *Red River*. I must have seen it fifteen times by the time I got out. That gun-comparing scene got me through a lot of cold nights, so it only felt right for a celebratory tattoo."

He'd been hoping to wheedle another laugh out of Adler, but it was looking like that was a one-time miracle. Instead, Adler was frowning at the horizon, his nose wrinkled in that uncharacteristically cute thinking face. Rainy wondered if he knew that he did that.

He was about to say something just to break the silence, when Adler finally blurted:

"I don't know how you do it."

It was soft and close-cradled, like a confession he hadn't meant to offer.

"Do what?" Rainy asked, mystified.

"I don't know how you—everyone—can do the things we do, and still be yourself."

There was a soft lostness to his voice that stole Rainy's breath. Adler's eyes were fixed on the water and glazed over with the past. He looked younger like this, and yet nothing like the younger self from the picture in Malia's file. Rainy thought of the quaver in his cigarette hand when he spoke of his scar, the dull resignation in his voice.

He thought of an empty gray apartment full of little nothings, and a family home he hated, and a world map full of places he'd never been, and a face in the mirror that he hadn't wanted to recognize since he was eighteen and a boy named Rafael, instead of a man called Rainy.

"Maybe I'm not," he said.

They stood in silence for a long time while the first brush of dawn turned the horizon gray and then a faint blush. The ache of a rough fight was settling into Rainy's body, bone-deep bruises and scrapes. The warm mugginess of the night was seeping into his skin where it was damp with sweat and blood, making him feel tacky all over. His joints smarted, and—okay, yes—his asshole was sore too. It was a pleasant, familiar ache from being pushed too hard, and his muscles kept clenching down around nothing. It made him acutely aware of the exact amount of extension it would take to reach out and touch Adler, and the tantalizingly close heat of his body.

He allowed himself a sideways glance. Adler's lean, graceful form was outlined in the light of the newborn dawn. And Rainy *didn't* want to kill him. He was spiteful, and vicious, and just sort of awful, but there was something about him that made those things feel charming. Maybe it was just that he was a novelty, a delightful little puzzle for Rainy to tease apart.

Maybe it was that they understood each other.

Whatever it was, Rainy just... he didn't know what he wanted. He was a creature of the moment, after all. What he wanted began and ended with laying his fingers on Adler's skin.

"Hey," he said. Adler glanced at him, uncertain. Slowly, because spooking him was probably a death sentence, Rainy closed a hand around his wrist and tugged him closer.

Adler was stiff but not resistant when Rainy pressed their lips together. It was weirdly tentative and chaste, like they were kids at their first school dance. But Adler softened against him, and Rainy felt a thrill of victory a thousand times better than besting him in a fight. The kiss stayed closed. It tasted like blood; Rainy had busted Adler's lip again at some point. Even with their mouths closed, there was a lingering hint of sweet-bitter smoke taste from Adler's cigarette. Rainy ignored it and eased him closer, curved his hands around his waist. It was so much narrower than his own, and his hands spanned it neatly. He hummed, pleased, and squeezed—

Adler gasped. Rainy jerked his hands away, burned, as Adler curled in around his broken ribs in that animal response to pain. He hovered ineffectively while Adler smoothed over the sudden exposed nerve of himself until he was arrow-straight and composed again, if a little too pale.

"You should get that checked," Rainy said, reluctant. He didn't want either of them to leave—it felt like this strange spell of truce would be broken the moment it was stretched beyond this enormous, half-finished house and the pale dawn that lit it, like a thread of gossamer pulled too thin.

"Yeah." Adler pointlessly straightened his vest, which was rather obviously a lost cause at this point. But it seemed to lend him the resolve to push away from the window alcove and move back toward the front door. "I'll talk to my people. You talk to yours. That's all."

"That's all," Rainy echoed, trailing after him. Temporary truce. Adler might very well come back tomorrow with orders to put Rainy in the ground as planned. And Rainy might get his own orders, and he... he would kill Adler. That had never been in question. It was just that, now, he was starting to think he might not like it.

And that was the other reason, he realized, that he needed this truce to work: Rainy wanted an excuse not to kill him. He needed a tiny, desperate sliver of hope that this could end in anything but their blood on each other's hands.

Adler stood in the open doorway, tall and precise and controlled. "Goodnight, Mister Rainy," he said, outlined against the early morning. And Rainy wanted him.

It gave him a sinking feeling in his stomach that whatever way this went, and however it ended, it was going to hurt.

Even after Adler disappeared, Rainy lingered in the construction site, resting on a workbench. He toyed with the tatters of his beautiful suit that had lasted exactly one night, and felt a sharp rush of satisfaction. There was a startling joy in dismantling and dirtying something expensive and gorgeous and too good for you. Maybe he should dress up for work more.

He found himself missing the familiar, secure weight of his Colt at his back again, and then remembered that Adler still had it, the bastard. Somehow, the thought didn't make him blind with rage. It was in hands that, at the very least, took proper care of things.

That didn't mean he didn't miss it. He aimed a contemplative kick at a staple gun on the floor that looked to be about its heft, flipping up with his toe. The tool arced up into his amazed hand, and he instinctively looked around for congratulation before remembering there was nobody around to see. He had an absurd notion of calling Adler back just to point at his foot and say, *I learned your trick, you smug bastard. It's not that hard.*

He found himself laughing, curled over on a bench in a half-finished house, body shaking with mirth until he tired himself out and sat still.

When the light outside was officially tipping over into morning, he pulled out his phone and brought up Lina Espinosa's contact.

One: Be advised that there is a small chance Andy Parish may be pressing some charges against me. I might have made a teensy mess at his house.

He paused, gnawing his lip.

Two: On a scale of one to ten, how good a mood is your dad in today?

Chapter 14

Florida Man Swept Up in Underworld Politics

T he Seong-Espinosa summit was held on the twentieth of October in the huge dining room of the Espinosa home. When Rainy arrived, the long polished-cherry dining table was set with a green-and-orange runner with little pumpkins stitched into it.

"'Tis the season," Jazz said delightedly, scattering tiny gourds in the center of the table while Felix tried in vain to whisk her from the room.

Emilio was already seated in the center of one side of the table, heavy and leonine. Rainy's smile petrified on his face when he caught his eyes and Emilio gestured to the seat at his right—an order, not a question.

"Don't think I'll forget that this was your idea," he said.

Rainy gathered calm around himself like a clean-cut suit. "When have I ever steered you wrong?"

"May every man's record stay as clean as yours."

Emilio's smiles, Rainy had found, weren't unsettling because the mirth in them was fake, but rather because the mirth in them was all too real.

"I know what I'm doing," Rainy assured him. He wondered how, exactly, his life had made the left turn into him making a habit of lying to crime lords.

The truth was that he had no idea what he was doing. He'd laid out the evidence from Parish with much more confidence than he'd felt, and convinced Emilio to send a runner to Seong. The runner returned without broken shins and boom—conversation opened. And now, here they were.

He'd tried to tell himself, as he'd gotten ready this morning, that the outcome of the meeting didn't really matter. Even if it went to shit, he'd only be back where he'd been a few days ago, ready to kill Adler at the soonest opportunity.

And yet, when he tried to reach for the righteous conviction that had been carrying him on his mission so far, the well seemed to have run dry. The anger was gone, replaced by the memory of Adler smoking a cigarette in the moonlight and offering Rainy a secret from his past like a tiny silver coin pressed discreetly between hands. A gentle, tentative kiss that Rainy had tucked away in his pocket like another glinting coin for him to reach down and guiltily run his fingers over in the quiet moments.

What Rainy felt now were nerves. Fizzing, humming nerves that had driven him out of the horrible, intimate quiet of his apartment hours before he needed to leave this morning. As much as he tried to reason his way out of it, he was desperate for this meeting to go well.

"Mi *vida*," Emilio rumbled. Jazz paused where she was trying to steal a baby gourd back from Felix. She was wearing a purple cocktail dress with an intense bustier, and her bleached hair was piled high. "Listen to Felix. These people are dangerous. The only reason I'm allowing them here is on Rainy's word."

Rainy shifted in his seat.

Jazz swept from the room, pouting. Felix started to clear away the rest of the gourds.

"No, leave them," Rainy blurted, hiding his laugh behind a cough. "Koreans love pumpkins."

"That's not—"

"It's true," Marco insisted, slinking into the room. Felix glared between the two of them helplessly, but dumped the gourds back into place. Marco exhaled a long, mango-scented puff of vape.

"Not in the house, Marcos!" Jazz shouted from the other room. Marco scowled and stowed the pen in his pants pocket. Lina entered the room behind him and cuffed him across the back of the head.

"Ow!"

"You're so stupid. Why'd you let Rainy kill half the Parish staff?"

"I wasn't even there!"

Lina just rolled her eyes and straightened her skirt suit before settling next to Rainy. It was immaculately tailored. Rainy thought she and Adler might get along.

"Why'd you kill half the Parish staff, Rainy?"

"I didn't! That was Adler."

The dining room doorway was suddenly eclipsed by Julian, who was one of Emilio's favorite enforcers and always called on for this sort of thing. He was nursing a black eye, but probably from a bar fight more recent than the one he'd gotten into when he'd been out with the group before. He leaned against the frame.

"They're here."

Emilio stood. "Have Alé bring them in. And try to look like you have some fucking dignity," he told his children, who continued to mill about like unruly cats. He scrubbed a hand through his thinning hair.

"No weapons," Rainy reminded Julian.

"No weapons."

"I know you have a knife on you."

"Don't."

"In your shoe."

Glaring, Julian bent down and pulled a short, thick-handled blade from the top of his boot. He tossed it to Rainy.

"You're such a fucking narc since you went freelance."

"Jesus, is this an oyster knife?"

"Ooh, gimme," Marco exclaimed, diving for it.

Rainy tossed the knife into a vase that stood in the corner. Marco looked crestfallen as it rattled and scraped its way to the bottom. "No weapons."

Footsteps sounded in the entry hall, and the Espinosas reluctantly fell into line. They faced the door as a united front: Emilio and Lina with stone-cold stares, Felix with a valiant attempt at one, and Marco with a weird little grin. Rainy stood off to the side, planting his feet and clasping his hands behind his back, but then he realized it was an awkward mirror of Adler's characteristic at-ease pose, and he shuffled nervously. The anxiety was still churning, making him queasy in this unfamiliar territory. He didn't know how he was supposed to present himself.

"Stop fidgeting," Emilio told him darkly. Rainy settled for leaning a hip against the table and folding his arms.

Two burly Korean gangsters entered the room first, both dressed all in black like club bouncers. Marco gave them a little wave. They just stared at him stonily and stepped to the side in unison to admit two more suits. The first was a middle-aged Korean woman with a hairstyle so smooth, it looked like it was made of plastic. The second was a man with light brown skin and a paisley tie that Rainy admired very much. They observed the Espinosas as Seong finally stepped over the threshold.

He was much the same up close as he was through binoculars—done up in a severe black suit that was unbuttoned a little at the collar, with a smile that crinkled his eyes and was oily as a politician's. Faced off against Emilio, he looked small and brittle. Seong might not have been as naïve as Andy Parish, but he was the same kind of man—one who had never had to do his own dirty work. Emilio might have been a bad man, but Rainy respected him for the scars on his knuckles.

All the concentration Rainy had went out the window once Seong stepped fully into the room, because Adler was glued just behind his left shoulder. He looked more put-together than Rainy had ever seen him, crisply ironed and neatly gelled and moving in precise military step. There was that gray-brown tweed from the first time Rainy had tailed him, and it was still embarrassingly sexy. Rainy didn't think it was his fault, though; Adler could probably make a hazmat suit look indecent.

Rainy tried to catch his eye, but Adler was very deliberately not looking at him.

Hmph.

Julian, still stationed by the door, circled in behind Seong's group. "No hard feelings, but we'll need to check you all," he said, and went to lay a hand on Seong's shoulder.

Adler caught his wrist. Rainy could see the outlines of his finger bones blanching white as he squeezed. Julian flushed angrily and tried to pull away, but Adler's grip stayed firm.

Seong's voice was low and smooth, only lightly accented. "Easy," he said. Adler dropped Julian's hand. Seong spread his arms, letting his jacket fall open to show he wasn't wearing any holsters. "We know how these things are done."

He looked directly at Emilio as he said this. Emilio nodded and spread his own arms.

Julian and Alé, another of Emilio's favorites, patted down Seong's entourage. Across the room, Seong's two bruisers ran their hands quickly and efficiently over the Espinosas. Rainy spread his arms and legs obediently when one approached him. The man checked him for weapons with a professional coolness. He seemed to receive special attention; the man even checked the contents of all his pockets. Rainy figured that Adler had something to do with that.

Adler also appeared to be receiving a uniquely thorough treatment from Julian, who looked gratified as he dug around in Adler's designer clothing. He slid his hands a little too high up the inside of Adler's thigh, smirking. Adler's jaw clenched so hard, Rainy was a little afraid his head was going to pop.

Eventually, both sides were satisfied. Julian nodded to Emilio, and one of Seong's men made a brief hand signal to Adler. Emilio spread his hands.

"Welcome to my home, Mr. Seong. Friends of Mr. Seong."

"A lovely home it is," Seong said. "Shall we get down to business?"

Emilio barked a laugh. "Direct. I like that." He held out a hand. "Call me Emilio."

Seong shook it. He gave a mirthful knife-blade of a smile. "Call me Mr. Seong."

Emilio nodded to his children. "This is my second-in-command, Felix Espinosa, and our counsel, Catalina Espinosa. My second son, Marcos. And I believe you're already familiar with Mr. Rainy."

Seong nodded along with each introduction, though it was nothing more than a nicety. He surely was already aware of the makeup of the Espinosa hierarchy. When Emilio finished, he folded his hands and nodded to the woman at his left.

"This is my director of business operations, Dr. Ryuk, and my head legal counsel, Mr. Gaumant." The man with the paisley tie held out a hand to Lina. She accepted it like an armed grenade.

"And, of course, Mr. Adler. My left hand, as it were."

"We're familiar," Emilio said.

"No hard feelings about the waterboarding, right?" Marco asked. Adler narrowed his eyes at him.

They settled at the long table in two parallel lines. Emilio and Seong faced each other like enemy generals in the central chairs, eyes locked on each other. Nobody missed the way Emilio leaned back in his chair with careful casualness.

Rainy was thwarted from securing the spot across from Adler when he stuck to Seong's right side, while Rainy was pushed to the edge of the Espinosas.

"It is a fair question," Seong said without preamble. "Whether we are willing to let go of the bad blood between us."

Emilio raised a brow. "I've found that, contrary to my daughter-in-law's expert opinion, the best salve for a wound is lots and lots of money. If we can move past our differences, this could be a very lucrative collaboration for both of us."

Seong looked pleased. "Indeed. Pierre?"

Gaumant the lawyer produced a stack of documents from his buttery leather briefcase and spread them out on the table. "This is a summary of Parish's recognized holdings," he said in a resplendent French accent. "The first issue is with this firm, Marquise."

As Gaumant spoke, Rainy tilted slightly in his chair to get a better look at Adler. He was sitting rigidly in his seat, the column of his spine arranged just a little off-kilter. Rainy had noticed his brow pinch when he sat, and again now as he shifted to get a better look at the photographs Julian had produced at Emilio's word. His ribs were still tender, then. There was a green-faded bruise under his eye and along his jaw. The sight made Rainy inexplicably antsy. He found himself absently rubbing the slight lump under his shirt where Nasrin had taped a square of gauze over the neat stitches she'd made, just over his heart.

"Rainy will take care of him," Emilio said authoritatively. Rainy turned to blink at him.

"What?"

Emilio's thick, dark eyebrows offered a remarkable impression of gathering storm clouds. "The contractor, Belko."

"Right, yeah. Easy."

"Perhaps it would be more prudent for Belko to be taken care of on our end," Seong said mildly. "I have my own channels."

"No," Rainy said. "If you want this to go smoothly, you'll want me. Adler's good at snapping necks, but he's lacking a certain... finesse."

Adler looked like he was considering leaping across the table and showing Rainy just how much finesse he was capable of. Rainy winked at him.

Seong looked displeased. "Nat?" he asked, and it took Rainy a moment to realize that he was addressing Adler. He had to turn his startled laugh into an awkward cough. Adler leaned in to mutter in Seong's ear, still glaring at Rainy.

"Very well," Seong said after a moment. "We'll trust you to take care of Belko. But that still leaves the matter of divvying up the spoils of war."

"Sixty-forty to us," Emilio said easily. "Seniority."

Seong laughed.

"Fifty-fifty," Emilio amended with false ruefulness.

"With all due respect," Dr. Ryuk said, her voice rough as a chain-smoker's, "that ignores the fundamental differences between our operations. We should make an equitable division plan based on asset type, to maximize our gains." She pulled up a spreadsheet on her tablet and slid it across the table. "We're willing to take a deficit in paraphernalia if we get sole claim to the two front holding companies."

Jazz had somehow weaseled her way back into the room with a tray of coffee, and now she was slinking around the back of the table out of Emilio's eyeshot, trying to eye the newcomers under the guise of playing hostess. Eventually, she decided to strike out and moved along the row of Seong's side, offering coffee. Seong and his two deputies declined politely, but Adler accepted a mug with two packets of sugar.

"Thank you, Miss Jazz," he said, accent indulgently syrupy. She flushed and fluttered, pleased. Rainy rolled his eyes.

Suck-up, he mouthed.

Idiot, Adler mouthed back.

Rainy tipped his head to the right and found Marco staring at him with a raised eyebrow. He glared back, then fixed his eyes firmly on the center of the table, trying to keep focus on the conversation.

He'd known it would be strange to see Adler in this new, unfamiliar context. Still, he hadn't expected to feel so... unsettled. Their spur-of-the-moment truce had been uneasy and fragile, but it had also felt clear and simple. Now, despite Adler's familiar open irritability, it felt a million miles away.

Maybe Rainy had just been delusional. Maybe seeing the delicate, sticky strands of what was between him and Adler here, in reality, was the problem.

He'd let Malia and Marco's stupid jokes feed into the idea that Adler was *his*. That he was some elusive wraith that appeared to tangle with Rainy and Rainy alone. Like his own personal white whale. Every interaction they'd had had been so far removed from everything else that it had felt like a dream with only the two of them in it.

This was the real world.

And this Adler, whose beautiful suits didn't look out of place nestled into Seong's lineup, who was called *Nat*—wasn't *his* Adler.

He had a sudden, stupid wish to have his version back, and all to himself again.

"We can draw up plans later, once our people have finished recon," Emilio told Seong.

"That depends on if we're able to come to an agreement." Seong folded his hands on the table. "I am under no illusion that we can be friends. But a partnership requires trust. Can we trust each other, Mr. Espinosa?"

"That is the question."

The light current of tension tracing its way through the air now thickened and redoubled, weaving a blanket over them all. The buzzing of a lightbulb in the corner echoed inside Rainy's skull like the scream of a klaxon. In the corner, Jazz allowed herself to be spirited outside without complaint, her tray clutched in a white-knuckled grip.

Emilio and Seong considered each other. On his side of the table, Emilio leaned in his chair, hulking and limned with silent threat. Opposite, Seong sat straight and unbothered, a slash of neatly tailored black against the lacquered wood chair. He examined Emilio with cool, shuttered eyes.

Slowly, Emilio smiled. He extended a hand to Seong across the table.

"I think this will be the start of a long and prosperous partnership."

Seong just gave him that oily politician smile. Their handshake was firm and final. Rainy's stomach curdled with the first, untrustworthy stirrings of hope.

The two sides of the table rose in unified lines, Seong and Emilio still locked eye-to-eye.

"If we're going to be working together, that means all wounds have to be forgiven," Emilio said. He jerked his head at Adler. "Rainy, kiss and make up."

Adler's mouth flattened unhappily, but Seong nodded at him, so he stepped around the corner of the table and stopped. Sighing, Rainy moved to meet him.

This close, Rainy could see the little stress fractures in Adler's posture where he was holding himself gingerly around his hurt ribs. The bruising on his jaw looked worse than it had from across the room. Rainy imagined more fading brown-green mottled across his chest and sides, over the smooth, lithe muscle of him where Rainy had trailed his hands before.

A strand of hair just above his ear was starting to come unstuck. He smelled like that same expensive cologne from the night they'd met.

Rainy held out his hand. Adler stared at it for a moment before shaking it.

"Sorry about the ear," he said drily. His face was smooth and un-affected, but in his dark eyes, there was a flicker of droll amusement that was held like a secret between them. Rainy wanted to tighten his grip, pull him in by the wrist, and kiss him again.

Emilio clapped his hands. "Good." Rainy blinked, startled, only then feeling the curious weight of all other eyes in the room. He hastily dropped Adler's hand.

Seong and Emilio were shaking hands again, and the rigid ranks dissolved into a flurry of hand-shaking, between Ryuk and Felix and Gaumant and Lina. It was a pageant of the type Rainy was used to in this house; genial smiles that contained blatant knives.

The hope in Rainy's stomach had hauled itself out of the muck and was shaking off its wings. *This might actually work.* He'd lose the money, but he couldn't bring himself to care when he might have a real excuse not to kill Adler. And if they didn't have to kill each other, maybe what had happened between them in the multipurpose room could happen again. The future was a soap bubble, shivering-bright and rainbow-hued.

"Looks like the terms of our truce are being extended," Rainy said.

"For now." Adler watched the flurry of movement, hands drifting behind his back and feet planted apart.

"For now," Rainy conceded, grinning. After holding out for a moment, Adler took the bait and looked back at him. When Rainy wiggled his eyebrows, he rolled his eyes. But the corner of his mouth twitched the barest hint of a smile.

The twinge of jealousy Rainy had been nursing the entire meeting ebbed, and the chatter of closing small talk lulled. He may have been tucked-in and polished here in front of the rest of the world, but Rainy's Adler was still there. He was a spark and a shadow behind Adler's carefully-built public exterior, a shimmer of feralness and mirth and lust that Rainy had managed to tease out from behind those walls. Maybe his Adler was the real Adler.

The Espinosas had finished saying their goodbyes, and Seong was moving for the door. Adler peeled away to return to his post at his shoulder without a backward glance. Rainy watched, aware that there was a stupid smile glued to his face, but unable to care.

Julian and Alé stalked after Seong's posse like a pair of rottweilers, seeing them off the property. The Espinosas immediately fractured into their typical chaotic pinwheel of activity. Emilio and Lina started quibbling over the documents spread across the table, while Felix tried to sneak a word in edgewise. Marco went digging for Julian's discarded oyster knife. Jazz slipped back into the room and over to Emilio with the capering dressage step of someone who knew they'd be instantly and indulgently forgiven for all trespasses.

"Marco, stop that," Felix insisted. Marco ignored him where he was testing the blade of the knife on the polished wood surface of the dining table.

"Let's relocate to my office," Emilio said, gathering a sheaf of papers. "If we're going to keep ahead of Seong's corporate bitch, we're going to need to draw up new plans."

Jazz laid a hand on his burly shoulder. "In a minute. Right now, I made margaritas in the kitchen."

"Jasmine."

Jazz pouted. "You can't take half an hour off, baby?" Her false lashes went downcast. "If you can't be bothered to give me a ring, you could at least give me a little of your time."

Emilio grumbled, but the trump card had been played, so he nodded at his children. "All right, fine. Kitchen now, study later."

"Fine by me." Lina plucked what looked like a list of stock options off the table and fanned herself with it as she strode toward the door. She looped her arm through Rainy's as she went. He was dragged along after her into the hallway.

"I think that went well," Rainy started cautiously.

"What the fuck was that?" she interrupted, continuing to march him down the hall toward the kitchen.

"It was awesome, that's what." Marco was suddenly at his other shoulder like some horrible, artificial-mango-scented manic apparition. "You've been holding out on me."

"What?" Irritation was starting to scratch at the inside of Rainy's skull.

"Malia and I thought you just had some weird little crush on the guy—"

"For the last time, I don't—"

"—but you didn't tell us he's fucking obsessed with you."

"We all totally thought you had some pathetic one-sided obsession," Lina said, straight-faced. "What a relief."

"Hey!" Rainy snapped. "Also, why the hell do you even know so much about this?"

"Rainy, please."

He pulled his arm away from her and was immediately ensnared by Marco. "This is going to be so great. It's almost as good as me and Tessa."

"It's going to be fucking terrible," Lina corrected. "You need to shut it down."

"I don't know what you're talking about." Rainy was really looking forward to that margarita. "Adler doesn't have a *crush* on me. Don't you guys have jobs you're supposed to be paying attention to?"

"Please," Lina said. "He was staring at you the whole time. I've never seen someone make fuck-me eyes that hard in a room full of that many criminals."

"We've fucked a few times. That's it. You're blowing this way out of proportion."

"A *few* times?" Marco's voice pitched up with delight.

"We've been trying to kill each other."

Marco sighed. "The course of true love never did run smooth."

Rainy shook them both off, hard. "Getting a little too friendly, aren't we? How about you two shut the fuck up about my personal life and do your jobs?"

There was something hard and prickly forcing its way up from his chest, and he just wanted them to stop. Stop tarnishing the luster of the image of Adler's tiny private smile, like a photo negative tossed carelessly into the ruinous light of day. Stop reminding him that this might end badly, and soon.

Lina shrugged and pushed past him, keeping on her heel-clicking path to the kitchen. "Your funeral."

Rainy turned his scathing look on Marco, expectant, and found him unusually somber.

"Look. I'm not trying to tell you anything, Rainy. I'm just saying that whenever you lay eyes on each other, it's like you're the only two people in the room." Marco moved him out of the way with uncharacteristic gentleness and followed Lina into the kitchen. "You should think about that while you still have time."

Rainy was left alone halfway down the hall, surrounded by green wallpaper and closed doors. He took a deep breath and tipped his forehead against the nearest door frame, feeling the white gloss paint soaking up the heat from his skin.

He pushed himself upright again when he heard Jazz clattering her way toward him and found her hanging off Emilio. Rainy pasted a careless smile on and peeled away to follow them in search of margaritas.

"Strawberry margs okay, Rainy?" Jazz asked in her thick Jersey roll.

"Sure."

"What is this, spring break?" Emilio scowled.

"Shut up, you huge fuck. I'm not talking to you."

Jazz toddled into the kitchen on her eight-inch stilettos, and Rainy made to follow her. Emilio caught his arm.

"A word," he said. It wasn't a question.

Rainy looked longingly into the granite-countered kitchen where Jazz and the Espinosas were already pouring drinks, then stepped into the alcove just outside the door.

"That went well," he said.

"Yes," said Emilio. "Let's hope there never comes a day when your luck runs out. Now, about Seong's man. The one I instructed you to finish. I've heard that you got a little distracted."

"Okay, seriously, what the fuck? Does this family sit around and have gossip sessions about my sex life?"

"Rainy, Rainy." Emilio clapped him on the back jovially. "I don't give a fuck how you get your dick wet. I just care that people keep their promises to me. And you promised no accidents. No distractions."

"He turned out to be a harder case than usual, and then something else came up. If you're worried I'm not still the best bang for your buck, don't be."

"I just want to be sure that if things go south, you aren't going to hesitate to put a bullet in his skull. Understood?"

Inside, everything felt quiet and still. The adrenaline hush before you turned a corner that might conceal a bullet.

"Are you planning something?" Rainy asked.

Emilio laughed, rumbling and deep and horribly mirthful. "Rainy. Please. You've always understood this business. So you know it's not a matter of *if* you'll have to kill him."

That shimmering soap bubble inside him popped. The fragile, lacy hope that had been tentatively growing evaporated in the cold that washed over him now.

Rainy stretched his easy smile until it strained the corners of his mouth.

"E, you know me. You have nothing to worry about."

Emilio ruffled his hair. "Good boy. Now, come have a margarita."

He lumbered into the kitchen without another word, leaving Rainy to lean against the wall of the alcove. He stared at the tiny dots of dust that clung to the shiny wood lacquer, dulling it. Everything inside him was leaden, sinking, dragging him down, down, down into the depths.

More than anything else, he was embarrassed. Embarrassed and ashamed, because he knew this life like the back of his hand, and he knew better than to let himself give in to that kind of stupid, naïve hope. The kind that didn't belong to people like him—not anymore. Not after the things he'd done, and the person he'd become.

Maybe Malia was right not to want to get in too deep with this world. Maybe she was just smarter than him. Rainy had never had the same doubts. He'd stepped right through that door and never looked back. Jumped into the ocean for the first time and swum like a fish. But maybe it just didn't work like that. Maybe this was what it felt like to be in over your head and never realize it.

Maybe this was what it felt like to be Miguel.

Rainy pushed off the wall and walked into the kitchen. He smiled when the Espinosas waved him over, and laughed when Jazz pressed a drink into his hand. Because he wasn't Miguel, and he wasn't Malia.

Rafael Perez had been a good, smart boy, who stayed out of trouble and was a recruiter's wet dream on the field. But Rafael Perez, like his brother, hadn't known how to swim.

Rainy knew that the trick to staying afloat was pushing someone else under. Rafael Perez had jumped into this ocean after Miguel, and he'd drowned. It was Rainy who came up for air. And he may have spent his life since afraid to look in the mirror, but he knew this much:

The day Miguel died, Rafa died too. He'd died, and become someone new. He'd found Miguel's killer and snapped his neck. He'd walked into this life and never looked back, given his parents the nice life they'd never had and outrun everything that might jeopardize it since. There were many things Rainy might have been, but only one that mattered.

He was a person who did what had to be done.

"Ah," Emilio said, "I almost forgot." He pulled something from the back of his waistband and held it out.

It was Rainy's Colt, familiar as his own arm with its pearled grip and the initials etched into the bottom. He'd last seen it when he was looking down the barrel, before Adler shot him with it. His ear itched where the skin had grown back, but the cartilage hadn't.

"Seong left this for you. Peace offerings, right?"

The weight of the pistol in his palm was like a handshake with an old friend who'd become a stranger. Rainy turned it over, tested its weight, ran a thumb up the grip where he could almost feel the warm ghost of Adler's hand. His ears rang with the echo of a shot.

Slowly, he released the magazine and turned it over in his palm. It had been emptied.

There was one round inside.

"I trust you know what to do with it," Emilio said lightly, turning back to his margarita.

Rainy slid the magazine home and tucked the gun away, where it fit as though it had never left.

"Yes," he said. "I know."

Chapter 15

Florida Man Ponders Romance; Chaos Ensues

The water of the bay lapped quietly at the concrete and corrugated metal of the docks. Black as ink. Rainy stared into it as he leaned against the grimy side of a loading bay, trying to see past its opaque surface. Overhead, a cloud drifted away from the face of the moon, and in the sudden light, he could see his reflection on the dark sheet of water.

He was wavering and insubstantial, like something unreal. He turned away quickly.

The group of Espinosa men were spread out across the dock like a tossed handful of dice, ribbing each other and shuffling with boredom. Felix, who was in charge, was trying to engage several disinterested men in a rousing pre-battle speech. At Rainy's side, Julian was checking game scores on his phone. Marco was attempting to do one-handed pull-ups off the side of the building. They were waiting for Seong's men.

It had been two weeks of frantic, hushed activity since the meeting at the Espinosa home. Lina had been working overtime with Gaumant and Dr. Ryuk to slice up Parish's legal holdings and move in with bids, and within days, Parish was ruined on paper—or so Rainy was told. What he'd been working on was a little more hands-on.

He'd easily offed his assigned target, Belko. Out a window, nice and neat. The rest hadn't been too difficult, a list of Parish's small-fish friends who propped up his operation like the bottom layer of a house of cards. Rainy plowed right through them all, until his arms were wet with blood to the shoulder. On the ground, the Espinosas had been circling closer on Parish's turf at the port, seizing small warehouses and a shipping yard and chipping away at Parish's men, until only one thing remained: a little cluster of warehouses, packed to the gills with Emilio's bread and butter. Guns, drugs, anything else that was illegal to import.

Seong had held up his end of the bargain; Parish's empire was in ribbons with the people who mattered. All that was left was the product that didn't exist on paper. And now, it was time to clean him out.

Rainy cast another glance around the midnight dock, empty save the Espinosa boys. "It's not like him to be late," he told Julian, leaned up against the bay next to him.

Julian shrugged. "What, like you and him are best friends now? The fuck do you know about what he's like?"

Rainy turned back to the water.

He hadn't seen Adler since the meeting with Seong. He'd tried and failed not to think about him. It was impossible not to worry at that ache like a loose tooth, feeling a part of him he'd once thought solid and immovable shift uncomfortably under the pressure. In some moments, he resented Adler for his apparent ability to wind his way down into Rainy's clockwork and make a mess of the gears and cogs that had run without fault for so long. He couldn't remember the last time he'd felt off-kilter this way.

Then again, maybe it was Rainy's fault. Maybe he'd held the door open and invited Adler in. He resented that idea even more.

There was an uneasy itch that had been spreading under his skin like an infection ever since the meeting. He always grew restless during a long streak of contracts, and the trail of bodies he'd accumulated these past weeks had turned the flutter of unease into a fever pitch that made his stomach turn and his head swim. Rainy was a master liar, but he couldn't quite convince himself that it had nothing to do with the tiny niggle of hope he'd allowed himself, which Emilio had shot out of the sky, an arrow protruding from its feathered chest.

There was a trick to living the way they did, on the underside of the world. When there was danger around every corner, you developed a second sense for when things were about to go south. Bad luck left a smell in the air. It had saved Rainy from more than one bullet.

He'd reloaded his Colt several times in the past two weeks, but the single round Emilio had given him was still safely burning a hole in his pocket. He slipped a hand in to thumb it now, over and over the tiny metal cylinder made warm by his skin.

"*Atten-tion!*" someone barked. Every man on the dock went rigidly straight with alarm, dropping what they were doing.

Rainy had heard laughter compared to the sound of bells, pealing or tinkling. Adler's laugh was more like a gunshot, sharp and mean and solitary. It made Rainy's heart do a little caper as Adler strode onto the dock sans jacket, in vest and shirt with sleeves rolled up to his elbows.

"I'm going to fucking—" Julian started, taking a threatening step toward him. Rainy caught him by the back of his shirt.

"We're all friends here," he reminded loudly.

Only four men followed Adler onto the dock, eyeing the Espinosas unhappily. Felix hurried forward to meet them.

"Where are the rest?" he asked.

Adler calmly checked his Beretta. "Sorry we're late. They'll be here in one minute." The clean, strong lines of his forearms were broken only by his watch. Rainy caught himself staring and deliberately wrenched his gaze away.

There was a sound of shifting water, and a motor. The Espinosas rustled in alarm as a small boat pulled alongside them. Adler waved off their raised weapons.

"That's mine," he said.

"We already have transport arranged," Felix said.

"I think you can understand that Seong might not trust you with *all* our loot," Adler replied. "We are who we are, after all."

Even though Adler didn't glance his way once during the exchange, or even put special emphasis on the words, the phrase still stuck in Rainy's throat, too big and awful to swallow.

Adler caught the rope that was tossed to him from the deck of the boat and knelt to tie it off, leaving his back exposed. The nape of his neck was a smooth, pale line against the black water. It would have been easy to finish him. Nobody made a move. When he stood, he was smiling.

The Espinosas pulled in tight as eight of Seong's men piled off the boat, filling out the ranks. Adler gave them brief, sharp orders in Korean, and they moved with military discipline.

"English, if you don't mind," Julian called.

"They're new. They don't speak English well." The corner of Adler's mouth was playful, and Rainy didn't like it one bit.

"It's fine," Felix said. "Let's just get moving."

"He's going to get us all killed," Julian hissed. He flinched when Marco appeared at his shoulder as though summoned.

"Watch how you talk," Marco said mildly, his eyes on his older brother. Julian ground his teeth, but lowered his hackles.

Adler had finished addressing his troops and strode up to Felix and his entourage now. He looked different at the front of a line of men, Rainy thought. Loose and authoritative. Like he wasn't just in control of himself, but everyone around him as well. *Sergeant Adler.*

"We'll go in from the east," Adler informed them. "Charlie warehouse is our first priority. My men take point. Those five, you send around from the southeast; those five stick to the waterline." He slashed with a flat palm, efficiently dividing up their force.

Felix looked beguiled by Adler's field-commander act. "That's—smart."

"You serious?" Julian pushed past Marco to Felix's shoulder. "He's not our fucking drill sergeant, Felix."

Rainy closed a hand around Julian's upper arm. "Just take it easy."

"You might be happy sucking this guy's dick, Rainy, but I don't take that shit."

"We're not enemies tonight."

"Don't be stupid," Julian spat. "We're *always* enemies with these fuckwads."

"Get your man in line," Adler told Felix impassively. He hadn't glanced Rainy's way even once throughout the entire exchange.

All eyes turned to Julian. He kept his eyes narrowed on Adler, but didn't say anything more. He just drew his Bowie knife from its sheath in his jacket and flipped it in his hand, blade over handle, handle over blade.

Satisfied, Adler turned his back on them and started off toward the easternmost warehouse, his men falling in behind him. The Espinosas looked to Felix.

"Split," he confirmed. The men peeled off into two groups, skirting opposite directions. Marco caught Rainy's elbow and nodded after Julian.

"I'm sticking to the bitch parade to make sure they don't get too out of line," he said. For a moment, he teetered on the edge of jogging off, looking uncertain. "Look, Rainy—this is need-to-know, okay?

And my father didn't think you needed to know. But things *are* going to go crooked in there. And I need you on my side, okay?"

There it was—the blow Rainy had been waiting for. Emilio was going to screw over Seong.

He couldn't feign surprise—he knew how this world worked, after all. They'd already gotten what they needed from Seong, and this shipment of spoils was the last thing on the table. It only made sense that Emilio would want to sweep it all into his basket. Still, anger boiled in his stomach. Emilio was planning to pull some shit on this operation, and he hadn't breathed a word of warning to Rainy.

"He doesn't trust me."

Marco waved him off. "He doesn't think you've turned. You've just been... flaky, lately. But I'm telling you now to get ready."

"Because you need my help getting it running smooth under Felix. And stopping Julian from blowing it by running his mouth," Rainy surmised.

"Because you're my friend," Marco corrected.

Rainy swallowed. "I'm loyal. You know I'm loyal."

"I know. I know that. Just... remember where *everyone's* loyalties lie." Marco stepped away and dipped a hand into his jacket. He flashed Julian's oyster knife with a grin. "See you inside."

Rainy was left alone on the dock, watching men melt into the gloom.

He was going to follow instructions. He was going to rejoin Felix's group, and carry out the warehouse sweep, and go along with the plan. And if Adler got in his way...

His hand dipped into his pocket again to fiddle compulsively with the bullet.

There was that now-familiar itch under his skin. Rainy just wanted to slit open his arm and drag out the clinging tendrils of it. He'd made up his mind—no, there'd never been a question. That was the core of his effectiveness—he was good at his job, and he'd never before felt conflicted about doing it. But now something was tugging at the edges of him, distracting and confusing.

He paused for a moment, fighting himself, then muttered a curse under his breath and took off down the center into the maze of shipping containers that separated Adler's men from Felix's.

He wasn't going to give in to the itch, but he needed to see, just to sate it. He wasn't hurting anything by scratching it just a little.

Corrugated steel boxes rose up around him like the walls of a labyrinth, blotting out broad geometric swathes of sky. Clouds drifted uncertainly overhead. Rainy struck a course for the border of Adler's group's path, moving at a clip and only pausing briefly at each junction to check for danger before forging ahead. He turned another corner toward the east, and then a strong arm was looping around his chest and yanking him back into the shadows. A broad palm clamped down over his mouth.

"Looking for someone?" Adler drawled in his ear before Rainy could throw him over his shoulder onto the pavement. Rainy bit his hand.

They were tucked into a little dim corner formed by a juncture of shipping containers. Under the clean linen-sandalwood scent of Adler's cologne, Rainy could smell the salt and garbage of the docks.

He wondered briefly whether Adler wasn't warm, even without a jacket. Despite the fact that it had been dark for hours, the air was heavy and oppressive in that way that trapped in the heat. He wasn't complaining, though. The snug fit of Adler's vest emphasized the lithe, deadly lines of him, and the bunched cuff of sleeve around his elbows was doing things to Rainy's insides. Careless was a very sexy look on Adler. Very sexy and very ominous. Rainy tilted forward into his space, against the solid steel wall of the shipping container.

"Couldn't resist giving everyone a show, huh?" He ran a hand down the lean muscle of Adler's side, down to where his pants were tailored snug as ever over his ass. The look Adler leveled at him felt dangerous. Rainy wanted to lap it up.

"This is how I dress when I need to get my hands dirty." Adler stepped away from him disdainfully. Rainy caught him around the waist and pulled him back, back into their little shadowy corner of the world.

There was a reason he'd come, he was pretty sure. There was a reason Adler was here, too.

"You didn't dress this way when you came to kill me," he pouted.

"Well. That's because I underestimated you."

"I think that's the nicest thing you've ever said to me."

"I'm sorry if I find it difficult to remain civil in your presence," Adler said flatly.

"Don't be." Rainy leaned in, pinning Adler to the wall with his weight. "I like it when you're mean to me."

Adler's lips were cool and a little chapped, and slid apart when Rainy pressed his tongue in insistently.

There was nothing chaste or tentative about this kiss. Rainy swept his tongue into Adler's mouth, confident and possessive, and groaned when Adler pressed forward to meet him. He fisted his hands in Adler's clothes, trying to get him closer, running his hands reverently over his ribs, his thigh, the delicate vertebrae of his neck.

Despite the adrenaline, he felt still. He was reminded of Adler murmuring, *It's not easy for someone like me to feel at peace, but there I just about managed it.*

At peace, at peace, at peace. It echoed there, inside his skull. The itch under his skin was gone—it always disappeared once he got Adler under his hands. As long as Adler was here, in Rainy's grip, he wasn't an unknown enemy element, off somewhere turning Rainy's world on its head. As long as Rainy had a grip on him, he could keep everything from spiraling out of control.

Remember where everyone's loyalties lie, Marco told him. In his pocket, Emilio's bullet weighed a thousand pounds.

Suddenly, he felt desperate, almost frantic. He sucked hard on Adler's bottom lip, bit down until Adler made a small sound in the back of his throat. This was all there was, this small, stolen moment in a hidden corner on their way to shoot up the place. Rainy wanted to make it last, to make sure he remembered it. He felt like his wandering fingers were curling deeper than Adler's skin, trying to pull off some figurative piece of him to hold and have and keep.

The moment was already over. Adler pushed him away.

When Rainy stopped kissing him, Adler looked himself—a perfect mixture of bored and amused, perpetually in on a joke that no one else knew about. It made Rainy want to shake him, and then kiss him again.

"You didn't answer the question," Adler said. "Why are you here?"

"I could ask you the same thing." Rainy smiled when Adler's mouth flattened unhappily. "*You* were looking for *me*."

Adler looked resentful at being caught out. "Maybe I was."

"Why?"

Thumbing his Beretta where it was nestled in a shoulder holster, Adler glanced around the abandoned corridor of crates before sucking in a long-suffering breath.

"You're smart," he began. "We both know what happens when we get inside."

Rainy tensed, but he wasn't surprised. Adler couldn't know the details of the Espinosas' plan; he was talking about something else. For all it suited him, sometimes Rainy hated this world, where backstabbing was the only real way to come out with anything worthwhile.

There wasn't a threat in Adler's voice, though. Instead, his words were hurried and tight, an undercurrent of urgency to them, even imploration. It occurred to Rainy that telling this to him, an enemy, pained Adler.

And yet, here he was.

"You said it yourself. You're not an Espinosa trained dog." Adler's face puckered, like the words tasted bitter. "You don't answer to their every whim the way you'd have to if you worked for them."

Rainy couldn't help the startled laugh that burst out of him. "Are you trying to turn me?"

"Don't be an idiot. I'm just telling you that I—" Adler's voice caught, caught off guard. Like whatever his next words were, he hadn't prepared them. "I don't wanna kill you. Don't make me."

The words shivered in the air between them. Rainy physically leaned away from them, like if he let them settle, they would mark his skin. He wanted to grab them out of the air, shove them back into Adler's mouth, and clamp his jaw shut like they'd never been spoken.

Don't make me. Like it was as simple as that.

Rainy felt painfully, colossally stupid. Because it *was* as simple as that. He'd deluded himself into thinking that it was complicated, that it was conflicting. But they didn't have that luxury. For them, it could only ever have been the simplest thing in the world.

He felt the frail, tremulous heartbeat of that hope he'd been nursing since their truce, just alongside his own. It was a feeling like humiliation, remembering the way he'd blindly fumbled for that kind of false hope, like a green amateur, like a child in a field of violets. He watched the pathetic hope Emilio had shot out of the sky struggle feebly. He would have to snap its neck himself. Of all the types he'd practiced over the years, mercy killing was the kindest.

"Right," he said, and even to himself, it sounded like a death sentence.

"Rainy—"

"Right. I'll see you inside."

The gravel crunched under his feet as he turned and walked away without another word, before he could try to memorize the way the low light gilded Adler's unhappy expression. He headed straight for the sound of one of the Espinosa groups moving a few containers away.

He waited for Adler to stop him—either with a hand on his wrist, or a bullet in his back. But nothing came. He didn't look back to try and read the reason why in the shadow of Adler's eyes.

He'd let himself indulge in the fantasy that this was thorny and complicated, but it was as simple as this: when the cards were down and the Seong-Espinosa alliance crumbled, they would be back to square one. Either one of them folded, or this ended the way it was always meant to. Yes, Rainy wasn't entirely beholden to the Espinosas tonight. But when the sun came up, he would still have a career, contacts and contracts and working relationships. *I don't want to kill you,* Adler had said, but the question had never been whether Rainy wanted to. It was whether he could. And the answer always had to be yes. He knew it was for Adler.

He couldn't think about the epiphany that Adler too, for whatever reason, had been looking for an excuse not to kill *him.*

It didn't matter. It was too late to think about that. It was too late for anything but this.

Felix's group of men came into view around a corner, and Rainy walked toward them calmly, despite the fact that he felt dizzy, that his pulse was thrumming too loud to hear anything else. This was what it felt like to be drowning. And when you were drowning, everything was black and white. The only thing that mattered was this: Rainy knew what it took to keep his head above the water. He'd learned a long time ago that to keep swimming, sometimes you had to push part of yourself down into the depths to die. He'd done it before. It had been simple then, too.

Rainy pulled out his Colt and released the magazine. Fully loaded, the way he'd made sure it was when he left his apartment that night, from the suitcase under his bed, the only thing in his big, empty room.

He thumbed a round out, let it drop to the gravel at his feet. The round from his pocket was hot to the touch when he fed it in. He slid the magazine home and tucked the gun away as he came level with Felix.

"They're planning something," he said in response to Felix's inquisitive look. "Be ready. God knows they are."

Felix absorbed this information gravely, but only nodded.

It was smart that Adler had sent them around the flank, because when Parish's men ran to deal with Adler's team entering from the east, they were there to catch them in the back. They put down three men, and the remaining two crouched to kick their weapons across the floor and raise their hands. Adler assigned a man to watch them and kicked the lid off a crate.

Several people from each team splintered off to start digging through the loot, taking stock. Rainy didn't approach Adler to see what was in his crate, instead leaning in to investigate one Eduardo had opened. Boxes of ammo, nine-millimeter hollow point. The rest seemed to be of a piece.

Outside, there was a sudden burst of shouting and gunfire that meant Marco had gotten bored and decided to get a head start on the next warehouse. Rainy sighed and jogged off toward the commotion.

They swept through the buildings quickly and with minimal difficulty. Parish's numbers were low—most of the rats having already jumped ship—and those who remained weren't eager to lay down their lives for a boss who might not be around much longer to make it worth their while. By the time they cleared the last warehouse, Rainy's magazine wasn't even empty. When he turned a final corner and came face to face with a Parish man, he didn't even have to raise his gun before the guy was haring out through an emergency exit and disappearing into the night.

He made his way cautiously back to the center of the warehouse, where Marco and Felix had converged with Adler. Rainy nodded reluctantly to Felix.

"Looks like we're all clean," Felix said, a slight ring of nervousness in his voice. Adler caught it like a bloodhound.

"Looks like," he replied. The lazy curl of the words in his accent, dry and bleakly amused, made something in Rainy ache. He wanted to press Adler between paper like a dried flower, and keep him frozen in this moment before the end until the pages crumbled to dust.

The air wobbled and stretched, the way it did when everyone knew what was about to happen, but no one wanted to be the first to tip their hand. Rainy caught Marco's eye. He ran a thumb lightly over and over the hammer of his gun.

"Well," Adler said finally, and then the eastern fire exit swung open.

A large posse of Seong's men swaggered in, ones Rainy didn't recognize—far more than Adler had arrived with. The boat, he realized. That's how they'd smuggled so many in past the Espinosas' lookouts. There had been far more on the boat than had first emerged.

They filed in and filled the mouths of rows and aisles around the central room, eyes grim and obedient on Adler. The Espinosas shuffled and tightened ranks. Rainy could see the pulse jumping at the side of Felix's neck.

"I think you see where this is going," Adler said drily.

He looked like he was about to continue, but he paused suddenly, frowning. He slipped a hand into his pocket and pulled out his phone.

"You should answer," Marco advised.

Glaring, Adler tapped the screen and issued a terse greeting in Korean. His face darkened further at the reply. A muscle twitched in his jaw.

"You're not the only one with friends," Felix said.

That was the Espinosas' play, then; while Adler's reinforcements had stuck to the action, the extra Espinosa men had slipped into the other warehouses, where Adler had left a few of his men and most of the goods.

Adler dropped his phone back into his pocket, expression flat. He sighed and unholstered his Beretta.

Marco looked at Felix. "My turn?"

Felix's mouth twisted unhappily. "Yeah."

"Thanks, *asere*," Marco said, and shot the man next to Adler between the eyes.

The room erupted into chaos. Gunfire echoed deafeningly in the enclosed metal space, and everywhere men were scrambling for cover. Rainy ducked and rolled to avoid a bullet that lodged in the crate where his head had been, and came up just in time to catch the burly Korean man who was coming at him with a switchblade. He slammed the man into a shelving unit until he went limp, then spun to pop off a few more shots into the fray.

The initial frenzied fire died off within a minute as the danger of ricochet made itself known, and it was replaced with grunting and thudding and the crunching of bone. People were rolling across the floor and darting through the shadows of the shelving aisles where someone had shot out an overhead light. One of the fire exits slammed repeatedly, echoing like a shotgun blast and setting off another panicked volley of gunfire. Someone tackled Rainy from behind, and he jarred the bones in his forearm catching himself on the concrete floor.

His attacker was strong, but Rainy was stronger. He rolled them over and threw a punch, reared up to strike again. Someone kicked him in the side, hard. He flew sideways and cracked his head on a metal shelf, and then his first assailant was up and on him again. A punch landed on his temple, sending his ear ringing and the still-tender missing tip smarting.

Someone yanked the guy off him and tossed him aside. Rainy looked up to find Alé standing over him, panting and bleeding from a split lip. He hadn't been part of Felix's original party.

Reinforcements had arrived.

Rainy took Alé's offered hand and leaped to his feet. The sound of violence was deafening, the ring of metal and thud of flesh and shouting in English and Spanish and Korean and something Rainy was pretty sure was Portuguese. He put down a guy who almost got one over on Alé and turned in a circle to try and get his bearings.

Felix was taking cover behind a reinforced crate, shouting orders which no one was listening to. Marco was brandishing his pilfered oyster knife where he'd pinned a terrified-looking member of Adler's group. Rainy couldn't spot Adler anywhere.

The fire exit opened and closed more quietly this time, and Rainy spun to face it, snarling.

Emilio stared back at him, a semi-auto clutched in his hands and his teeth set grimly. Here, like Napoleon, to ensure his troops secured victory. Rainy made eye contact with him, fingers tingling on the grip of his gun.

A heavy, dark eyebrow arched. Rainy swallowed, and nodded.

Before he could take a breath to second-guess himself, he dipped into the shadows in search of Adler.

Chapter 16

Florida Man Locked in Battle to the Death

H e found him framed by the towering shelves of one of the aisles, holding an Espinosa pup by the hair as the kid's feet scrabbled on the concrete, trying to find purchase. The kid was dropped unceremoniously when Adler spotted Rainy, and he scrambled away toward the exit.

As the sound of battle crashed and lurched around them, Rainy held Adler's cool, assessing gaze. The tumult of sound and movement washed over him and receded as a sense of perfect stillness set in. He watched the lines of tension in Adler's body, the minute angles of him. Fluid, predatory, deadly.

Still.

On the grip of his Colt, his palm was slippery with sweat.

If he let himself think, he would be lost in the memory of the few gentle moments between them, the confessions Adler had handed him in the secret dark of night, and the flutter of Adler's eyelashes as he slept under the safety of Rainy's watch.

So he didn't let himself think. He just breathed, felt the steady expand and release of his ribs, willed the frantic rush of his pulse to slow.

He raised his gun.

The moment his wrist twitched, Adler was moving. He was down the aisle in half a second, and Rainy dropped his gun hand to brace.

It wasn't the smartest play Rainy had ever seen from Adler. A lot of men would probably have been shaken by being rushed full tilt, but Rainy had played varsity linebacker for three years. He caught Adler's full weight, swung it, and slammed him against the shelf at their right.

Adler made a sharp noise of pain, the impact jarring his still-healing ribs, but he didn't stop moving. There was a shimmy and twist almost too fast for Rainy to follow, and then his elbow was being twisted so sharply that he had to step out to stop it from breaking.

As soon as Adler was free, they were really fighting. He lunged straight for Rainy's face, pummeling him viciously so Rainy had to deflect him rather than using his gun before Adler could get his own free. Rainy dodged a knockout punch to the temple and caught it on his wounded ear.

"*Fuck!* Seriously?"

Adler's play was clearly staying too close and moving too quickly for Rainy to shoot him with the Colt still gripped in his hand. Well. Rainy was resourceful. He swung his gun hand up and smashed the pistol against the side of Adler's head.

Adler reeled back, stumbling into a shelf and sending small boxes clattering. Blood trickled down his jaw where the gun's hammer had gouged a small furrow. It cut across his scar, perpendicular. With dazed eyes, Adler reached up to touch it, then stared at the blood on his fingertips.

"Hey!" Rainy shouted. He wasn't really sure why—Adler's eyes sharpened right away, and Rainy lost his chance to end it with a quick shot right then and there when Adler tackled him.

Still better than seeing that look on his face, Rainy thought as his back hit the concrete and the wind was knocked out of him.

They rolled a violent somersault through the open central floor, hands scrabbling and nails gouging. Rainy was dimly aware of the other combatants in the vicinity pausing to watch as they crashed to a stop against a wooden crate, the Colt flying out of Rainy's hand.

He went for a pin, but he was too slow. Adler had him on his back already, forearm against his throat and full weight bearing down. Rainy choked, feeling his Adam's apple grind into the cartilage of his trachea. White patches spread in his vision, like holes being eaten in celluloid film. He fumbled at Adler's sides, hands ghosting over his shoulder holster to find the tender spot on his ribs, and dug his thumb in with everything he had.

Adler hissed and faltered just enough. Rainy threw him, and he went rolling into the aisle at their right.

The worst part was that, deep down, the thrill was still there. This was what chess masters must feel, Rainy thought as he scrambled to his feet. He'd never felt it quite like this before—the joy of an opponent who was his equal. It was a kind of intimate connection. A fucked-up one, maybe, but one all the same, and that didn't diminish the delight of seeing whatever Adler next pulled from his sleeve.

Now, though, when he faced off in the mouth of the aisle and watched Adler roll gracefully to his feet, the delight was choked in dread. Scalding, dark, sticky, like tar seeping down through his insides.

Adler's hand went to his shoulder holster. His face went stiff when it came away empty.

"You should really keep better track of your stuff." Rainy brandished the Beretta. *Your move.*

It did not disappoint. Adler took a running start toward Rainy, then leaped up onto one of the shelves that made up the walls of the aisle. He used the momentum to launch himself off the opposite bank of shelves, moving too abruptly for Rainy to shoot him, and grabbed hold of a crossbar at the top of the aisle.

Rainy just had time to think, *You magnificent bastard*, before Adler dropped down on him legs-first.

They went down in a clumsy tangle. It was all knees and thighs for a moment—at one point, Adler got a leg locked around Rainy's neck, and Rainy wriggled out and went for a pin of his own, only to get his wrist bitten bloody for his trouble.

"The biting," he hissed, trying to trap Adler's arms with his shins.

"The teeth are an underutilized weapon," Adler told him, miffed, and drove a knee up into the small of his back to knock him off.

The Beretta had slid off somewhere, lost. Rainy pulled himself out of the tight-woven trap of their limbs. Adler followed on his heels and immediately aimed a kick at Rainy's head that he only narrowly avoided.

They ebbed and flowed along the edge of the open central space, blocking and countering in a seamless dance whose steps they each knew too well to be tripped up by the other. Rainy dodged a series of low abdominal hits and a blow that would have spun his head around like a cartoon character's if it had connected. He could feel Adler growing more unhappy, his strikes turning more clinical and brutal, subsumed in mindless efficiency.

Most of the men in the center of the warehouse had warily spaced away from each other, pausing their own battles to watch. The glance Rainy spared to confirm this fact nearly cost him a broken jaw, so he didn't look again. Someone was shouting in Korean, presumably cheering Adler on.

"Hey, Rainy!" Marco shouted from somewhere off to his right. "Catch!"

Fortunately, Adler was just as distracted this time, so Rainy didn't get his neck snapped when he turned incredulously to watch Marco brandish Julian's oyster knife and toss it overhand. The blade flashed under the harsh overhead lights before it was snatched out of the air. By Adler.

"Shit," Marco called. "Sorry, bro!"

Rainy was too busy trying to avoid getting his throat slashed to reply.

He was on the defensive now, retreating as Adler wielded the knife in long, slashing arcs at his throat, his belly, his brachial artery. When Rainy threw up an elbow to block a jab at his carotid, he got a deep laceration on the back of his forearm. Adler didn't let up, driving in with the knife again and again, until Rainy's sleeves were ribbons and his skin from wrist to elbow was scored with tally marks like a cell wall. Blood spattered across the concrete floor, forming a smearing red trail under their shoes. Rainy yelped as another burning line carved through the mess of pain, and he saw Adler flinch minutely.

"Just," Rainy gasped, stumbled back again. "Just—"

Adler's eyes were black. There were lines carved deep around them, making him look so old.

"I told you." There was a scratch in his voice, like someone had scored the inside of his throat. "You can't put this back in the box."

The blade darted out quick as a careless word. Rainy lurched to the side this time, the tall, dark walls of shelves reabsorbing him. He backed up blindly down the aisle, his sneakers dragging and catching on the concrete. Adler stopped in the mouth of the aisle, backlit by the harsh lights. His face was grim, his jaw set. Something dripped off the tip of his blade.

It hit Rainy then, more strongly than ever before, that this was the moment he died. There was regret, swirling thick and heavy, behind Adler's eyes. But he was still going to take those few steps forward and finish this. Because, in the end, they were the same. Adler was like Rainy. He'd do what he had to.

Pain was squeezing into Rainy's arm, a latticework of red-hot razor wire. He focused on the bite and sting of it, trying to clear his head. He was going to keep fighting. Until the very goddamn end.

An oyster knife. A fucking *oyster knife.*

The walls of the aisle formed a neat one-point perspective, narrowing Rainy's world to the vanishing point in the center of Adler's chest. He watched the knife turn over, contemplative, in a broad, strong palm. There was blood sprinkled lightly across the front of Adler's pristine white shirt, a red splotch on his collar where it had run down from the cut on his face. Rainy could see the rise and fall of his collarbone.

He was suddenly overcome with the desire to kiss the curve of that collarbone, to trace it gently with the pad of his thumb. And then the apprehension and adrenaline were undercut by a flash of sadness from the knowledge that from the very beginning, from the very first moment they'd met, nothing good or soft could have ever come of this.

He wondered what might have happened if they'd met in that hotel bar in another life, where Rainy had stayed home that day in the rain and Adler had taken the ticket back to America that Seong had offered him.

The knife made another small circle in Adler's palm, then his thumb settled on its edge, sure and steady.

"I'm sorry," he said, quiet enough that only Rainy could hear. He started forward.

Rainy took another shuffling step back. The rubber heel of his sneaker tapped against something lying on the floor. Out of the corner of his eye, he saw a shimmer of gunmetal and pearl.

His Colt.

It must have slid through the open space under the shelves when it was knocked out of his hand and come to rest here.

Adler was almost on him now, the knife glinting in his hand. There was no time. No time for anything at all.

Rainy kicked, dug in, and flipped up with his toe. The gun leaped up into his hand, and he swung it up. Adler halted, the barrel pressed to his forehead.

They stood frozen an arm's length apart. The silhouette of the gun divided Adler's face neatly in two; on either side, an eye, both staring unflinchingly into Rainy's. One side smooth and unbroken skin, the other furrowed deep with the same old scar.

Rainy could see the breakneck calculation shimmering across the reflective surface of Adler's eyes. He was weighing the merits of ducking, grabbing, slashing, trying to wrestle away the gun. Rainy could see the options wash in and out like the tide, each rejected.

The oyster knife clattered to the concrete at their feet. Its handle bounced off the rubber toe of Rainy's sneaker, spattering blood.

They considered each other evenly. Silent.

"Well," Adler said finally. "Go on, then."

He closed his eyes.

Rainy's next inhale stuttered against his will. He rolled his shoulder forward the tiniest bit, until the skin of Adler's forehead pressed white, until his neck tipped with the force of it. His eyelashes fluttered a little, but he didn't open his eyes. Rainy could feel the heat of his breath on his wrist.

All it took was the flex of a single forearm muscle, a tug on the tendons in his index finger. Curling the tip of his finger in toward his palm like a homecoming he'd made a hundred times before. Just moving one finger. The simplest thing in the world.

Rainy's arm was still a razor net of pain. Blood dripped down his elbow, fell from the point to splatter on the ground. The grip of the gun was slippery with it. Another drop rolled down Adler's neck.

One movement. One that cost so little, in the end. There was one bullet in the chamber. There was one bullet between Adler's eyes. Here and there. Dead and alive. Pull, click, bang.

Magic bullet.

Pull the trigger.

Adler's chest rose and fell, measuring out a countdown of breaths. Which one was best to be the last? The bullet would spray blood and brain matter across the shelves. Adler would be dead before Rainy could catch his body. And he *would* catch it, he realized.

He would catch him as he fell.

Do what you have to do.

Adler was a handsome stranger, leaning against the bar while he made Rainy's drink. He was asleep against Rainy's shoulder, limp and helpless, face slack and peaceful.

Everything around Rainy was still, but he had never felt anything further from peace.

Behind his eyes was a deep black sea where everything went to drown.

His head was an empty gray apartment, where nothing grew and nobody had lived for years and years.

His hand trembled. The barrel of the gun wavered and bobbed against Adler's skin.

Do it.

Adler's eyes flew open so suddenly that Rainy almost pulled the trigger from sheer surprise. His dark eyes found Rainy's like a compass point to true north, round and shiny with shock. His mouth dropped open, but no sound came out.

What? Rainy almost asked, and then he noticed a bloom of color out of the corner of his eye and let his gaze drift down.

On Adler's stomach, below his ribs and just left of center, the fabric of his shirt and vest bowed out a little. A pinprick of blood soaked through and, like a dam bursting, it began to spread, a soaking dark oil spill of red.

The pressure below the fabric disappeared, and there was another soft, wet sound and the grind of metal on bone. Adler made an involuntary noise.

Julian stepped back, coming into Rainy's view in the narrow space of the aisle. His Bowie knife was slicked red. Blood ran down the handle of it and onto his hand, wrapping around his wrist in happy red tendrils.

"Try giving me orders now, you piece of shit," he said.

When Adler crumpled like wet paper, Rainy caught him. They landed on the ground hard enough to bruise his kneecaps and the Colt bounced off somewhere, forgotten.

"Shit, fuck," he said, scrabbling at Adler's clothes, hands slippery with blood. There were two distinct dark patches on Adler's back, spreading fast. Rainy pressed his hands down, and blood ran up between his fingers and over his knuckles. First, lower, intestines. Blood blooming on the front of Adler's shirt. Second, higher, between the ribs. Kidney. Liver. Bad, bad, bad.

"*Fuck.*"

Adler's fingers were tangled in his shirt tightly, like he was drowning and trying to use Rainy to pull himself from the quicksand. His eyes were still wide. Rainy pressed harder against the wounds, ignoring the way Adler groaned and tried to shift away. The blood was coming too fast, spreading, soaking. *Aorta*, Rainy thought in a panic. *Vena cava. Blade scraping bone.*

Julian wasn't blocking the light anymore. There were voices, murmuring, tense arguing. Rainy didn't think they were speaking a language he understood. Adler's face filled his whole vision, and the rest was white noise.

There were lines of pain carved deep around his eyes. The sharp light of terror in them was dulling too fast, turning sleepy.

"No, no, no," Rainy insisted. He shoved his hair back out of his eyes, felt the smear of blood his hand left there wet and hot on his skin. A drop rolled down his brow and collected on his lashes. He pressed down harder. Stop the bleeding. That was it, stop the life from draining out of Adler's limpening body. But Rainy's hands were made for the opposite, for tearing and breaking. He didn't know how to fix things. He didn't know how to fix this. Panic was a wild beast inside him, shredding its way up through the soft meat of his organs with frantic claws, trying to wrestle its way out of his mouth.

Adler felt fragile in his arms, slim and getting slimmer, like he was dwindling before Rainy's eyes. There wasn't enough of him left to hold on to. His eyelids were drooping.

"Hey, fucker," Rainy snapped. "Don't fall asleep on me. Talk to me. Tell me how stupid I am. Tell me how much you hate me."

Adler shook his head. His eyes fell closed. Rainy shook him.

"Talk to me, Adler."

"What were you gonna study?" Adler murmured.

"What?"

"You said you were going to college." His eyes were a little un-focused, like he was staring through Rainy's head at the ceiling beyond. "What were you gonna study?"

Rainy's fingers were cramping, they were locked so tight. "Psy-chology," he admitted. "I wanted to study psychology."

"Hm." A half smile tugged at Adler's mouth, and the ghost of a dimple appeared.

"What about you?" Rainy asked. He needed to keep him awake, keep him talking.

Adler snorted. "I was never gonna make it to college."

"If you had. Anything you want."

Adler fell silent for a long moment, and Rainy was about to shake him awake when he realized that he was just seriously considering the question.

"I always liked math," he said finally. Rainy couldn't help the laugh that burst out of him.

"Of course you fucking did."

A pair of shoes appeared at the edge of Rainy's vision, but he didn't care. Couldn't. Adler's eyes were drifting closed again.

"Why'd you like math?"

Adler did smile this time. It had a delirious, dull edge to it. "I liked knowing the rules. Harder to get in trouble when you understand the rules."

Rainy's hands had gone nerveless. He wasn't pressing down on the bleeding anymore, or trying to elevate. He was just holding, now.

I've almost died on concrete floors more times than I can count, Adler had said. Rainy felt like he was choking on the unfairness of it, the wrongness, that it should end like this. Bleeding out for nothing on another concrete floor.

Adler was shivering. Rainy held him tighter. He wrapped his arms around his shoulders, cradled his head, stroked a hand through his hair.

"I'm not going anywhere," he whispered. "I promise. I'm not going anywhere. I'm so sorry."

Adler made a tiny gesture, and it took a moment for Rainy to realize that he was beckoning him close. He leaned in, using his chest to shield them from the rest of the world. Adler's lips pressed against the ruined shell of his ear.

"Don't ever apologize, Mister Rainy. It don't look good on you."

Before he could reply, Adler's head slipped down into the crook of his neck. His breath was hot and shallow, and damp like a kiss just under Rainy's jaw.

The shoes moved closer, attached to a pair of legs now, insistent for his attention. Rainy looked up dully and found Emilio standing in the aisle. Across from him, holding his gaze, was Hyun-woo Seong. Rainy didn't think to wonder where he'd come from. In the central space, the fighting had stopped. The men were spaced and slumped, weary and warily watching Seong watch the blood spreading across Adler's back and down Rainy's arms. He turned his eyes silently back up to Emilio.

He called something in Korean, short and sharp. Every gun in the room held by one of Seong's men was out and trained on an Espinosa man in half a heartbeat. The three nearest to the aisle all pointed their weapons at Emilio's chest. The Espinosas jumped into motion, fixing their own guns, and the room became a statue garden bristling with weapons.

What we have here is a good old-fashioned Mexican standoff, Rainy thought, and an inappropriate giggle bubbled in his chest. He dug his fingers tighter into Adler's arms.

"You should not have done that," Seong told Emilio. "I would have been satisfied with victory. Now, I will take blood."

Emilio's jaw ticked, but he didn't humor the guns pointed at him with a glance. Instead, he looked down to where Rainy knelt by his feet, still wrapped around Adler's limp form. Their eyes met. Rainy felt sick, sick and infinitely tired. Emilio's gaze was dark, and heavy with a weight that felt all too much like that old, familiar disappointment.

"I don't think you want to do this," Emilio told Seong. "Element of surprise out of the way, you're outnumbered. If you back down now, the only further thing you lose tonight is the loot."

Seong's face was pale—with rage or with fear, Rainy couldn't discern. He didn't particularly care, anymore.

"You misunderstand," Seong said. "I will burn this warehouse to the ground with all the merchandise inside just to make sure you are among the ashes. The *loot* is nothing. There is no scenario in which you walk out of here unruined."

They sized each other up for a long, long moment, while the room held its breath. Rainy prepared himself to curl over Adler's body to protect him from gunfire. Emilio's eyebrows were low as he searched Seong's face for the bluff, but he didn't seem to find it.

"I have an alternate proposition," Emilio said finally, without dropping Seong's gaze. "Felix?"

"Yes?" Felix asked, from where he was in a triangular standoff with the two nearest Koreans.

"Call Nasrin," Emilio ordered evenly.

Felix wavered. "I don't think she—"

"Call Nasrin."

Felix paused another moment before reluctantly lowering his gun and stepping away to pull out his phone.

"My daughter-in-law is the best trauma surgeon in the city," Emilio told Seong. "There are no better hands, if you want your man to survive the night."

Rainy's heart jerked painfully against his ribs. It felt dangerously like that feathered thing. He squeezed Adler, feeling his waning, shallow breathing and the threadiness of his heartbeat, echoing Rainy's own.

Seong considered Emilio for another eternity. Finally, he nodded.

"Lower your weapons," he called to his men. "We're finished here."

Chapter 17

Florida Man Has Breakdown, Redecorates

I n the end, two Espinosas had to drag Rainy off of Adler so they could hurry him off to meet Nasrin. He tried to fight them off half-deliriously as Adler was pulled from his arms.

"No," he insisted. *Who's going to hold him? Someone has to hold him.*

"Rainy," someone said in his ear. It was Eduardo, holding his shoulders. "Rainy, easy."

They don't know that someone needs to hold him.

"It's okay."

Adler disappeared, fragile and pale. Rainy was left standing in the aisle, his hands shaking. He only registered that other people were moving around him when Seong spoke again, still looking at Emilio.

"You have my attention, Mr. Espinosa. Now, let us hear the rest of this proposition."

"If there's a chance for him to live," Emilio said, "my daughter-in-law will take it. You have my word."

"And how much is your word worth?" Seong asked stiffly. His men had put away their guns, but two of them still pulled in close to him, shooting threatening glares.

"You turned on me first," Emilio pointed out.

"Only because it was obvious that you would betray my trust. I am a prudent man."

Emilio shrugged, half-apologetic. "So am I. You know the business. Can't trust or be trusted."

"I have found," Seong said, "that the only man who can be trusted in this world is the one who can be trusted to do what you suspect he will, not what you wish him to. I suppose that makes us both trustworthy men."

Emilio paused for a moment, considering. Then he tipped his head back and boomed out a laugh.

"I suppose it does," he said. "Since we are both trustworthy men, here is my proposition: either we can keep fighting to the last man, as you've made it clear you're willing to do—or we lay down our arms and each walk out with something. As per our original agreement."

"Mm." Seong's mouth curled into a thin smile. "I have also found that the only way contracts are carried out as written is if both sides test the limits and lose. I suppose we have found ourselves in such a situation."

Emilio held out one of his large, scarred hands, stretched like half a bridge across the void of the warehouse aisle.

"We call a truce and split the pot."

Seong shook his hand. Rainy felt tension he hadn't realized he was holding flow out, and he slumped against the shelves.

"I think," said Emilio, "that this may be the start of a long and profitable business partnership, Mr. Seong."

Seong sized him up. "It might seem that way," he said, voice going cool again. "But only if he lives."

Then he turned his unguarded back on Emilio and walked off to bark orders at his men.

Emilio directed Felix to scramble the men. The commotion would draw cops sooner or later, and they wanted to get the crux of their business done first. Rainy was just wondering whether he was meant to follow Felix when Emilio turned to him. Rainy froze. They were alone in the dim aisle. Emilio walked over to him with measured steps and held something out.

It was Rainy's Colt, retrieved from where he'd dropped it to catch Adler as he fell.

"Looks like your luck hasn't run out just yet, Rainy boy," Emilio said. "If you're still a praying man, you might want to fold those hands and start kissing ass."

Rainy looked numbly down at the proffered handle of the gun, shimmery with pearl. He reached out to take it. Before he could, Emilio flipped it up so his finger was on the trigger and the muzzle was pressed right into Rainy's stomach through his blood-soaked shirt.

He leaned in so his mouth was just next to Rainy's ear and said, quietly:

"The next time I see your trigger hand shake like that, I'll make sure you never work in this state again." Rainy felt Emilio's jovial smile like a tap against his jaw. "And if you ever let your dick get in the way of my business again, I'll cut it off myself. Understood?"

He pulled the gun away from Rainy's abdomen and released it so it dangled from his finger again, handle up.

"We can discuss how you'll make it up to me later. I don't take broken promises lightly."

Obediently, Rainy took the gun. Emilio left him there in the aisle staring at it. He ran a finger down the stock, scratched with a nail at the etched initials on the bottom. RP.

He stood there until he managed to get control over the shake in his hands, then tucked the gun away and walked out into the tumult of men and crates. Eduardo waved him over with a roll of bandages. Rainy was confused until he looked down and remembered the dozen vicious slashes up and down the backs of his forearms. The pain rolled back in with the knowledge. Blood was still oozing from the cuts, but nothing urgent enough to require immediate stitches. He allowed himself to be hastily wrapped up before joining the loading process.

Normally, after a fight, he felt electrified. Now, he was only hollow. He walked and carried and supervised where he was told like a windup toy. Somehow, he blinked and found himself with a crate in his hands, carrying it to a truck. When he handed it up, there were bright red handprints smeared over the lid.

One trip, two trips, four. On the way back to the main warehouse, he split off from the group and stood in the center of the gravel shipyard, breathing in the night.

Overhead, the tentative clouds had slunk away, leaving the stars glaring down unusually bright and cold. Their light prickled like needles sinking below his skin. Their gaze felt invasive and prying, unwelcome. Rainy stared back, unseeing.

His hands squeezed and released at his sides. The fingers were stiff and cramped from being clenched too hard in Adler's clothes. Drying blood across his knuckles cracked and flaked.

The voices of the men were distant. Silence gathered in the clearing like a crowd of onlookers.

Rainy caught a glimpse of his own face in the flat glass surface of a puddle. There was a broad smear of red across his forehead, left from a swipe of his hand through his bangs. His hairline and right eyebrow were gummy and crusted with blood. It flaked off his eyelashes.

A metal claw closed around his ribs, squeezing and sinking in through the slots and piercing his lungs. He yanked the hem of his shirt up to frantically scrub at his face. The blood smeared and flaked. He scrubbed until his skin burned and his eyes watered. When he dropped his hand, his face was new.

Gravel crunched and pinged against metal. Rainy's head snapped up.

"Sorry, bro," Julian said. "Didn't see you there."

He leveled an easy smile at Rainy, the well-greased rapport of years of friendship. Rainy didn't return it.

His arms were red to the elbows. The blood only stained Julian's knuckles. His hands were nearly clean.

Julian read the tension in his expression, and the smile slipped.

"Do we have a problem, man?"

Rainy clenched his fist at his side until his sore knuckles creaked. He felt still inside, but this was beyond the usual adrenaline-readiness of a fight. This was what he imagined a lion crouching in the grass felt. The stillness of a predator in which nature had never bred doubt.

This was how he imagined Adler felt all the time. The thought was like... well, a knife between the ribs.

"Come on, Rainy, are you for real?" Julian folded his arms and leaned against a nearby shipping container. "You didn't want the guys to see you faltering, did you? I was doing you a favor."

Rainy looked down at his bloody trigger hand, remembering the shake in it.

"Yeah," he said. "I know you were." Then he crossed the narrow strip of gravel and punched Julian in the face.

"*Fuck* you!" Julian shouted. There was a smear of red on his cheek now from Rainy's bloody fist. He tried to swing back, but Rainy deflected easily and hit him again.

Julian had always been clever with a knife, but he'd never been much of a brawler. His defenses crumbled like the siege walls of a sandcastle under Rainy's hands. Rainy slammed him back against the shipping container, smashed his fist into his face over and over until he felt bone crunch and his knuckles were wet with fresh blood.

"I'm sorry," Julian gasped, mouth thick from a broken nose. "I'm sorry, I didn't—"

Rainy didn't want to hear it. He couldn't. He grabbed a fistful of Julian and threw him down onto the gravel.

"I'm sorry," Julian gasped again. All Rainy could see was Adler's blood, the way he'd crumpled. All he could feel was the ghost of breath against his ear. He drew back and kicked Julian in the stomach, hard. Again. Again. He remembered bringing his heel down on Adler's ribs and hearing the crack. He paused.

Julian was curled on his side in the gravel, retching and bloody. Rainy felt wild; unmoored, unmade, like the atoms of him were breaking apart and all the meaningful pieces of him were sliding and shifting. He crouched and hauled Julian closer by the front of his jacket.

"Either I kill him, or nobody does," he said. "He's mine. Got it?"

Julian's face contorted, and Rainy didn't want to hear a reply. Instead, he slammed him down into the gravel, then raised him up and did it again, and again, and again, and—

Hands were hooked through his elbows, pulling him off, dragging him back. Rainy fought them, vision red.

"Rainy," Marco said in his ear.

Julian was trying to scrabble away, pressing back against the shipping container. Rainy started to throw Marco off and go after him.

"*Rainy*," Marco murmured again, close enough for only him to hear. "He's okay. He's in surgery, but Nasrin says he's stable. He's going to be okay."

The fight ran out through his feet and into the gravel like he'd sprung a leak. He slumped back, and Marco loosened his grip.

Julian pushed himself up against the wall and glared as Marco pulled Rainy to his feet.

"Get him away from me."

"Shut the fuck up, Julian," Marco said. "Don't pick fights if you're going to be a little bitch about it." Then he fished in his pocket and emerged with the fallen oyster knife, its blade haphazardly cleaned of Rainy's blood.

"I think this is yours," he said, and tossed it. Julian had to dodge to avoid the blade.

Marco turned Rainy by the shoulders and guided him out of the shipyard.

"Fuckin' hate that guy," he said cheerfully, making a show of dusting off his palms. "Now, where's your car?"

"Why?"

"I'm driving you home. Come on, there's nothing left for you to contribute tonight."

Rainy allowed himself to be led out of the complex of warehouses in the direction of the garage a few blocks away where he'd stowed his car. The inside of his head felt empty and sticky, like something syrupy had filled him up and then been poured out.

"You are my friend," he told Marco. "Sometimes, you're even a good one."

Marco laughed. "Selfish reasons; don't worry. After seeing what you did to Julian for stabbing the guy, I'm just trying to keep your mind off my little water torture incident."

A whip-thin Espinosa kid Rainy didn't recognize ran up to them, mop of brown hair flopping comically. Emilio must have really called out everyone to break everything down in time.

"The cops are here," the kid told Marco. "Eduardo sent me to tell you. They're keeping them occupied at the south end."

"Did he tell you which district?" Marco asked.

"Uh, yeah. Central."

Marco's face broke into a slow beam that Rainy had come to know and dread. "Central, you say?"

Sometimes, Rainy thought Marco was like one of those pull-string toys; something would give a little tug on his chain, and suddenly he would be bouncing from foot to foot and moving his hands at a mile a minute. He was transparently raring to race off in search of his beloved Sergeant Tessa, the rest of the world forgotten. Then his eyes landed back on Rainy, and he winced.

"Tell Eduardo..." he hedged.

Rainy rolled his eyes. "Go. I'll be fine."

"Yes! Thank you, Rainy!" Marco grabbed Rainy's head in both hands and planted a smacking kiss on his cheek. Then he sprinted off, spraying gravel.

"Um," the kid said awkwardly.

"Go make sure he doesn't get shot," Rainy sighed. The boy's eyes widened and he gave chase.

The walk back to his car was quiet. This part of town was empty this time of night, and he didn't pass a soul. It felt like striding through a city post-Rapture. Everyone else had gone and left Rainy behind in his own little personal perdition.

There was a tiny metronome in the back of his brain. Every few moments, it ticked, and an image of the light fading from Adler's eyes flashed through his mind.

He was okay. That was what Marco had said. He was in surgery, but he was going to live.

He was going to live.

That small, silly hope gave a tiny flutter of its wings.

When Rainy got to the garage, he crawled into the back seat of his car to get at the fresh clothes in his emergency duffel. Each piece of clothing he peeled off felt like a piece of plate armor removed after battle. Everything was stiff and dark and half-damp with blood. The enclosed space reeked of copper and brine. The pain in his arms crested and ebbed like the sea.

Back in the front seat, he flicked on the headlights and pulled out of the garage. The ticking of the metronome in his head was getting louder and faster, like gravity was running in reverse. It filled up and reverberated through the empty space in his skull, until it was all he could hear.

He made another turn onto a dead and empty city block. He cursed and pulled the car over.

He couldn't hear himself thinking over the noise. He just wanted quiet. He just wanted it to stop.

He slammed his fist into the dash. The plastic groaned. Rainy felt immediately repentant. His faithful car hadn't done anything to deserve it; he didn't want to hit it. He scrambled to find who the urge was directed at, who he *did* want to hit. But he didn't want to hit anyone. He was so fucking tired of violence.

He was so tired of bloody knuckles and black eyes. He was so tired of breaking things in ways that could never be fixed. But there was nothing else he knew how to be. There was nothing else out there for him. He'd forgotten how to be a person.

He'd forgotten how to want to be one.

Once upon a time, Rainy had known how to pray. He'd measured out the words carefully in the tiny room he and Miguel had shared, his little hands clasped in his lap and his eyes screwed shut to keep out any interference with his direct connection to God. And then, one day, that room that could barely contain two burly teenage boys felt massive with only one left. Rainy hadn't forgotten. Miguel had taken all the prayers with him. He'd grabbed one silken end and run until the last of it slipped through Rainy's fingers and he was left totally empty.

"You did this," he said to the gray predawn silence.

Once upon a time, he might have been talking to his brother's soul, up there in the ether. Once upon a time, he might have prayed. But Rainy wasn't Catholic anymore. The only thing listening was the sound of his own voice reflected back off the windshield.

"You dragged me down with you, Miguel." His voice cracked. "You dragged me down with you."

The ticking was still there, but he recognized it now. Because it was always there. It was the reason behind all the running, the late nights and flashy clothes and different beds and the hiding and the lying and the metamorphosing. It was the sound he heard whenever he was left sitting alone with himself.

It was an echo. The click of a pebble dropped a long time ago. The sound bounced off the tracery and ribbed vaults and flying buttresses, a hundred million tiny facets of masonry and stained glass. It bounced and reflected and doubled over itself infinitely in the flawless echo chamber of a perfectly empty cathedral.

It was the sound of total emptiness.

Rainy was tired of running from it. He sat and listened.

He stayed parked haphazardly in a fire lane as the sun rose over the city, tentatively and then all at once. When the world was light, he turned over the ignition and put his hands on the wheel, and discovered he didn't know where he was going.

He wanted to go home, he realized.

Not to his empty, lifeless apartment. Not to his parents' house.

For the first time in a long time, he wanted to go home to a place that *was* home.

But that place didn't exist. It hadn't for nine years. He didn't know what that place would look like for him now. He didn't even know where to start.

He didn't know where he was going. He just started driving.

He ended up at a hardware store.

Rainy stared at the door until the open sign flicked on, then rested his forehead against the steering wheel and laughed.

When he got back to his apartment, the sun had fully risen. It illuminated his living room where he'd left the curtains open. Rainy closed his eyes and felt it warm his face before setting down with a thud the approximately one hundred pounds of hardware store merchandise he was carrying.

The girl at the paint counter, irritated at having a customer so early, had grown even more annoyed when he hadn't been able to tell her what color paint he wanted.

"What's your favorite color?" she'd asked, exasperated.

"I have absolutely no idea," Rainy had realized aloud. "Just give me one of each."

So that was how he'd ended up with seven gallons of paint in wildly different colors. Rainy didn't know anything about paint, but that was probably enough for four rooms, right?

He planted his hands on his hips and surveyed the main area of his apartment. The dove-gray walls blended into the gray vinyl plank floor blended into the stiff, uncomfortable couch. There wasn't even a floor lamp in the living room; Rainy wasn't sure he even knew where all the outlets were. The longest he'd ever actually stayed consecutively within these walls was a three-day period a few years ago when he'd been knocked out by the flu.

Taking in the empty space felt absurdly like staring up at the peak of a mountain he was meant to climb. With no gear, in flip-flops.

"This is stupid," he said, and stayed frozen to the floor.

Eventually, he made himself cross to the kitchen and tug open the drawer where he tossed all the accumulated crap that other people might have displayed on tables or shelves. He buried his arm in to the elbow and dug around.

His fingertips found a cool, crimped ceramic edge. He drew out the small bowl his mother had given him two weeks ago.

Nine-year-old Rafael stared out at him from the bottom of it. Miguel beamed in the sunshine.

Rainy walked over to the front door, where there was a little alcove between the wall and a support beam.

"This is stupid," he repeated to the empty room.

He stared at the bowl in his hand. Two brothers stared back, innocent and forever the best of friends. The empty alcove loomed. Rainy's hand was shaking violently, the way it had when he'd held the gun to Adler's forehead.

Slowly, almost fumbling it, he placed the bowl inside the alcove.

The walls didn't come crashing in. The water didn't come rushing into his lungs.

He dug a hand into his pocket and fished out his keys, then placed them in the bowl.

"Oh," he said.

Then, something did come rushing in. Not violent, but steady and inexorable like the tide. Rainy was bowled over by it. He needed... he needed...

He snatched up a brush and a can of paint without checking the label and marched over to the nearest vast expanse of blank wall. Cracking open the can, dunking the brush in. No time for a drop cloth. He slashed the brush across the wall, but not the way he would slash a knife. This, for once, didn't feel like breaking.

The paint was purple. It broke through the gray-white like the first hint of spring through snow. Like a field of violets rising from the forest floor. Rainy brought the brush down again and again. His shoulders were shaking, and he realized that he was crying.

Crying, and laughing, and smiling so wide his cheeks ached.

The gray disappeared, slowly and then all at once, like the rising of the sun.

That was the feeling, he realized.

Peace.

It felt like peace.

Chapter 18

Florida Man Romances Stabbing Victim

"Goodbye, security deposit," Malia said the moment Rainy got tired of her pounding and finally opened the door to let her into his apartment.

She stared with wide eyes at the living room and kitchen, where every wall had been painted a different vibrant color. The room was packed with mismatched furniture he'd grabbed at flea markets and antique stores; anything he'd found interesting or hadn't wanted to leave there alone and unwanted. The counter was stacked with secondhand books. There were holes drilled in the ceiling where he'd decided he wanted to install a new light fixture.

"My God," she said. "You know, before, your apartment screamed sociopath. And now, somehow you've managed to go so far in the other direction that you ran right back into sociopath territory."

"Already regretting letting you in."

"Too late." She dropped onto his new couch, which was upholstered in an incredibly loud floral pattern and was deliciously comfortable. "You really did all of this in, what, two and a half weeks?"

Rainy shrugged. Over the several years that he'd owned the place, he'd never wanted to spend more than a night there. In the interval since the disaster down at the docks, he'd ordered in for every meal and only left to go shopping.

"Okay," Malia said, "ignoring your obvious and mildly concerning manic episode—I bring tidings."

She flashed her phone screen, where a news article was pulled up. The headline informed him that the sale of Andy Parish's Miami properties to Hyun-woo Seong had been finalized that morning, and Parish was leaving the city for Louisiana indefinitely.

"Marco says his dad's in a very, very good mood," she told him.

Rainy grimaced. "We'll see."

In the intervening time, Emilio had sent him a message that made it clear in no uncertain terms that Rainy would be his cut-rate errand boy for the foreseeable future if he wanted to get back into the good graces of his main source of revenue.

"Did he deposit my cut of the liquidation yet?"

Malia nodded. "I'll funnel it to you tomorrow."

"Good. All this stuff was expensive as fuck."

He could use the money from the successful Seong-Espinosa venture, especially now that he wouldn't be getting the payout for delivering Adler's head.

Malia was toying with the flared hem of her pant leg where it was crossed over her lap.

"Did you come all the way here just to show me the front page of the *Herald*?" he asked.

She scowled. "No, you big lug. I came to say I'm sorry."

"Wow, come again? The wise and mighty Malia—"

"Don't push your luck." She jabbed a finger at him. "I'm not sorry for what I said. I meant all of it. But I'm sorry it drove a wedge between us."

Rainy grabbed a bag of chips off the counter and dropped into an overstuffed armchair nearby. He crunched a chip loudly. She took this as an invitation to continue.

"I'm going to graduate in the spring, and I am going to get out of this line of work. I'm not taking that back, and I mean it. But as much as I might not want this life, you're still my friend. I'm sorry I've been a crappy one."

"You haven't been. You were right," he admitted. "I was miserable. I—I am miserable, maybe. But I'm not going to hide from it anymore. I can't keep living like that."

He tilted back in his chair, let the legs drop back down with a heavy thud. "Did I ever tell you what happened to my mentor, Rezakova? She was before your time."

Malia shook her head.

"She was the best there ever was. Stone-cold scariest bitch you'd ever meet in your life. Taught me everything I know. And then, when I was just a year or two older than you are now, it all finally caught up to her. She disappeared one night and ended up chopped up into bits scattered all around the city dumpsters. They identified a finger they found in the landfill."

Malia was starting to look a little queasy.

"You know what she always told me, right up to the day before she died?" Rainy stared up at the ceiling, which he'd painted a pale blue like the summer sky. "She always said that the only way out of this business is through the grave. Maybe she was right. Maybe even if you could get out, the stain would never leave you. Maybe they'd find a way to drag you back in."

"I have to try," Malia said.

"I know you do. And when the time comes, I'm going to help you. However I can."

He lowered his gaze to find Malia smiling at him, soft but firm. He smiled back. Old wounds were forgotten. In the new light of his apartment, things felt fresh and possible.

If anyone could get out of this life scot-free, it was brilliant, iron-willed Malia.

"You really are acting super different," she said, then drummed her nails on the arm of the couch. "Does it, by chance, have anything to do with the total fucking freak-out Marco said you had down at the docks?"

Rainy winced. "The rumor mill's gotten hold of that one, hasn't it?" It never failed to amaze him how much career criminals loved their gossip.

"Oh, yeah. Everyone thinks you lost your marbles, and you haven't really shown up to dissuade them in the past two weeks. Marco says Julian's managed to turn his buddies against you."

The comment blew in a few clouds to darken his sunny mood. He'd have to go back soon, and when he did, he'd have to deal with being in Emilio's bad graces and the ruins of whatever friendship remained between him and Julian. The thought made him want to hole up in his apartment forever.

Malia eyed him. "Have you, ah, made any visits to the hospital?"

"Really?"

Malia shrugged. "Don't play dumb. I wasn't there, but I have reliable sources. I'm told there was tearful clutching."

"How much has Marco been running his mouth about this?"

"So much. He's convinced that you and Adler are going to have a double wedding with him and Sergeant Tessa."

Rainy scowled. "For the last time: there is nothing going on between us. We fucked a few times. That's it."

"God, I didn't need to know that. But let's be real, Rainy. I've never seen you as obsessed with another human being as you have been the past month. You *like* him."

Unbidden, the image of Adler outlined against the dawn, offering him that small, secret smile, flashed through Rainy's mind. He felt a warm squeeze in his chest, the same one he'd felt when Marco forwarded him a text from Nasrin two and a half weeks ago, letting them know that Adler was out of surgery and expected to make a full recovery.

"Okay," he admitted, "I like him. But don't go full Marco on me, okay? That doesn't mean I'm in love with him, and it definitely doesn't mean we're going to date."

"But it does mean you want to visit him at the hospital."

God, Rainy was starting to remember why he *hadn't* missed her. "I don't think Seong would be too pleased to see his recent ex-enemy's favorite hitman show up at the sickbed of his right-hand man."

"Oh my God," Malia laughed, "you're being a total pussy about this, aren't you?"

"That is a misogynistic expression, young lady."

"Pussy."

"For your information, I've been busy. Going to see Adler when I already know he's fine hasn't exactly been at the top of my list because, again, we're not fucking dating."

"So it won't be a big thing if you just pop over to Mount Sinai to see him."

"UHealth," Rainy corrected offhand, and then scowled.

"Right. Hasn't been on your mind at all."

Rainy flicked a chip at her.

"You're such a little shit. This is why Marco's my favorite."

"No, he's not."

"God, no."

Malia crossed her arms and legs at the same time as though in a choreographed dance. "Clearly, you're being a baby about this, so I'm going to stay and bother you until you agree to stop being an idiot and just go talk to him."

"Oh, really?" Rainy smirked. "Then I guess you'll have to hear all the nasty details of how he and I fucked in the multipurpose room at work."

"*Ew*, you did not!"

"Oh, yeah. I faced him toward the mirror and put him in my lap and—"

"Ew, God, Jesus, okay, I'm going." Malia threw her hands up in defeat and then clapped them over her ears as she made a beeline for the door.

"And at Parish's house," he called at her retreating back, "he ate me out so hard—"

"I hate you so fucking much," she said, and closed the door behind her.

In the ensuing quiet, Rainy returned to his chips in peace. He stared at all his new furniture and crunched thoughtfully.

"I'm not going to the fucking hospital," he said, and got up to get ready to go to the hospital.

He was definitely not nervous to see Adler again after what had transpired at the docks. That definitely wasn't why he changed his shirt three times before leaving and even dug out some styling mousse to stall for another few minutes by fiddling with his hair. When he arrived at the hospital, he circled for twenty minutes until a parking spot near the front opened up. He was finally driven out of the car and through the front doors by the fact that the sun was almost setting, and visiting hours would probably be over soon.

He felt weird and shaky, like someone had hit a pressure point. The thought of seeing Adler again was thrilling and nerve-wracking and fizzling in a way that made him feel like he needed to slam the lid down on it before it bubbled over.

The lobby reminded him a bit of an airport, with its gray-flecked linoleum floors and long check-in counter. Rainy sidled up to the front desk, sucking hard on a grape-flavored lollipop to mask his nerves.

Apparently, it didn't work, because the woman behind the desk immediately gave him a sympathetic smile.

"Here to see someone?" she asked. She was wearing scrubs printed with a half-familiar cartoon character that gave Rainy a brief flash of childhood nostalgia. He felt a pathetic urge to let her wrap him up in her big, soft arms.

"Yeah. Um, yes." He cleared his throat and took out his lollipop, rolling the stick between his fingers. "Nathaniel Adler?"

She clacked away at her keyboard. "Can I ask your relationship, honey?"

Rainy paused. "Friend."

"All right, friend it is. Real sweet of you to come and visit, especially at the end of the workday." She clicked her mouse, then frowned. "Looks like your friend's being released. His bill's been settled, and he's being checked out now. He'll probably be through here in a moment or two, if you want to have a seat and wait."

"Oh," Rainy said dumbly. "Oh, okay." He retreated from the counter and stuck his lollipop compulsively back into his mouth.

Adler was leaving the hospital. It made sense, after over two weeks. Adler was leaving the hospital right *now*. Probably not by himself. God, why had he let Malia talk him into this? It was a terrible idea.

He was just about to try and make a covert exit when a pair of men turned the corner into the lobby. Rainy clocked Seong first, looking incongruous in a charcoal pinstripe suit with a small duffel slung over his shoulder and a paper pharmacy bag crinkled in one hand.

It took him significantly longer to recognize that the man walking next to him in worn jeans and a crewneck sweater was, in fact, Adler.

Rainy froze like a deer faced suddenly with a mountain lion, standing in the middle of the lobby with one damning foot angled toward the door and the other toward the front desk. They halted and stared at him. Adler's eyebrows inched up toward his hairline. Seong just wrinkled his nose, muttered something, and peeled off toward the counter. Rainy had never wanted to melt into the floor more than he did at that moment.

He was too dumbfounded and embarrassed to reconsider the option of running until Adler was already right in front of him.

Rainy had refused, on the drive over, to rehearse what he was going to say. That had just felt pathetic. Now he was deeply regretting it, because when he opened his mouth, the first thing that fell out was:

"You're not wearing a suit."

"I'm not working," Adler said, and gave him that familiar look that said that Rainy was the dumbest motherfucker to ever live, and Rainy felt like a weight was lifted off his chest.

"You, uh, look good, considering," he said lamely.

It was true enough, but it didn't mean Adler didn't still look like crap. His casual clothing hung off him at starvation angles, and his cheekbones stood out in the pale, gaunt cast of his face. There were dark smudges under his eyes, and his usual sharp air was more queasy and subdued. Instead of predatory, his movements were tentative and unambitious. His hair was greasy. He had a five-o'clock shadow. Rainy wanted to kiss him.

Suddenly, it wasn't enough to hold on to the text from Marco, to see Adler here in front of him. Rainy needed to reach out and touch him, feel the smooth completeness of his skin and the warmth of his pulse. He hadn't realized how sick he'd felt, stuck on the image of Adler going limp in his arms, the tactile memory of his blood, hot and sticky, with nothing to replace it.

"I thought I'd drop by," he explained when Adler didn't bother replying. "Check up on you."

"Right. Here I am."

"Here you are," Rainy agreed, and it came out on a puff of relief that startled even him. Adler's face changed at that, softening slightly, but Seong was already back on top of them.

"You're all cleared to go," he told Adler. Then he gave Rainy an unimpressed once-over and shot Adler a look that transparently said, *Really? This one?* "I'm afraid we don't have time to stay and chat. Leo's waiting with the car. I'll call to postpone my dinner another thirty minutes, so—"

"I could drive you home," Rainy blurted, because maybe he really was the dumbest motherfucker to ever live. When Seong and Adler just stared at him, he blundered on, "I came all this way. And I'm headed uptown anyway." Which wasn't true, but Adler shrugged.

"Why not? Then nobody needs to move their schedule around."

Seong deadpanned his displeasure. "Nat, you know I've learned not to underestimate you, but you're not exactly at full capacity right now. Do I need to remind you who this man is?"

"You planning on killing me tonight?" Adler asked Rainy.

"No."

"Great. Then it's settled." Adler took the duffel and bag of drugs from Seong and dumped them unceremoniously into Rainy's arms. Rainy had to fumble to keep from dropping them.

"Nat," Seong protested.

"I'll be fine," Adler assured him. "Thank you."

Seong frowned, but squeezed Adler's shoulder and nodded. He gave Rainy a dirty look on his way past that threatened the full force of retribution an angry and legally dubious multimillionaire could bring to bear. Then he pulled out his cell and started a call as he ducked out of the lobby.

With his hands occupied with Adler's stuff, Rainy had no defenses when Adler reached out and stole the lollipop from his mouth. He stuck it between his own teeth with a pleased groan that felt very inappropriate for a hospital waiting room. Rainy raised a questioning brow.

"Doctor says I got to quit smoking again," Adler explained. Then he gave another satisfied suck and, well, Rainy couldn't complain.

He deposited Adler's things in the back seat of his car, politely ignoring the grunt of pain that came from the front when Adler settled into the passenger's side. Dusk was beginning to fall as he climbed in and started the car.

"Do we need to make any stops?"

Adler shook his head. "I assume you remember where I live?"

Rainy smiled ruefully. "I remember."

When he pushed up his sleeves to start driving, he felt Adler's eyes snag on the maroon latticework of scabs down the back of his forearm. The cuts were healing cleanly, but not prettily.

"It's nothing," Rainy said, to counter the apology he could see forming on the tip of Adler's tongue.

As they inched along in traffic, he began to regret more and more not planning some kind of speech. The silence between them was heavy and brittle, full of unspoken things. Even though neither of them had said a word yet, it felt like the aftermath of an argument. That moment on the warehouse floor, where Rainy had held Adler as he died, had said too much, revealed things that couldn't be reeled back in. They swelled the atmospheric pressure of the car until Rainy's temples throbbed.

"So," he said finally, unable to sit in silence any longer. "You and Seong seem... close."

"Mm."

"I have to admit, I didn't really get it before. I mean, I understand loyalty—"

"Do you?"

"—but seven years is a long time to stick around out of loyalty to your boss." Rainy glanced at Adler. "There's something else there. I mean, he must have done something to earn that."

Adler stared straight ahead out the windshield. The city's first flickers of nighttime neon reflected off the surface of his eyes. "He took me in when you could count all my ribs, when my face made children cry and I needed all the lights on just to sleep, and all he asked in return was that I be loyal and good at my job."

Rainy wondered, sadly, if that was the most kindness anyone had ever shown him.

They lapsed back into silence for a while as Rainy struggled to think of a neutral direction to steer the conversation in. After five minutes of dead air, Adler flicked on the radio, wrinkled his nose at Rainy's presets, and immediately started flipping through stations.

"Uh, excuse me? Hands off my car."

Adler ignored him. He found a country station and settled back, looking pleased. Rainy stared at him, horrified.

"Oh my God."

"Eyes on the road."

"What is this?"

"Music," Adler said, offended.

"Is it?"

Instead of replying, Adler turned up the volume and pointedly started humming along.

"Wow. Remember the ketchup and hot sauce? This is *my* ketchup and hot sauce."

Adler just flipped him off and slapped his hand away whenever he attempted to change the station.

As they drew further uptown, a knot of anxiety began to grow in Rainy's stomach that Adler would just ask to be dropped off before Rainy got up the courage to say... whatever it was he was going to say. His fears were alleviated when they reached Adler's street and Adler directed him to a covered off-street parking spot. He gathered Adler's things from the back seat and followed him inside.

Adler only lived on the second floor, but by the time they got to the top of the stairs, he was winded and a little queasy-looking again. Rainy debated whether stepping in to offer him an arm to lean on would result in a black eye or vomit on his shoes or both. In the end, Adler caught his breath on his own and opened the door.

They were immediately rushed by two low, furry shapes. The dogs. Rainy had forgotten about the dogs. They were both German shepherds, one very creaky with a white muzzle and the other bobbling happily along with one leg strapped up in a complicated silver brace.

Adler crouched, wincing, to ruffle their ears and accept disgusting, sloppy dog kisses all over his face.

"This is Dolly," he told Rainy, indicating the older dog, "and this is Martina."

"Pleased to meet you," Rainy told them as they snuffled curiously around his pants.

When Adler instructed them to go, both dogs obediently trotted off to lie down. Rainy paused before following him into the apartment. This was what he'd wanted in the car. It wasn't like he hadn't stepped into a hundred strangers' apartments—whether to fuck them or to kill them. And yet, this felt more intimate than any of those times. Rainy shook himself off and stepped over the threshold before Adler could question him.

It was pretty much what he'd envisioned when he'd tried to imagine a place Adler might live—modern and scrupulously neat. Black leather couch, stainless steel appliances. In the corner was a large potted ficus that was pretentiously healthy. The dogs watched Rainy from a pair of plush beds that took up a questionable amount of the living room.

Rainy trailed Adler into the kitchen, where he set the pharmacy bag down on the counter and started rifling through it while Adler clattered about.

"They hooked you up with the good stuff." Rainy shook a little orange bottle of oxy at him. "On a scale of one to ten, you want some?"

Adler shook his head. "I'll wait."

His tone was brusque and businesslike as ever, but he was moving gingerly. Rainy ached just watching him.

"I'm gonna take a shower," Adler said. He opened a drawer and took out a roll of plastic wrap. "It's been weeks of sponge baths and shitty hospital bathrooms, and if I don't get under hot water in the next five minutes, I'm gonna break something."

Rainy wavered at the counter, unsure of his place. That wasn't exactly a demand for him to leave, but it wasn't an invitation for him to stay, either. He shuffled from foot to foot. This was worse than when he'd been thirteen and walking a date home for the very first time, agonizing over whether to kiss her at the door.

"Should I order a pizza?" he hedged, trying to gauge Adler's reaction out of the corner of his eye.

"No solid foods yet," Adler lamented. "Apparently, Su-jin left some soup in the fridge, though, if you wanna heat some up."

Rainy very smoothly and casually avoided fist-pumping in victory and set the opioids down to focus on his new task. Before he could make it to the fridge, though, he was distracted by Adler's grunt of pain. He'd tried to pull his sweatshirt off and gotten stuck.

"Here." Rainy carefully removed each of Adler's arms from the sleeves and lifted the sweater over his head. Adler's expression when the fabric moved out of the way reminded him of Patoso, utterly indignant at receiving any kind of assistance. Rainy was distracted from mocking him, though, when he looked down.

Under the sweatshirt, Adler's chest was bare. There was a small white surgical dressing pad stuck on his stomach, just above his navel. Rainy must have made an involuntary sound, because Adler's expression softened and he allowed himself to be turned. His back was taped up more, two white dressings secured over careful sutures. Rainy's hand hovered over the skin, hesitant to touch. When he finally laid his palm on Adler's side, careful to avoid the damage, the puff of breath he let out ruffled the hair at the nape of Adler's neck.

"You're okay." He hadn't fully believed it until this moment, until he could feel the warmth of Adler's skin, his tiny shiver as Rainy ghosted a thumb up and down his ribs.

"I'm okay," Adler confirmed.

Neither of them moved for a long moment. Rainy's hand stayed heavy on Adler's side, soaking up the warmth and the small movements and rhythms of a living body. He watched Adler's shoulders rise and fall with his breath, felt his ribs expand. There were words welling up inexorably from somewhere in Rainy's chest, filling his throat and pressing against the back of his teeth.

Adler handed him the roll of plastic wrap. "Waterproof me?"

Together, they got his abdomen cocooned in several layers of plastic wrap. Adler padded off, and Rainy lingered in the kitchen.

"You know," he called, "I almost feel bad. Here I am, left alone to snoop through your stuff, while you haven't even been in my apartment. Sort of a power imbalance."

"What makes you think I've never been in your apartment?" Adler called from the bathroom.

"What does that mean?"

The door closed.

"Adler, what does that mean?"

The only answer was the sound of the shower turning on. Rainy shook his head and turned to the fridge.

There was a large pot of delicious-smelling soup, which he placed on the stove and set to heating. When he closed the fridge, he noticed that there were a few pieces of paper stuck to the door with magnets. The clumsy, colored-pencil drawings of small children, labeled in lopsided Hangul. On one, a wobbly English hand had written *For Uncle Nat*.

Rainy poked his head out of the kitchen. The shower was still running, and he could hear the slap of water on skin and tile. In the living room, the two dogs watched him with cocked heads, but didn't move from their beds.

Rainy went snooping.

One wall of the living room was lined with books that, when approached, turned out to mostly be those crappy spy thrillers they sold in airport convenience stores. There were a few thicker, older tomes of classic Russian literature sprinkled throughout. Rainy pulled one out and flipped it open. On the inside cover, there was a short inscription scrawled in permanent marker. Rainy was pretty sure it was in Russian, but the bold clumsiness definitely signaled a man's handwriting. He felt a spike of jealousy toward an imagined sexy Russian mafia ex who gifted Adler volumes of Dostoevsky, then promptly realized how stupid and pathetic that was and retreated to the bedroom.

Adler had a king-sized bed with a very tasteful, boring comforter and a plush blanket spread over the foot that was covered in dog hair. Rainy was startled by the click of nails on wood, but it was just the dogs following him from the living room. They leaped up and settled on the blanket, and Rainy stepped back, uneasy. But they just lay there watching him with curiously tilted heads, so he felt safe to resume his invasion of their master's privacy.

There were condoms and a loaded Glock in the nightstand. The closet was full of suits hanging in crisp garment bags. The dresser was full of T-shirts and jeans. Rainy found a false back in the wardrobe, behind which there were several semi-autos, a large collection of knives, and the case that contained Adler's sniper rifle. Rainy was about to close the door again when he noticed something glinting on a hook in the gloom. He lifted off the chain and stepped backward for better light.

The dog tags clicked together in the cup of his palm. They were black, with rubberized edges to stop them from clinking too loudly. Rainy smoothed a thumb over one, feeling the shallow indentations in the metal.

ADLER
NATHANIEL T., JR.
9354176954
A POS
BAPTIST

In the bathroom, the shower turned off. Rainy hastily returned the tags to their hook and fled the bedroom for the kitchen, where the soup was just starting to bubble. The dogs followed him and lay back down in the living room.

He'd located some bowls and was ladling out soup when Adler emerged in a cloud of steam. He was wearing an old T-shirt and sweats, and his hair was wet and curling around his ears. He'd shaven. His feet were bare, for Christ's sake.

"You're staring," he observed.

"Yeah," Rainy said.

Adler wordlessly accepted a bowl of soup and perched on a stool to dig in. Thank God; he looked like he'd lost fifteen pounds in the hospital. Rainy observed him over his own bowl.

In well-worn sweats and bare feet, Adler looked like a totally different person. Warm, soft, touchable. Frighteningly human. Even his scar seemed different, a more natural part of his face. But even in this new and unfamiliar form, Rainy could still see the hallmarks of *his* Adler. The impeccable posture, the defensive set to his shoulders. The way he watched Rainy closely without actually looking at him, and the slight smug curve of his mouth that meant he knew Rainy was watching him back.

It felt comically obvious now that the Adler whom Rainy had considered his, and the put-together professional one he'd been jealous of at the meeting, and the one here in this apartment weren't separate people. There had been no reason to be jealous in the first place, because all of those things had always been his Adler. They all fit together, even if he didn't yet understand all the joints and seams.

Wandering his apartment had been a stark reminder that, as vivid and tangled as this thing between them had grown, Adler was still something of a stranger to him. Rainy knew how he fought and how he fucked, what his nightmares were about and what he asked for when he was about to die. And yet, he'd learned more actual details about Adler's life in the past hour than he had in the entire time they'd known each other before today.

A *positive blood*, he thought. *Baptist.*

Rainy wanted to learn the rest. The thought sat warm and secret, tucked safely behind a rib.

"I think I could use a drink," he admitted.

"That's just cruel. I'm not allowed to drink right now."

"Sad as it may be for you at first, if you get me liquored up, I might let you do all kinds of dirty things to me."

Adler smirked and stirred his soup. "Sounds like a good time. You sloppy drunk and me with my guts full of stitches."

To Rainy's surprise, he stood and crossed to the wooden hutch cabinet that was lined with neatly organized bottles of liquor. He pulled down a shaker.

"What's your poison?"

"Please, God, anything but absinthe."

Adler laughed that full, rusty laugh. He filled the shaker with ice and started pouring liquor, hands moving with that professional carelessness Rainy had clocked in the bar on that night that felt like a lifetime ago. In a minute flat, Rainy had a tumbler of hazy, dark-gold liquid sitting on the counter in front of him. Adler batted his hand away when he tried to reach for it.

"Not yet."

He dug in the fridge and came out with a jar of cherries. He dropped one into Rainy's glass, then tossed a second in a high arc and caught it in his mouth.

Rainy felt a flash of fondness like a kick in the chest. It punched the breath right out of him.

"What?" Adler asked, catching his expression.

"I was just thinking that I really tried my damnedest not to, but I still can't help but like you."

Adler's smile, for once, wasn't mean-spirited at all. It crept onto his face shyly and then all at once, like he'd tried to catch it but it had slipped his grasp. The dimples made him look younger.

"Try your drink, Mister Rainy."

"You're not trying to payback-roofie me, are you?"

"I guess we'll see."

Rainy took a sip and raised his eyebrows. "This is delicious. What is this?"

"Amaretto sour with bourbon."

"All right, I'll bite. How did you learn to make drinks like that? There's nobody who's that dedicated to a con."

Adler settled back on his stool. "I used to work as a bartender on the side when I was a kid. It's still a useful cover, on occasion."

Rainy jotted this down on his mental list of facts about Adler. It had doubled in length this night alone. Rainy was starting to think he might want it to go on forever.

Thank God for Malia, he thought, and finished his drink.

Chapter 19

Florida Man Yet Again Drugs, Robs Date

When Rainy was nearly finished with his soup and Adler was still picking at his full bowl, Adler's phone rang and he stepped away to answer it.

"Had to assure Seong that I'm still alive," he explained upon returning. "He don't think much of you, by the way."

"He should. I gave up a shitload of money by not killing you."

"Sad. I didn't kill you and still got paid. Perils of going freelance, I guess."

"I hate you."

Adler smirked. "No, you don't."

No, I *don't*, Rainy thought.

"So," he said. "Seong and Espinosa are working together now, at least tentatively. I think that means we need to renegotiate. Extend the terms of our truce."

"Does it now?"

"Sure. If we're going to be stuck working together on occasion, we might as well be friends."

Adler let out that sharp, familiar rifle crack of laughter. "You wanna be friends."

"With the most generous package of benefits."

"There it is." Adler rolled his eyes and started to shift away, but Rainy caught his arm. He turned it over and traced his finger up the blue stripe of vein from the delicate skin of Adler's wrist to the IV bruise on the inside crease of his elbow.

"It would just be cruel to make me watch you prance around in your slutty little outfits without the knowledge that I can drag you into the nearest broom closet and take you out of them once you finish barking orders at everyone," Rainy said.

Adler extricated his arm carefully. "What makes you think I'd even be interested now that it's not breaking the rules anymore?"

Rainy faltered. In the past two weeks, he'd turned this thing between them over and over in his head a million different ways, but it had never occurred to him that, without the adrenaline rush of violence, Adler might be done with him. Now, it seemed... painfully obvious. The humiliating part was that he had never hesitated. The taboo thrill had been removed entirely, and Rainy had barely noticed. He was still as attracted to Adler as he had been the first moment he laid eyes on him.

He looked down to where Adler's hand rested in his lap, removed from Rainy's grip. Just the possibility of reaching out and reclaiming it was—not thrilling. Grounding. Steadying. It was the sense of calm he'd felt at the docks, kissing Adler despite the danger hanging over their heads. The first breath of peace, the delicate feather-tickle of hope. *Let me keep it*, he thought.

"Then I'd just keep trying to win you over," he said. "I can be very persuasive."

"So I recall. Maybe if I'm bored or drunk enough, it'll even work."

And then Adler made that expression that said he'd just won a game nobody else knew they'd been playing, and Rainy thought, *Thank God*, because until that moment, he hadn't realized how afraid he'd been that he'd never see it again.

"I can work with either of those," he said. "Just name a time and place, sweethea—"

He cut off with a wheeze when Adler drove an elbow into his stomach.

"What did I tell you about calling me that?"

Rainy smiled at him. Not a flirty grin, not a smirk—just a plain, sunny smile, because at the moment it felt hard to do anything but.

"Worth it," he said.

Adler blinked at him, a surprised flush coloring his ears. His mouth fell open a fraction, then he snapped it closed and his eyes fell to his bowl. Rainy ducked his head to try to catch his gaze, and beamed at what he found there.

"You like me," he accused.

"Are you for real right now?" Adler was frowning, but there was a dimple at the corner of his mouth.

"I'm onto you." Rainy poked an interrogative finger at him. "Anyone else, you would have killed as soon as you got a clear shot. At the bar, on the roof, at the Rattrap. But you kept letting me go. Because you're *smitten* with me."

"Oh, fuck off. I just like to play with my food before I eat it."

"Oh, no, you think I'm *charming*."

"Ha."

"Adorable, then," Rainy conceded.

"Delusional is what you are."

"Deny it all you want, but you can't fool me." Rainy shook his head, something finally sliding into place. "Here I was, puzzling over what kind of weird mind games you were playing, having sex with me in a wine cellar instead of just killing me—and that's all it was, wasn't it? You just *liked* me."

Adler was properly flushed now, whether from embarrassment or irritation Rainy couldn't tell. "Your ego is truly astounding."

"Just admit it. What was it? The pickup line? The pet name? My raw sexual magnetism alone?"

"I just figured I'd get it out of the way. I'm a practical man," Adler said, reaching up to press his thumb against the corner of Rainy's smile, "and that includes knowing my weaknesses. You are special, though. I've never met anyone else I was so equally attracted to and desperate to punch."

Rainy laughed and held out a hand. "So, then, what do you say? Indefinite truce?"

Adler tipped his head and considered the proffered hand like the bones of Rainy's fingers might hold hidden knives. Finally, he reached out and took it.

"Truce until further notice," he conceded.

"I promise you won't regret it."

Adler's mouth tightened. "Don't do that."

"Do what?"

His gaze had gone so rapidly distant that Rainy felt like something precious had been pulled from his hands. The wear and tear of the past few weeks was painfully obvious again in the pallor of Adler's skin and the hollows under his eyes.

"You know this business ain't one you can make promises in. You can't promise we won't be at war again in a week. You can't promise that in a month, you won't be trying to kill me again. You know we can't... keep them. So don't."

His face had taken on that strange quality Rainy recognized from their predawn heart-to-heart—the angles of his characteristic grimness softened, pensive and a little sad. It made something squeeze and flutter uncomfortably in Rainy's chest. It was vulnerability. It was terrifying. Rainy wanted to pull a curtain shut around them to hide that look on Adler's face from the rest of the world.

Where the frown lines on his face softened, youth collected and pooled. Rainy ached to reach up with a thumb and smooth it all away. He wondered again what it would have been like if they'd met in a different life, one where they didn't lead the lives they did. Maybe he would have asked Adler out on a date, and Adler would've said yes. Maybe they would've fallen in love, gotten married, adopted two kids and lived in the suburbs.

But then they would've been different people, wouldn't they?

Hesitantly, Rainy took Adler's hand in both of his. He looked down, traced over the scars and freckles on his knuckles. He imagined them smooth and unblemished, but found the image didn't suit.

"You're right," he said. "I can't make many promises. And maybe it's sad that this might be all we could ever have, but there is one promise I can be certain of, if you'll promise the same to me."

Adler half met his eyes, cautious. Rainy swallowed.

"No matter what happens, who does it or how, even if I'm the one who kills you, I won't let you go alone. No matter what, on the day you die, I'll be there to hold you."

"That's not a small promise," Adler murmured.

"No."

Adler looked down at where Rainy's hands covered his. His lashes brushed the freckles on his cheekbones, and his hair was drying soft and wavy around his ears, and he was so lovely it hurt to look at him.

"If I ask you a question, will you answer it honestly?" he asked.

Nerves fluttered in Rainy's stomach. "Okay."

"If your Espinosa friend hadn't cut in, would you have done it?"

Rainy didn't need to ask what he meant. He could still feel the grip of the Colt in his hand, warm and slippery with blood. He could still see the tip of it pressed between Adler's eyes, wavering slightly back and forth.

Like a metronome.

"No," he whispered. "No, I don't think so."

Adler looked up at him, eyes dark enough to curl up and sleep in. "That's the wrong answer."

"I know," Rainy said, and kissed him.

Adler sank into it. His lips were chapped but warm, and the hair at the nape of his neck was downy-soft under Rainy's fingers. When he tried to push forward, Rainy kept it slow and languid. For once, there was no rush.

They made out pressed up against the kitchen counter until Rainy grabbed Adler by the waist and lifted him up onto it. He huffed with pain, but Rainy was already mouthing soothing kisses down the side of his neck. He sucked on the pulse point under Adler's jaw and reveled in the feeling of him, close and warm and smelling of lemon soap and aftershave, with no ultimatum hanging over their heads.

"I was so glad when Marco told me you were okay," he admitted into the secret space behind Adler's ear. "Nobody drives me crazy like you do."

"Mm."

"With your stupid giraffe neck and your smart mouth and—"

He cut off with a yelp when Adler pinched him on the ass, hard. Adler laughed at him, sharp and cruel, and Rainy's clothes were suddenly chafing and dragging everywhere. He curled his fingers into the waist of Adler's sweatpants and tugged them down. Adler frowned at him, affronted.

"That's disgusting. This is a kitchen; I prepare food here. Didn't your parents teach you manners?"

"Didn't the army teach you to shut up?" Rainy countered, and took Adler in hand. He was already flushed and hard, and his skin slid so smoothly under Rainy's palm. Adler tilted his head back with a groan, already dripping precome.

Rainy laughed. "Two weeks with no conjugal visits allowed?"

"That's prison, not the hospital, idiot."

"Mm, am I hearing a little prison roleplay? What are you in for? No, let me guess—tax evasion?"

"I hate you so—"

Adler cut off with a hiss when Rainy bent down and sucked him into his mouth.

It had been a while since he'd given a blowjob, so he let himself play around with it. He stroked his tongue up and down the shaft, slid down slowly until the blunt head nudged his throat. Adler was long, and trying to take him in all the way made Rainy's eyes water.

It was worth it when Adler's hand came down to play with his hair, petting his bangs back. When his fingers found the stiffness of styling mousse, he paused.

"Got all dolled up to see me, huh?"

He gave a throaty chuckle, affectionate and condescending, and Rainy's dick jumped in his pants. It was all he could do not to grind his hips against the cabinet for friction. He started to bob his head more eagerly, sucking Adler in deeper until his eyes were stinging and he could swallow around the tip. With each stroke, Adler rewarded him by absently trailing his fingers through his hair, teasing out the product until it was a mess.

He kept going until his throat felt raw and Adler was panting, his lip caught between his teeth and his head tipped up to the ceiling. Rainy pulled off a particularly masterful swirl of his tongue and saw the muscles in Adler's stomach tense up.

Adler grunted in pain. "Fuck. Damn."

"Relax," Rainy murmured into the crease of his hip. He ran a soothing hand up Adler's shirt. "Just sit back and relax, and I'll take care of you."

He ducked his head back down and kept going until Adler's thighs were trembling under his hands and it became impossible to ignore his own desperate need for friction, for heat and movement and release. He pulled off with a wet slurp and found Adler already looking down at him with a strangely soft expression. His hand came down to cradle Rainy's jaw, a calloused thumb swiping a drop of spit from his bottom lip.

"Should we move this to the bedroom?" Rainy asked.

Adler wrinkled his nose, rueful. "I don't think you can fuck me tonight. My insides aren't feeling particularly hospitable at the moment."

"That's not what I had in mind." Rainy looked up through his lashes, the way he had when seducing Parish. But this time, it felt right. "I've been thinking about Parish's."

"Oh?"

"When he was inside me, all I could think about was you."

"I know." Adler's voice was hoarse and dangerous.

"So, here's my proposal: I take you to bed, and you lie back and relax while I ride you, and then I load you up with oxycodone and rub your shoulders until you fall asleep. How's that sound?"

Not breaking eye contact, Adler slid off the counter. Without bothering to pull his pants up, he led Rainy out of the kitchen and down the hall.

The dogs followed in a clatter of claws on hardwood. They leaped up onto the bed and settled on the blanket, until Adler ordered, "Privacy," and they both somberly retreated to the living room.

Adler sat on the bed and kicked off his sweatpants, but left his shirt on over the bandages. Rainy floundered out of his own shirt and fumbled at the zipper of his jeans until his dick was free of its denim prison and he groaned in relief. Adler reached for him, but Rainy swatted him away.

"Bedrest. Doctor's orders."

Adler glared at him but laid flat on the bed. Rainy crawled onto the duvet and submitted himself to Adler's curious hands. They slid up the ridges of his abs to trace over his tattoos, coming to rest lightly on the patch of violets over his heart. The pressure sent a throb through the still-healing knife scar there, a line of pink new skin that cut through the flowers. Adler's fingers were gentle now. Rainy tried to hide the stutter in his breath.

"Like what you see?" he asked.

"Eh. I've seen better."

Before Rainy could protest, Adler slid his hands down to his ass and squeezed, earning a stutter of his hips.

Rainy fumbled for the nightstand, pushing aside the Glock to find a condom and lube. Adler raised his eyebrows.

"Snooping, were we?"

"Shut up." Rainy struggled with the cap of the bottle until Adler took it from him and slicked up his own fingers.

"Scoot up," he ordered, and Rainy obediently shuffled forward until his knees were on either side of Adler's chest.

"Brace your hands on the headboard."

"Fuck, okay, yeah." Rainy tipped forward until his fingers were splayed on the cool, dark-lacquered oak, his elbows locked and triceps straining. Adler's breath was hot on the inside of Rainy's thigh. His tongue traced over the tattoo there, and Rainy shuddered.

Adler didn't waste any time pushing one slippery finger up into him. Rainy hissed, a full-body clench rolling through him until he forced himself to relax. Adler worked him gently with that one finger, stroking until he was sighing and pushing back into it. He'd forgotten how good it felt to be the one filled up and fucked, letting himself surrender.

Adler added another finger, starting to stretch him open. Lazy flares of lust popped low in Rainy's abdomen, little landslides that shook loose stones and tugged like gravity. Long fingers curled inside him, calloused pads finding his prostate and pressing in, rubbing hard. The first twitches of pleasure morphed into a spasm of it, a quake that grabbed Rainy by the hips and yanked him down into warmth and heat. He dropped his head down to rest on his shaking arms. Adler pressed another wet kiss against the tattoo on the inside of his thigh while his fingers kept working him.

Finally, Adler let his fingers slide out. Rainy felt himself clench around the loss. The slick of the lube felt cold in the empty air, tingling against the burning hot of his muscle. He pushed off the headboard and scrambled backward. In his haste, he jostled Adler's bandaged stomach, earning a grunt of pain.

"Sorry, sorry." Rainy hunted for the condom among the dunes of the rumpled duvet and ripped it open. He didn't have the patience to be gentle as he rolled it onto Adler. "God, okay, are you ready?"

He positioned his hips, braced up on his knees, and lined them up. A burst of nerves flared in his stomach when the head of Adler's cock nudged his entrance, but he swallowed hard and sank down.

Adler's clever fingers had done their job, and he took it more easily than he'd expected, feeling himself stretch pleasantly as he lowered himself down. In fact, he took it a little too easily. Adler wasn't particularly thick, and with the added weight of his hands on Rainy's hips, he slid in fast. Rainy's thighs were bent at an awkward angle, so he couldn't slow himself as he slid all the way down until their hips were flush, letting out a startled gasp.

They were in the center of the bed, which meant there was nothing for him to hold on to except the sheets. He fisted his hands in them until his knuckles went white. What Adler lacked in girth, he made up for in length, and the pressure pushed so far inside so suddenly that Rainy was overwhelmed. He'd never been filled and stretched so *deep* before. It made him whine, the pleasure lapping up over his head and threatening to pull him under. He tried to focus on Adler's thumbs rubbing soothing circles into his hip bones.

When he could marshal control of his limbs again, he flexed his thighs to rise up and sink back down, and groaned at the pure sensation of slide and push inside him. Adler's eyes were locked on his, hazy and liquid. He bit down on his lip when Rainy moved his hips again, and that was all the encouragement Rainy needed to start gliding up and down in earnest. He watched every thrust play out on Adler's face, each roll of his hips, and then he had to pause a moment because little spasms of sensation kept making him clench down and feel how tight they fit, how deep and slick, and he was going to come right now if he went too fast.

He found his rhythm, alternately riding hard and then languid. One hand stayed on Adler's sternum to remind him not to clench his abs again and hurt himself. Rainy didn't make it easy on him, though. He worked his hips until Adler was panting, until he brought a hand up to lace with Rainy's, squeezing so tight that the small bones of Rainy's hand popped.

Rainy thought of the dog tags hanging in the wardrobe and grinned.

"You like that, Sergeant?" he asked. "You going to teach me how to follow orders?"

Adler rolled his eyes, which Rainy found rather impressive considering how hard Rainy was riding him. "You're doing it wrong."

Rainy scoffed. "I'm doing it *wrong*?"

"Yes, you're doing it wrong." Adler's voice shifted, turning deeper and more authoritative. "Slow down. Take it deeper."

Despite his irritation, Rainy found himself obeying, sinking down further until his stomach muscles jumped and a bead of sweat rolled between his shoulder blades.

"Good. Now, what do you say?"

"What? Yes?"

"Yes, *what*?"

"Yes, sir," Rainy bit out, annoyed.

"Good. But I want it slower."

Rainy slowed the rocking of his hips. Adler raised an eyebrow and slapped him on the ass, hard.

"Yes, sir," Rainy hissed. He was definitely not going to be turned on by this. He refused to be.

Adler made a lazy, approving noise that went straight to Rainy's dick. He tilted his chin down, shamelessly watching where he slipped up into Rainy.

"Speed up," he ordered.

Rainy ratcheted his hips and hissed, "Yes, sir," and, fuck, he was turned on by it. His own neglected cock was throbbing now, precome beading at the tip, begging for friction. He ground down harder onto Adler, chasing the sharp tug of pleasure in his belly. "Fuck, God."

"Did I give you permission to speak freely?"

"No, sir," Rainy gasped. He was moving at a frantic pace now, plunging himself down with abandon, eyes screwed shut. He reached for himself, desperate for sensation.

"Hands off," Adler's voice told him sharply.

"Yes, sir," Rainy whined.

There was a vibration under his thighs and against his palm where it was pressed to Adler's sternum. When he opened his eyes, foggy with arousal, he found that Adler was laughing at him.

"*That's* how it's done," Adler said.

Rainy's intense, tingling high was washed away in indignance. He swatted Adler on his still-clothed chest, drawing out a wince.

"Why do you have to be like this? You're the worst fucking person I've ever met."

Adler just batted his lashes. "I'm the worst fucking person you ever met, *sir.*"

Okay, fine. Two could play at that game. Rainy set his jaw and moved his hips in a new rhythm. Adler's lips parted involuntarily at the motion.

He reached for Rainy's hips again, but Rainy grabbed his wrists and pinned them to the bed at his sides. Adler struggled, but they didn't budge as Rainy kept working him, chasing each new rhythm based on the way it made Adler gasp and squeeze his eyes shut. He kept at it mercilessly until Adler's nose scrunched in an expression endearingly reminiscent of his thinking face, and Rainy leaned in to kiss him and ordered him to come, and he did, gasping into Rainy's mouth while he pulsed deep inside him in a way Rainy would be feeling for hours.

As his orgasm faded, Adler went loose and syrupy, brown hair rumpled on the bedspread and body lax, and Rainy desperately, desperately needed to come. He reached down and started stroking himself, thrusting back onto Adler's cock before it could start to soften. He was right on the edge; it would only take a second to get himself off.

Adler's hand closed around his wrist and pulled it away. Rainy whimpered in frustration.

"Don't think I don't know what you're doing," Adler said. "I just took my first real shower in weeks. I am *not* letting you come all over me."

He grabbed Rainy by the hips and dragged him forward. Rainy protested as Adler slipped out of him, but he was appeased quickly when he was pulled up the bed until his knees framed Adler's shoulders and his cock was buried in Adler's mouth.

He braced his hands back on the headboard and fought the animal instinct to thrust into Adler's throat as hard as he could. His mouth was so wet and hot and talented, just like it had been that night in the wine cellar, and the only thing missing was the way Rainy's body was now clenching down around the empty space inside him. Then Adler's fingers came up, slipped in and filled him and went straight for his prostate. The pleasure hit Rainy like a punch in the gut and he came with a shuddering gasp.

Instead of releasing, the white-hot wave of it seemed to crest and crest as Adler's fingers kept working him through his orgasm, until Rainy was a shaking mess with his sweaty cheek pressed against the cool wood of the headboard, whimpering nonsense. Finally, the sensation settled evenly like fallen snow, and Adler let him go.

Rainy sprawled out on the sheets next to him, everything feeling melty and liquid. His bones and muscles had given way to warm honey. He lay there and let everything slowly swirl back into place, listening to the sound of Adler's breath in the close air of the bedroom.

When he got his arms under control again, he propped one under his head to look at Adler, whose chin was tipped back. The tendons in his neck made strong lines from the soft crook of his jaw to his scarred collarbone, and his Adam's apple stood out sharply.

"On a scale of one to ten," Rainy started.

"Give me the fucking drugs."

Laughing, Rainy tapped out two tablets from the bottle on the nightstand and passed them to Adler, who swallowed them dry. He dropped his head back onto the pillow with a grunt.

"I believe I promised you a shoulder rub."

"Hmm." Adler closed his eyes and wrinkled his nose.

Rainy laughed again, then hesitated a split second before leaning in to kiss him.

"I'll be right back." He hopped out of bed, wobbling a little as his legs deliberated over whether to support him.

In the bathroom, he found a washcloth and cleaned himself up. He sucked in a breath as the textured fabric dragged over his sensitive, swollen skin. Gleaming eyes regarded him from the living room, where Dolly and Martina reclined on their beds. Rainy grabbed a fresh washcloth and shuffled back toward the bedroom.

"I think your dogs might be perverts," he said, ducking inside.

Adler was already asleep, limp as a rag doll on his back among the rumpled sheets. His head was tipped away from the light, mouth hanging slightly open and a bead of drool gathering at the corner of his lip.

"Jesus Christ," Rainy said. "Why couldn't you have knocked out this fast the first time I drugged you?"

He wiped Adler clean with the washcloth and manhandled him into his pants. Adler only snorted and twitched a little in his sleep. Gently, Rainy tugged his T-shirt down to cover his stomach and shook out the sheets and duvet, pulling them up to his neck.

He settled on the edge of the bed, admiring his work. He'd always thought Adler's face looked softer in sleep, but here, in an old T-shirt and familiar, homey sheets, the effect was magnified. He looked so soft you could almost love him.

Rainy's earlier thought had been wrong; Adler didn't look younger this way, not exactly. He didn't look like the picture of his younger self Rainy had seen, at least. Instead, it was that he looked gentled, softened by kindness. At peace.

Rainy wondered if, one day, he'd see that look on Adler's face when they were both awake.

With a careful thumb, he swiped away the drool that was about to fall down Adler's cheek. *I watched over you while you were sleeping*, he thought. It brought a sense of déjà vu so strong it made him reach up to touch his damaged ear just to make sure he hadn't dreamed it all. The skin had healed back completely, smoothing the ragged edge of missing cartilage.

He was glad, he realized, that it was there. He was glad that there was a physical marker of the change in him since he and Adler had met, the way his magnetic poles had flipped. A mark on the outside to prove what had happened on the inside. An empty space where Adler had taken a bite out of him.

Adler twitched in his sleep, wrinkled his nose, and muttered. Rainy smoothed his hair back from his forehead.

"Goodnight, sweetheart," he said.

He wasn't really sure what the etiquette here was, but he didn't think he should pump the man full of opioids and then leave him unmonitored. Also, he wasn't in any particular hurry to clear out. He went to the living room and selected a random thriller from the shelf, then returned to bed with his prize. The dogs followed him and jumped up onto their blanket, and Rainy let them stay because he couldn't really see any reason not to. He turned off all the lights except a floor lamp near the bed and settled in.

The book was, as expected, nothing special. But it kept him occupied as he sat propped against the pillows next to Adler, occasionally glancing over to watch him twitch and mumble in his sleep. By the time the alarm clock read one, Rainy was almost finished with the book. Next to him, Adler shuddered in his sleep and made a low noise. Rainy looked over, amused, only to find that Adler's face was pinched, his chin jerking. His eyelashes were damp.

"Adler, hey."

Adler's leg darted out and struck him in the shin. The contact seemed to alarm him, and he started to roll away. Rainy dropped the book and leaned over to stop him, grasping him by both shoulders.

"Adler."

He stirred, relaxing under Rainy's hands and staring up at him, half-comprehending. His eyes were still glassy with the pain meds, pupils dilated.

"You were having a nightmare," Rainy told him. "You're okay."

He sat back. Adler just blinked up at him, still looking confused. There was a pillow mark on his face. His eyes came to rest on the book in Rainy's lap.

"Just wanted to keep an eye on you," Rainy said, feeling awkward. "I can head out soon, if..."

"Stay," Adler murmured, already falling back asleep. Except a heavy dose of painkillers and several layers of unconsciousness had turned his accent near-incomprehensibly molasses-thick, so it came out more as *Shhttyyyy.*

Rainy set his book aside and turned off the lamp. He sank beneath the covers into the soft and dark made warm by their shared body heat. The mattress was memory foam and the pillows were that awesome self-cooling kind. He wouldn't have pegged Adler as someone willing to splurge on comfort, but maybe spending a few months in a dank Syrian jail cell made you more invested in good sleeping arrangements.

The minutes stretched. Each slow blink gathered the cottony dark in closer. When he was certain Adler was asleep, Rainy slipped his hand into the space between them and linked their fingers together.

He woke at five in the morning to the violent beeping of the alarm clock. Cursing, he threw an elbow over his eyes, but Adler just grumbled and rolled over, so he sat up and turned it off, then figured he might as well get up.

Fifteen minutes later, he was in love. He was in love with Adler's coffee maker. It was shiny chrome and had all kinds of fancy settings and probably cost a million dollars. It made the most delicious coffee Rainy had ever had. He could have sworn there was a hint of cinnamon in it. It was so good that he made himself a second cup, and then a third for the road in a swiped travel mug.

The dogs were sitting by the door staring at him expectantly, so he shrugged and found a leash. He took them downstairs one at a time to do their business. When they came back inside, they went straight to a neatly organized mat near the kitchen with bowls and a tall canister of food, so Rainy gave them each a scoop and called it good. This pet ownership thing wasn't so hard.

Once that was accomplished, he lingered in the kitchen. Adler was still dead to the world and probably would be for some time. Rainy wasn't sure if he should leave a note or something. It was in that moment that he realized that he didn't have Adler's phone number. The thought was oddly jarring. He knew so little about Adler that he might as well have been a stranger, and, at the same time, he felt like he knew him better than he'd known anyone in years. He leaned against the counter, thoughtful.

Helping himself to the kitchen before dipping out was pretty typical fare for him after a one-night stand. Except it didn't feel the same. Rainy was looking around this near-stranger's apartment with the deep, comfortable certainty that he would be back. He would figure out a way to get back, even if he had to stand outside Adler's window and throw pebbles.

The other unusual thing was that, this time, he was actually looking forward to going home. Before Malia had shown up yesterday, he'd bought an enormous haul of cat stuff from the pet store, and he was planning on spending the morning assembling the cat tree and then trying to lure Patoso inside for good.

He was looking forward to the day so much that he was whistling.

In the fridge, he found a carton of eggs and whipped up a scramble. He doused it in sriracha, because that was the only hot sauce Adler appeared to own, and covered it with an upside-down plate to keep it warm. Then he hunted down a pen and pad of sticky notes and stood poised over the island, considering what to write.

He found himself glancing consideringly at the coffee maker.

Twenty minutes later, he was in his car, working his way through pre-rush traffic. He had a message from Emilio on his phone, with a target's name and a simple directive. *Time to start proving to me that you can still keep a promise.* Rainy forwarded it to Malia, along with the assurance that he'd be back to work tomorrow.

The next message was from his mother. He called back as he drove, but she didn't pick up.

"Hey," he said after the voicemail tone. "Sorry it's been a while. I'm ready to talk about Thanksgiving now, though."

He tipped his head back, feeling the warm breeze through his hair, and let out a breath.

"See, I was thinking, why stay in Miami at all? Why don't I buy us all tickets to go somewhere for the weekend? Anywhere in the world you want to go; it's my treat. Anyway, ah, call me back later. Love you."

When he reached home, he ascended the stairs with his newest household acquisition cradled in his arms. Inside his apartment, which was so full of things that he nearly tripped on his way through the door, he nudged aside a stack of books and a standing mixer on the kitchen counter to make space for his new coffee maker.

It fit like a dream. He started to brew himself a celebratory cup.

In the now-empty spot on Adler's counter, he'd left a note which read:

Now we're even on the tires. Eggs not poisoned. Promise.

And then, after a telling space:

See you around.

In the bottom corner, he'd left his phone number.

Sipping his cinnamon-flavored coffee from a colorful homemade mug he'd found at a flea market, he crossed to the alcove by the door. In it, his mother's bowl still stood, its treasured picture at the bottom. Miguel was half-covered by Rainy's keys. Little Rafa beamed out into the future. Rainy wondered if it was possible to track with perfect accuracy the exact hour and minute and second he'd lost that. But the crack in his chest when he looked down at the photograph wasn't only despair.

It felt a little bit like hope.

It certainly wouldn't be today, or probably anytime soon. But one day, in the not-too-distant future, maybe Rainy would be ready to be Rafael again.

The feeling in his chest was still unfamiliar, but he was getting used to it. Rearranging himself around the weight of it. A fledgling hope, a tentative peace.

The stillness he felt when Adler was in his arms, smiling his whip-crack smile.

He wondered at that—that Adler could bring so much chaos and upheaval into his life and, at the same time, bring him peace for the first time in nearly a decade. Perhaps it wasn't so strange, though. Rainy was a Miami kid, after all. He knew hurricanes. He knew that there were things in this world that could bring all the violence and destruction of God's wrath, and also the small heart of peaceful tranquility at their center. Maybe Adler had dragged him through the wind and floods to bring him to the eye of the storm, where all was calm, if only for a moment.

Maybe if he played his cards right, he could stay there for a little while.

He reached into his pocket and pulled out the second item he'd stolen from Adler's apartment. The dog tags were cool in the palm of his hand. He squeezed them until they went warm, then let the chain slide through his fingers. They clinked into the bottom of the bowl.

Rainy looked at the name *Adler, Nathaniel T. Jr.*, jumbled in next to his apartment keys and his childhood and a ticket stub from a basketball game he'd found in his pocket yesterday, and he smiled.

For the first time in a long time, it felt like the start of something.

Rainy and Adler will return in

Gratuitous Violets Book #2: *Always Something*

Coming spring 2025

American Spirit

An exclusive short story from Adler's POV!

Nat wanted a cigarette.

Once upon a time, you'd have been hard-pressed to find him without one in his hand. Back at Camp Mackall, his SFAS instructor had called him "tar and feathers" because he smoked like a chimney and weighed approximately five pounds soaking wet. The habit had lasted him from age fifteen to age twenty-two, when he'd smoked his final cigarette just before turning in for bed ahead of an early morning mission, watching the stars burning fat and hot in the skies north of Raqqa. He hadn't touched one since. As far as quashing bad habits went, spending three months in hell was a pretty effective, if unpleasant, method. That was seven years ago. The urge struck rarely nowadays, and when it did, it didn't bother him much.

Except today. Today, it was really fucking bothering him.

It probably had something to do with the fact that he was sitting on the tarmac at Miami International Airport, staring out the window and not moving from his seat. Seong had insisted on lending him the private jet for his flight from Busan. Nat had only accepted in the end because it was more comfortable for Dolly and Martina, and he had a great many possessions that were difficult to move through customs.

The problem with flying that a private plane couldn't alleviate was that the changes in pressure made Nat's bad ear ring like a motherfucker for fifteen minutes after every ascent and descent. He was sitting in his seat now listening to it, the high-pitched hum that felt like static across half his skull, like he'd lain on it funny and it had gone dead. It felt like a kind of blindness of its own, even after all these years. It kept him company as he stared out the window, fingers itching for a cigarette.

It was time to get off the plane. They'd stopped moving ten minutes ago. Nat had gone through the motions of unbuckling his seatbelt, tidying away the glass of now-flat ginger ale he'd been nursing for the past three hours, and returning the battered paperback spy thriller he'd bought in a Buenos Aires airport newsstand last week to his bag. Now he was just sitting, having run out of reasons to stall.

The pilot emerged from the cockpit and stood at the front of the cabin, smiling blandly.

"Would you like any help with your things, Mr. Adler?"

"No, thank you," Nat said, taking the hint. He straightened, joints creaking, and picked up his bag and jacket.

The door at the front of the cabin was open, blaring white sunlight, and the glowing rectangular portal of it gave a striking impression of Saint Peter's gates. Nat knew it couldn't be, though, because ever since he was little, he'd known that if he was ending up anywhere after he died, it sure as hell wouldn't be there.

The stairs leading down onto the tarmac were glossy white, covered with black, sandpaper-like grip strips. Nat kept his gaze firmly on them as he descended. The heat rolled in, but only as an afterthought. What hit first was the humidity, a wet slap of it, like trying to shoulder his way into a bank of fog. It was familiar, the muggy air like the taste of childhood in the back of his throat. He was glad he'd shed his jacket and rolled up his sleeves during the flight.

When he reached the bottom step, he halted.

Tarmac looked the same all over the world. Flat, black, dusty, hot. There was no reason this patch of it should be any different from the hundreds that Nat had stepped down onto in the past seven years.

Here was the thing:

The last time Nathaniel Adler had set foot on American soil, he'd been twenty-two and hopping a plane to his latest deployment, which he didn't yet realize would be his last. His boots had lifted off a patch of tarmac just like this one, and that was that.

All these years, he'd avoided returning here, even for work. Seong either hadn't noticed or had been willing to indulge him. In any case, Seong's operation hadn't gotten a foothold in the States until very recently. Most of Nat's time had been spent in East Asia and South America. But three years ago, Seong had started expanding to new ports and relocating every year or so to keep a closer watch on newer operations. Nat went where Seong went, and where Nat went, people died. Apparently, there were a lot of people in Miami who needed to die.

The tarmac yawned like a chasm just beyond the brown leather tips of his shoes. Nat stared into it, dizzy. He didn't know why the urge was hitting him so violently in this of all moments, but he was just fucking dying for a cigarette. His fingers were restless, and there was a phantom taste of tobacco at the back of his throat when he licked his dry lips.

"Is everything okay, Mr. Adler?" the pilot asked behind him, and Nat startled.

"Yes. Yes, everything is fine."

He stepped down onto the tarmac.

He hadn't been sure what he was expecting. The sole of his shoe felt the solidness of pavement, the heat radiating off of it. His legs held him. He stood on the ground.

Still, it struck him. The symmetry of it. Completion. Shoes off American tarmac, shoes back on. Like he'd never left. Like the years between had been erased.

The gravity of it stuck in his throat like a bad drag, smoke-rough. He thought, with dreadful, awed certainty, *Something is going to happen now.*

Nothing happened. The moment passed. Nat looked to the back of the plane, where a pair of men were already starting to unload his things, and went to help. He let the girls out of their crates and had them trot around to stretch their legs before getting them situated in the moving truck and helping to load up boxes.

They drove into the city. Nat hadn't brought much; just half a dozen boxes. Apparently, the furniture had been taken care of, and most things could be bought here. All he'd brought with him were the things that weren't interchangeable—clothes, books, keepsakes, Dolly and Martina's things, and, of course, his tools of the trade. Most of it had been in Buenos Aires, the last stop on Seong's world tour, but he'd stopped over in Busan for the rest.

He had a new apartment on the Upper East Side, which he hadn't yet been to see himself but Su-jin had toured and given her stamp of approval. The Seongs had been in town for several weeks now and seemed to have settled into the city well. They'd requested him over for dinner that night, and Nat had agreed. He wasn't too keen on getting started with unpacking right away, not when he'd spent the past week continent-hopping.

His building was nice, set back a bit from the street on a walk lined with bushes that dripped fat blossoms. Nat let the girls out first.

They investigated the greenery happily before he led them inside and up the stairs.

It was a good apartment. Dark hardwood floors, spacious, plenty of light. As Seong had intimated, a full set of very expensive-looking modern furniture had already been moved in. Nat gave Dolly and Martina the go-ahead to investigate and watched them sniff around, disappearing down the hall toward the bedroom. After a minute, they returned and sat at his feet expectantly, tongues lolling.

"What do you think? Feel like home?"

The words felt strangely weighty, dragging and dropping off his tongue and rolling across the floor. He half expected the dogs to give chase.

Instead, they lay down on the floor. Martina whined and licked her lips.

"Yeah," Nat said. "I thought so, too."

The two movers Seong had sent along helped him carry his boxes up the stairs and deposit them in the living room. When there was only one box left in the truck, he set it on the curb and tipped them, then stood with his hands on his hips and watched them drive away.

Miami looked and smelled like a city.

It's not any different from anywhere else in the world, he told himself.

Except. He could dig through his fakes for a valid US license and rent a car. He could put it on this very road and drive straight north, and this road would turn into other roads, but there would be no oceans to cross. There was a single ten-hour drive between him and Hedrick, Alabama; between him and his parents and the things he once was.

He knew they were still alive. He checked up, once a year on his birthday or Christmas, when it got the worst of him. Sometimes he thought part of him would always be stuck there, as a child, waiting. He'd never learned to stop poking it. He kept waiting for it to stop hurting. But every time he pressed his finger there, to the raw wound of it, it ached and it bled.

Nat felt sometimes like he had been walking around with a cannonball-sized hole in his chest. The suits didn't cover it, and everyone could see, see the meat and splintered bone on the inside where it had cut right through him, and the sky on the other side. Every year, he tapped a finger against the raw edge and thought, *Yes, still tender.* He waited for it to heal, like the newer wounds, but it never did.

He wanted to smoke, but that was par for the course when he thought about his parents, so he got over it and walked inside.

The last box was full of knives and disassembled firearms, packed neatly into their padded cases and taped together. It was heavy, and Nat's back ached. He stopped at the bottom of the stairs just inside the building's entrance to take off his tie and slip it into his pocket. Footsteps shuffled across the tiled floor behind him, and his fingers closed around the butterfly knife strapped to his wrist.

When he turned, he found a man with his hands crammed into his own pockets, smiling sheepishly. He was wearing Bermuda shorts. Nat was tired of him instantly.

"Hi," the man said. "I'm Tristan. You must be in 2D."

Nat released the knife and faced him fully. He clocked the twitch in the man's features, the way he tried not to flinch when he spotted Nat's scar.

"John," Nat offered, using the name on his lease.

Tristan smiled at him with straight, white teeth. He had dark skin, curly hair, and broad shoulders, and was actually quite pleasant to look at, once you got past the shorts—which Nat wasn't sure he was willing to do.

"You need help with that?" Tristan asked.

Nat looked down at the box of extreme and highly illegal firepower sitting at his feet.

"No, thanks," he drawled. "I'm a big boy."

"Oh, I know." Tristan's eyes were heavy on him. Nat knew exactly how he looked—flushed and sweaty, collar open, hair probably a mess. In some situations, he would have been flattered to be undressed by someone's eyes. At the moment, between the humidity and the nicotine craving, he felt more like jabbing Tristan in the throat and watching him roll around on the floor.

"If you wanted, I could show you around the neighborhood," Tristan plowed on. "We could grab some drinks."

Nat gave him an unkind smile. "I'm kind of busy right now."

"Later, then, maybe. I'm in 1B, if you ever want to swing by."

"Great." Nat picked up the box and stepped onto the stairs. "I'll keep that in mind."

He unpacked the girls' beds and bowls, arranging them in his best approximation of his Busan apartment. They were ex-military like him and were used to moving around, but familiarity would make them more comfortable. He watched them mill about before calling them over to lie down. He lay on the floor between them, staring at the ceiling, allowing them to kiss him on the face until his eyebrows were sticky with dog saliva. Then he unpacked a change of clothes, showered, and left for the Seongs' downtown penthouse.

The sun was just barely starting to set, and Miami sparkled against the sky like a bioluminescent reef that had crept its way up out of the Atlantic. Nat supposed it would be swallowed by the sea again soon enough.

The Seongs' penthouse was classy, modern, and half glass. Under Su-jin's ministrations, it was already practically identical to every other place they'd lived in the past three years. When she opened the door, Su-jin beamed and pressed a kiss to his unscarred cheek.

Her customary greeting was a kiss on both, because she thought it made her seem international, but they'd negotiated this compromise during his early days in Busan because the right side of his face had been swathed in bandages, and then big, ugly stitches, and then tender new skin that burned when it was touched.

Yi-joon and Ji-soo ran up and flung themselves around Nat's middle so he stumbled against the doorframe. He was immediately bombarded with information about the beach, the penthouse, and their new American school. They spoke in flawless English now, but both retained the slightest Southern twang to some words because Nat had been their earliest and most beloved conversation partner.

Seong greeted Nat warmly with half a hug and a handshake. They all migrated to the kitchen, where Nat was saddled with a glass of wine and subjected to an alternating merry-go-round of conversation in which he was first assaulted with questions—*Was the flight smooth? How do you like the new apartment? Did you see the leftovers I left in the fridge?*—and then with anecdotes about being an eleven- and/or eight-year-old in Florida—*You can see sharks in the water sometimes, and alligators in the swamp. We're taking a class trip to the Everglades next month. Did you see the beach yet?*

The kids quieted down while they ate dinner, and Seong and Su-jin started exchanging looks—their plotting looks, which always meant that they had certain opinions about how Nat should be living his life, and they were trying to manipulate him into following them.

"It must be good to be back in your homeland," Seong said.

Nat made a noncommittal noise. Seong had always had strange ideas about homelands. Nat had never been much of a patriot. The army had been an escape route, and then it had been a home he could avoid being kicked out of by earning his keep. The old US of A had never done much for him.

It was clear that the Seongs expected it to mean something, him being here. That it would change something about him, or make him want to change. The thought made him uneasy.

On his way out the door, Su-jin smiled at him and squeezed his arm.

"Maybe this is the place," she told him.

And he didn't know what she meant—honestly, he wasn't sure that *she* knew what she meant—but still he was reminded of the rug-pulling feeling of stepping back onto American soil, and his irrational certainty that *Something is going to happen now.*

"Yeah," he said. "Maybe."

Back at his apartment, he prepared for bed by hunting through the entire place, vents and all, for every possible entrance and exit. Once he was satisfied, he dug up some sheets and made the bed, then spread out a blanket for Dolly and Martina to lie at the foot of it. They leaped up and settled down to sleep, Martina curled into a tight ball and Dolly sprawled across half the bed, and Nat smiled and kissed their heads and called them good dogs. He lay down himself, but it didn't last long. Su-jin had put up thick blackout curtains, and the darkness squeezed in tight. It was a black wall over him, just an inch above his nose, that he would hit his head on if he tried to sit up.

He forced himself to get up and sift through one of the boxes until he found his night-lights, then plugged one into each outlet in the bedroom.

He went to sleep.

The dreams always started with something unassuming—he was tending a bar, playing cards with his squadmates, walking the dogs. It was their way of leaking insidiously into the safe parts of his life, he supposed. This time, he was getting off a plane, but not in Miami. It was some faceless, shifting amalgam airport made up of a dozen he'd seen in the past few years. He walked across the tarmac, rifling through the duffel slung over his shoulder.

The dream turned, the way it always did—abruptly.

He saw the flash and heard the bang, felt the concussive force of it. He flew through the air, limp like a rag doll, deafened and blinded, but he felt it again and again, what he imagined standing on the surface of a star going supernova would feel like, the whole world collapsing in on itself and then exploding outward again, burning everything in its path.

The tiny cuts hurt, and then his shoulder, his chest, and then the whole right side of his head was gone, evaporated in pain. He heard the voice of Niemann, their medic, telling him, *You feel the worst one last.* He thrashed on concrete. It skinned his elbows and knees, slick with blood, and he could taste it in his mouth. It was running down from the wound in his face, clogging his throat and bubbling up into his sinuses.

He opened his mouth to scream, and it opened all the way—all the way back to his ears.

Nat woke in darkness, disoriented. His mouth tasted like blood, hot copper, and it was happening again, he was back in that place, like he'd never left. Like it had all been a delusion of the fever. He flung out with his arms and legs, but they were trapped, pinned to his sides, and he couldn't breathe—

But they were trapped because he was tangled up in sheets, on a soft mattress. Not the hard floor of a cell. He could hear the breathing of the dogs, their unhappy rustling. When he forced himself to lie still, the sheets didn't squeeze in. They just laid there, damp with sweat.

There was blood in his mouth and his cheek was stinging, but on the wrong side. He'd bitten the inside of it in his sleep.

He lay still for five minutes, then ten, as the panic subsided and his breathing slowed to an even rasp. He got out of bed and went to the bathroom on wobbling legs to rinse out his mouth, then sat on the couch. He never managed to go back to sleep for hours afterward. He stared at the ceiling for a long time. His hands were still shaking. A cigarette would help. There might be a corner store open somewhere nearby.

He dismissed the thought in favor of turning on the TV. At some point, he fell back asleep upright on the couch, and woke with a crick in his neck.

He spent the morning unpacking boxes, getting everything squared away. It was soothing, to make the place feel more like home. He unpacked the books last, organizing them on the shelf in the living room in alphabetical order by author. His copy of Turgenev's *Fathers and Sons* slid out of the stack, and he flipped open the cover. The inscription stared up at him in Vanya's bold, tilted Russian cursive.

A reminder not to be such a cynic, it said.

He remembered the first time they'd met, when Vanya had been trying to fence a stolen Repin through Seong, and Nat had decided to meet with him first. Vanya had looked him up and down and grinned, and said:

"I always wanted to fuck an American."

"American soldier," Nat had added.

"Even better. My grandparents would be disgusted."

And that was all it had taken, really, because Nat had always been easy that way.

They'd dated earnestly for a couple of months. Vanya was loud, confident, expressive, with a braying laugh. He was bright in a way that Nat liked, because it felt like some of the light reflected off of him, made him shine a little, too. And then, at the end of two months,

Vanya had looked at him and said, "We're never going to be in love, are we?"

Nat had shrugged. Even if they had been, he wouldn't have known how to tell.

They'd dated very casually for two years after that. Whenever their cities lined up, they'd stay together. The sex was great, the conversation almost as good. Nat also appreciated that Vanya was easy to get rid of, when it was wanted. All he had to do was say something needling and caustic, and, rather than engaging, Vanya would just shake his head and walk out for a few hours until Nat had cooled off and was ready to act as though nothing had happened. They both slept around freely in the months between meeting up, and it suited them both well enough.

Every once in a while, though, Vanya would look at Nat with this probing expression, searching for something. Nat would wait for the verdict. Each time, Vanya would say, "Still not love, I think."

The last time had been in Tokyo, three years ago. Vanya had met him at the airport and they'd driven to a hotel together, where he'd followed Nat into the shower and let Nat fuck him against the wall. Then he'd spread Nat out on the bed and spent an hour working him with his fingers until Vanya got it up again and fucked him there in the sheets. Just missionary, slow and deep, with his nose pressed into the curls behind Nat's ear. And he'd touched him so tenderly, Nat had thought, *Something is different. Something has changed.* When they finished, Vanya kissed him, gentle and searching, and then he propped himself up on an elbow and looked down at Nat and said:

"This has to be the last time. I met someone."

Nat, not understanding at first, had rolled his eyes. "We both meet lots of someones. That's the beauty of the arrangement."

"But, this time, I'm in love with him," Vanya said.

And wasn't that a kick in the teeth.

"Okay," Nat had replied, and that was that.

He traced the inscription with his finger now, then closed the book and placed it on the shelf, in its own carefully organized place.

He spent the afternoon wandering the city, familiarizing himself with the landscape of it. He'd already been studying up on the local underworld politics, and he scoped out for himself now the borders of the Espinosas, the Vees, Andy Parish's Brickell District. By the time he returned home, he felt strange, floaty and disconnected. The need for a hit of nicotine had been building all day, and he'd figured out why.

The last time Nat had been in America, he'd been a person who smoked. He'd done it constantly up until his last deployment, and as long as he'd lived in the States, he hadn't stopped smoking since he was in the tenth grade. It felt like such a natural part of existing in this place, almost vital.

He was pretty sure that was the brunt of the issue, but it was still nagging at the back of his mind, making him antsy. Being antsy made him want to smoke all the more. In compromise, he took down a bottle of bourbon from the liquor cabinet and made himself an old-fashioned.

The familiar motions of it soothed him, lessened the craving. Unfortunately, once he'd finished and it was sitting in front of him, he realized he didn't actually want it. He sat staring at it for several minutes. Then he shrugged, picked it up, and left his apartment.

Tristan opened the door of 1B, shirtless. He was almost bearable when all his muscles were on display.

"I made an extra," Nat said. "Can't drink it by myself. Thought maybe you could help."

Tristan grinned. "You thought right."

Nat watched Tristan drink his drink on the couch, and then he let Tristan kiss him, and then he let Tristan lay him out on the couch and strip him out of his clothes. He fingered Nat a little too clumsily, a little too rough. He fucked competently enough, because it was hard to get that wrong, but he just sort of stared at Nat the whole time, or buried his face in Nat's neck when he apparently got too overwhelmed. There were murmured endearments, but most of them were in Nat's bad ear anyway, so he didn't have to suffer through them.

There was a point where Tristan pinned Nat's hands at his sides and Nat thought, *Yes, okay, this is interesting*, but Tristan gave up on it quickly and just reached down to jerk him off. Which was fine with him; the performance wasn't exactly inspiring enough to warrant a marathon.

He came in a floaty, hot rush, gasping and clenching down because Tristan had him in a death grip, and when he came down from it he was relaxed. Easy and bone-deep, the way he'd been looking for. Tristan came soon after, which Nat almost missed in his own comfortable haze, then lay down to nuzzle his face into Nat's neck.

"That was great," he panted. "Was that great for you?"

"Mm," Nat said vaguely.

"I'm starving. You want to go get food?" Tristan's voice was hopeful.

"Already ate," Nat lied.

That was one of the many things that hadn't come with him when Seong pulled him from hell—the hunger. Starving did that sometimes, a doctor had told him once. Nat hadn't had an appetite in years.

He extricated himself after several awkward attempts at conversation and, on his way out the door, dodged an invitation to brunch.

Back at his apartment, he showered, put on sweats, and lay in bed, and then cursed when he realized he'd left the glass at Tristan's.

Sleep evaded him. He lay on his back for hours, staring at the ceiling, thinking about nothing at all. There was a sort of trepidation that had been dogging him all day, a certainty that he was just waiting for something that was going to creep out of the bushes and pounce on him at any moment. Not another nightmare—they weren't nightly anymore. Something else, that he didn't understand and didn't want to think about.

At two, he gave in and picked up his phone, because it was either that or actually walk down to the corner store this time.

It was just past noon in Yekaterinburg. Vanya picked up on the third ring.

"Nat?" he asked. He'd never quite gotten the hang of the flat *a*, so it came out more like *Net*. Nat closed his eyes.

"Hi. Thought I'd give you a ring, check up."

He could hear the smile on the other end of the line like static in his good ear. "*Where have you moved to now?*"

"How'd you know?"

"*Because you only call when you move to a new city.*"

"Miami," Nat conceded.

Vanya paused. "*Back in America, then. How is that?*"

Irritation licked in hot, because he wished people would stop asking. "It's another fucking rock in the ocean. What am I supposed to say? Want me to whistle 'To the Colors'?"

"*Sometimes I can't recall why I miss you, and then you say sweet things like that,*" Vanya replied. Nat's jaw clenched.

"How's Maksim?" he asked.

"*Maks and I are good, thank you.*"

Nat's fingers had drifted down to where he was still sore from Tristan, and it was easy when he pressed into the sting to remember better soreness from better sex. The way they had stumbled into hotel rooms and Vanya had pushed him up against the wall and they'd scrabbled at each other, frantic to get on and around and inside. In those times, when Vanya hadn't been able to refrain from touching him another second, he'd thought, deep down, *If this isn't what it feels like, I don't know what is.*

He wondered if Vanya fucked Maksim that way or not. He didn't know which possibility was worse.

"I'm surprised you haven't gotten bored of him yet."

Vanya sighed. "*You know why I always pick up the phone when you call? Because I know you. I know you need to keep checking. It makes you feel safe. And I'm happy to do that for you. But you don't get to talk about him that way.*"

The words settled into Nat's skin like napalm. He hated that—being psychoanalyzed. He hated being made to feel like he was transparent to everyone but himself.

"You were a decent fuck," he said coldly, "but if you think you ever knew me, you're as stupid as you look."

And, back then, that would have been all it took to make Vanya hang up, walk out. But he didn't. He just sighed, like he'd expected nothing less. And Nat realized that somewhere in the intervening years, Vanya had changed, and he had not. That was what stung most of all when Vanya said:

"*One day, someone will feel for you what I feel for Maks. I promise.*"

Nat hated a lot of things, but he hated most of all when people were exactly right about him. He set the phone down on the pillow next to his face and stared at it, breathing in the dark.

He felt like he'd spent his entire life waiting to be loved. It had been easy with Vanya. All he had to do was sit there and be looked at and wait for the verdict. And, each time, he'd thought, desperately, *Maybe I finally figured out how to make it happen.*

And even now, if one day he picked up the phone and Vanya said, *Yes, I think so*, none of the rest of it would matter. He would lie back and spread his thighs, because he had always been easy that way.

"*Call again the next time you move continents*," Vanya told him gently. His voice was tinny through the speaker, insubstantial in the darkened room. "*Now, go to sleep, Nat.*"

Nat let him hang up and kept staring at the black screen of his phone.

He felt it so acutely, that hole in his chest that let people look right through him. More than anything, he felt the hollowness of it, the bubble of empty in the center of his body. The spot where, a long time ago, before he'd even been old enough to understand, something had been scooped out. Now everyone could look right in and see that all the vitals had been damaged, heart most of all. And nobody would bother pouring something as finite as love into the bottomless fucking hole of him, just to watch it run out the other side.

In the dark, he shifted onto his side and drew his knees up to his chest until he finally fell into a dreamless sleep.

The next day, he went to Seong's office and begged to be given work to do. Seong gave him a disapproving look, but he didn't argue.

Nat spent the next week getting to know the ins and outs of the new operation. He criss-crossed Miami like a field commander surveying the troops, checking the fortifications. It was good that he did, because the men needed whipping into shape. That was part of why Seong liked bringing Nat along with him—people were afraid of him, and they obeyed when he gave orders. Seong said that it was the soldier in him and his general menacing aura. Nat thought it was probably mostly the scar.

A few days in, Seong sent along the kind of orders Nat specialized in, and he went hunting. He slunk through Vee territory, easy and strong, and put bullets where they needed to go. On the second hit, he let the tall, burly guy notice him first so he tackled Nat to the ground and they fought hand-to-hand. It was a swimming, tie-dye blur of catharsis when the man slammed Nat's skull against the concrete and his ears rang and he tasted blood. When he'd dispatched the man with a knife in the carotid, he sat and touched his split lip and bloody nose and breathed, and breathed.

At home, he showered the blood off. Contrary to what most people thought of him, Nat had never *enjoyed* killing. It made that hollow yawn in him more, made him twitchy and tired, made sure that the following night was one of the nightmare ones. But it felt good to be necessary. It felt good to be good for something.

A week after his arrival, he appeared in Seong's office with coffee for their customary morning meeting only to find Seong fuming. The Vees, who Nat had been working on, were not proving to be much of an issue. It was the Espinosas who were testing them, looking for weakness in the new blood. Emilio Espinosa had had three of Seong's new Miami hires dispatched by a favorite mercenary hitman of his, and Seong wanted to draw a hard line.

"Send me the details," Nat told him. "I'll fix the guy right up for you."

Later that day, while waiting for the details on the new assignment, he killed another man. It was an easy job, a bullet through the back of the skull. As he walked away, he found himself fumbling through his pockets and realized he was looking for a cigarette.

"Goddamnit."

The nicotine craving had been growing in him like a malignance for the past week. He'd figured it was just being back in the States, but some moments he wanted a smoke so bad he felt like chewing off his own fingers.

He would go back to his apartment, where there would be a file on his new target waiting for him, slipped under the door. He would open it and start to make plans. He would do his job.

On the building next to him, there was a banner whose corner had been splattered with blood. It was advertising the upcoming Veterans' Day celebration, with a woman dressed in red, white, and blue saying the emblazoned tagline, *Welcome home, soldier!*

Nat closed his eyes and pressed his face against it. He breathed in the humid air, the smell of grime and garbage. When he straightened up again, he went to find a corner store.

What he found first was a gas station, bounded on two sides by freeway, in a block of fast food restaurants. He was so stricken by the image that he sat down on the curb outside and just watched.

Cars flashed too fast over the cracked pavement, between the wavering glaze of heat and the thick black nerve bundles of power lines overhead. The air smelled like gasoline and greasy food. Even busy, everything in sight felt abandoned.

He thought about Vanya, who'd once told him, *Wherever you go in the world, you're always American.*

He'd never been to Miami before, but he felt like he'd sat on this exact corner a thousand times. It felt like home, the ugly kind of home that you only loved when you had to consider hating it.

Maybe there was something to Seong's nonsense about homelands. Maybe what he'd been feeling this past week was the motherland welcoming him back to her doughy, feverish bosom. *Welcome home, soldier!* He'd been all sorts of people all over the world, but a part of him would always be stuck here, and he'd stepped in it and now it was stuck to him again.

He considered the feeling of stepping onto the tarmac, really considered it this time. Boots off, boots on. It didn't just feel like symmetry, like completion. It felt like resuming something. Like he'd lifted the needle off a record, and only now dropped it back on. He hadn't just been a smoker the last time he'd been in America. He'd been changing, on a set trajectory, hurtling toward some manifest destiny. All that time away, he'd put it on pause. He'd been frozen in time, avoiding this next big thing that was sitting here waiting for him.

There had been a story to him at twenty-two, a trajectory to his life that he only saw now in its absence. One that he'd put on pause. And now, he'd wandered his way back into it.

He thought, *Something is going to happen now.*

Maybe it was the healing that hadn't happened because all these years he'd been in suspended animation. There was going to be a billboard on the side of the highway telling him what to put inside the hole in his chest. Something was going to show him how to stitch up the edges.

"Maybe this is the place," he said out loud.

Then he went inside to buy himself a pack of cigarettes.

At the checkout counter, there was a sign taped to the wall that said *Discounts for veterans.*

"I'm a veteran," Nat told the clerk, a Black man in his early sixties, going gray across the dome, wearing a sweat-patched Navy T-shirt.

"Afghanistan?"

"Syria."

The clerk saluted him, grinning. "Thank you for your service. Can I see your VIC?"

"Do you really need to?" Nat asked, gesturing to his face.

The clerk's lips made a thin line, like he was going to laugh and then thought better of it. "You know what, man, you go ahead and take them for free."

When he got outside, he realized he'd forgotten to buy a lighter, and he didn't carry one anymore. With a sigh, he stuffed the cigarettes into his pocket and set off in the direction of home.

When he got back to his apartment, he stepped right on the folder that had been slid under his door and nearly slipped. Scowling, he picked it up and tossed it onto the kitchen counter, next to the corkboard he'd set up to pin things to—addresses, business cards, photographs—over a map of Miami he'd snagged from a tourist stand on the beachfront. He left it there and went to dig in the kitchen drawer for a lighter. Once he scrounged one up, he set it upright on the counter next to the pack of cigarettes and dropped wearily onto a stool.

Dolly came over to lie at his feet. He pet her head idly with a toe as he stared at the cigarettes. The minutes passed, the sun through the kitchen window sparking off the brushed steel surface of the lighter.

He looked at the manila folder.

He looked at the cigarettes.

"Fuck everything," he said. Then he opened the drawer at his elbow, swept the cigarettes and lighter into it, and closed it. He pulled the folder toward himself and flipped it open.

He read the details: description, name—what a stupid fuck-ing name—and movements. All the easy intel picked up off the streets, where everyone in this city knew something about everyone else. Scanning down the notes about style, habits, and known vices, the start of a plan began to stitch together in his head. This man was a lot more dangerous than the Vees he'd been picking off so far—which meant this was going to be a lot more interesting.

Good. If he wasn't going to smoke, then what he needed to sate this itchy, hungry feeling under his skin was a challenge.

His fingers were still twitchy and restless, so he drew the small butterfly knife from the strap at his wrist and spun it over his fingers—open, closed, open, closed.

Under the next sheet of paper, there was a photograph. It was a candid, taken at a bar somewhere, and the man in it was looking off to the right and grinning. He was handsome, square-jawed and thick-necked, with broad shoulders. Light brown skin, shaggy black hair pushed back carelessly from his forehead, open and confident and arrogant. His smile was like a spotlight, eyes crinkled, front teeth a little crooked. Nat disliked him instantly.

It didn't stop him from running a finger lightly over that smile, frozen in time and bright as the sunrise.

He took the photograph and smoothed it out on the corkboard, right over Riverside on the map. Then he jammed the knife into it to hold it in place. The blade stuck right through the man's forehead, edge cutting down between his big, brown puppy-dog eyes. Nat took in the sight with grim satisfaction.

"Sorry, Mr. Rainy," he said, getting back to work.

"It's nothing personal."

Acknowledgments

This book owes its life to the ceaseless support of my friends, family, and other loved ones, most of whom I hope will never, ever read it. I've dreamed about putting my first novel out into the world since I was about five years old. I definitely never expected it to be this one, but that's the way life goes, sometimes. This book turned out to be the little manuscript that could.

My first and biggest thanks goes out to my sister. M, you have always been there to help, encourage, and inspire me. It's genuinely astonishing that, despite the fact that I have now published a novel, you're still the bookish sister. You will always be my book club, road trip, and readathon buddy. You remind me every day why books are magic. I love you.

I also want to thank all the friends who have supported me along the way. Even when you didn't quite see the vision, you nodded along and gave me a thumbs-up, which is all a girl can ask for, in the end. You make my life bright. A special thanks goes out to my very first writing group, all the way back in middle school. Even though I haven't spoken to many of you in years, I still think of you each time I see that blinking cursor, and am grateful for how you encouraged me to start putting words on paper, even if they were cringy ones about teens with heterochromia saving the world.

Of course, this love letter wouldn't be complete without acknowledging my #1 beta reader, Brianna. You were the first complete stranger to read and love my dumb little book, and I will always consider you my first fan. Thank you for showing me and my idiot boys some love when I really needed it.

Thank you to my editor (myself), copyeditor (myself), typesetter (myself), cover artist (myself), marketer (myself), and social media manager (myself). You rock, myself. Thanks for believing in me.

Thank you to my mom. Mom, you were the one who gave me my love of reading and the courage to share my silly stories with the world. I'm sad that you'll never get a chance to read this, but also kind of relieved. You were pretty open-minded, but this one might have been a stretch, even for you.

Finally, thank you to my readers. You make my world go round.

About the Author

R. J. Piper is a villain, a rogue, and a scourge upon society. Her favorite pastimes are hiking, playing with her dogs, and doing stupid things solely for the sake of the bit (like writing this book). This is her first novel. You can berate her for corrupting the morals of America on any of the following platforms:

Instagram: @rjpiper_writes

TikTok: @rjpiper_writes

rjpiper.com